DISCIPLINE

DISCIPLINE

PACO AHLGREN

GREENLEAF
BOOK GROUP PRESS

Published by Greenleaf Book Group Press, LP
4425 South Mo Pac Expwy., Suite 600
Austin, TX 78735

For ordering information or special discounts for bulk purchases, please contact Greenleaf Book Group LP at: 4425 South Mo Pac Expwy., Suite 600 Austin, TX 78735, (512) 891-6100.

Design and composition by Greenleaf Book Group LP
Publisher's Cataloging-In-Publication Data
(Prepared by The Donohue Group, Inc.)

Ahlgren, Paco.
  Discipline / Paco Ahlgren. -- 1st ed.

  p. ; cm.

  ISBN-13: 978-0-9790842-0-1
  ISBN-10: 0-9790842-0-2

1. Parapsychology--Fiction. 2. Enlightenment--Fiction. 3. Cosmology--Fiction. 4. Time travel--Fiction. 6. Science fiction. 7. Occult fiction. I. Title.

PS3601.H54 D57 2007
813./6   2007923696

Printed in the United States of America on acid-free paper

10 09 08 07   10 9 8 7 6 5 4 3 2 1

First Edition

*This book is for Mr. Toler,
who is my Jefferson.
And for Nim, who is my Jack.*

MISPERCEPTION

AUSTIN, TEXAS

SPRING, YEAR NINETEEN

ELLISON TOOK DEEP breaths, sobbing, sending clouds of vapor into the freezing air, his body trembling—as much from terror as from the cold. He hung over the tub in the dark bathroom, semicircles of fatigue under his eyes. A droplet plummeted from the faucet and exploded into the half-full tub.

I watched him reach into the water with his left hand and splash his face. He babbled quietly to himself, his eyes twitching. A pistol rested in the palm of his right hand, which lay limply on the floor. His index finger stroked the trigger slowly, rhythmically. "I can't do this," he mumbled. "I can't."

His fingernails were clean and well manicured, but that was all that remained of his usual neat appearance. He wore an expensive suit—appropriate for an accountant in his mid-twenties—well-pressed not long ago, but now rumpled and stale. His hair was a tangled mess. For days, he had endured a fever so intolerable that he had shut off the apartment's heat, hoping to find some respite, but even the icy air in the bathroom failed to stop the perspiration that ran down his forehead. Trails of sweat, tears, and mucus ran through his developing beard, soaking the sleeve of his shirt.

He was going insane, and there was nothing I could do to help him.

A few days ago, I had watched him slipping. I was aware of almost the exact moment the voice had begun talking to him—the rumbling distortion in his mind

I had known only too well so many years ago. Ellison started muttering to himself, and soon after had tried to drown the voice with booze and muscle relaxants, but it was clear that neither chemical had diminished its persistence, nor allowed him even a minute of sleep in the last seventy-two hours. As it grew worse, he had reacted by locking the front door, ripping out the phone cords, and barricading himself in his bathroom.

He had no way of knowing I had been here through it all—was here now, watching him, fighting every impulse to appear to him, to help him endure. His desperation tore at me, and at times, I wondered why I remained—why I didn't just leave him to face the inevitable alone. But I couldn't abandon him; I was as responsible for this as anyone, and I would stay with him, suffer with him, even if he didn't know.

Now panic was setting in, and I watched as Ellison started openly negotiating with his own mind, trying to convince himself that it was all just a temporary glitch in his software. "If I can . . . just last a . . . little longer . . ."

So Ellison sat in his bathroom, accepting what seemed to be imminent insanity. But at the very moment it looked like he would cave to the onset of his own madness, he sat bolt upright, and I knew that the whispering must have stopped. He lifted his head and scanned the floor in front of him, and the relief seemed to wrap around him like his mother's arms. He drew in a long breath and held it, unable to understand what was happening. I wondered how it could possibly get any worse. And yet I knew without a doubt that it would.

The old man simply appeared in the corner of the bathroom, a specter forming out of brumal emptiness. I had wondered for so long what he would look like in this moment, but even after all the wicked things I had watched him do over the years, I wasn't prepared for the hideous thing before me, and I felt an icy shiver trickle down my spine.

I had expected him to make a dramatic appearance, but he arrived silently, unceremoniously, a shadow shifting with the moonlight, moving across the bathroom walls. He climbed up onto the counter, his stringy gray-black hair hanging in front of his face as he stared vacantly at a blade in his right hand. He twisted the knife back and forth, as though puzzling over some complex issue, and were it not for the slight movement, he might have passed for a vulgar statue.

Light glinted off the blade and danced on the bathroom wall in front of Ellison like rippling water, breaking the blackness with restless brilliance. Ellison twisted his head in a panicked reflex, and when his eyes reached the old man perched on

the edge of the counter, he shrieked and scrambled into the far corner of the bathroom. He lifted his arm and pointed the pistol at the man. "Whoever you are, get
out of my house or I swear to *God* I'll blow your fucking brains out!"

The old man stopped twisting the knife and lifted his head. His face was a mask
of hatred. Ellison recoiled at the sight but continued to point the pistol unsteadily
at the bent figure, who squinted and smiled a mouth full of sharp rotting teeth.
The old man sucked air into his throat and let out a wheeze, which transformed
into rattling laughter. He pointed the blade at Ellison. "You are a craven piece of
human filth, and you're not going to shoot anybody."

"Get the *fuck* out of here!"

The old man's smile hung for a moment and then abruptly disappeared. He
leapt from the counter and landed hard on the floor, arms spread wide. *"Do it,
motherfucker!"*

Ellison squinted and fired twice. Tile shattered on the wall and the old man
staggered backward, staring at his chest as the echoes of the gunshots faded. He
lifted his head, his eyes wide with surprise. Then his face slipped back into a mali-
cious grin. "You missed."

Ellison fired two more rounds, but the man just waved his hand dismissively,
vanishing into nothingness, and while he was nowhere to be seen, his voice
echoed in the bathroom. "I know you're here," he said, and I knew he was talking to me. "Why don't you come out and show yourself to the boy." The voice
exploded in another fit of harsh laughter. I remained still, watching the scene
with increasing dread.

Ellison trembled as his eyes darted about the bathroom searching for the grisly
creature at whom he had just fired four shots, almost point-blank. "Oh fuck! Oh
fuck!" he said, his voice quavering. "What's happening to me?"

He slid his back up the wall and crab-stepped to the doorway, holding the shaking pistol in front of him. The faucet released another droplet, which cracked like
thunder when it hit the water. Ellison's head turned left and right, his wide eyes
sweeping every inch.

"I don't want to hurt you." The old man appeared for an instant to the left of
Ellison, and then vanished again.

Ellison wheeled and stumbled backward, falling hard on the floor, pointing the
pistol at the doorway. No one was there.

He started weeping again, taking a large handful of his hair and pulling it hard.
"What the fuck is happening to me?" He pushed his back against the tub, his body

succumbing to exhaustion and fear. And I knew, with every second of this madness, that he came ever closer to the only way out.

"It doesn't have to be this way." The old man was back, sitting in the darkest corner of the bathroom, gently running the edge of the blade over his pants. He stared at it impassively. "This can all end," his head remained bowed but his black eyes drifted up to Ellison, "if you want it to."

Ellison shrank against the tub and pointed the pistol at the old man again. Although he knew it would have no effect, he fired one more shot, shattering the mirror on the wall behind the scraggy body.

"Jesus," the old man said. "Will you please stop doing that? Somebody's going to call the police." He broke into another fit of gravelly laughter, and I winced, knowing the police would be here soon enough.

"Why are you doing this to me?" Ellison moaned.

"Don't be so maudlin," the old man said. "You don't mean anything to me, you piece of shit. You're a pawn. I just need you to do one little thing and then I'll leave you alone." He paused. "I need you to help me find him."

"Who?" Ellison said.

The old man scanned the room, looking for me. He chuckled and a drop of saliva seeped from the corner of his mouth, stretching toward his shirt. He sucked hard, pulling it back in, and his neck began to pulsate, making a gurgling sound in his throat. He opened his mouth, the lips curling back in a snarl, dilating, spreading ever wider, struggling to give birth. A geyser of black liquid exploded from the hole in the old man's face and landed on the floor with a sickly splash.

He crouched down, hunching over the mess to examine it. He put his finger in the puddle, stirring it, and after a few seconds the pool of black vomit began to roil and bubble. Tiny white worms squirmed in the substance, then separated into thousands of smaller puddles, turning into an army of insects, scrambling in every direction. They scratched at the floor with their spindly legs, looking for any crevice.

Ellison writhed, frantically trying to avoid the bugs speeding toward him. The old man put his hands behind his back and began pacing slowly, crushing hundreds of the insects with each step. "The thing is, I'm not from around here, and I really need your help."

He paused midstride and turned his head, squinting menacingly. Then, with a low snarl, he launched himself, driving the younger man further into the corner. But just before he reached Ellison, he froze, hovering, slowly bringing the blade toward Ellison's face, stopping less than an inch from the younger man's eye.

I tensed, fighting the urge to do something—*anything*. But I knew exposing myself to this monster would be an incalculable mistake. Everything would be lost.

"This is how it's going to work," the old man said, slowly twisting the blade in front of Ellison's eye. "If you do what I ask, I'll go away." His mouth stretched into a broad smile, the wrinkles on his face pinching into the appearance of scales. "And if you don't help me, I'll cut your fucking head off." His grin broadened. "Here's what I want you to do . . ."

After days of relentless agony, Ellison had no choice but to listen, clearly hoping it would bring some end to the lunacy. But soon he began to shake his head, becoming nearly hysterical. "No, *no*! Leave me *alone*! *No*!"

"That's not a very promising attitude."

Ellison stopped crying, the last vestiges of sanity pushing him into defiance. "You're not even real."

The old man chuckled and shrugged, holding the knife up to his own face, examining it. "This is real . . . at least it was when I fucked your sister and ripped her guts out."

Ellison began to tremble again, emitting a piercing scream, "*Get out!*"

The old man yelled, "*Shut the fuck up!*" He sprang from the counter and jumped up and down on the floor in front of Ellison. "*Shut the fuck up!*"

Ellison covered his ears and squeezed his eyes shut. "Get out!"

Then they both suddenly stopped screaming and became still, panting and staring at each other. The old man began chortling again quietly.

"What did you do to her?" Ellison said.

The old man put his hand on his hip, rolling his eyes in mock frustration. "How many times do I have to tell you? I *fucked* her . . . and ripped her *guts* out. Then I put her uterus in a box and mailed it to you."

"This isn't real."

"And what if it isn't?" the old man asked, and leaned over Ellison. "I can stay as long as it takes. I'm part of you now."

Ellison's eyelids fell, his lower lip wet with saliva. "I can't . . ."

I stood behind the old man. Ellison looked up slowly, and I allowed myself to appear for an instant. His eyes widened when he saw me, my face twisted with sorrow, trying to tell him with my eyes to cling to hope. But there was no hope to be found, and I knew it.

"What are you doing here?" he asked.

The old man whirled around but I faded too quickly for him to catch a glimpse of my face. "Get the *fuck* out of this!" He screamed in my direction, his expression furious. He turned back to Ellison and said, "You do what I tell you to, you little shit!"

Ellison stared at the old man for a moment, and then his eyes filled with resignation. He raised the pistol. "I can't."

"Don't do that," the old man said.

But Ellison put the barrel of the pistol under his chin, closed his eyes tightly, and pulled the trigger.

The old man didn't even blink at the explosion. He merely tilted his head and gazed at the body—the eyes fixed open, red lumps of tissue and brain sliding down the wall. He crouched and brought his face close to Ellison's. "I needed you, you little fucking worm. What a goddamn waste." He sniffed twice, stood erect, and grunted. Then he turned around and scanned the room, still looking for me, his eyes black with rage. "I'm going to find someone, you *cunt*, and when I do, I'm going to delight in watching you die."

A drop of water fell from the faucet to the tub, pealing for a million years. Then the old man was gone—a thread of smoke dismissed by the wind.

I stared at Ellison's body, a part of me dying with him in that moment. A tear rolled down my face, tickling my skin. *The first in decades*, I thought, almost puzzled by its appearance. I touched it, and then looked at the moist tip of my finger. *Will I ever be ready?* Then reality descended on me with the full magnitude of its crushing weight. *As though I have a choice . . .*

I leaned my head back and closed my eyes, breathing deeply as I fell into the void.

INDICATION

YEAR UNKNOWN

If you caught a glimpse of your own death, would the knowledge change the way you live the rest of your life? You might think the answer is obvious, and in my youth I might have agreed. But that was before I learned how elegant—and misunderstood—the universe really is.

My perspective has changed. We fatuously measure our tenure in this place, individually and collectively, using the concept of time. But it is a profound mistake—the first of many we have made as a species so embryonic and unprepared, yet so self-satisfied with our level of achievement that we are oblivious to the magnitude of our ignorance.

With the concept of time, we have manufactured a monster. It is the bane of our existence, measuring the span of our days as they drain away, drawing its strength from our bodies, leaving only withered, rotting shells to bury. We despise time for what it steals from us, and yet we covet it, trying to preserve every ounce of its substance—as though it has substance. And so, despite our best efforts, we have resigned ourselves to the futility of time's preservation. But this resignation is perhaps the biggest mistake of all.

It seems so simple as to be a cruel joke, for it is the effort itself that makes understanding time so elusive. But time does not exist; it is no more than a myth created to comfort us as we come to terms with looming mortality—or, more succinctly, imminent death. And yet we continue to impose this linear temporal construct on a universe that has no such boundaries. The foundations of immortality, however, lie not in preservation, but rather with the understanding of how absurd the concept of time is to begin with.

The years have caught up to me now, and I am tired. There is so little left that shocks or inspires me. After all that I have seen, I am reluctant to pour out these experiences to an audience that will largely reject the content as science fiction or fantasy. And yet something new compels me—something I don't quite understand. It isn't an urge; it's something bigger, deeper, and I know with every grain of purpose in my soul that I am supposed to give this away. It is my debt to the past, and to the future, so I will pay it here.

What follows is not difficult to understand; the concepts are basic—utterly effortless in their application. But the human spirit thrives on creating complexity where simplicity would do as well, and I have accepted that most people will close themselves to what I will say.

Still, a few will understand. It is to them I most owe this story.

JEFFERSON

AUSTIN, TEXAS

DECEMBER, YEAR EIGHTEEN

I WAS EIGHTEEN the day I met Jefferson Stone, and even considering my state at the time, I still remember almost every detail.

I sat at a table next to a window in the coffee shop watching big snowflakes drift softly to the pavement. They said it never snowed in Austin, but here it was, filling the air, a billion cotton fibers floating softly to the ground. They melted as they hit, and the scene filled me with delicate sadness. My eyes blurred a little as my mind drifted through memories. I felt the familiar tightening in my stomach, and then reflexively allowed reality back in, seeking comfortable distraction in the room around me. And with its kitschy decor and eclectic patrons, Cardinal Yorkshire's—or the Cardinal as it was commonly called—had plenty of distraction to offer.

I had spread my chessboard in front of me hoping to find a game, but the Cardinal was uncharacteristically empty, so I read from a tattered paperback until my mind began to drift. I turned back to the snowfall and took a sip from my fourth pint of beer. I leaned back, pulled the glass close to my chest, closed my eyes, and breathed deeply through my nose, holding the air in my lungs for a moment.

Behind me, a scream cracked the silence. Beer splashed onto my shirt as I craned my head around. The outburst had come from Barney, one of the Cardinal's resident homeless. "Sorry. I'm s-sorry, so sorry. Scared me," he said. Like many of Austin's homeless, Barney had a mental disorder, which manifested most prominently through outbursts like this one.

I smiled through my irritation. "It's okay, Barney." I rose from my chair and started toward the counter.

"He's coming," Barney said. "He sees us." He pointed a filthy finger at me. "He sees you. But I won't help him." He shook his head rapidly, speaking quickly, like a little boy recounting a nightmare.

"Yeah . . . Try not to worry about it too much, man."

"I try." He coughed, his head twitching as he squeezed his eyes shut.

What happened to you? I thought as I walked past him.

The bartender, Saul, smiled and shook his head. "You can't keep your back to Barney." He handed me a towel from behind the bar.

I returned the smile, patting the front of my shirt with the towel. "I'll try to remember that. Can I have the bathroom key?"

He reached for it and held it out to me. "Here you go."

"Thanks, Saul." I returned his towel and headed to the bathroom. As I emptied my bladder, I decided it was time to go home. I had been at the Cardinal for hours, and I was probably getting too drunk to play chess. When I returned the key to the bar, I lifted my eyes and stopped short.

At my table, at the other end of the coffee shop, I could make out the silhouette of a man against the bright falling snow outside. Something about his form seemed familiar, but I couldn't place him, and I suddenly began to feel a little anxious.

As I crossed the shop, the details became clearer to me. The man was perhaps in his mid-sixties, wearing pressed wool pants and a white button-down shirt, with sleeves neatly rolled up, revealing lean forearms. He had one leg tossed casually over his knee, a clean leather shoe dangling off the floor. One elbow was propped over the back of a chair, and in his other hand he held my paperback, gazing at the pages through small, round, wire-rimmed spectacles.

He was bald to the back of his head, and the little bit of gray hair that remained on the sides was cut short. A scar trenched its way from the top of his forehead to the middle of his exposed scalp like the mark of Ahab. The man looked up from the book, and our eyes met. I tried to pull my gaze away, but something held me there. "Is this your table?" he asked.

I nodded.

He gestured at the chessboard in front of him. "How about a game?" He ran his fingers gently over the scar on his head.

"Actually, I was about to leave."

"I hope you don't mind that I was looking at your book. I marked your place."

I looked at him almost suspiciously. "That's okay."

"Well?" he said. "One game?" He looked briefly at the coffee counter, and I turned to follow his gaze. Saul was back now, wiping down the bar.

I looked back at the man in front of me. "Sure."

He extended his hand. "Jefferson Stone."

"Douglas Cole," I slurred, gripping his palm. "I'm just going to get a beer before we start."

"Go ahead."

I walked to the counter to order another pint, and when I returned Jefferson was still watching me strangely—almost as if he were looking for something. The familiarity struck me again, but I still couldn't pinpoint it. "Have we met before?"

"I don't think so," Jefferson said, straightening in his chair.

"I thought maybe we had played a game together?"

He shook his head. "No, I think I'd remember."

"I guess so," I said, shrugging. I grabbed two pawns from the board—one white and one black—and mixed them up. I hid one in each fist and extended my arms for Jefferson to choose. He pointed to my left hand, and I opened it to reveal the white pawn, which he returned to its place on the board. He opened with his king's pawn.

Considering the number of beers I had had, I thought it might be wise to move slowly, so I mulled over my positions carefully. Jefferson, however, paid almost no attention to the game, making his moves quickly, then shifting his attention to our surroundings, examining the Cardinal's decor with an almost childlike fascination. After several moves he said, "So Douglas, are you a student?"

"No, I trade futures." The words spilled out with effortless haughtiness. "They're kind of like stocks."

"What contracts do you trade?"

I looked up, surprised that he knew enough about futures to ask the question. "The financials mostly."

He nodded casually, and I looked back at the board for a little while longer before moving my king's knight out. "How do you know about futures?" I asked.

"Oh, I guess I've picked up a little here and there. I'm impressed someone your age can handle that kind of risk." He looked at the board for a moment, then at me again. His brow suddenly creased. "Douglas?" He pointed at the middle of my face.

"What?" I looked down as the word left my mouth, and a crimson droplet hit my shirt. Blood began to pour from my nose. "*Shit!*" I stood up abruptly, knocking over my chair, and grabbed a napkin from the table to catch the stream. I was about to turn and head for the bathroom when I glanced at Jefferson, our eyes locking again. He almost seemed disappointed, and the thought tugged at me.

I tore my eyes away, looking instead at Barney, who shrank into his seat as I hurried past him to the counter. Saul looked worried. "Here," he said, offering me a handful of paper napkins, along with the key to the bathroom.

"Thanks," I pushed the stack against my nose. I rushed to the bathroom, where I threw the blood-soaked napkins onto the floor, grabbed a few paper towels from a stack next to the sink, and reapplied the pressure to my nose. I leaned my head back, holding the position for a few minutes until the bleeding stopped.

I left the bathroom carrying some fresh paper towels, in case the bleeding started again. "Are you okay?" Jefferson asked when I got back to the table, his eyes fixed on the blood staining my shirt.

I grabbed the sweater on top of my bag and slipped it over the mess. "Yeah, I'm fine." Jefferson had righted my chair, and I sat in it. "Whose move is it?" I asked, trying to redirect the conversation.

"It's yours. I moved my bishop here." He pointed to the board, then looked up at me, still concerned. "You should see a doctor about that."

"I'm fine, really. It's just a bloody nose." I hastily moved a rook, and he seemed content not to push the issue, so we played in silence.

The game didn't last long. "Checkmate," he said.

I searched briefly for options, but there were none. "Looks like it." I drained the last of my beer and said, "You're really good. Are you sure I've never seen you in here before?"

"No, I've never been here." He looked uncertain for a moment and then added, "How about you? Do you come here much?"

I laughed. "I live here, man! I'm here just about every day."

Jefferson rose from his chair, picked up his bag, and put on his coat. "Okay, well, thanks for the game." He extended his hand again.

"You should come back," I said. "You can usually find a lot better competition than me in this place."

"Well, then, maybe I'll see you." He smiled and turned to leave. I followed him with my eyes as he left the Cardinal.

Outside, snowflakes drifted over Jefferson, and he tightened his coat around himself, walking slowly away, disappearing into the snow.

As I watched him slip into the white afternoon, something stirred in me—an uneasy feeling that even the alcohol in my bloodstream couldn't suffocate. It was the first grain of a question forming in the recesses of my mind, but I dismissed it easily, because there was no way I could have known how significant it was.

It would be an incalculable misstatement to say that Jefferson merely influenced my life. He did begin as my friend and teacher, and I will cherish those aspects of our relationship for as long as I live, but they seem irrelevant in light of his real purpose that day. It still takes my breath away to consider everything he knew as he shook my hand and looked into my eyes for the first time.

On the surface, hell might seem like a strange place to plant the seeds of transcendence, but for those who can endure its wrath, its soil is fertile and deep. Jefferson knew all of this, and so much more. He knew that he would rigidly define my future, but he also knew that in order to do it, he would have to save my soul.

A soul, however, is a delicate and complex thing, and the path to redemption is far from straight. When I look back now, I am most intrigued by the fact that on the day of our introduction, Jefferson knew that before I could be saved, I would have to step to the edge of my own annihilation.

And perhaps the most unnerving part of it all, was that he would—with complete discipline and self-restraint—do nothing to stop me.

CHILDHOOD

The pursuit of truth and beauty is a sphere of activity in which we are permitted to remain children all our lives.

—ALBERT EINSTEIN

Durango, Colorado

ALMOST EVERYONE KNEW my father as Max—a simple name that suited his easy nature. His full name, however, was Thomas Maximilian Cole, and my mother seemed forever compelled to deride him for it. "How can anyone have such an aristocratic name and still be so unmotivated?"

Dad was a freelance writer for magazines around the country and, while he didn't make much money, it was enough to keep us comfortable. He loved his job because it gave him the freedom to live where he wanted to and to make his own schedule. As long as he met his deadlines, his editors were happy.

Outside of work and family, my father had only one real interest: he loved to play chess. He could often be found in coffeehouses and bars, concentrating in front of a board or reading from strategy books, memorizing openings to improve his game. I loved to watch him play; I was always proud when he won and took it hard when he didn't.

He was unequivocally honest, a trait that permeated every aspect of his life, including his passion for chess. Other players often challenged him to wagers, but he never accepted. He played only for the love of the game and he encouraged me to follow the same path. "Chess is its own reward, Douglas," he told me. "You should do it because you love it. That's the way everything in life is—if you aren't doing something because you love it, you're wasting your time. Do you understand that?"

I nodded. It made sense to me.

"You don't need to gamble, son," he added. "I never once saw a gambler come out a winner, but I've seen people lose everything they have and then some because they couldn't walk away."

My father claimed I started playing chess when I was three, but to me it almost seemed as though it had been with me since birth. Like him, I loved the game—the intricacy, complexity, and subtle grandeur. But more than anything, I loved the game's finality. Chess leaves no dispute—even a stalemate is irrefutable, turning what might have been an almost certain victory into a loss of sorts.

Dad loved teaching me. He worked hard to show me the fundamentals, and we regularly played together for hours, the time slipping by unnoticed. We often played with his old double-faced timer, although sometimes we just worked through a game with no time limit at all. But either way, we never played our games in silence. "Don't open on the edges," he would instruct. "Capture the center of the board, son!" Or, "Don't bring out your queen so early! Why are you being so aggressive?" Or, "Don't stack your pawns. You'll plug that file. Be careful!"

Dad let me win the first or second game whenever we played. I always knew he was giving me the victories, although neither of us ever acknowledged it. The joy of winning overshadowed the fact that it wasn't genuine, and it made me try even harder to make it real.

◆

WHEN DAD WASN'T writing or playing chess, he spent a lot of his time with his best friend, Jack Alexander. I don't know when Dad and Jack met, but they seemed inseparable.

Jack had a magical sense of humor, enhanced by a southern accent no one could quite place—which ranged from nearly imperceptible to downright antebellum, depending on his mood. He had a marvelous talent for twisting his face into complex expressions that seemed painful, and he chewed gum constantly, with such skill and enthusiasm I sometimes wondered if his charisma wasn't entirely dependent on his ability to smack as he spoke.

It was rare for Jack to show up at the house without toys or candy for my little brother, Thomas, and me. But the gifts came at a price: Jack got no end of pleasure from telling ridiculous jokes. He began calmly, with an air of false dignity and seriousness, but he always delivered the punch line at his most boisterous and animated, his accent growing more pronounced with his excitement.

Thomas soaked up every drop of Jack's humor and, while I thought the jokes were stupid, I always laughed too. Jack somehow made them funny, even when they really weren't.

"Hey, Thomas?" he would say, chewing his gum mechanically, his eyes beaming, "Why don't ducks fly upside down?"

Thomas would shrug dutifully, smiling in anticipation of the well-worn punch line.

"Because they'd quack up, that's why!" Jack would throw back his head, bellowing with laughter, and Thomas would join right in, imitating the raucous braying and snorting. They'd both guffaw entirely too long, and once the laughter died Jack would tell another.

Jack worked for a small computer company in Durango, and he helped us set up our first system, always encouraging us by bringing over new software—stuff to make Dad's writing easier, or games for Thomas and me. Dad and Jack would talk about computers for hours, lost in conversation about the latest developments in gadgetry and software.

The discussions between Jack and my father were by no means limited to computers, however; they had endless debates on everything from philosophy to mathematics. Politics and economics were always hot topics, and sometimes the conversations became lively, although they never degenerated to anger. Jack had an obvious, deep respect for my father, and whenever he was close to angering Dad, he would skillfully redirect the conversation.

Wherever we went, women stared openly at Jack. He usually returned the regard, grinning a little, often earning a furtive smile. A few times, I even noticed my mother watching him, which seemed to make him uncomfortable. He never responded as warmly to her as he did to other women. I assume that my mother stared at Jack for the same reason every female did—because he was good-looking—and yet, for all her apparent appreciation of his physical attributes, my mother seemed to detest him. "There's something wrong with him," I once overheard her say to my father. "He's . . . *strange*."

"What's so strange about him?" Dad asked, surprised. "He's got a good job. The whole town loves him. He's great to Thomas and Douglas—"

"Well that's another thing. He's *too* nice to the boys. What if he's got a thing . . . you know, for *children*, or something like that? I mean he's not married. Don't you think that's a little odd?"

Dad erupted with laughter. "Lots of people aren't married! That doesn't make them pedophiles!"

She scowled. "Well, I don't like him. His language is disgusting. Do you think it's okay for Thomas and Douglas to hear those things?"

"Denise, I haven't noticed that your language is particularly chaste."

"Well, it's better than Jack Alexander's."

My mother had a point—filthy language spiced almost every sentence from Jack's lips, most of which I probably wouldn't have otherwise learned for years. Still, my mother's problems with Jack didn't keep the rest of us from loving him. He was more than a close friend—he was like a second father to my brother and me.

Year Six

ONE DAY, MY mother took me shopping with her to a small boutique on Main Avenue, where she browsed among the racks of clothes and trinkets. Thomas was only an infant at the time, and had stayed home with Dad.

I quickly grew bored and asked her if I could get some ice cream. "Get my purse," she said distractedly. I assumed she would take me to the shop herself—it's what Dad would have done. But she was too engrossed in what she was doing, so she just handed me some money and sent me off.

I walked a few blocks south along the sidewalk until I saw the shop directly across Main. Without looking, I stepped off the curb between two parked cars and emerged into the street. I caught a motion in my peripheral vision and twisted my head, seeing what should have been the last image ever to enter my brain—the front end of a car about twenty feet away, rushing toward me.

The driver pounded the brakes, the tires screamed against the asphalt, and smoke spilled out from behind them. I froze.

A fraction of a second before the impact, something pulled me back. My feet landed on the sidewalk and my knees buckled. I felt hands beneath my arms, picking me up and spinning me around, and when I finally found the courage to open my eyes, I saw Jack Alexander's face a few inches from mine. He smiled. "That was close," he said in a low voice.

I burst into tears. The relief of safety and the realization of what had almost happened too much to bear.

Jack pulled me to him. "You're safe now."

I threw my arms around his neck, the coins in my hand spilling to the ground. Understandably, the miraculous coincidence of Jack's appearance didn't cross my mind; in that moment, he had simply and irrevocably become my savior and hero. He squeezed me a little tighter. "Everything's fine." he said. "You can calm down now, kid." He extended his arms enough that our eyes could connect, and when they did, the impact nearly knocked the wind out of me. Jack wasn't smiling anymore. "I'll never let anything happen to you. Do you understand? Not ever."

I stopped crying as a peaceful feeling rippled through my body. I suddenly felt more secure than ever before in my life.

His face broke into another smile. "So you're okay?"

I nodded.

A few onlookers pointed and stared, as the car that had almost hit me drove slowly past, the driver scowling. Jack waved him on and then returned his attention to me. "What's all this money for?" He began gathering the coins.

"Ice cream."

"Ice cream? Is that what caused all this fuss?" He smiled again and scooped me into his arms. "Well, if that was your mission, Sir Douglas, I feel like I should help you complete it!" He carried me across the street, but just before we reached the shop, he put me down and knelt in front of me, taking my shoulders in his hands. His expression was serious. "Why don't we just keep this between us, okay?" he said, holding my gaze.

I was already looking forward to telling my father about how Jack had saved me; I could imagine how grateful and happy he would be. But Jack's solemnity told me this needed to be a secret, and while I didn't fully comprehend the gravity of his expression, I at least understood that to reveal what had happened would be a violation of his trust. No force in the universe had enough power to cause me to do that.

I nodded slowly, and I never spoke of it.

Summer, Year Nine

My mother's animosity toward my father puzzled me. She often threatened to leave him, after which she almost always sought some sort of misplaced conciliation that I don't think my father—or anyone, for that matter—was capable of giving her. When it failed to materialize, her voice would grow gradually louder until she finally started throwing around the word "divorce."

"You aren't even listening!" she would yell. "We barely keep these boys fed!"

My father would simply look at the floor. "They have enough." And he was right—despite all her frustration, we seemed to have everything we needed.

When my mother's anger turned to the subject of money, I sometimes wondered how we seemed able to afford what she lightly called the "little gifts" she bought for herself. She shopped for entire afternoons, accumulating rows of shoes and racks of clothes.

My mother didn't have a college degree, but she was fiercely independent and beautiful. Her charm could be disarming, so when on occasion she decided to take a job—usually at apparel stores or boutiques—managers and owners were always eager to hire her. But none of the jobs ever lasted more than a few months, and the money she made was far less than the money she spent.

Despite the assaults he endured, the way my father stared at my mother made it clear he loved her deeply. Nonetheless, by the time I turned nine, I knew that if ever two people were mismatched, they were my parents. Maybe my mother felt some affection for my father at one time, but in my memory, she didn't love him the way he so obviously worshipped her. Still, I persisted in the belief that, because Dad adored my mother so much, they would stay together forever. But it wasn't meant to be.

If I had to speculate, I would say that my mother probably only stayed married to my father because she feared being alone. There's little doubt in my mind now that she found whatever she needed outside of their relationship, although I was somewhat oblivious to it as a child.

I'm almost certain Dad stayed faithful until the end. His integrity would never have allowed him to cheat on my mother under any circumstances, regardless of how much she abused his faith in their marriage. Even as the cracks began to appear in their life together, he supported her in every way, overlooking the progressive signs of their failing relationship.

Alcohol didn't yet control my mother, but on most days, she had usually started drinking by lunchtime. She could be mean, sometimes losing her temper for no apparent reason. She never hit me or my brother, but Thomas was afraid of her—she often snapped at him. She seemed to understand, however, that I wasn't intimidated by her the way Thomas was, so she didn't come after me much. We left each other alone, and that worked well enough.

From an early age, I felt that Thomas was my responsibility. He had severe asthma and, while most big brothers are hardwired to pick on their younger siblings, his fragility terrified me and drove me to an almost obsessive protectiveness. Other kids found it odd that I spent so much time with my little brother, but I could never leave him to fend for himself. And because I spent so much time with him, children my age didn't want to have much to do with me.

Thomas's asthma landed him in the hospital several times a year. The first signal of an attack was laborious wheezing, which progressed until he couldn't get a breath of air. We had a breathing machine for him, and whenever an attack started to get bad we poured medications into the apparatus, turned it on, and shoved a tube into his mouth. Sometimes it helped. Sometimes it didn't.

I can still picture him sitting on the couch or his bed, the machine next to him, its motor humming. Rarely did a week pass that I didn't hear its familiar rattle in our small house. Gases flowed from one end of the mouthpiece as Thomas exhaled, and disappeared when he inhaled—provided he still could inhale.

If all else failed and Thomas's breathing became too dangerously labored, we bundled him into the car and took him to Mercy Medical Center's emergency room. There, doctors started IVs and continued the breathing treatments. They asked questions about his allergies and his history, and administered epinephrine injections.

If none of this worked, the last resort was intubation—a process that involved stuffing a plastic hose into Thomas's mouth, forcing oxygen into his lungs. The painful process terrified Thomas. It terrified me too.

I'll never forget how his eyes would widen as his panic escalated. He would cry, but the muffled sobs just gurgled around the tube in his throat. Tears would stream down his cheeks, and I would hold his hand tightly to let him know I was with him. But no matter how strong I tried to be, inevitably I broke down too.

The summer when I was nine was especially tough for Thomas. His breathing was almost always raspy, and the purr of his breathing machine seemed perpetual. Dad and I would sit with him—or at least stay within earshot—when the attacks occurred, checking on him frequently. My mother, however, seemed increasingly annoyed by the episodes, and once the initial crisis of one of his attacks was addressed, she would leave him with one of us—or sometimes even alone—so she could make calls or run errands. I suppose she felt the attention my father and I gave him was enough.

For several days that July my father's freelance work demanded he leave town on assignment, which meant that while he was away, I was forced to care for Thomas to a large extent. And one afternoon, two days into Dad's absence, I was confronted with the thing I dreaded more than almost anything in the world: Thomas started wheezing.

At first, it looked as if it would be a routine attack, so I loaded medicine into his breathing machine and handed him the mouthpiece. My mother had characteristically disappeared that morning without telling us where she would be, so I sat with Thomas, idly thumbing through a comic book while keeping an eye on his condition, which seemed to be worsening. More than anything I knew that I would have to call an ambulance if things didn't improve, and while I was more than prepared to do it if I had to, I didn't want to jump the gun and face my mother's wrath. This would be a delicate judgment call for anyone, but being saddled with such an enormous responsibility at nine years old was terrifying.

About twenty minutes later, I heard the front door open and close, followed by the click of my mother's shoes on the hardwood floors. Thomas was genuinely struggling to get air into his lungs, his face beginning to show signs of the desperation that was almost always followed by panic. I was more scared than ever, but at least now I'd have help. "I'll be right back," I said. "I'm going to get Mom, okay?"

Thomas nodded bravely.

I met my mother as she was heading out the front door again. "Mom, Thomas is really wheezing."

She stopped and turned. "Did you give him a treatment?"

"Yeah, but he's bad." I looked past her and saw an unfamiliar car idling at the curb, a large figure at the wheel. She moved slightly, as if to block my view. "I think he's getting worse," I added.

"Douglas, your brother is fine. I have some things to take care of. I'll be back in a few hours."

"What if he has to go to the hospital?"

"He's not going to have to go to the hospital. How many times has he had trouble this month?"

I shrugged.

"And have we had to go the hospital?"

"No, not for awhile."

"Exactly. He'll be fine. Just keep an eye on him until I get back." She turned and walked out, leaving me standing in the living room. I heard the car's door shut, followed by the engine fading into the distance.

I ran back to Thomas's bedroom, where he lay on his bed, struggling to pull in the medicated vapor. I sat next to him and held his small hand.

"Where's . . . Mom?" he asked around the plastic mouthpiece.

"She'll be back later." I stared at him for a few more minutes, my worry deepening.

Suddenly he said, "Douglas . . . I . . . need . . ." He lifted his chest off the bed, trying to get oxygen into his lungs. ". . . hospital." The fear in his eyes had turned to panic.

This was the most frightening part—the self-perpetuating cycle that defined the nightmare Thomas might have to face at any moment of his life: the asthma causes the panic, which increases the heart rate, which in turn increases the amount of oxygen the body demands. And in that instant, I knew if I didn't get my brother to a hospital, he would die.

Thomas's grip on my hand was almost painful now, his eyes wide, his chest heaving, begging for breath.

"Thomas, you gotta calm down. You're going to make it worse." Now I was starting to panic too.

I hovered over him, tightly gripping his hand as he gasped for breath. His eyes were starting to bulge, filled with terror, his lips darkening along with his skin tone. It was obvious what I had to do, but just as I started to rise to go for the phone, Thomas convulsed, his back arching high off the bed. He lost consciousness, and the mouthpiece fell to the floor. An ambulance would never get here in time. He was still struggling for air, but I could tell none was getting into his lungs.

I grabbed his shoulders and started shaking him. "Thomas! Thomas, wake up!" His lips were blue. "*Thomas!*" I screamed. "*Wake up!*" Tears were rushing down my face, and my vision blurred. "Thomas, if you don't wake up, you're going to *die*!" And it was with this thought that I saw a clear image of my brother lying in a casket. It was more than I could take, and at the very instant I thought I was going to submit to the panic—dangling me over the very edge of insanity—something inside just shifted.

All at once, I felt a tremendous calm, and I realized I was no longer crying. I wasn't scared anymore, and I had lost the urgent sense of purpose. Somehow, I knew everything was going to be all right; the fact that my brother was dying in front of me seemed almost incidental.

I released his hand and gently touched his forehead. I ran my fingers down his face, and I felt a tingling sensation in my hands and arms. My breathing was deep and relaxed.

Thomas abruptly convulsed again, inhaling sharply. I could almost feel the oxygen flowing into his lungs, copious, easy. He began crying, and I scooped him into my arms, squeezing him, crying with him. "It's okay," I said.

And I knew, with a feeling approaching certitude, that it was true—by some miracle, he *was* going to be fine. Yet, through my relief, I felt a deep uneasiness, because I couldn't deny the fact that I had been responsible for the miracle—that I had somehow saved my brother's life—although I had no idea how. I pulled him away from me and watched his color return. He stared at me, but I had to look away, and suddenly, I was confused and frightened again.

Thomas and I looked at each other for a moment, and I wondered if he was aware of what had just happened. I searched his eyes deeply, hoping for some clue, but I found nothing there, and we said nothing.

When Mom got home, she checked in on us. Just to be safe, I had put Thomas back on the respirator. She stood over him for a moment, watching his breathing. She switched off the machine and removed the mouthpiece. "Are you okay?" she asked him.

Thomas nodded, glancing quickly at me, and I wondered if he would say more. I was almost certain he could have no awareness of what had happened; he had, after all, lost consciousness. And yet there was something in his eyes—something resembling understanding, or maybe even empathy. His eyes moved back to my mother, and he remained silent.

She turned to me. "See, I told you everything would be fine."

I stared at the pattern on the bedspread. I had nothing to say.

Dad came home a couple of days later, much to my relief, and that evening, after he had unpacked and gotten organized, we sat down to play some chess. For the past two days, I had been nearly traumatized—not only by watching my brother almost die, but also by trying to understand why he hadn't—and I was comforted to be sitting across from the person I trusted most in the world, even if I could never tell him what happened. How could I explain that Thomas had almost suffocated and then suddenly, inexplicably, recovered fully? And more importantly, how could I broach the subject of my mother's neglect? How would Dad react? No, I would say nothing to him.

We were about halfway through our fourth game when I took one of Dad's rooks. He had no reprisal and fell silent. At first, I thought he had given me the piece, as he always did when he let me win, but then I realized I had taken the piece because I had earned it. My heart began to race.

Dad tried to recapture the piece, but I took my time, playing a game of attrition, and soon we had traded several more pieces. Finally, I took his queen and marched his king down the board, where I cornered it—an obvious and indisputable victory.

An awkward silence hung over us while we stared at each other. Then Dad gave me a broad smile. He began to set up the board again, pushing the white pieces toward me, tacitly confirming my victory. In that moment, I was tempted to tell him what had happened with Thomas, but I stopped myself. It was better this way.

April, Year Eleven

ONE DAY, NOT long after my eleventh birthday, my English teacher stopped me in the hallway after school. "Douglas, could you come to my office?"

I gave her a puzzled look. "My brother's waiting for me on the bus," I said.

"It'll only take a moment. Could you take the second bus?"

I shrugged. "Okay. Let me go tell him. I'll be right back."

I found Thomas and told him to go home without me—that I would catch up with him later. I returned to the classroom and found Mrs. Kellerman busy behind her desk, and when she heard me enter the room, she looked up from her work.

"Did I do something wrong?" I asked.

She smiled. "No, no. I want to talk about your grades, Douglas."

I was confused. "My grades are okay."

"That's exactly why I asked to see you. I can't figure out why you're making Bs and Cs instead of As. I know you have more in you than that."

I thought about it for a moment and then decided to tell her the truth. "I hate school. It's boring." It was an honest response, but I was afraid she would be angry.

She leaned back in her chair and set down her pen. "Did you know that I teach advanced placement?"

I nodded.

"I'd like to get you involved. It will mean you'll be in a smaller class, you'll read more, work at your own pace, and it will give me a chance to focus on you. There will be more homework, but I think you'll enjoy the challenge."

That didn't sound like something I wanted; I hated homework, and I didn't mind the absence of challenge. Besides, my math skills were bad enough that I wasn't sure even a miracle could improve them. "Can I think about it?"

"Sure," she said. "Take a day or two."

I left the classroom and caught the second shuttle about ten minutes later. During the twenty-minute ride, I thought about what Mrs. Kellerman had proposed. I wasn't sure I wanted the increased responsibility, but I loved reading, and the chance to do more of it sounded wonderful.

As the bus approached my stop, I reached down for my pack. When I looked back up, my eyes were drawn to a motion outside the window. What I saw nearly knocked the wind out of me.

Thomas was about twenty-five yards away, sitting on the ground, crying. Even from that distance, I could see that he was wheezing, his chest heaving as he tried to get each breath.

The driver opened the door, and I flew from the bus, landing hard on the street. Adrenaline flooded my body. I dropped my pack and ran, fury burning like acid in my veins.

Two boys stood around Thomas, laughing and throwing stones at him. Any compassionate person would have been appalled by the scene, but watching the boys torment and humiliate my little brother enraged me like nothing I had ever felt.

I plowed into the first boy with so much force that I knocked him against the second boy, toppling them to the ground. They scrambled to get up, but I didn't allow it. I hit the first boy in the face, bloodying his lip. Then I bounced to my feet and swung at the other boy.

My fist connected with the face of Rudy Buck. Our eyes locked, and I froze, suddenly uncertain about what I had done. He moved his hand to his face and rubbed it slowly, staring at me venomously.

Rudy Buck was a year older than I was, and while I didn't really know him, he had always been just odd enough for me to be vaguely aware of his existence—even if only distantly. He was a burly boy, with pale unhealthy-looking skin, eyelids that always seemed to hang at half-mast, crooked, discolored teeth, and atrocious smelling breath. In fact, he carried a general sour odor about him—something like milk gone bad.

As Rudy and I faced each other, the other boy, Mark Evanston, grabbed me from behind and held me. Rudy moved forward and stuck his face in mine. "You *dumb*fuck." He pronounced each syllable slowly, giving me a wicked sneer. Then the smile just disappeared from his lips, and he stared at me blankly for a second— almost as though he no longer knew where he was. His eyes appeared to glaze, and even in the midst of my fear, what happened next seemed eerily incongruent.

Rudy brought his face closer to mine, his expression curious, as though he were an animal about to sniff me. One of his eyes drifted toward his nose, giving him a cross-eyed, unstable look. "What do you think about this . . . *Medicine Man?*" he whispered in a gravelly voice, stretching out the final two words until they became almost a growl.

I felt a chill crawl through my body. I could find no response to the question. While Rudy had sometimes seemed a little strange to me, I had certainly never considered him hostile or violent. But now his expression held a mixture of disgust, anger, and hatred. I stared at him, uncertain what to do, my fear turning mercilessly into terror.

Another second passed before I heard Mark, still holding me from behind, say, "What are you talking about, man?"

Rudy jerked his head back, looked over my shoulder at Mark, and screamed, "*Shut your fucking mouth!*" Then he drew back his arm and delivered two hard blows—to the side of my face and to my stomach.

Mark let me go, and I fell to my knees, staring at the ground, trying to catch my breath. I looked up, first at Mark—who seemed a little frightened and shaken himself—and then at Rudy, who appeared to be reeling, as though he was having trouble keeping his balance. He put a hand on either side of his head and squeezed his eyes shut for a moment. When he opened them again, he stared at me—not with venom, but with uncertainty.

I heard a distant shriek and I turned to see my mother in front of our house. I couldn't make out what she was saying, but now she half-jogged, half-pranced toward us in her heels. When she finally reached us, she went immediately to Rudy. "Oh, my *God*! Are you okay?"

Rudy looked at her but didn't respond.

My mother turned her head to me. "Go home, both of you! *Now!*" she ordered.

But we weren't going anywhere. Thomas was still wheezing—badly.

Suddenly, whatever confusion Rudy had experienced had evaporated, replaced by an uncharacteristic hubris. "Yeah, you *faggot*. Take your little pussy brother home."

My mother didn't seem to hear him.

Rudy touched his cheek where I had hit him, then pointed his finger at me as if to say, *I'll be watching you.* Then he and Mark walked away.

I was groggy and my stomach ached, but I managed to crawl to Thomas, who was crying and wheezing almost uncontrollably. "Thomas, stop," I said gently. "They're gone. Where's your inhaler?"

My mother just stood there, hands on her hips, staring at us. Thomas's sobs diminished, but the wheezing didn't. "They took it . . . away from me . . . They wouldn't give . . . it back."

I got to my feet and scampered to where I had dropped my pack, reaching in and pulling out the spare inhaler I kept there. I ran back to Thomas. "Take a puff and hold it for me."

He put it in his mouth and squeezed. The atomizer released the prescription medicine into his throat, and he managed to hold it for several seconds. He exhaled, and I grabbed him, pulling him close. He shuddered a few times before I let him go. He stopped crying, and his breathing began to improve.

I glared at my mother. I was disgusted with her, and she knew it.

For a moment, she looked apologetic, but then her expression hardened. "Did you hear me?" She raised her voice again. "You get your brother home!"

I grabbed my pack, helped Thomas to his feet, and we started walking toward the house. I stared at her as we passed. She tried to hold my gaze, but failed.

I took Thomas inside the house and examined him carefully. His breathing had improved; thankfully, his asthma wouldn't be more of an issue this day.

The rest of the afternoon was tense. My mother didn't seem to know what to do with herself. She paced from room to room, mumbling angrily. Eventually, she came into the den to rant for a minute or two at Thomas and me about how lucky we'd be if Rudy's parents didn't sue us. Then she walked away, only to return a few minutes later to continue her tirade. "You could have broken his nose!" she shrieked.

Thomas and I listened for a while as she alternately paced and yelled, but finally I couldn't take anymore. "Thomas was getting beat up, Mom. I don't see what your problem is."

"Don't you *talk* to me that way!" she yelled. "I'm your mother! Do you understand?" Her hysteria silenced me. She stayed in the room for a minute longer, and although I was too intimidated to say anything more, I stared at her defiantly. "And don't you *look* at me like that either!" she seethed.

She continued pacing about the house. A few minutes later, I heard her in the other room talking on the phone. Her voice was surprisingly gentle, considering how harsh she had been with me only moments before. "I won't be able to meet you," she said. "There's been some trouble with my boys. No, he'll be home soon. I'll call you tomorrow. I'm sorry. Okay, bye."

When my father got home, my mother had calmed a bit, but tension still permeated the small house, and Dad sensed it. "What's going on?"

"I'll tell you what's going on," she said, folding her arms. "Your son attacked one of the neighborhood kids. He broke his nose, and if I hadn't gotten there when I did, he would have hurt him much worse."

"What?" I said. "I didn't break his nose!"

She glared at me and Dad gave a surprised laugh. "Hold on! What are you talking about?"

"I told you, goddamn it!" she said.

"Denise, please, calm down. Did Douglas just attack some kid for no reason?"

"Just about! They were teasing Thomas a little and Douglas hit the boy."

"Well, that doesn't make much sense." He looked at me. "Why were you fighting, Douglas?"

My mother became indignant. "I told you want happened!"

Dad twisted his head toward her and narrowed his eyes. Something seemed different about him. "And now I'm asking Douglas." He pronounced the words slowly.

She stood there, furious, but said nothing.

He turned back to me. "What happened?"

"I stayed after school. I sent Thomas ahead on the first bus—"

My mother interrupted. "Why did you stay after school?"

"Denise!" Dad barked.

Shock briefly replaced her anger. My father never acted this way. She started to say something, then thought better of it.

Dad looked at me again, silently urging me to continue.

"Mrs. Kellerman asked me if I want to be in the advanced class."

"Really?" he said, raising his eyebrows. "Are you going to?"

"I guess so."

He smiled. "Tell me what happened with the fight."

"I took the later bus, and when I got off some kids were throwing rocks at Thomas. He was wheezing, and I just went crazy I guess."

"See!" my mother yelled.

"*Denise*," my father said, a new, more ominous warning in his voice. He looked back at me. "And then?"

"I don't know. I was just so mad—"

"I got there just in time to stop him!" my mother said. "*That's* what happened!"

Dad winced angrily at the newest interruption, but this time he only said, "Douglas, is that right?"

I looked at my mother. "Well, no . . . One of the boys held me, and the other one hit me." I remembered Rudy's eyes and I almost shuddered.

My mother let out an exasperated sigh, and my father shot a glance at her. She didn't say anything. Dad picked up Thomas. "Are you okay?"

Thomas nodded.

"I can't believe this!" my mother said, her lips tightening. "I'm not blind. Douglas started a fight. He's too protective of his little brother, and I wonder if that isn't a big part of Thomas's problem. Maybe he just needs to take care of himself for a change."

Dad put Thomas down and turned to my mother, fire in his eyes. "If it weren't for Douglas, I have no idea what Thomas's life would be like. Try to remember that next time you're out performing your duties as the town courtesan." His eyes didn't waver from hers.

She looked as though she had been slapped. Dad narrowed his eyes again. "You didn't think I knew?"

Her lip trembled, and her face twisted with rage. She exhaled strongly, air hissing through her clenched teeth, and stormed from the room.

Dad looked down at the floor. I could see how much effort this moment had required of him. Finally he turned to me. "Have you guys eaten?"

Thomas and I shook our heads.

"There are some leftovers in the fridge." He looked at me. "Heat them up for you and your brother. If you boys have homework I want you to do it." He smiled reassuringly and walked out of the room.

Thomas said to me, "Douglas? What's a 'cort . . .'" he hesitated. "What's that thing Dad called mom?"

I had never heard the word myself, but I had an idea what it meant. "I don't think it's important, Thomas." I looked at him for a moment longer. "Let's get some dinner."

The next few weeks were a firestorm. The incident brought about an enormous change in my father, as though a crack had appeared in the shell that had confined him for years. I suppose he had simply had enough of my mother's volatility, not to mention her irresponsibility with her family. I could see the intense love he still felt for her, but he no longer backed down from her aggression, which only caused the tempest to grow.

My mother stuck it out for a while, although she spent less time than ever at home. Eventually, she seemed to realize that my father was no longer going to capitulate to her anger. She asked for a divorce about two months after my fight with Rudy Buck and Mark Evanston. The request seemed to devastate my father, yet he agreed to her wishes without protest.

About two weeks after the announcement, Dad moved in with Jack Alexander. Thomas and I stayed with my mother, although I wasn't sure why, and I hoped it was only temporary. I was relieved that my parents had separated, but I worried about where Thomas and I would wind up. A couple of weeks later, however, my father sat us down and alleviated my concerns.

"Your mother and I have decided that you boys will live with me," he said. "I've rented a small house for us downtown."

"What'll Mom do?" I asked.

"I'm not sure, but I want you to be clear about something: it isn't that your mom doesn't want you, you understand? You're living with me because we decided that's what's best for you and your brother."

I think Dad knew I didn't believe him. I felt sure that my mother's decision had far less to do with our well-being than Dad tried to make us believe, but we left it at that.

Not long after the separation, we found out my mother was seeing someone regularly. The news didn't bother me, but I think it crushed Dad. For the next few months, he just wasn't his usual self. Gradually, however, his spirits lifted, and he returned to normal—or maybe even better than normal. Eventually he even started dating a little too.

When the divorce was final, Dad got a loan and bought my mother's half of our old house, where she had lived since the separation. She moved into an apartment, and Thomas, Dad, and I moved back into the old place.

My father told my mother she could see us whenever she wanted, but Thomas and I only spent time with her about once a month, if that, and the visits were always awkward. Essentially, she just disappeared from our lives.

Fall, Year Eleven

I DECIDED TO take the advanced placement courses Mrs. Kellerman had suggested, but I wasn't prepared for the level of the material, or the pace at which we studied it. I was allowed to read more than ever before, which I enjoyed tremendously. Unfortunately, I was also introduced to algebra a full year earlier than I otherwise would have been, and despite the extra attention I received from my instructors and tutors, I did poorly. I had never been mathematically inclined, but now the numbers were totally defeating me, and I started to wonder what Mrs. Kellerman had seen in me.

The school required one music course, and at the beginning of that school year, the symphony teacher visited each classroom to talk about what he called "musical magic." The whole concept sounded absurd to me, and I never would have considered joining the symphony if the only alternative hadn't been choir. But there was no way I was going to stand up and sing songs every day, so the symphony it was.

Once I got used to the idea that I was going to have to play something, I opted for a stringed instrument. I shied away from the violin and viola because only girls played those, and I didn't want to lug around a bass. So I decided I would play the cello.

On the day I made my decision, Jack and Dad were sitting on the porch when Thomas and I got home from school. Jack immediately jumped up and grabbed Thomas, picking him by the ankles and lifting him above the ground.

"Hey, Thomas!" Jack said, smacking his gum exuberantly. "This duck walks into a pharmacy, right?"

Thomas giggled as he hung upside down. "Let me down, Jack!"

Jack ignored the demand. "So, Thomas, this duck says to this pharmacist, 'I need some lip balm. Just put it on my bill!'" Jack bellowed with laughter and Thomas cackled with him. Then Jack laid him on the ground and tickled him.

Thomas was giggling so hard he almost couldn't talk. "Jack, stop!" he managed to yell. "I'm going to piss all over myself!"

"Goddamn it, Thomas! Where did you learn language like that?" Jack said, tickling him some more.

"I wonder," Dad said. "Jack, leave him alone. He's going to start wheezing."

Jack relented, and Thomas sat up, catching his breath.

"And how was your day, Douglas?" Jack said, sitting down next to me.

"It was good. I joined the symphony."

"The symphony?" Dad said. "What instrument are you going to play?"

"The cello."

He looked at me skeptically. "And I suppose you want me to buy you a cello?"

"Is that okay?"

"Will you be serious about it?"

"The only other choice was to sing in the choir."

Jack's face twisted. "Oh, hell. Do they want you to wear a dress, too? I guess we better go to the goddamn music store right now."

Dad said, "Hold on a second—"

"Hold on nothing," Jack said. "Let's go." And before Dad could protest further, we all piled into the car and drove downtown.

When we got to the store, Dad started looking at the used cellos, but Jack would have none of it. "Max, this is absolutely no time to be a tightass. This boy could be the next Pavarotti."

Dad looked annoyed. "Pavarotti's an opera singer, Jack."

"Be that as it may, we owe this child the opportunity to excel at his talent." Jack gestured toward me with a broad sweep of his arm. "We should provide him an instrument with which he might make us proud!" He put his hand on top of my head as though anointing me.

"What's this 'we' crap, Jack?" Dad said. "Are you planning to pay for it?"

Jack started to answer, but then looked at the price tag and closed his mouth. He rubbed his chin for a moment. "Perhaps my enthusiasm is premature."

"Yes," Dad said. "Perhaps it is."

In the end, I came away with a moderately priced used cello. It was dinged and scratched in a few places, but it was good enough to get me started.

Our music teacher was Robert Dickey, but we just referred to him as "the Dick." He was a chain smoker, and while he never actually lit up in class, he did smoke just about everywhere else on campus, in direct violation of any number of rules. But Dickey had worked at the school so long that he outranked everyone in unspoken tenure, if not in fact. No one was about to tell the Dick he couldn't smoke a cigarette.

The Dick wiggled when he walked and spoke with a slippery, distinctly feminine patois that caused a lot of speculation about his sexual orientation. He had a high-pitched voice, and when he got excited, he almost seemed to squeal.

The Dick's left eye was made of glass. Someone once told me that he lost it in "the war," although I never heard which war, specifically. The orb floated around in his head as though it had a mind of its own, like some exotic pet he kept with him all the time. It was ghoulish.

When he moved his head, his good eye went precisely to where he directed it, but the glass eye just slid around sluggishly in its socket. It reminded me of the compass on the dashboard of our car, the directional ball forever bobbing around in its liquid-filled glass container, indicating a general direction but never firmly committing to a solid point.

The Dick had an unpredictable temper that sometimes resulted in dramatic tantrums. "Are you playing in A minor?!" he would howl, swinging his gaze in the general direction of part of the class, the glass eye making it impossible to determine exactly whom he was addressing.

Two or three of us would glance at each other with puzzled expressions and barely perceptible shrugs. The glass eye would bob gruesomely, like an egg with a bull's eye painted on it floating around in a bowl of water. "Yes, I'm talking to you!"

"Which one of us?" someone would whisper.

Then he would squeal again, even louder. "*Are you listening to me?*" His glass eye wiggled excitedly in its socket, and those of us in the approximate area of his gaze would exchange confused glances again. Finally we *all* just nodded, and that usually satisfied him.

"Well it doesn't sound like you're playing in A minor!" The Dick would stare at us silently for a while longer to drive home his point. Then he would strike his music stand theatrically with his baton, and we'd begin again.

In spite of the Dick, I enjoyed playing the cello more than I thought I would. I fell in love with the richness of the sound, and almost immediately I began to hear unique patterns in the music I played. I invented my own progressions that were simple initially, but grew in complexity—my first attempts at true creativity. They came to me of their own accord, changing and growing over time, emerging from my emotions, which only made them more beautiful to me.

But I was no virtuoso. I loved the spontaneity of actually playing, not studying music on sheets of paper, which was tedious and only diminished the experience. Our practice exercises seemed dry and cold to me, too calculated and precise— exactly the antithesis of what made me love the music itself. I found the relation- ships between keys and scales intimidating and laborious, reminding me a little too much of my problems with math.

I struggled with the lessons, mechanically repeating the notes written on the sheets in front of me until I got so frustrated I had to push it all aside. I would close my eyes, lean my head back, and fall into one of my own compositions, soaking up every note emanating from my cello. The music soothed me, even if I didn't understand the theories behind it, and the instrument gave me com- fort—an escape from reality.

I didn't know it at the time, but this was my first glimpse of the passion that would drive me to the brink of my own ruin and force me to examine the darkest places in my soul. Yet this same energy would offer me a deeper understanding of my place in the universe, opening my perception in a way I could never have imagined, pulling me back to the surface.

My cello would be with me through almost all of it, its music a manifestation of the turmoil that would consume me. And in the end, it would be there to help me find my way home.

April, Year Fourteen

IN THE WINTER, the Rocky Mountains are a desolate, ice-covered wasteland. The views are majestic, but it is a long, frigid season of short days, seemingly devoid of life, and for two kids growing up in the mountains, spring and summer are gifts beyond measure. Wildflowers emerge—patches of living fireworks exploding in every imaginable color, blanketing meadows and fields. The trees, with their new leaves, create deep shade, and the rivers and streams swell with melting snow.

One spring day just after my fourteenth birthday, Thomas and I went to one of our favorite spots on Junction Creek, about a quarter of a mile from our house—one of our many after-school haunts. Here, boulders had fallen down the side of a sheer cliff, partially blocking the stream and creating a large, deep hole. Tree trunks and branches further clogged the passage of water, which formed a beautiful silver cascade that danced through the detritus. When the creek was down in the warm summer months, we loved to splash around in the hole. But in April, the water was still too cold, and the current too strong for swimming.

This afternoon, we went a little farther upstream, looking for a shallow pool to explore. We were on the rocks along the banks of the creek, watching the water surge in the center, when I caught movement in my peripheral vision. I turned my head and saw a dog walking toward us.

It was a black Labrador retriever, and he quickly made it clear he was friendly. Thomas threw a stone into the creek, and the Lab enthusiastically bounded after it. After spending some time searching for the rock, he swam back to us. Thomas and I began throwing sticks for him, which he would dutifully return to us.

After a few minutes Thomas said, "Can I ask you a question?"

"Sure."

"What does it mean when a boy and a girl are 'going' together?"

I turned to look at my little brother and grinned. "You got a girlfriend, Thomas?"

He became indignant. "No! It's just that some of the boys and girls at school are, you know, going together."

I nodded and threw a small branch into the stream, trying not to laugh. The Lab leapt into the water with a splash, chasing down the stick.

"Douglas," he said after another moment, "Have you ever gone with a girl?"

"No."

"Why not?"

"Mmm . . . I guess I've never met anybody I've wanted to *go* with."

"Do you have to be in love with somebody if you go together?"

"I don't think so."

Thomas thought about that for a minute. "Do Mom and Dad love each other?"

"I think they used to."

"Why does Mom look so mad at Dad whenever she comes over?"

I picked up another stick and threw it for the dog. "I think sometimes people just don't get along, and so they have to . . . sort of . . . get away from each other."

"Do you think she's mad at him?"

"Yeah, I think she might be a little mad."

"Is she mad at us too?"

"No, I just think she's got a lot of stuff on her mind, that's all." I took a deep breath and let it go slowly. The Lab was back, panting and looking eagerly at me. "We should get home soon." I picked up the stick the dog had dropped at my feet, heaving it into a deeper channel of the creek.

There were few places on Junction Creek where the stream was so deep that a dog would need to swim, but this was one of them. The Lab seemed strong and comfortable in the water, and it didn't really occur to us that it might be dangerous. I was about to turn and begin the journey home when the current pulled the dog under, near the deep hole downstream that Thomas and I had so carefully avoided. The dog surfaced, but the creek sucked him under again, forcing him into the trunks and branches that formed the small waterfall at the edge of the hole.

A chill wrapped around me and I yelled, "Get out of there!" as if the command would somehow solve the problem. But the dog was in trouble, snagged in the tangled debris of the cascade, and there was no way for us to get to him without endangering ourselves. He pawed furiously at the water, but the current was strong, sucking him under again and again. He came up for air intermittently, whining and yelping. I'll never forget the sounds—desperate, panicky. "Get out of there!" I screamed again. But the dog couldn't break free. His head began going under more frequently.

Thomas stayed next to me, his hands on his head in absolute helplessness. "Douglas, get him *out* of there!"

The dog went under a final time and my body tensed. I was completely powerless, my mind racing in frustrated agony, searching furiously for a way to save him.

We waited for what seemed like hours, pacing the edge of the creek, nearly hysterical. I tried to convince myself that the dog was still alive, that somehow he had held his breath, or had surfaced beyond our vision. But in a more rational part of my mind, a cold voice droned, reminding me that no matter how hard I tried to resist the truth, there was no hope.

I rubbed my face for a moment, and when I dropped my hands, I saw a black mass pop to the surface downstream. I ran along the bank, following the unmoving body as it drifted to the shore, until it lodged on some stones a few feet from the edge. I jumped into the water and grabbed the lifeless heap, dragging it to land. Foam flowed from the mouth and the eyes were fixed open, glazed, staring at nothing.

Thomas stood next to me, tears flowing down his cheeks.

"I'm sorry," I said, not really knowing who I was apologizing to. I kept thinking of how the dog must have suffered, and I couldn't accept that I had thrown the stick that had caused this. I had killed him.

With a last desperate effort to change the outcome, I put my hands on the dog's chest near his lungs. I didn't know CPR, but I had to try something. I frantically pumped the chest and more foam gurgled from the mouth with each push. I sobbed, "Please, dog . . . *please*, live."

The imminence of death is never more disturbing than to children—blinded by innocence, still oblivious to the true intensity of mortality. And yet, death is, by any human definition, natural. But therein lies the foundation of human arrogance: our myopia leads us to believe that we actually know what nature is, exclusive of our own inextricable roles in its complex, yet elegant production.

The universe, however, is an unpredictable and boundless realm—an infinite *suchness* that so transcends our insignificance as to be comical. And no matter how much our hubris instills in us the belief that our deficient senses might explain its reasons—as though the universe needs reasons—there are still so many things we don't understand.

What happened next was well beyond anything my experiences could have prepared me for. It addressed much more than my innocence; it called into question my very perception of reality.

A gentle warmth filled my hands. I thought I felt—or maybe heard—a distant vibration. I stopped pumping the dog's chest, feeling the tremor as it ran through my body, stimulating every sense. I gave in to the odd, almost familiar peace descending over me, pushing out the fear.

And then I remembered: This was the same sensation I felt when Thomas had nearly suffocated, only amplified. Chills ran the length of my body, and my vision grew dark for a second. I felt a vacuum develop in my mind, a distinct lack of anything, blocking my ability to reason, opening my mind to its true magnitude for the first time ever. There seemed to be no way that I, a creature of substance, could resolve this emptiness—this absolute nothingness.

Whatever this was, its presence suddenly made me realize that my understanding of the world around me was flawed, and the epiphany rolled over me like a speeding bus. The more I tried to reconcile the problems before me, the less important they became, and I found strange comfort in this.

And still, I looked for substance, just beyond my reach: how could this place in which I exist be so vast, so utterly beyond my comprehension, so complex, and yet so simple? Something stirred in me, and what followed didn't come to me as mere words, but as an entire concept:

This is who you are.

An electric current of warmth spread through my body. A smile came to my lips, and I looked at Thomas, who stopped crying and took a few staggering steps back. He sensed something powerful was happening to me and it terrified him. My smile faded a little. I looked tentatively at my little brother for a moment longer and then back to the dog's corpse under my hands.

The body moved.

Thomas let out a little gasp, stepping back further.

The dog coughed, foam sputtering from his lungs. He spewed and hacked for a moment, before raising his head, confusion clouding his face.

The tension in my body melted, replaced by relief, and then by utter exhilaration. But then, just as quickly, a landslide of reality descended, and I took a deep breath, my eyes widening with fear. The dog and I looked at each other, and a new feeling began to seep in.

My smile disintegrated. This was not normal.

The dog rose to his feet unsteadily, looking at me, his eyes full of confusion and fear. He shook his body and then staggered away.

I turned to my little brother, forcing another smile, but he looked at me strangely, unable to articulate his questions. I rubbed my face. "I . . . don't . . ." I couldn't get my mind around this thing, to accept that it had really happened. "Maybe he wasn't . . ." But we both knew the dog had been dead only a few seconds ago.

Thomas just gawked at me, his lips parted slightly.

I put my hand out. "Thomas . . .?"

He stood very still.

"Thomas?" My voice cracked.

He continued to stare at me.

I tried to inhale as deeply as I could, but my breathing was shallow and strained. I sat on the pebbles and rocks on the bank of the stream, put my face in my hands, and began to cry. I stayed like that for a few minutes, grasping for some explanation.

I felt a hand on my shoulder, and I looked up. Thomas stood over me, his face still blank. But there was something new in his eyes now, a sort of compassion. "We won't talk about it," he said. "We just won't tell nobody."

I didn't know how to respond, but the kindness in his eyes comforted me. It reminded me of the day Jack had pulled me out of the path of the oncoming car.

Finally I smiled a little. "Yeah, okay." He held out his hand, and I took it, pulling myself up. "We really ought to get home," I said. "Dad's going to be worried."

Eventually I surrendered to the mystery, because no matter how hard I tried, there were no answers, and nobody would believe us anyway. It was probably just some fluke. I wasn't, after all, a doctor. Anything might have explained it. *Anything.*

I simply pushed the memory into a dark corner of my mind, hoping that I would never have to think about it again.

◆

I CONTINUED TAKING advanced placement classes through middle school and into my first year of high school. While other kids were experimenting with drugs, alcohol, and their sexuality, I avoided it all; I had neither the time, nor the desire. Instead I stayed buried in my books and music.

I played my cello almost every day, but I no longer made much progress. The passion I had discovered seemed to have dried up, and, although I still forced myself to practice, music theory never stopped giving me trouble. I couldn't seem to break out of old patterns—I was mired in the same old scales and runs, and so my interest waned. The big picture eluded me. No matter how much I studied, I was unable to grasp it.

I began to take an interest in science, especially physics. I found a more tangible mathematical theory there, with concepts that I could easily visualize. The revolutionary discoveries that drove scientific progress fascinated me. But despite this newfound passion, rudimentary math—like music theory—still confounded me. Science helped bridge the gap a little, but the numbers failed to come clear for me. I would have small breakthrough moments, as if for a millisecond a huge screen had been illuminated in front of me, giving me the critical elements I needed to understand the complex calculations, but the revelation would soon fade into blackness, leaving me as frustrated as ever. Understanding math became almost an obsession: how much peace would I find if I could only grasp it?

I would have to find inspiration, a new way of thinking about numbers and music, but the more I struggled to discover that perspective, the more unobtainable the objective seemed to be.

Late April, Year Sixteen

IN THE SPRING after my sixteenth birthday, I told Dad I wanted a job. He seemed to like the idea. "Where are you going to apply?"

"I want to work with Jack," I said.

MacGregor's Electronics was the small technology company that Jack worked for, and while it didn't have many employees, it still accounted for a large share of the computer business around Durango. For decades, MacGregor's had sold radios, CBs, and other electronic products, but with the recent onset of the digital revolution, the store's focus had shifted to the exploding computer industry. So if consumers or companies around Durango had computer needs, MacGregor's was the place to go for help. It wasn't the most advanced shop in the world, but it was sophisticated for Durango.

From the day Jack brought us our first computer, I had been enthralled with it, and I gradually learned how to use all of the programs he had given us. Dad didn't take to it as intuitively as I had, and struggled with most of it. But by watching Jack carefully when he encountered various problems, I was eventually able to troubleshoot, helping Dad through just about any technical obstacle.

After Dad gave his approval, I went straight to MacGregor's to talk to Jack. I found him in the back of the shop, in a repair room, with his head nearly hidden inside the casing of a computer. He heard me and looked up. "Hey kid, what's going on?"

"Not much." I nervously put my hands in the front pockets of my jeans. "I wanted to ask you something."

"I'm all ears, chief."

"Do you think maybe you could help me get a job here?"

"Sure," he said, putting his head back into the computer's chassis.

That was easy, I thought.

Jack didn't add anything, so I said, "Um . . . do I need to talk to somebody about it or what?"

"Nope."

"Oh. So . . . what do I need to do?"

"Nothing."

"Okay." I rocked back and forth on the soles of my shoes. "So . . ."

"Look, kid, you have a job if you want it. I've already talked it over with everyone here."

"But how did you—?"

"I didn't. But I've seen the way you are with that computer at your house, and I figured it was just a matter of time before you showed up looking for work."

I looked at him, puzzled. "Well, when should I start?"

Just then, Jack dropped something inside the box he was repairing. He looked down in frustration. "Fuck. You start right now, that's when. Hand me that screwdriver over there."

I stayed and helped Jack for the rest of the day, returning the next morning as an official employee of MacGregor's Electronics.

My earliest childhood memories included Jack, but working with him at Mac-Gregor's exposed a side of him I had never seen before. For instance, Jack had always been pretty fashionable, as far as I could tell, but at work, he looked nearly impeccable—at least by Durango's standards. The only exceptional note in his otherwise carefully constructed wardrobe was a collection of dilapidated baseball caps, all bearing filthy slogans. To his credit, he did seem to find the good sense to remove them—with lightning speed—whenever clients, or, God forbid, Carlisle MacGregor appeared.

The whole routine seemed perfectly moronic to me, and finally one day, I could bear it no longer. "Jack, why do you wear those stupid hats?"

"Huh?"

"They sort of make you look like . . . an idiot."

His face became pained. "You think I look like an idiot, Douglas?"

I smiled. "Well, yeah."

Jack furrowed his brow and waved his hand dismissively. "Well, that shows how much you know, you unrefined little cretin. Let me explain something: the world is full of people who think it's their job to impose decency and virtue on the rest of us, and I simply prefer to keep things balanced."

I stared at him blankly, not quite sure how to respond.

"Fuck all of 'em," he said. Then he patted my head and walked away.

Jack and his coworker, Pete Collins, formed MacGregor's technical crew. Pete was in his late twenties, tall and lean, with a pronounced stoop and long, straight, sandy blonde hair. He smoked inordinate amounts of pot and listened to punk all day through a set of ratty headphones that seemed as critical to his wardrobe as the shoes protecting the soles of his feet. He wore a full, scraggly beard and sported a tattoo of a marijuana leaf on his upper right arm. Pete was quiet and smiled all the time, with happy, squinty blue eyes that radiated crows' feet at the edges. He wore only jeans or corduroy pants, always accessorized by a well-worn T-shirt and filthy tennis shoes. Sometimes he looked positively homeless.

But Pete's image belied his talent. Despite appearances, he was astonishingly brilliant. Around MacGregor's, Pete and Jack were the guys who made things work—the techies. They were strange bedfellows, to be sure, but they worked extremely well together, creating a partnership I envied.

Most of the work at MacGregor's took place in "the Cooler"—a big room with workbenches along the walls. The tables were full of tools that we used to fix the boxes that came and went. I don't know how the Cooler got its name, but that summer, I spent a large part of my time in that room, helping Jack and Pete.

Jack rarely called Pete by his given name, preferring instead to address him as "Ass," or, occasionally, the more formal "Anus." Jack seemed interminably puzzled by Pete's very existence. Sometimes, for no apparent reason, he would cock his head and stare at Pete with a perplexed expression. Pete, however, would have no part of Jack's foolishness—his standard response was no reaction at all.

All of the repartee aside, Jack and Pete were good friends; there was no mistaking the intellectual and professional bond between them. But Jack never seemed to cease taking delight in harassing Pete—whether Pete was around or not—and this behavior, like all the rest, began to gnaw at me.

"Why do you call Pete that?" I asked Jack one day.

"Call him what?" Jack said, sorting through a pile of cable and chomping his gum. His baseball cap read: *Jesus loves you. Everybody else thinks you're an asshole.* It sat loosely on his head, cocked at an odd angle.

"Anus."

Jack stopped chewing his gum. His expression became confused, bordering on worry. "You don't know?"

I shook my head, and he resumed chewing, slowly. "Oh, you'll find out soon enough, I guess."

The wait wasn't long. A few days later, we were in the Cooler testing some network boxes when Jack wrinkled his nose. "Jesus *fucking* Christ!" He stepped back from the workstation, his face contorted. "*Fuck!* Was that you, Ass?"

Pete tapped on the keyboard in front of him, his face expressionless.

"How do you make that smell?" Jack asked. "Did you shit your knickers?"

Then I smelled something like a mixture of rotten eggs and garlic. I gagged.

Jack folded his arms and glared at Pete. "You're going to make the child vomit."

"I can't help it," Pete said, his face still emotionless.

"Bullshit!" Jack said. "Your turd vapor is giving us lung cancer. Has it ever occurred to you that you could go outside?"

Pete just pecked at the keyboard.

I started moving quickly toward the door and Jack followed, keeping his eyes on Pete. "You're repugnant, you filthy hippie. You ought to see a goddamn doctor about that."

Early June, Year Sixteen

ONE FRIDAY DURING lunch, Pete and I were in the alley, in the middle of a chess game, when Jack opened the door slightly. "Hello, girls."

Without taking his eyes from the board, Pete said, "Hello, Jack."

Jack stepped into the alley and mussed my hair. "Who's winning, kid?"

"Not me."

"What? Douglas, don't tell me this freak is beating you."

Pete leaned to his right, resting his elbow on his leg. "Who would miss you if you died, Jack?"

"I know you would, Anus. Listen, I have to go to Pagosa to fix a network, and I'm going to need some help."

Pete sighed. "Well, I guess that means I'm coming. You'll just fuck it up if I'm not there."

Jack looked at me. "Do you want to come, kid?"

"I have plans with Dad and Thomas later. Will we be back by six?"

"I don't see why not. It shouldn't take more than a couple of hours."

"Okay, I'll go."

"Get your stuff together and meet me at my truck." He started to go back into the building, but then added, "Hey, Anus, can you get that stuff I asked you about?"

"Yes, Jack," Pete said, looking back at the board in mock frustration.

Jack nodded, turned, and closed the door.

"What stuff?" I said.

"I have a friend who has some acid," Pete said. "Jack wants some."

"What kind of acid?"

"What do you mean, 'What kind of acid?'"

"I don't know. Why would Jack want acid?"

"You really don't know, do you?"

I shook my head, and Pete gave me a quizzical look. "It's a drug, dude. It's LSD."

"Is he going to take it?"

"What else would he do with it?"

"Have you done it?"

Pete laughed. "Yeah, once or twice."

"What's it like?"

"You see shit, hallucinations. I don't know. It makes you think about a lot of stuff."

My eyes were wide. "Isn't it dangerous?"

"Water's dangerous! Electricity's dangerous!" He moved a rook and stood up. "Checkmate."

I stared at the board, but the outcome meant nothing to me. I had a strange sensation in my stomach. My teachers had hammered into my mind the sinister and deadly nature of drug abuse; even getting used to Pete's nearly constant pot-smoking had been difficult for me, although I had come to accept that the habit probably wasn't as bad as everyone made it out to be.

But LSD? I knew almost nothing about it—what form it came in, what effect it had. And Jack was using it? Somehow it just didn't seem right.

Pete said, "Let's get going." He went back into the building and I followed slowly. We grabbed our bags along with some tools from the Cooler, and met Jack in front of the shop, where we loaded our gear into his truck. I hopped into the cab between Jack and Pete, and we left for Pagosa Springs.

About half an hour into the trip, Pete said, "Pull over at that gas station, Jack. I gotta pee."

"You know, Anus, you're like a goddamn child. Why didn't you do that before we left?"

"*I'm* like a child?" Pete shook his head and glared at Jack. "Just shut up and pull over."

Jack sighed, easing into the gas station.

After Pete got out, I looked at Jack, trying to find the courage to ask the question needling at me.

"What is it, kid?" he asked.

"Jack, are you really going to take LSD?"

He looked surprised. "Who told you that? Pete?"

I nodded.

He stared hard at me, smiling. "Why do you want to know?" I shrugged, and he said, "I don't know, I might take some."

"Does Dad know you do drugs?"

He chuckled. "Well, I don't really *do* drugs. But your dad and I haven't discussed it, if you must know. Why? Were you planning on telling him?"

"No." I looked at the floor for a moment and then said, "What's it like?"

His eyes swept the horizon. "That's a tough question. I guess it just changes the way I look at the world."

"Pete says it makes you think about stuff."

"Hmmm . . . is that what he says? Well, for starters, Pete doesn't think at all. Anyway, it's more accurate to say that LSD makes you think differently. Why are you asking me so many questions? Are you thinking about becoming a chemical dependent, Douglas?"

"No! Come on, Jack! I was just wondering—"

"I know, I know." He nodded toward the gas station, and I saw Pete approaching the truck. "I want to talk to you more about it later, but maybe when we're alone. Cool?"

I nodded, and Jack smiled.

About five miles outside Pagosa Springs, we turned onto a small farm road and drove another six or seven miles, until we reached a large group of warehouses. The company was a distributor of farm equipment, and without access to their inventory databases, through their network, they were nearly powerless to function. The manager stepped out of his office, looking relieved that we had arrived. He took us into one of his warehouses, and we got to work.

It took about an hour to fix the problem, and when we were finished, I finally looked at my watch. It read almost four-thirty. Jack said, "I guess we'd better get out of here if you're going to make that date with your dad and Thomas." The manager thanked us profusely as we packed our gear and then headed out.

We had driven a few miles along the small road leading back to Pagosa Springs when Jack's truck began to sputter. It jolted several times before the engine died. Jack coasted to a stop by the side of the road. "God*damn* it!"

"What's wrong?" I asked.

"I don't know. I should just trade this fucking thing in. It gives me more trouble than anything I've ever driven."

Pete laughed. "That's because it's older than you are."

Jack ignored him. He tried to turn over the engine, but it wouldn't start, so he popped the hood, and we got out. "What do you boys think?"

Pete looked skeptically at the engine. "I think your truck is a hunk of shit."

Jack scowled at him. "Why don't you shut up, you fucking hippie? Do you know anything about engines?"

"No."

Jack sighed. "Well, it's about four or five miles to Pagosa, so we might as well start walking and hope somebody picks us up." He looked at me. "Sorry, kid, it looks like you're going to miss dinner with your dad and your brother."

"It'll be okay. I'll call when we get to a phone."

We began our hike toward Pagosa Springs. Although several cars passed us, no one stopped to give us a ride.

It took about an hour and a half to get to there, and we headed straight to the only gas station we saw. While Jack spoke to the mechanics, I used a pay phone to call Dad.

"What time do you think you'll be home?" he asked.

"I don't know. I guess it depends on how bad the problem is."

"I could come pick you guys up."

"It's okay. Jack says the truck does this sometimes, but it doesn't take long to fix."

"Well if it looks like you're going to be really late, give me a call."

"Okay. I'll see you later, Dad."

Jack and Pete were standing by the tow truck, in conversation with the mechanics. "It'll probably take about an hour to get the truck hitched up and back to the garage," one of the mechanics said as I approached. "Why don't ya'll grab a bite to eat, and we'll go have a look." The two mechanics got into the tow-truck and drove away.

We picked a small diner not far from the garage. We found a quiet table in the corner and gazed at our menus until the waiter came to take our orders. After a few minutes of silence Jack said, "Well, you two are just full of interesting discussion tonight."

"I'm sure you'll be running your mouth soon enough," Pete said.

Jack gave him an empty stare, but Pete just shook his head and looked absently out the window toward the service station. Jack turned to me. "I guess I'll have to get my conversation from you, kid. What should we talk about?"

"I don't know."

"Hmmm. How's school? Are you still doing that advanced stuff?"

"Yeah, we just finished exams."

"How'd they go?"

"I don't know . . . okay I guess. I've been having trouble with math."

"You don't like math? What the hell's wrong with you?"

"It's not that I don't like it. It's just hard, that's all. I like physics a lot, though. It's helped me with math a little."

"Physics, huh?" Jack brightened. "Have you started studying quantum mechanics?"

"No, I think we start on that next year."

"Well, you'll enjoy it. It's a real mind-fuck."

"And I'm sure you're going to tell us *all* about it, aren't you?" said Pete.

Jack turned to him, smiling broadly. "Now that you mention it, Anus, I guess I just might."

Pete looked at me and rolled his eyes.

Jack glared at him and took a sip of beer. Then he looked at me. "You've learned about Newton and Einstein and all that?"

I nodded. "Uh huh, some. We've been reading about them."

Jack held his bottle up to the light, tilting his head and closing one eye. "Everybody knows that stupid story about Isaac Newton getting knocked on the head with an apple, but most people don't know much about Einstein. Oh, sure they know he was a goddamn genius, and that he had a fucked-up haircut and all that. But they don't know anything about his theories."

He put the bottle down and began to peel the label. "Einstein was the first to point out that time and space are really just one unified thing, which oddly enough," Jack smiled at me, his eyes twinkling, "he called 'space-time.'" He looked at the ceiling for a moment. "It's really elegant if you think about it. I mean, how do you travel through space without taking time to do it? And how do you move through time without taking up space?" He suppressed a burp. "I may not have that exactly right, but that's about the gist of it."

Jack's eyes, however, told me that he *did* have it exactly right. I got the feeling that any mistakes he made were by design, and I wondered how much he kept hidden from the world behind his mask of silliness. Every time I thought I knew everything there was to know about him, he surprised me with something new. He was like a big brother, a dad, a best friend, and a great teacher all rolled into one. But more than anything, Jack was my hero. I didn't take my eyes off him as he spoke, and even Pete was listening closely now. "How do you know all this stuff?" I said.

"I don't know. I've read some books. And I watch those educational TV shows too. They always have all those German bastards on there." Jack narrowed his eyes and stared at me advisedly. "You know, Germans are the smartest fuckers on earth—they invent everything."

"Like fascism," Pete said.

"The Italians invented fascism, Peter, and this illustrates why I'm telling the story and you are not. You are a foul human being with no education and you would do well to absorb as much as possible from your intellectual superiors."

Pete shook his head and smiled. "Doesn't your tongue ever ache?"

The waiter appeared with our food, and after he distributed the plates, Jack pulled the wad of gum out of his mouth and stuck it under the table.

Pete glared at him. "That's so bourgeois."

Jack took a bite of his sandwich and resumed his lecture. "Anyway, Einstein knew that energy and mass are essentially the same thing. He discovered that as you go faster, time slows down for you, but not for anyone who isn't moving as fast as you are.

"There were some other guys in there too—one named Bohr and another one named Schrödinger. The person who did the earliest work, though, was Max Planck." Jack pointed his bottle at me now. "Planck is the guy who came up with the word 'quantum' or 'quanta' or whatever it is.

"So then this *other* German named Heisenberg came up with this idea that blows my mind more than all the rest. He called it the 'uncertainty principle.' He said that while you could measure a particle's velocity—"

"What's a particle?" I asked.

"It's one of the things inside the atom, like protons, neutrons, and electrons. So anyway, this Heisenberg character noticed that we couldn't simultaneously measure a particle's velocity and position in space-time. He saw that if you measure where the particle is, you can't know how fast it's going because whatever you use to measure it also changes the particle's speed. On the other hand, if you try to measure how fast a particle is going, you can't know where it is because whatever you use to measure it also moves it."

"I don't get it," I said. "Why would measuring where it is affect its speed?"

"Because whatever you use to observe it bounces off it. Think about it this way: If a car is going seventy miles an hour, you can measure its location and speed. But just because you look at the car doesn't affect where it is or how fast it goes. The operative word here is 'look.'" He paused, waiting for me, and I nodded slowly, tentatively.

"Okay," he said. "Now pretend I just pushed a marble across the table. What if you want to know where that marble is and how fast it's going?"

"I guess I would just measure it."

Jack lifted his finger. "But what if you can't actually see the marble? What if the marble is in a box, and the only way to measure it is to shoot a second marble into the box, bouncing it off the first one?"

I nodded again. "So the second marble comes back . . . and when I measure what it's done, it tells me where the first one is . . . and how fast it's going?"

"That's what you would think, right? But what if, when the second marble comes back, it can't tell you both those things?"

"I thought you said it could?"

"What if it can't? What if, when you bounce the second marble off the first, the direction and speed of the first marble changes? You wouldn't know where it is now—you would only know where it was when the two collided. The first marble is still somewhere in the box, but you don't know where, because it was moving when the second marble hit it. Actually, that's just a crude analogy—it's a little more complicated than that. But what's important is that, at the quantum level, whatever you use to observe things also affects the things you observe. So by the time you think you've got it figured out, everything has changed again.

"But the coolest thing about subatomic physics is the way it has affected our thinking. After all these smart Germans created these theories, some modern philosophers got interested in what was happening—especially in Heisenberg's uncertainty principle.

"For thousands of years, men looked for proof of this and proof of that. Really, the only exception was a bunch of Asians who decided they just didn't give a shit about anything." Jack threw his hands in the air. "Who cares if there's proof? It's all that Zen Buddhist stuff. They said you should just live your life and hope for the best . . ." He paused for a second. "Well, that may not be exactly what they meant." He flapped his hands dismissively in the air in front of him. "But never mind all that. Anyway, these modern philosophers are all freaked out about the uncertainty principle because, if we can't know with certainty what a particle does at the subatomic level, then how the hell can we really know anything at all? I mean, how do I know for sure that you're really even here with me? Hell, how do I know that I'm really here, for that matter? You can see how uncertainty takes subjectivity and crams it right up your ass.

"So anyway, because of the uncertainty principle, some scientists and philosophers, including Schrödinger, decided that everything in reality is up in the air.

They said that, because we can't know the exact velocity and position of subatomic particles, those particles must only exist as probabilities.

"Then some other scientists pointed a beam of light at a wall and put a piece of paper, with some slits cut in it, between the wall and the beam of light. Basically, when the light came out through the other side, it didn't act the way it was supposed to act. Part of it disappeared for some reason, and the real problem was that they couldn't *find* the reason. And if it wasn't confused enough before, that really fucked everything up.

"Then another guy named Hugh Everett came up with an explanation for why the light disappeared. He called it the many-worlds theory, and it's probably the most disturbing one of all. Later, another scientist named David Deutsch advanced Everett's ideas. They said that because part of this beam of light had disappeared, the photons had been affected by what was called 'shadow photons,' which were thought to be part of parallel universes."

"Parallel universes?"

"Yeah. Deutsch says there are an infinite number of universes out there similar to ours. He refers to the many universes as components in what he calls the multiverse, which is all universes combined. He said that in every instant of time, a new universe is created, and that every possible outcome exists as reality in another universe."

"How?" I asked.

"What, you want the equations?"

I laughed. "No, I just don't know what you mean. Are you saying different realities exist?"

"No. I'm saying one reality exists, but that parallel universes exist in that reality. For instance, there are some versions of earth where no life exists, and there are some versions in which life is completely different, because one universe took a right turn a billion years ago, when our universe went straight. And there are some versions in which the earth is almost identical to ours.

"Deutsch said that an infinite number of outcomes are developing out of every instant. In one outcome, I'll have a heart attack and in another, a bear will eat you. In still another outcome, a guy wearing a cute little summer dress will run into this diner and sing a song from *Oklahoma*."

"Oklahoma?"

He gave me a curious look. "It's a shitty musical, Douglas. Don't you know anything?"

I shrugged and took a sip of my drink.

"Anyway," he said, "that doesn't matter. What does matter is this: anything that's physically possible, at any instant, will happen in some universe, somewhere. And now there are even scientists who have discovered holes in the fabric of space and time at the quantum level. They believe the holes are actual connections to parallel universes, and they believe that the holes connect us to the dimension Deutsch theorized about. Some scientists think it's not only possible to go to another universe, but that we might be able to travel through time, because space and time are the same, right?"

"I guess so."

"Well, they are," Jack said. "So a few years ago some scientists used light, or X-rays, or something like that to do an experiment, and they shot a beam through what they believed was a hole in space-time at the quantum level. A fraction of a second later, the beam came back, but they couldn't explain where it had gone during the time it wasn't visible."

"Did it go into another universe?"

"That's what they say."

"Do you think it did?"

"Yeah, I think it did." Jack was looking at me curiously. "You're interested in this stuff, aren't you?"

"It's really cool." I thought about all of it for a moment. "Jack, does LSD make you think about stuff like this?"

Pete and Jack looked at each other for a few seconds, and then broke into laughter. Jack said, "Yeah, kid, it makes you think about stuff like this."

I drank the last of my drink and said, "If I ever wanted to try it, would you guys do it with me?"

Their smiles faded and they exchanged concerned looks. Finally, Jack said, "I don't know if we'd *do* it with you, but if you've got to try it, I guess I'd want to be there to make sure you were okay." He turned to Pete. "Does that make me complicit in the corruption of a minor?"

Pete nodded. "Yep."

Jack became serious. "I'm not sure it's the greatest idea, and I'll probably go to hell for saying this to you, but I'd rather you be with us than a bunch of jackass kids."

"You were going to hell a long time before this," Pete said, straightening. "Hey, look, they're back."

We watched the tow truck pull in, followed by Jack's truck.

"I guess they fixed it," Jack said. "That was fast."

We quickly ate the rest of our dinner, paid, and walked back to the garage. "So what's the diagnosis?" Jack asked one of the mechanics.

"I don't know what to tell you—we started her right up. I let her run for a few minutes and then drove her back myself. There ain't nothin' wrong with that truck that I can see."

Jack looked puzzled. "Nothing?"

The mechanic shook his head. "You boys heading back to Durango tonight?"

"Do you think it's safe?"

"Tell you what." The mechanic took out a card and scrawled on the back. "Here's my home number. If y'all have any more problems, you call me and I'll tow you to Durango myself. I can't find a thing wrong with that truck."

"Well, we can't ask for a fairer deal than that," Jack said.

We got in the truck, and Jack positioned it in front of one of the gas pumps, instructing me to fill the tank. Then he went back inside to pay the bill, and when he returned, we headed for Durango.

As we pulled out of Pagosa, the sun hovered silently, a ripe piece of fruit waiting to plummet to Earth. It would sink before long, dimming and dripping rich colors of red and orange all the way to the horizon. But for now it proclaimed its sovereignty over the summer sky with a radiant, almost defiant display of brilliance, hot against my skin as I turned my arm up to look at my watch.

It was a little past seven-thirty.

Whatever caused the breakdown must have been temporary because the truck got us home without a problem. We pulled into Durango just before nine and drove to MacGregor's, where we unloaded our gear for about half an hour. I usually rode my bike to and from work but since it was dark, Jack offered to give me a ride.

As we drove down my street, something seemed out of order. Even in the dark, I could see several unfamiliar vehicles parked in front of our house, one of which was a police car.

I looked at Jack, and he shrugged, but his face was concerned too. My heart started to pound.

Jack parked in front of the house, and we got out. A few people milled about near the front door, including a cop who presumably belonged with the cruiser. The entire crowd turned to face us in unison, their expressions desperate.

My mother was there, which made me even more uncomfortable. She looked haggard.

"What's going on?" I asked.

Everyone continued to stare at me, their faces empty, hopeless. I began to panic. "Mom, what the hell is going on?" I walked in the front door, looking around frenetically. I was about to walk through the house when I felt a hand grab my shoulder firmly. I turned to find the cop restraining me. "Hold on, son."

"What's going on?" I asked for the third time, my voice growing louder. "Where are Dad and Thomas?"

My mother said, "Please calm down. I have to talk to you."

I caught my breath. "Okay, tell me what's happening."

"There's been a car accident," she said.

The blood rushed from my head.

"Douglas, your father and Thomas were killed." She said it with as much compassion as she possessed.

My mind clogged, and my skin melted to my bones. *It has to be a joke. Why would they do this to me?*

"Mom, don't fuck with me," I said, forcing a smile to let her know it was time to let me off the hook. "Mom? Don't *fuck* with me!"

People were everywhere around us, staring at me sympathetically.

"Mom?" The word barely came out as a whisper. My legs buckled, and I fell to my knees. I tried to pull air into my lungs, but I couldn't quite get my breath.

Jack stood over me. A tear rolled down his face.

"They're dead," I said, trying to hold a smile. "How did that happen, Jack?"

CONDEMNATION

June, Year Sixteen

Just after my phone call, Dad had taken Thomas to Gateway Park to throw a frisbee. Then they went for pizza. On the way to the restaurant, a man ran a red light going about seventy miles per hour, and hit Dad's car on the passenger side, killing Thomas instantly. Dad hung on for about half an hour, but died on the way to the hospital.

Jack told me the other driver had been jailed, but I didn't get many details after that. Everyone was hesitant to discuss it, and in truth, I didn't want to know too much about it, even going out of my way to avoid the news coverage. About two days after the crash, someone told me the man had committed suicide, and that was all I wanted to know about any of it. I just pushed it from my mind.

The following week passed in a haze. There was a funeral, but I was barely aware of it. Jack refused to leave my side, driving me everywhere, making decisions for me, and comforting me when I broke down. Neither of us got much sleep.

I don't know exactly where my mother was through most of it, but she was definitely around, flitting in and out like a ghost, watching. She moved some things into the house, taking up residence again. It didn't occur to me that this might be permanent, but a few weeks later, she gave up her apartment and had the rest of her things delivered.

My father's lawyer, Fred Rausch, asked me to come to his office for the reading of Dad's will. My mother, now my only legal guardian, accompanied me, although she seemed more concerned about the content of the will than with supporting me emotionally. The two of us drove to Fred's office in silence, which was now the way we spent most of our time together.

Fred and Dad had been friends for a long time, and I was glad he was in charge of the estate. I was numb during the reading of the will, comprehending none of it. When Fred finished, I said, "Can you explain it so I'll understand it?"

He looked at me sympathetically. "Okay. Your dad didn't have a lot of money when he died."

"Of course he didn't," my mother muttered.

Fred ignored her. "I've taken care of the bills, and the cash that's left should be enough to cover your expenses until we're through probate. There are some stocks, mostly in retirement accounts. They don't amount to much. The house carries a mortgage, but that will be covered by your dad's life insurance policy."

"What am I going to do?" I asked.

Fred smiled gently. "I'm not finished. The life insurance policy names you and Thomas as beneficiaries, and since your brother's gone . . ." He gave me a pained expression. "It's a lot of money."

I was taken aback by the amount. I looked from Fred to my mother, who suddenly seemed very interested, like a hungry animal about to be fed. Fred glanced at her, and then looked at me again. "Your dad wanted everything left in trust until your eighteenth birthday. He wanted the house paid off and put in your name, but again, it won't become yours until you are eighteen."

"What will I live on?"

"There's a stipulation in the will that your guardian—your mother, in this case—will receive a check every month for your care. The judge has also agreed to let you have enough money to buy a car. It won't be fancy, but at least you'll be able to get around."

"How much money are we talking about every month?" my mother asked, her eagerness a little too apparent.

"We'll have to figure that out."

We were silent for a moment, and I asked the next question carefully. "Do I have to have a guardian?"

My mother's head snapped around and she glared at me with a mixture of panic and fury.

"Until you're eighteen, yes," Fred said.

I sat in silence for a few moments. My mother started bouncing her knees, but Fred waited patiently.

"What are my options when I'm eighteen?"

"You can do whatever you want. You'll get the remaining money from the trust—plenty to go to college, if you choose. You'll be comfortable for a long time."

We spent the next half-hour deciding on the amount of the monthly check. My mother kept arguing for more, but Fred diplomatically explained that it couldn't exceed my basic living expenses. When we finally came up with a number, I told my mother I wanted to speak to Fred alone.

She stared at me for a moment, her lips pursed. "Fine," she said and stalked out of the room.

When the door closed, I said, "Mr. Rausch, does my mother have to be my guardian? Can't I get someone else?"

"I can only imagine what you're going through right now, Douglas, but I have to be frank with you: in order to do something like that, I would have to convince a court that your mother is unfit, and that wouldn't be easy. I have to make the checks payable to her for the next eighteen months, but if she isn't taking care of you, come see me and I'll take it to a judge."

The ride home was so tense it was almost unbearable. When we finally arrived, I went straight to my room. A few minutes later, my mother came in unannounced. "What did you say to Rausch?"

My mouth was sticky-dry. This confrontation terrified me, but I knew if I didn't stand my ground in that moment, I would lose every future battle—and the battles were sure to come. "It's none of your business."

Her eyes were black with anger, her lips quivering. "Just remember something, you little shit, I'm still your mother, and for the next year and a half, *I'm* in charge, not you. Do you understand?"

"Mr. Rausch is waiting for any excuse to go to court." My words were strong, but inside I was petrified, and she knew it.

She glared venomously at me for a moment, then sneered wickedly, turned, and left the room.

It was one of the last conversations I would have with my mother. After that, we kept our distance, serving out our sentences in solitude under the same roof, avoiding each other as much as possible.

———◆———

Mr. Rausch had said the checks would be mailed at the beginning of each month, and when the time came to receive the first payment, I checked the mail as often as I could. But my mother stayed around the house most days, and I rarely beat her to the box after the postman's delivery. So I waited, hoping she would let me know when the money arrived, but she didn't.

After about a week, I gathered my courage and approached her in the kitchen one morning. She sat on the counter painting her toenails and didn't bother to acknowledge my presence.

"Has our check come?" I waited for a moment, but she didn't respond, so I said, "Are you going to answer me?"

"It came." She continued her task without looking up.

"Where is it?"

"I cashed it yesterday afternoon."

"It's not your money, Mom. I have to eat."

She painted her toenails with slow, meticulous strokes. "You obviously think you're still running this show, don't you?" She pushed out a dismissive snort. "Well, you just go ahead and believe whatever you need to."

"I'll call Mr. Rausch."

"Good. Why don't you just do that, you little asshole?"

I went to my room, pacing back and forth, wondering what to say to Fred. I had no idea what my mother would do with the money, but I was fairly certain groceries weren't a high priority on her shopping list.

About twenty minutes later, I heard the front door slam, and I paced a while longer, wondering where she had gone. I picked up my cello, hoping that the music would give me clarity.

I had been playing for about forty-five minutes when my mother burst into my room. I jumped in my chair and we stared at each other coldly for a few seconds before she said, "I'll split the check with you every month. Do what you want with your half." She threw some cash on the floor next to me and waited while I counted it. It was exactly half the agreed-upon amount of the check. I hoped my expression told her I was fine with the arrangement.

She appeared to understand and left the room. I suppose she concluded that half the money was better than no money at all, and she kept up her end of the bargain: from that moment on, I found the same amount of cash in my room, in an envelope, the first week of every month. My relationship with my mother had degenerated into a precarious economic stalemate.

◆

I CONTINUED TO work at MacGregor's a few days a week after school, which meant I didn't have to spend as much time at home. But I was late for work a lot now, and when I finally did arrive I couldn't concentrate. I was apathetic, distant, and bitter, often lashing out at Jack and Pete—my closest friends in the world, as well as my last tethers to a reality that was rapidly disintegrating around me. They had become my surrogate brothers, the closest thing to family I had, tolerating my petulance remarkably well. They handled me gently, the jokes and teasing all but vanishing from our interactions. Pete and I played chess once in a while, but my heart wasn't in it, and our matches gradually diminished. I tried to find enjoyment in the game, but it only reminded me of Dad.

The first few months after the car crash were especially empty, cold, and lonely. My mind toyed with me, convincing me that the slightest noise—any knock or creak—was Thomas or my father in the next room.

Soon enough, even noises weren't necessary to evoke the memories. They came on their own, uninvited, obsessively persistent. Ghostly images of my father and brother would appear anywhere, anytime—Dad sitting on the bench in front of our house, or setting up the chessboard in the dining room, or maybe Thomas playing in the yard. They seemed so real, so alive. I suppose they should have offered me solace—a connection to these two souls whom I missed so dearly. But the ghosts were anything but comforting. Even in their most serene manifestations, they sickened me with nostalgia, crippling me with the desire for even five precious minutes with my dead family.

But if these gentle memories were hard to endure, they were nothing compared to the nightmare visions my imagination invented when I thought about the accident. I would see Thomas's mangled body in the street, Dad screaming, his head ripped open. I knew almost no details about the crash, yet my mind forced these gruesome images on me, and the more I tried to drive them out, the more they persisted. Some nights, the ghosts kept me up for hours, and when sleep finally did come, they took over my dreams as well.

And one perpetual thought made the visions all the more unbearable. It was true that I had no way of understanding the phenomenon that had allowed me to save Thomas the day of his asthma attack, or that had allowed me to bring the dog back from drowning. But I couldn't deny that these things *had* happened, and as much as I had tried to hide the knowledge from myself and the world, I also couldn't escape the feeling that, had I been with my father and brother, I might have somehow saved them. I even fantasized that maybe there was still a way to bring them back, but in the deepest recesses of my mind, I knew it was too late. And worst of all, the thing that might have made it possible—the energy I had connected to, whatever it was—now seemed to be gone forever. After the crash, I tried repeatedly to find that repose within myself, believing it could somehow end the pain, but it was as lost to me as my father and brother.

The loss was intolerable, and nearly impossible to accept; in an instant they had been ripped away, along with almost every bit of security and stability I had ever known, replaced with a cold and abrupt mandate that I mature instantly, with no negotiation or preparation. My life had become a hopeless tragedy, and it was quickly becoming clear to me that I would have to find some way to deal with the psychological and emotional torment that gnawed at me almost every waking moment. If I didn't, I wasn't at all certain I was going to make it.

Fall, Year Sixteen

WHEN THAT DREADFUL summer finally melted into autumn, I hoped the new school year would help distance me from the tragedy that had eroded almost every grain of happiness in my life. I stayed away from the house as much as possible; there was so little there for me anymore, and the sadness of the place was stifling—a dense vapor that hung in every room.

Distraction was critical to my state of mind, so I kept myself as busy as I could. I stayed with the advanced program, and between school and working at Mac-Gregor's, I had little free time. When I did find a few spare minutes, however, I devoured books about theoretical physics, driven by the seeds Jack had planted in my mind.

In truth, I was searching for an explanation: surely when my father and brother had so suddenly disappeared, they must have gone somewhere. I struggled to understand what that place might be, and somehow the concept of multiple universes was more comforting to me than the idea of heaven. A part of me even believed that maybe they weren't really dead—maybe they were simply in another universe. And although my more rational side told me this probably wasn't true, I still clung to the idea, building fantasies about seeing Dad and Thomas again one day.

I interrogated Jack on virtually everything, from the rigid scientific axioms of subatomic physics to the more amorphous philosophical and spiritual implications of the theories. He, in turn, seemed to delight in teaching me about the endless paradoxes. I relished tearing into the abstractions he threw at me, attacking them from all angles, trying to find illumination, but the more I learned, the more confused I became. Still, Jack's knowledge about the subject was, as far as I could tell, limitless, and he never tired of watching me struggle to comprehend the complex ideas. Plus it gave us something to talk about—it was an effective way to avoid the other, more oppressive subject neither of us wanted to address.

Through my cello, I found some respite from my grief, but the more effort I put into the music, the more the richness of the compositions that I had once loved seemed to elude me. I attacked the instrument with a renewed determination to understand the relationships between the sheets of music and what emerged when I played. I had an intuitive grasp of the elegance with which the components connected and overlapped, but something crucial was missing, and the whole picture was like a fading dream, shapeless and alluring—a thousand shattered pieces, unformed and incomplete.

On the day of the fight at the bus stop, Rudy Buck had pointed his finger at me, silently warning me that our business that day wasn't finished, and in the years after, he had fulfilled the tacit promise, making an almost enthusiastic effort to haunt my life. At first, he had limited his aggression to angry glares from a distance, but over time, he—sometimes along with Mark Evanston—had taken to taunting me whenever possible, and as the years had passed, the two of them had become bolder—sometimes pushing me around, or tripping me as I walked past.

As awful as things had been that summer, I had at least avoided Rudy and Mark. But my life had become nothing more than a nearly inscrutable set of psychological variables, forming an equation that seemed to grow exponentially more complicated by the day, and when school resumed, I had no choice but to add the old fear and intimidation back to my growing list of problems.

Everyone knew Rudy was strange—that he spent most of his time alone and didn't quite fit most people's definition of normal. Occasionally, he showed up at school with a black eye or a swollen lip, and when it happened, everyone knew why.

Jim Buck, Rudy's father, was an alcoholic of the worst breed. He had once been a successful plumber in Durango, building his business from the ground up, earning the respect of the community. The Bucks—Jim, Sally, and their son Rudy—appeared to be a stable, happy family, but when Rudy was about six, his mother was diagnosed with advanced lymphoma. She didn't last the year.

Jim didn't seem to know what to do without Sally, so he just shut down. He sold his business and sent Rudy to live with an aunt, trying to find some relief from the maelstrom his life had become, and soon enough it became apparent that the respite he so desperately sought would come primarily from liquor and idleness. It didn't take long for Jim's savings to dry up, so he began taking odd jobs here and there. And by this time, most people had just concluded that his melancholy was probably permanent—mostly because he now spent almost all of his time and money in bars.

Understandably, when Rudy returned home a couple of years later, he wasn't quite the same. But Jim wasn't quite the same either, and Rudy's presence brought back nothing but hard memories. Jim didn't much know how to fit the boy into his despair and solitude, and soon enough he began to resent the interruption of his private grief. He reacted by slapping Rudy around with an incautious enthusiasm.

Social workers stepped in a few times, but Rudy never spoke a word of incrimination against his father. Jim showed his appreciation by beating his son with increasing severity. Neighbors were either ignorant of the facts, or more likely simply didn't want to get involved.

It was easy to understand how a boy living in that environment might turn out a little odd. But while his story was tragic, Rudy had seemed to prefer dealing with his situation in solitude—the occasional exception being the companionship of Mark Evanston. For so many years, Rudy never lashed out at the world the way one might have expected—that is, until the day at the bus stop when I defended Thomas. But from that point on, Rudy was different—his moods varying from dark and angry to downright predatory. And for the last few years, as far as I could tell, harassing me had been his primary objective.

On the third day of the new school year, I left my fifth period class and started walking down the hall to my locker. When I looked up, Rudy and Mark blocked my path.

"Hey, you little pussy, did you miss us?" Rudy asked. His cheek was bruised a deep shade of purple and his lip was split. His father had been busy.

I took a long breath. Rudy and Mark grabbed me and threw me into a row of lockers. I landed hard, pain shooting through my spine.

"I heard you had a shitty summer, you little faggot," Rudy said, grabbing my collar, pulling me to my feet. He put his face in mine, his breath as foul as ever. "I know you missed me, shithead."

"Why do you hate me so much?" I asked, my voice cracking. "What did I do to you? All I did was protect my brother!"

"You know what you did, fuckface. I won't never let you forget it . . . not never." His eyes were maniacal, almost too cruel to be real, and for a moment, I almost didn't recognize this boy I had known—even if only casually—for most of my life. I glanced at Mark, who again seemed uncomfortable at how quickly Rudy's anger seemed to consume him.

Rudy smiled sadistically, his teeth discolored and crooked. He let me go, and I slid back to the floor. The two of them stared at me for a moment, and then, as if to confirm his power over me, Rudy kicked me in the stomach.

A small crowd had gathered, everyone gawking in disbelief. One girl said, "Just leave him alone."

Rudy glared at her as he walked away, the wicked smile never leaving his face.

I didn't want to cry, but I couldn't hold back the tears. I buried my head in my arms and wept.

Early Spring, Year Sixteen

ALTHOUGH I TRIED to achieve some normalcy, every aspect of my life was getting progressively worse, and the diversions of school, work, and cello were quickly losing their power to distract me. I needed more.

My introduction to alcohol didn't come in the way it does for most kids— hanging out at friends' houses, using fake IDs to get into bars, or going to parties on weekends. My first drinking experience occurred a month after school started, when I meticulously calculated and executed a plan with one single objective in mind: to escape, by any means possible, the unbearable bleakness of my loss.

My mother was drinking more than ever now, and kept a lot of liquor around the house. She wasn't focused enough to notice a little missing here and there, so I began with vodka—which seemed to have the mildest bite—and worked my way through her supply.

I loved the way alcohol diminished the power of the ghosts, and while the apparitions never went away altogether, the booze certainly weakened them—at least at first. I drank hard every night, until I was drunk enough to forget the pain, wishing the numbness could last forever. But it didn't last forever, and I found myself craving something more intense.

There were two reasons I decided my next experiment would involve LSD. First, since my conversation with Jack and Pete on the day of the accident, I had become nearly obsessed with quantum physics, and since they had both implied that I might understand the theories better under the influence of LSD, I was anxious to try it. Somewhere in my mind, I still believed that if I could just wrap my mind around these concepts, I might yet find a way to come to terms with the deaths of my father and brother.

The second reason, however, was somewhat less justifiable; I smoked pot for the first time with Pete just before school started that year, and I enjoyed it—a lot. So, now I had been smoking, as well as drinking, the ghosts into submission. But with the inevitable sobriety that followed, the apparitions returned with as much force as ever, refusing to be appeased by anything milder than yet another round. I decided I needed a more permanent solution, and I believed that LSD, being the mind-altering drug it is, held a great deal of promise.

One morning that spring, I approached a kid who had sold pot to me a few times and asked him if he could get me some acid. He shrugged and said it wouldn't be a problem. The next day he gave me a clear plastic bag containing a quarter inch square of white paper. In return, I gave him some cash, and I was on my way. It was just that easy.

Later that day at MacGregor's, I found Jack working alone in the Cooler. "You got a minute?"

"Sure," he said, raising his head, eyeing me carefully.

"You think we could go camping this weekend—maybe just you, me, and Pete?"

His expression became concerned. "Do you need to talk or—"

"I just want to get away. It'd be nice to spend a night hanging out with you guys."

He nodded. "Sure, kid. I'll talk to Pete."

Pete, of course, thought it was a great idea; both he and Jack would have done anything to help me. It didn't occur to me that I should discuss the rest of my plan with them.

After school that Friday, I went home, grabbed my overnight bag, and headed to MacGregor's, where I helped Jack and Pete install some hard drives for about an hour. At five, we quit working and packed our gear into the bed of Jack's truck. Then we started driving north, ascending into the Rockies.

I sat between Pete and Jack, just as I had the day we went to Pagosa Springs. The memory made me uncomfortable, especially on top of my already escalating nervousness about what I planned to do. Jack turned on the truck's radio, and the tinny sound of an old country song filled the cab. He began singing along with the music in an intolerably discordant voice.

"Shut the fuck up, Jack," Pete said.

Jack leaned forward, raising his eyebrows at him. "You don't like my singing?"

"No. I don't."

Jack looked at me. "I guess you don't like it either."

I shrugged, and he rolled his eyes, settling back against the seat.

After about fifteen miles, we turned onto a gravel road, heading east, deeper into the pines.

"This piece of shit truck better not break down again," Pete said.

"Pipe down, Ass," Jack said dryly. "It'll be fine."

We passed several sites occupied by campers, but after a few minutes, Jack brought us into a broad meadow and pulled into an empty site—a dirt version of a cul-de-sac, with a fire pit in the middle. He cut the engine. "I guess this'll do," he said.

I stepped out of the cab and looked at the western horizon. The sun was setting behind a mountain peak, sending out brilliant rays of red, melting into a dark, twilight-blue sky. I held a deep breath for a few seconds and then released it, shuddering from the evening chill. My heart was pounding.

We unloaded our stuff and built a fire as the sun continued to go down. Jack and Pete carried a cooler from the bed of the truck and positioned it near the fire.

"Let's cook," Pete said. "I'm starving."

Jack gave him a wry look. "Anus, has it ever occurred to you that your appetite might not be so voracious—nor, therefore, your vaporous output so repulsive—if you didn't smoke such copious amounts of dope?"

Pete stared at Jack, cocking his eyebrows. Jack looked back at him and stopped what he was doing, sticking out his chin. "What's your fucking problem?" They continued to stare at each other for a few more seconds. Finally Jack shrugged and began to stack wood next to the fire.

Pete reached into the cooler and pulled out two beers, handing one to Jack. "The things that come out of your mouth just astound me." He sat next to the fire, set down his beer, and as if in defiance of Jack's comment, pulled out a pipe and started smoking pot. Then he leaned to his left and let out a fart that started as a wet hiss but graduated to a high-pitched whistle, like a tea kettle going off.

When it finally ended, Jack shook his head slowly, not even bothering to look up from his task. "And you talk about the things that come out of my mouth?"

I tried to smile, but it was forced—I only had one thing on my mind. It's *now or never*, I thought. "I'll be back . . . I'm just going to pee."

"Don't get eaten by a bear," Jack said, setting steaks on the grill. "And hurry back. Dinner will be ready in a few minutes."

I walked until I was out of their sight, reached in my pocket, and pulled out the LSD, putting the small square piece of paper in my palm. I stared at it for a moment, more scared than ever of what I was about to do. Smoking grass was one thing—everybody did it at one time or another. But taking acid was different; stories abounded about bad trips and permanent brain damage. This was serious experimentation, and as I stared at the square, I wondered if I should do this.

I put it on my tongue before I could talk myself out of it. I stood there for a minute, staring at the stars that were just beginning to appear in the gloaming, listening to the melody of a stream flowing a few feet away, accompanied by the steady chirping of crickets around me.

After a few more minutes I walked back to the fire, where I sat down and stretched my legs.

We all settled back, watching the flames, talking idly. After a few more moments, Pete handed me a plate and some utensils. We served ourselves, and Jack and Pete began to eat, but my appetite seemed to have disappeared. I merely toyed with some asparagus and potatoes with my fork.

"What's the matter with you?" Jack said. "Aren't you hungry?"

"No," I replied, looking down. "Not really."

He eyed me oddly, but didn't say anything else. I stared at my plate, anxiously wondering what to expect, and how I would react.

After about thirty minutes, everything started to feel a little bit different, and then, in my peripheral vision, I thought I detected movement. My heart rate increased a little, and I suddenly wondered if I had made a huge mistake.

The first ghost to appear was my father. His face filled my mind, smiling, looking peaceful, and I felt a brief sense of tranquility. I stared at his image, no longer aware of my actual surroundings. Distant whispers filled my head, an unintelligible chorus of muttering voices, chanting as if in prayer.

Then, without warning, my father's face became contorted, changing to sorrow and then to pain. His expression puzzled me, and then he turned his head slightly. A wound stretched along the side of his scalp, his brains hanging out, reaching his shoulder in long strands of blood and pink tissue. "Douglas!" He screamed. He stretched his mouth wider than I would have believed possible, his face contorting, his eyes turning into solid, empty blackness.

I put my palms against the sides of my head and pressed hard. My mind felt like it was stretching beyond its physical boundaries, pulling apart.

My father snarled, "Why did you do it?" He turned his head to look at something and my eyes followed. Thomas's body lay in the middle of a street, sprawled and broken in a pool of coagulating blood.

My soul expanded and contracted with my lungs. My identity was shredding—I no longer knew who I was. My existence in the universe had simply ceased.

The earth trembled, and I started to scream.

Now Jack's face was inches from mine. His hands gripped my shoulders, shaking me. "Douglas! What's going on?"

Pete stood next to him, deeply concerned.

"I . . . I don't know!"

"Yes, you do," Jack said. "Tell me what's happening."

"I . . . saw Dad and Thomas! Jack, they're dead!" Tears streamed down my face.

"What's going on, Douglas?"

"They were in front of me . . . on the street!"

"Kid, listen to me. Did you take something?"

"Jack? I'm scared."

He took a deep breath and even more calmly repeated, "Douglas, did you take something?"

I nodded. "Yeah . . ." I shook my head, confused. Dad's face appeared again and I screamed.

Jack shook me and yelled, "Douglas! Stay here with me! What did you take?"

I opened my mouth, confused. "I took acid."

"God*damn* it! What made you think you were ready to do that?" His voice was stern but level. "You told us you'd talk to us—"

Pete put a hand on Jack's arm. "Come on, man, he's scared to death. Let's just get him through it."

Jack looked at Pete for a moment and then said to me, "Okay, we're going to take care of you."

I nodded rapidly.

"Your dad and Thomas aren't here."

I looked around nervously. "They were there—"

"No. It's just us—nobody else. You understand?"

I nodded again. Jack took his hands from my shoulders and placed them on either side of my head. As I looked into his eyes, I saw something change within him, a measured preparedness, as though he had rehearsed this scene a thousand times. He was suddenly in total control.

I closed my eyes and relief rushed through my body as though it were emanating from the tips of his fingers. My face tingled, and I opened my eyes, looking deeply into Jack's. I leaned my head back.

The sky was clear, the night air cool and soothing against my skin. Another ripple of energy swept over my body, calm and sweet. Jack removed his hands from my head. "I think he's going to be fine," he said to Pete, his confidence making me more peaceful still. He and Pete sat down, watching me cautiously.

My body was tense—my jaw tight, my stomach constricted. Suddenly every grain in my soul pulled me back to that day on Junction Creek—to the dog's drowning. *And then he was alive,* I reminded myself.

I ground my teeth and, with all the abruptness of a lightning strike, I was suddenly abjectly aware of how little significance I had in the universe. This was the same feeling I'd had in Thomas's room, the day he stopped breathing, and also on the bank of the river, hovering over the dead dog's body.

I looked up at sky full of countless stars forming streaks of light across the sky, smearing through time and space, and I became even smaller in the vastness of the universe, the tiniest mote swimming through an endless black sea.

Yet I wasn't alone; I felt whole, as though I *were* the emptiness itself, a deep sense of potential, standing on a cliff, ready to take the step that would allow my mind to soar in any direction—or maybe even in *every* direction. I wasn't sure where to go, or what to do, so I simply let the ideas run—rivers of possibility spilling over me.

I am everything, and I am nothing . . . It was a fleeting thought, a wisp of smoke, gone almost before the words could fully form in my mind.

It is easier now for me to articulate what I felt that night, but at the time, I doubt I could have described it to anyone so fluidly. It was direct and experiential, almost pure—my most profound taste yet of the connection that has defined me throughout all the seemingly countless years that have passed since.

My focus stretched to the limits of its capacity, pulled in infinite directions, my vision bouncing from object to object. The needles of a pine tree fused into fuzzy masses, swirling on their branches. I thought at first it was the wind, but there was none—the needles themselves vibrated like a throng of bees. The tires of Jack's truck roiled like thick black liquid, and I got up and walked toward the vehicle.

"What are you doing, Douglas?" Pete asked.

"Let him go," Jack said. "He'll be fine."

I turned to look at them, smiled, and resumed my walk to the truck. I looked into my own eyes in the side-view mirror. My pupils were big and black, and they looked strange, which made me giggle for a second. But then I saw something new—an energy of some sort, tranquil and unborn, both beautiful and alien. And although I didn't understand it, it was comforting and familiar.

I looked back at Jack, barely recognizing him. His face was different, no longer solid, but moving like everything else, a trillion atoms vibrating against one another. I saw everything he was with more clarity than ever before—his essence and his gentle kindness.

But there was something else—something frightening I had never seen before. I tried to look deeper but the vision collapsed; it was as if Jack knew what I was looking for and had erected a wall to shut me out. He shook his head slowly, smiling. I walked back to the fire and sat down again.

A new thought appeared. It came from something I had learned in physics, that energy is neither created nor destroyed. But the concept was no longer abstract; now it had weight. We are everything—part of a system that binds us, transcending human concepts of life or death. The universe is a zero sum game, nothing created nor destroyed, and while things change, nothing dies. I felt physically struck by the insight.

I thought carefully about my role in the vastness of space and time, and my uncertainty gave rise to the futility of human interpretation. We are not a unique and separate part of our universe, and our opinions concerning it have no meaning apart from it, because we are in it. The interpretations are ours—by us, for us, and utterly meaningless without us. Even the word "meaning" depends on us for viability, and when we are gone, the universe will still exist, heedless of our perceptions.

Perhaps this sense of futility should have scared or intimidated me, but it didn't. If anything, the sense of wonder and expansiveness pushed me toward the realization that, in this vastness, I could do anything, *anything at all.*

Suddenly I understood numbers with new clarity: like language, they are nothing more than metaphorical constructs. The blueprint is not the building, and the language is not the event; description is not the described, and so experience is everything. To see something begets familiarity, but to know something, one must *become* the thing—or at least come as close as possible.

I took a deep breath, threw back my head, and allowed the universe to crush me beneath its enormity. *I am so small, and yet I am everything...*

In that instant I understood how completely perception defines our interpretations, despite the fact that our perspective is so thoroughly meaningless to the universe.

Experience defines our perspective, yet our perspective is meaningless to the universe. We can only truly understand through direct experience, not by *attempting* to perceive. The concept wasn't foreign before, but it had only been a fleeting notion until this moment. Now it was a blinding epiphany, concrete and elegant in its salience: the concept of *perspective* is far more than merely the light that hits our retinas, or the temperature that affects our skin.

Experience is everything . . .

More streaks of light melted above me in the sky, and suddenly I was living within the music. It made sense! The richness and texture of its fabric were part of me again, but music theory was no longer some amorphous concept; it had become experiential. I now felt the circle of fifths, the modes fitting together seamlessly in different keys. I clearly understood how the transpositions fit together mathematically, and beyond.

And then, as though a thousand spotlights had been trained on me and ignited all at once, I recognized one clear concept about everything I saw that night: this is the *state* of the universe. It, and everything in it, merely exists—independent of human thought and interpretation. The universe simply *is.*

The words, letters, numbers, music, and all the other countless constructs we use to navigate our lives are nothing more than descriptions. But the actual conditions themselves—often residing beyond our perception—*do* exist in the universe, in *spite* of human interpretation. These physical manifestations are pure, direct, and if we let go, we can experience them as such.

I thought about great composers and musicians, how easily they slipped between modes, effortlessly intertwining them, and I realized in that moment music becomes great only when the artist *is* the music. I knew then I would only be a good musician when I *became* the sound that flowed through my hands and body. Training is the foundation, but once the foundation is finished, the artist must become the art. Anything less is simply mechanical repetition. I realized playing my cello would never be the same after this moment, and suddenly, I ached to have it with me.

All these thoughts came to me simultaneously, instantly, as if the concepts had always been there, hidden in some vault in my mind. And now, finally, I had opened the correct door. I breathed deeply, letting the cool oxygen fill my lungs and feed my bloodstream. My heart beat heavily in my chest, pumping the rich red liquid through my body, and I was aware of every drop of it.

I heard a voice, faint but growing louder. "Douglas? Hey kid! Hey! Are you with us?"

I turned to Jack and Pete and smiled. "Hey!"

"Where have you been?" Jack said. "You've scared us enough for one night."

"I was thinking."

"Oh *really*? Well we never would have guessed that! You were drooling on yourself too!"

I rubbed my chin, wiping away a stream of saliva. "This is incredible."

Pete smiled. "What were you thinking about?"

I rocked back and forth, folding my hands between my knees, staring at the fire again. "About how meaningless this all is."

"Meaningless?" Jack said.

"Not exactly meaningless I guess. It's just that we're just so . . . small. I know it probably sounds stupid."

Pete looked at me earnestly. "It doesn't sound stupid." For an instant, I thought I saw a deep respect in his eyes, but I dismissed it.

"The experience is so important," I said.

"How do you mean?" Jack said.

I thought about the question for a moment. "I knew this girl in school. We took Spanish together. We sat in class for three years, trying to learn the language, but we were only learning another way to speak English. I mean, the teacher would say, 'casa means house.' But we weren't learning 'casa,' we were just learning another word for 'house.' Then during the summer, this girl and her family went to Mexico, and when she came back, she *really* spoke Spanish. I asked her how she got so good in three months, and she told me that she started thinking in Spanish. And I understood—a casa wasn't a house to her anymore. In her mind, a casa was a building with doors and windows and floors. A casa was a casa. Does that make sense?"

Jack and Pete stared at me with their mouths open. Then they erupted with laughter. "This is what you think about when you take acid?" Jack howled. "You're just a goddamn philosopher!"

And before I knew what was happening, I joined them in their laughter—effortless gales that sent tears running down my cheeks. When we calmed down, I sat in silence for a moment, once again staring at the fire. "I understand it all better now," I said. "I see the connections."

"I thought you might," Jack said. There was something warm and familiar in his eyes, and the idea returned: *He's holding back—there's something important he doesn't want me to see.*

But as quickly as the thought had appeared I realized how silly it sounded, so I let it pass.

◆

When I got home the next day, I played my cello for hours. It was as though I had opened a window and fresh air now permeated the room; the way I played hadn't changed, but my ability was somehow different, better. The compositions that had so long been part of my soul, that I had created early on, came as easily as peaceful sleep. The music was a state of my being, rich and beautiful—unique again.

Within a few days I realized my work in math was different too; something inside my mind had shifted, and the way I now saw numbers was complete. It was like learning to ride a bicycle: one day I couldn't do it and the next I could. Variables and constants jumped off the pages at me, inviting me to connect them in equations, balanced and elegant. The patterns were so obvious that I couldn't understand how I had missed them before.

I had little doubt the discoveries I made in the woods would reshape my perception forever, but I was disappointed to find that the deep vacuum left by my family's death remained. I took LSD several more times, each experience unique and enlightening, but never like the first night. And each instance exacted a huge toll, exhausting me afterward for a day or more. Eventually I decided not to use it anymore.

Acid may have inspired me, but it had done little to eradicate the ghosts, who redoubled their efforts to pollute my mind with their grizzly images whenever I didn't have a distraction. I played my cello more often, but I also drank and smoked more pot than ever. My mornings were hell, and although my understanding of physics, math, and music had evolved, my grades didn't improve, and my attendance suffered badly.

May, Year Seventeen

MY MOTHER WASN'T working, living instead off half the check that came from Mr. Rausch every month. She stayed out late most nights, sometimes not coming home until very early in the morning, if at all. On the mornings when she actually did make it home, I would walk into the living room to find her door closed—and it was usually still closed when I returned in the afternoons. She and I merely coexisted, living our lives like planets orbiting a star, held together by the same forces that kept us apart.

More and more often, I would wake up to see unfamiliar cars parked in the driveway. A few times I bumped into strange men in the living room. They struggled to put their clothes on, stumbling out the door, always embarrassed, offering me a "Good morning," trying to make small talk. But I never responded. I wasn't about to become friendly with my mother's lovers.

She was almost always drunk by this time, and she started to violate our unspoken rule of isolation, stumbling unannounced into my room with increased frequency, spewing her filthy vitriol at me. If I ignored her, however, she would eventually go away—for a while.

She saw one man regularly—or more often than the rest anyway. His name was Chuck, but I never knew his last name. He was a carpenter or bricklayer or something like that, tall and muscular, unshaven, and always reeking of cigarettes. He wore plaid button-down shirts with the sleeves cut off, exposing a tattoo that twined around his right bicep—something between a rose stem and a strand of barbed wire.

One night I came home from MacGregor's and noticed Chuck's truck parked in the driveway. I walked in the front door and heard his raised voice. "Just tell the little fucker that he has to let you have it!"

My mother slurred something in response that I didn't catch. I edged through the entryway and was nearly to my bedroom when my mother said, "Is he home?" and then more loudly, "Come here, Douglas, we need to talk to you."

I went into my bedroom and locked the door, but about a minute later they began knocking loudly. I knew ignoring them would be futile, so I opened the door, and I was immediately struck by how much she'd aged; her expression seemed frozen in perpetual anger. She was emaciated, frail.

"I locked my door for a reason," I said.

Chuck was agitated and couldn't seem to keep still.

My mother said, "Have you forgotten who's in charge here, you little shit?" When I didn't respond, she added, "I have a question to ask you. I'm having some trouble this month. I want you to give me some money."

"That's not a question."

"I don't give a shit *what* it is! I need you to give me some goddamn money!"

"That's not our agreement."

Her eyes flared and she growled, "You'll do what I tell you, *Douglas*." My name almost sounded like profanity passing between her lips.

"I'm not giving you any money." I thought about how my father had, for so many years, acquiesced to her anger, and the memory made me resentful. "Just get out of my room."

Before I could react, Chuck lunged at me. He hit me in the face, knocking me backward. I struck the wall hard, crumpling to the floor. He started to come at me again. "You don't listen too good, do you?" he said, his eyes glowing maniacally.

He's enjoying this, I thought as fear slithered through me.

Suddenly my mother screamed. "Stop it! Get away from him!" At first I thought she was talking to me, which seemed a little absurd. Then she stepped between us, facing him, her back to me. Some maternal instinct must have kicked in from the deep recesses of her fogged mind.

"Where's the goddamn *money*, you little fuck?" Chuck yelled.

"Get the hell out of my house!" my mother shrieked, her fists clenched. She shook her head violently, causing her stringy hair to swing in a tangled mass.

Chuck was puzzled by her sudden disloyalty, uncertain what to do. Finally he said, "I don't need this shit." His eyes shifted between my mother and me, and then he stormed from the room.

When he was gone, my mother turned to face me, her eyes devoid of their usual cold anger, replaced by a desperate pleading look. She crouched and put her arms on my shoulders, as if to assess the damage. "Douglas?" She started to weep. "Douglas?"

I pushed myself up from the floor, breaking loose from her grip. My eye was swelling where Chuck had hit me. I brushed past her, walking toward the kitchen to get some ice.

She followed me. "Douglas? I'm sorry, baby. I didn't mean to—"

"I'm going to Mr. Rausch tomorrow after school," I said, turning to face her again. "You should start packing your stuff."

"I'm sorry," she sobbed. "Please don't do this."

As I look back at the moment, I realize I never knew what my mother wanted out of life. We never discussed her dreams or regrets, or how she felt about Thomas's and my father's deaths. What I do know, after many years of deep consideration is that she was almost certainly driven by demons—the sources of which died with her. Wherever they came from, they tortured her with every bit as much cruelty as my own ever imposed on me. I also know that much of her substance passed into me, and if I have contributed anything to this universe, I owe much of it to her. I am forever grateful for that.

Much later in life, I forgave my mother for the things that happened between us. I harbor few regrets about my experiences, but one of the strongest I still cling to is that I didn't have the strength to find that forgiveness when I looked into her eyes in the kitchen that night.

I looked hard at the woman in front of me, at the shell she had become, unable to fathom that she was begging me for mercy. I opened my mouth, finally armed with the ammunition I needed, ready to release years of resentment, to castigate her for all her irresponsibility and recklessness. But just as I was about to let her have every vicious ounce of my anger, something stopped me. The storm inside me disappeared, replaced by little icicles crawling up my arms, raising the hairs on the back of my neck.

Something in my mother changed in that moment. She stopped crying, and her face melted into an eerie relaxation. She cocked her head slightly, looking deeply into my eyes, her expression puzzled and vacant, and for a second I was sure a fuse had finally blown, sending her over the edge. A drop of saliva seeped from the corner of her mouth and ran down her chin. Her head twitched convulsively, just once. Her eyes rolled back in her head for an instant before reappearing, growing wide. She smiled, and in a gravelly whisper said, "They're coming to get you, *Medicine Man*. They're gonna suck every *fucking* drop of blood out of your veins."

I inhaled sharply, pinpricks of fear stabbing every square inch of my scalp. *Rudy Buck called me that name…*

My mother looked so demented, and her words were so ludicrous—so out of place in this context—that for a fraction of a second, I wondered if she wasn't trying to turn the entire thing into a joke. But there was no mistaking what I heard. I stared at her in disbelief, almost unable to form the next question. "What did you say?"

She shook her head as if to clear her mind, and then she sobbed again. "Douglas, *please!*"

"What the hell are you talking about?" The confusion was overwhelming. Had she heard Rudy say it? *No, she had been too far away.*

She didn't answer me because she couldn't. She wasn't aware of the words that had come out of her mouth. It had nothing to do with her or Rudy; they were only conduits—mere voices for something so inconceivable I could not have even begun to imagine its origin. But I now know one thing clearly: if I somehow could have perceived the source of those words, I would have turned and sprinted from the house, because that moment marked the beginning of the most destructive and terrifying chapter of my life.

I stared at her, unsure of what to do, uncertain of her stability. Finally, I left the kitchen for my room, her pleading sobs fading behind me. I was beyond caring about her plight; my only thought was that I was finally going to get her out of my life.

Several minutes later, I heard her bedroom door close.

ALTHOUGH I HAD threatened to go to Fred Rausch, I put it off the next day. After what happened, I worried about starting a battle I might not win; I needed a day or two to consider exactly what I would say to Fred. I went to work after school and returned home just after five that evening.

My mother's car hadn't moved, and the first thing I noticed when I got inside was that her bedroom door was still closed. Her slothfulness disgusted me; she hadn't left the house all day.

I unloaded my books in my bedroom, took out my assignments and arranged them to begin studying. I was slipping further and further behind, and I needed to catch up or I knew I would be kicked out of the advanced program. But I before I dived into my books, I needed a drink.

I went to the kitchen and poured half a glass of vodka over ice, topping it off with water. I took some more ice and filled a small plastic bag, to put on my swollen eye. On the way back to my room, I looked at my mother's closed door and shook my head. She almost never stayed in there all day.

I started studying but the process was slow; my eye was almost swollen shut and it hurt badly. I muddled through my homework, as well as a couple of drinks, and once I had fulfilled my academic obligations for the evening, I took out a bag of weed and smoked a bowl. It was time to commence, in earnest, with chasing away the ghosts.

I left my room in search of more alcohol, but stopped when I passed my mother's room. The door was still closed. Something wasn't right.

I put down my empty glass and forced myself to knock lightly on the door. "Are you in there?"

There was no reply. My heart began to beat faster. *This is stupid. I'm high, and I'm scaring myself for no reason.*

"Mom? Are you in there?"

Again, no response.

I tried the doorknob. It turned easily. "Mom?" I pushed the door open slowly.

Her room was dark and smelled of mildew and sweat. Clothes were strewn everywhere. I moved forward cautiously. "Mom?"

Still no answer.

I made my way further into the room, and my heart began to beat faster. My eyes adjusted to the poor light, and then I saw her, lying on the bed, sunken eyes half open staring up at nothing. Her skin was bluish-gray, the color of raw chicken, and her mouth fixed ajar. She was beyond her troubles now.

An opened bottle of bourbon sat on the bedside table. Empty plastic prescription bottles lay scattered about, pills strewn around the body like tiny white maggots preparing to feed.

I had never seen a human corpse, and although I had no great love for my mother, the sight of her now was more than I could handle. I stumbled backwards, a sharp yelp escaping my mouth. I stepped on a shoe in the middle of the floor, lost my balance, and smacked my head hard against the wall.

It would be reasonable to suggest that the confluence of events at that moment might have led to any number of visions; after all, I was in shock, stoned, a little drunk, and I had just hit my head. And it so happens that I did, in fact, for some time, use my disoriented state as a convenient explanation for what I saw next.

An old man stood in the corner of the room beside my mother's bed. He had long, greasy gray hair and black eyes. He stooped, staring at my mother, smiling with a mouthful of sharp black teeth, waving a bony finger over her corpse. His head snapped up, his cold, hateful eyes melting with mine. He opened his mouth, pointed the curled finger at me and hissed, "You're next."

Then the image vanished.

Terror, disbelief, and nausea converged on me. I scrambled to my feet and bolted from the room. I stood outside my mother's bedroom door trembling, unable to comprehend what I had just seen, fighting panic. Insects crawled all over my body, and I shuddered violently, trying to rid myself of the vileness creeping over me. I put a hand on either side of my face stretching my skin downward as a quaking moan gurgled from my throat.

I caught my breath after a moment and half walked, half ran to the kitchen, stumbling over furniture, and bumping into a doorjamb along the way. I grabbed a bottle of scotch from the counter and took a long pull, the harsh liquid burning my throat.

I put the bottle down hard on the counter and took several deep breaths. I picked up the telephone and dialed the police, managing to remain calm enough to summon them to the house.

Then I dropped the phone, slid down the wall to the floor, and let the tears come.

◆

"WHEN GOD CLOSES a door, he opens a window."

The words came from a smiling fat woman, whose name I hadn't caught. She said she had been my parents' friend years earlier—before I was born. She, along with about twelve other people, including Jack and Pete, had come to pay their respects.

I muttered thanks to the woman, and then watched my mother's coffin slowly descend into the earth. *She lived in Durango for years*, I thought as I scanned the small crowd, *and so few people are here . . .*

As the priest's monotonous voice buzzed in my ears, one thought wouldn't leave my mind: *I have no family. I am alone.*

Fred Rausch stood next to me for the ceremony. When it was over, he said, "Are you okay?"

I nodded.

"I know this probably isn't the best time to bring it up, but we need to think about what you're going to do now. You're not eighteen yet and you need a legal guardian. Give it some thought and we can talk about it in a few days."

I looked at the ground. "I'll find somebody."

After the funeral Jack dropped Pete off at MacGregor's before driving me home. As we pulled into the driveway, I cringed, dreading entering the house.

"I'm going to need some help," I said.

"What is it?"

"It's a pretty big deal; I need a guardian. It'll only be for a year, but you might have to go to court with me a few times."

Jack stared vacantly out his window, but his face broke into a smile. "That's all? Hell, I thought you were going to tell me you were pregnant." He turned to me. "Of course, I'll do it."

I managed to smile back. "Thanks, Jack. It means a lot to me."

When I got in the house, I went to the kitchen to get a beer, and then walked into the den, intending to fall back on the couch. It had been a long day and I wanted nothing more than to numb myself from a future that was more uncertain than ever. But as I stepped into the room, I stopped short.

A cello rested against the sofa, a red ribbon tied around its neck. "What the hell?" And then I knew. *Jack.*

The instrument was old, its color rich and dark. I ran my fingers along the beautiful finish, remembering the day when Jack, Thomas, Dad, and I had gone to the music store to buy my first cello. Jack had wanted to get one that would make everyone proud.

I gazed at it for another moment before I sat down and removed the ribbon, resting the neck against my left arm. I picked up the bow beside it, checking its rosin, giving it tension. I plucked each string; the tuning was right on, so I pulled the bow slowly across. The resistance was perfect, sending rich vibrations up my wrists and arms, into my chest, and through my body.

I wasted no time slipping into my music—the themes that had inspired me for so long. The cello was a flawless masterpiece. The notes I played resonated gorgeously, caressing me in passionate, melancholic tones, surrounding me with all the warmth and comfort of a mother cradling a sleeping infant. As I played, I wondered about the instrument's history. Where did it come from and who made it? And how did Jack get it?

I stopped playing, walked to the phone, and dialed Jack's number.

"Hello?"

"There's no way you could afford something like that. Where'd you get it, Jack?"

"Who is this?"

"Where'd you get it?"

"Where'd I get what, you little bastard?" he said. "What the hell are you talking about?"

"Quit fucking with me, Jack. It's beautiful."

He didn't say anything.

"Jack?"

Nothing.

"Jack!"

"What? Jesus Christ, stop squealing at me!" I could feel him smiling on the other end of the line.

I hesitated a moment, and then I said the only words that made sense. "Thank you, Jack."

———◆———

I ENJOYED LIVING alone; I wasn't happy my mother was dead but I was relieved not to have to put up with her rage any longer. I finally felt that I could move on, and although the ghosts still constantly invaded my thoughts, I believed I was doing a pretty good job of managing my life.

But in reality the foundation was beginning to crack. At first, my teachers were sympathetic—if I was late to class or even absent altogether, the transgressions usually went overlooked. But eventually, my grades began to reflect my lifestyle.

One day, my counselor called me into her office. "A few of your teachers have asked me to talk to you about your absences and your grades. You've been given a lot of latitude because of the uniqueness of . . . your situation." She took off her reading glasses. "Douglas, we're all aware of your circumstances, but some of us are worried that you've withdrawn—that you might need to talk to someone about the issues you're facing. What do you think about that?"

I pretended to consider what she said for a moment before I answered. "Some bad things have happened to me, but I'm trying to get through them the best I can. I'll think about seeing somebody."

She was quiet for a moment. "All right, we'll give it another few weeks, but if your performance slides any further, we're going to have another conversation."

So, for the next few weeks, I made it a point to get to school on time and turn in assignments when they were due, but I was just going through the motions; nothing really changed. I certainly didn't stop drinking or smoking pot, and I put no more effort into the work than I ever had.

And so it was as easy as that. People voiced concern and I simply told them what they wanted to hear, or showed them what they needed to see so that I could move on with my lifestyle, unimpeded. The truth was nothing more than an incidental detail.

———————◆———————

ONE AFTERNOON IN the late spring of my junior year, I went to see my chemistry instructor during his conference period, to compare my calculations to some of the class notes. The classroom was empty, but the teacher had left the documents open, as he promised he would in case he needed to step away. As I waited for him, I stood at the desk, furiously trying to reconcile a problem.

I didn't see Rudy Buck and Mark Evanston walk in the room. "Whatcha doin', you fuckin' geek?" said Mark. He had a slight lisp, giving his words a serpentine edge as they slid from his mouth.

I jumped in my seat, startled, my heart thumping in my chest. I stared at them, frozen, as they moved into the room.

"He asked you a question, fuckhead," Rudy said. One of his eyes was black and nearly swollen shut.

I shrugged, allowing my shoulders to slump, looking down at the floor to avoid eye contact.

"You scared?" Rudy yelled sharply.

The sudden noise made me jerk my head up. I looked away again, and he laughed. He picked up a container of paperclips and began throwing them at me, one at a time. I felt stupid and vulnerable, and tears started to well in my eyes.

"What should we do to the little prick today?" Rudy asked.

Mark looked at him and said, "Let's do something different."

Rudy walked to the door and kicked it shut, turning the lock. When he turned around, something about him had changed, and it sent a chill through me. I was no longer just some kid Rudy liked to push around. No, he stared at me now like a wolf fixated on a crippled calf, and I knew that I was in a lot of trouble.

Rudy reached into his back pocket and pulled out a knife. He unfolded the blade, which locked into place with a loud click. He narrowed his eyes at me and smiled.

Mark said, "Rudy . . . man—"

Rudy turned his head violently. "*Shut the fuck up!*" His eyes were wild, and I remembered that day at the bus stop, years before. This was the same look I had seen then, but now the glint carried a hint of greater instability.

Mark defensively raised his palms in front of his chest, taking a step back.

Rudy was teetering on the threshold of something new; he seemed ready to explore fresh levels of cruelty. I fixated on the blade in his hand. The various possible outcomes raced through my brain as fast as my heart pumped adrenaline through my bloodstream.

He turned his gaze to me, and his face relaxed, his eyelids drooping. He was breathing through his open mouth, his lower lip moist, hanging limply. He inhaled and held it. Then, in a scratchy, throaty voice I barely recognized, he said, "Well, here we are again, *Medicine Man.*"

My eyes widened, and I felt a bolt of pure fear rocket through my body. I had to be going insane. *Did I hear him correctly?*

Then, something shifted inside of me. The importance of the moment descended on me—a thousand bells chiming at once. I don't know where the thoughts came from or why they were so clear, but I knew, inexorably in that moment, that I *had* heard Rudy correctly—just as I had heard my mother correctly the day before she died.

This is important. Pay attention.

A new explosion of awareness broke through, illuminating everything—a little like LSD, but different in a way that I couldn't quite identify. My body relaxed as a wave of peace passed through me. My vision blurred and something entered my mind, not as a fragmented thought, but as a whole concept, intact:

Everything is changing . . .

It came as more than mere words; it was a presence, offering the most intimate whisper, and now my fear became insignificant. My mind cracked open to infinite possibilities. *The day the dog drowned in the river . . .* A trickle of energy had guided me then, trying to show me something . . . *something. But I buried it.*

Now it was back, surging—a contradictory deluge of tranquility and momentum. I leaned my head back, collapsing into the universe. My vision went black, and I fell through space, carried by the force of an enormous wave.

The feeling spread through me, like the comfort of a fire on a freezing night. The hairs on my arms rose, saluting the electric air. I breathed deeply, slipping away from the moment. And yet something distant demanded my attention, pulling me back to reality. Rudy stood in front of me, unmoving, no longer looking like any sort of threat at all. He held the knife inexpertly, not quite sure what to do with it.

I wanted to smile but something stopped me—an embryonic humility assuring me that any arrogance would destroy this balance. I felt more solid and stable, more certain of my path than ever before in my life.

"Hey, *fucker*!" Rudy said. "Are you listening to me?" I was frustrating him. I wasn't playing my role.

Our eyes met again and suddenly I knew who he was. I felt his absolute terror of life—of his fate. He couldn't hide it anymore; I was over his wall, and he knew it. And yet, there was something else there, something hidden that I couldn't quite get to.

With fading confidence, he said, "Are you fucking listening to me, you pussy?"

I narrowed my eyes slightly. "Why do you use the word 'fuck' so much, Rudy?"

He let out a nervous laugh. "Do you know what I'm about to do to you, you dumbshit?"

The corner of my mouth turned up in an almost involuntary smile. "You aren't going to do anything."

His fury snapped its last restraints. "You don't think so, asshole?" He rushed at me, the knife extended before him.

My breathing eased and my heart rate slowed to a steady rhythm. Everything decelerated, as though a spell had been cast, restraining the engine of the universe. I searched Rudy's eyes, and I watched the last of his bravado desert him, turning instantly and without mercy to indecisive fear. He didn't slow his pace or change his direction, yet his resolve was gone.

I stepped to my right. I spun, connecting with his back, using my energy with his momentum to increase his speed. He hit the wall behind me with a loud thud and fell to the floor, the knife clattering beside him.

He didn't get up.

I felt the smile spread across my face, and suddenly I was bursting with a seductive ecstasy, single-minded and pure, born of something new. I was furious, yet all at once thrilled by fury itself: I felt *powerful*.

I looked at Mark, his eyes full of fear, and he said, "How did you do that?"

My smile, now almost maniacal, stretched even wider across my face. I began to walk toward Mark, slowly, imagining all the ways I could end his life. I was acutely aware of how vulnerable he was—like a little boy, paralyzed by the danger in front of him and yet wanting nothing more than to get away. I stood there, knowing I could do anything I wanted to him. He had no power to stop me.

The humility and peace that had guided me to this point dissolved, the stillness slipping away in the face of an overpowering disgust, fueled by the euphoric rage rushing through me. I wanted desperately to destroy Mark, to punish him for the years of suffering I had endured at his and Rudy's hands. My mind raced with vile ideas, visions of torture and cruelty that I couldn't quite believe were originating in my own mind.

The terror in Mark's eyes made me hungry, and I moved closer, smiling insidiously now. I was going to kill him. I had never been more certain of anything. Mark, suddenly realizing just how dangerous the situation had become, was on the verge of tears, and I further delighted in his terror and misery. I took another step toward him and then stopped.

Something is wrong... I sucked air through my teeth, looking around the room. *Something is so wrong here.*

I shook my head, consciousness cutting through—bright light awakening me. The peace slowly seeped back in, chasing away the rage. Mark saw the change and his expression turned briefly to relief, and just as quickly to raw fear again. He collapsed against the wall, his breathing rapid, whimpering, never taking his wide eyes off me.

I looked down at my tightly clenched fists and allowed them to relax. I stretched my hands, submitting to the stillness, allowing it to quell my wrath. When I looked at Mark again, I felt only pity.

I scanned the scene, calm, but confused. Rudy Buck lay sprawled on the floor in a grotesque heap, barely conscious, groaning. His nose was bleeding into a small puddle under his face.

Everything had happened in less than a minute; the transition from terror to calm to ecstatic rage had been easy, the way a drug enters the bloodstream and conquers the body's functions, dictating feeling and thought. I pulled oxygen deep into my lungs, thinking about what I should do next. But the answer came as easily as everything else: there was nothing to be done.

I gathered my books and papers from the table where I had been working and walked out the door, leaving Mark and Rudy in the chemistry lab. They could explain to the world how this had happened. I wanted no more of it.

◆

I suppose I should have been overjoyed, but I wasn't. In fact the more I thought about the incident, the more confused and frightened I became. The fight—if you could call it that—had been at once voluntary and involuntary, and this paradox may have been the strangest part of the experience. I had been aware of every detail, but I had controlled none of it; everything had just fallen into place—almost too elegantly. And yet I knew that it hadn't been predetermined; my decisions and reactions had been critical to the outcome.

And where had the humility and tranquility come from? How could I have been so serene at the same time I was creating so much violence? Of course the reality was that I hadn't actually *created* anything—I had merely helped Rudy and Mark complete their own undoing, and I felt strangely unaccountable, as if things had simply happened the way they were supposed to. Yet, however adequate that explanation appeared on the surface, I knew it was incomplete, and the more I tried to accept it, the more uncomfortable I became.

And then there was the other element—the unmitigated loss of restraint that had descended on me, and that I had barely resisted at all. I had never known such hatred. For a few seconds, I had breached the limits of reason, tumbling into a cesspool of madness, and while most of it had likewise happened beyond my control, an element of it had been equally calculated. It wasn't enough to say that I had been capable of killing Mark—I had *wanted* to kill him. And that terrified me more than anything else.

Within an hour of the fight, my confidence left me and I found that I was as scared as ever of Rudy and Mark. I doubted I could replicate what had come over me in the chemistry lab; I didn't even know if I *wanted* to replicate it.

In the coming days, I became introverted, shuffling around school in a semi-stupor, feeling alone in every classroom. It didn't take long for the news to spread, and many of the other students—and even some teachers—cast sideways glances, as if I had some contagious disease. That I had been able to do such things seemed unnatural to everyone—including me.

In the end, I convinced myself that I had simply experienced some fleeting insanity, or maybe even a flashback, but none of these conclusions left me with a lot of conviction. What had happened made absolutely no sense, so, as with every other inexplicable and terrifying event in my life, I merely left the questions alone.

In the end, my renewed fear proved unwarranted. Rudy and Mark never bothered me again. And the strange feeling, or whatever it was, didn't come back either—at least not for a very long time.

May, Year Eighteen

By the time I finished high school, I had improved my grades and my attendance, although, considering my lifestyle, I'm not sure how I did it. The brutal shock of my family's deaths had faded, replaced by a dull ache that never left me completely, and I depended on chemicals regularly to get me through the long days and nights.

My new cello provided another release from the strain, and I frequently played for hours, the notes vibrating through my body, conciliating the ghosts for a while, offering me a little relief. The cello isn't often used as a happy instrument, although I wouldn't call it a particularly despondent one either. But when it chooses to be sad, it weeps with a profound joylessness, and the cello I received on the day of my mother's funeral could stretch the saddest note for an eternity, pulling from me the deepest emotions. We had a bittersweet relationship, but it was one I couldn't live without.

My past was a graveyard of agonizing memories that I avoided with meticulous efficiency, finding more and more distraction in drugs and alcohol. But battling the past didn't leave a lot of time to think about the future, and I gave little serious thought to life after high school. In fact, for a long time I thought I would just stay in Durango and work for MacGregor's until I found another path.

As I moved through my senior year, my advisers and teachers began to pressure me about attending college. I vacillated, as usual, but they persisted, and the more I thought about it, the more my future troubled me. I loved Durango, but deep inside I knew I had to move on if I ever wanted to escape my past.

"I've been thinking about what I should do after high school," I said to Jack in the Cooler one day.

"Uh huh." He had his head shoved nearly all the way into a computer, looking at the motherboard with a flashlight.

"I've been wondering about whether or not to stay in Durango after I graduate."

He pulled himself upright. "Why the fuck would you want to stay here?"

"I don't know. Where else would I go?"

"To college, maybe?"

"I could do that here."

"Douglas, there's a lot more to the world than Durango. Don't you want to see other places?"

"You sound like my teachers. Where'd you go to college?"

He stuck his head back in the computer. "I didn't."

"Then why should I?"

"Because you're smarter than I am."

"But I don't know what I'd study."

"Study computers, you little bastard. Hell, you almost know more about this shit than I do now."

"So where did you learn so much about computers if you didn't go to school?"

"I worked for a few technology companies in Austin when I was growing up."

Jack had never spoken much of his youth in Texas. "What's Austin like?" I asked.

"It's hot as fuck in the summer, but it's a fun town, and the University of Texas is a great school." He pulled his head up again. "The women are ass-sexy, and now that I think about it, I'm not even sure you've ever had a girlfriend."

"So?"

He looked at me suspiciously. "Are you a virgin, Douglas?"

"No!"

"I think you are."

"I am not!"

"Are you gay?"

"Shut up, Jack!"

"Maybe you should think about applying there—you know, get yourself some sweet stuff, along with an education."

Ultimately, I applied to several schools and, ironically, the University of Texas accepted me right away. So I decided I would leave Durango after all, and Austin seemed to hold the most promise. Now it was simply a matter of finding the strength to say goodbye, and although I would miss my friends—especially Jack—I didn't dread leaving as much as I had thought I might. I was ready to get away, to start again somewhere new.

Jack had dutifully handled my checks each month until I turned eighteen, at which point I received the balance of my father's estate. At the urging of Fred

Rausch, I hired a financial advisor who invested the money, holding enough aside to cover the cost of college and my living expenses.

I held a yard sale that summer, ridding myself of almost everything I owned. Then I put the house on the market. It sold quickly, so Jack let me stay with him for about three weeks until it was time for me to leave for Texas.

One day I sat in the Cooler leafing through an Austin apartment guide. "Do you know anybody who can show me around Austin?" I asked Jack.

He shook his head. "I don't know a soul in Texas anymore."

"Nobody?"

"No." The way he said it this time carried an edge of sadness.

"I didn't mean to—"

"It's nothing, kid. I haven't been there in a long time, that's all."

I flipped through the guide for another moment and then said, "I'm nervous."

He smiled. "We'll always be here for you. And you know, everybody comes back to Durango. Nobody stays gone forever."

A few weeks later, Jack helped me load my things into a trailer hitched to the back of my car. We headed to MacGregor's where Pete waited for us. The three of us laughed and talked for a while, exchanging requisite pleasantries, but the situation was awkward, as goodbyes so often are. Their faces looked distant. Jack wouldn't even make eye contact with me.

"Come visit me, you two," I said, trying to diffuse the discomfort.

"You know we will," said Pete.

"Yeah." Jack's voice was strange, and he still wouldn't look at me. "We will. Now get out of here, you little bastard."

"Okay then," I said, lifting my hand to wave. I smiled and slowly pulled away.

Pete watched me as I left, but Jack walked back into MacGregor's. I knew he wasn't upset with me—this was just hard. He had become my surrogate father, and now I was leaving. I extended my hand out the window, and Pete waved back.

Then I turned the corner and MacGregor's was gone.

FOUNDATION

Now do you say you are going to make Right your master and do away with Wrong, or make Order your master and do away with Disorder? If you do, then you have not understood.

Obviously it is impossible.

—CHUANG TZU

Austin, Texas, June, Year Eighteen

IN THE EARLY afternoon of the second day of my drive, I reached the central Texas hill country and immediately understood Jack's preoccupation with the summer weather. Texas is oppressively hot, made worse by the humidity—nothing like the cool, arid summers in Colorado. But this was my first adventure in the world, and I wasn't going to let a little heat and humidity dampen my spirits.

Before I left Durango, I had arranged to rent a small apartment in Austin, near the university. When I found the complex, I peeled myself from the seat back, and went in search of the manager.

I located the unit and knocked, and after a moment the door opened. I looked down at an old woman, bent with age. "Ms. Richmond?"

She stared at me for a moment.

"I'm Douglas Cole. I'm here for—"

"I know who you are," she said with a thick Texas twang, reaching in a pocket on her shirtfront, pulling out a set of keys. "I've been expecting you." She stepped out of the door, locking it behind her. "Come with me."

I followed her along a maze of walkways winding through the complex. "How old are you?" she asked.

"I put it on the application I sent—"

"You coulda lied. Wouldn't be the first time somebody tried it. Now how old are you?"

"I'm eighteen."

"Uh huh." She turned a corner and stopped. "This here's yours."

She unlocked the door to my unit, and after quickly walking me through it, said, "This ain't no orphanage, and if I find out you're lyin' 'bout your age, I'll throw you out in the street, you hear me?"

I nodded.

"Good. Now I don't want to hear no late night partyin' or nothin' like that. Too many you young folk think God put you on earth to keep people like me up all night, but I won't put up with it. I want the rent paid by the fifth of every month—you can just slip the check under my door if you want. I'll bring a lease by in the mornin', and I expect the first month's rent then. You got any questions?"

I shook my head.

"That's your parkin' space yonder. After you unload your trailer, you can park it on the street tonight, but it needs to be gone by tomorrow. Have a good evenin'."

Then Ms. Richmond walked away, leaving me bewildered and standing alone in front of my new apartment.

Welcome to Austin, I thought.

I spent the next few hours unloading boxes and furniture as the sun floated westward, descending weightlessly toward the horizon. The temperature reached its unforgiving climax, while I dripped with the sweat that the heavy, drenched air refused to absorb from my body.

As I unloaded the last box from the trailer, certain I couldn't endure the heat another minute, the sun dropped below the trees and a breath of cool air reached me. I put the box on the ground, straightened, and closed my eyes. A few seconds later, I opened them to the sound of a group of kids about my age walking toward campus. I followed them with my gaze, wondering who they were, and where they were going.

I rushed into the apartment, recharged by their laughter, suddenly wanting more than anything to be with them, to explore this new place. I took a quick shower, threw on some clothes, and walked out the door.

In the years I have known Austin, it has exuded a magic I have rarely found in other places. From my first day there, I was struck by the rare intellectual and spiritual symbiosis that has always pervaded that section of Guadalupe Street running beside the University of Texas, known as the Drag. I cannot remember a time when it didn't afford a kind of scholarly reprieve for thousands of untested voices, clamoring for their places in the growth of knowledge, begging for the respect they have yet to earn. For these young minds, the Drag is a place to bloom, almost completely free from stifling judgment.

The Drag has always pulsed with an awareness most easily perceived by those yet to understand its depth—an awareness not derived from intention or design, but rather, by the random product of innumerable theories, colliding in critical mass to form a chaotic bridge between that which is demanded, and that which will never be accepted—the ownerless terrain between uncompromising dogmatism and discontented youth. This was the Austin into which I was initiated.

Throngs of young people moved purposefully past me, fed by the heat of the summer evening. I stood transfixed on the sidewalk, spellbound by their faces, struck by the intelligence in the eyes that looked back at me. These people weren't here merely to be educated, they were here to experience life.

And at that moment, I realized what a mistake it would have been to stay in Durango. The instant my feet touched the pavement on which I now stood, I became wedded to Austin forever. I belonged here.

Fashions ranged from postmodern punk to conservative casual, but no matter what they wore, the people were gorgeous. Record stores pumped out waves of esoteric underground music, and I caught the enticing scents of exotic foods drifting from more restaurants that I could count. I ambled down the street, soaking in every detail. I stopped to have dinner at a small Vietnamese café, and then continued my tour.

I crossed the street and entered the vast campus, where endless walkways and streets wound between enormous limestone buildings shaded by the twisted boughs of towering oak trees. After a couple of hours of aimless wandering, I made my way back to the Drag for a cup of coffee, or maybe a beer. I stuck my head in two or three shops before I finally came to one that grabbed me. It was serving an eclectic mix of people, from students, to professionals, to the homeless—the drag worms. I got in line to order a cup of coffee and my eyes fell on two men sitting across from each other, staring intently at their table.

Chess!

I ordered and sat down to watch them play. As I took my first sip of coffee, the words on the cup caught my eye. I pulled it away from my lips and read: *Cardinal Yorkshire's American Coffee Emporium: Serving the Drag for over 15 Years.*

The Cardinal was a smoke-filled rat-hole lit by long fluorescent tubes hanging across the ceiling. Newspapers and magazines littered every corner, and the furniture looked like the spoils of a hangover-inspired Saturday morning garage sale adventure—a collection of reclining chairs, sofas, rickety tables, and other discarded heirlooms. The stained, pea-green carpet could easily have served as the turf at a miniature golf park, and on the walls—painted an equally reviling shade of green—hung garish artwork, burning into the backdrop like acid. The place was a visual manifestation of an LSD experience gone horribly wrong, and yet somehow its nauseating decor lent to a relaxing, comfortable atmosphere.

The Cardinal's aroma was a sour combination of coffee, beer, cigarettes, mildew, and human refuse. The music was loud, eclectic, and unpredictable, competing with the chattering din of a clientele every bit as diverse, their faces displaying a fusion of cynicism, apathy, and intelligence.

Soon I was in my first game, followed by several more. I ordered beers for the table, striking up conversations, asking questions about the city and the university. Everyone was friendly and helpful, offering me as much information as I could digest. I liked this place and I thought to myself, *This isn't going to be so hard.*

I played and lost several matches. I could easily have stayed until the shop closed but I had too much to do, and I was exhausted from my two-day drive. There would be time for chess later, and I knew I would be back.

I found a liquor store near campus where I bought a bottle of scotch with the fake ID Pete had given me after my mother died. I returned to my new apartment, set up my bed, organized a few other necessities, fixed a drink, and pulled out a bag of weed. It was a Friday, and summer session started Monday, so I resolved to get my apartment in order over the weekend.

But first things first: I got into bed and filled my body with the chemicals that would help me slip away.

———◆———

FOR THE NEXT week, I rose early to attend classes. As soon as I finished with those obligations, however, I explored Austin, walking for hours, visiting coffee shops and restaurants, touring the capitol, perusing art galleries and museums. And after each adventure, I found myself back at the Cardinal, which was quickly becoming my new home, always pulling me back for another pint of beer, one more game, or one more conversation with new friends.

The university's social structure was not what I was used to—it was driven by those innumerable eager young minds, so hungry for new discoveries and often independent for the first time in their lives. Within days of my arrival, I began to meet all sorts of interesting people, in class or in coffee shops and bars. I was invited to clubs and parties, and the fact that I had plenty of money only made the process of making friends easier. My phone was soon ringing regularly, and while many of the friendships were superficial and transitory, I didn't care; I was a college freshman with a lot of time and cash, and I enjoyed being surrounded by people—always having something to do. I had never had many friends before, so I was more than happy to spread my wealth among those who were willing to help me break out of my shell. I even believed that I might be able to put my past behind me.

I tried to immerse myself in the academic life of the university, but not surprisingly, I kept getting distracted. At first I found myself putting off studying for a quick lunch or dinner with friends, but after a while the procrastination extended into entire evenings. The endless diversions began to take control and partying became my priority. Somehow it didn't concern me much; academia couldn't compete with this new life—this never-ending sea of fun, drowning the painful memories.

For me, Austin was a world of inexhaustible hedonism. At night, students and young professionals would pour into its nucleus, shuffling, stumbling, and crawling through clubs, drinking, taking drugs, and endlessly debating the implications of just about everything imaginable.

And they *lived*—virtually exhaling creativity and innovation. Just looking at them was like peering through a window into the future. Austin was never a city of tourists or monuments; it has always been a place of dark learning and art—a living canvas, dripping with passion and driven by thought.

Here, I discovered that there are more paths to numbness than cannabis and alcohol—a *lot* more. Before long, I was exposed to a cornucopia of drugs that I had always considered too dangerous even for my desperate quest to escape. Aside from the few times I took LSD, I had avoided pumping my body full of synthetic chemicals. But in this climate of wanton, youthful exploration, my curiosity overwhelmed my caution, and soon I was experimenting with every drug I could get my hands on, although ultimately I didn't become enamored with most of them.

Ecstasy was fun, but it didn't inspire me much. It seemed artificial, and like LSD, left me exhausted. Heroin was the most popular drug in my crowd, but it required too much equipment, and I never got past the idea of jamming needles in my arms, no matter how good it made me feel.

But soon enough, I found cocaine, which hit me hard and fast. Unlike LSD, it didn't demand my participation. In fact, it required almost no effort at all; it simply washed through me, vigorous yet serene, eradicating my pain and crippling my inhibitions. From the instant I inhaled my first line, the drug took me in its arms, and I offered no resistance, sliding into its sweet comfort as easily as nestling into a warm bed on a cold night.

September, Year Eighteen

THAT SUMMER CAME and went like a cyclone, torrential, and so quick I would have missed it had it not been so intense. For a few weeks in August, I tried to gear up for the fall semester, and I even convinced myself that I could maintain this new lifestyle and still find the time to study, but I had become too entrenched in self-gratification to be serious about school anymore. And so my grades suffered even more that autumn than they had during the summer session. The lifestyle was finally starting to assume control.

In the beginning, cocaine gave me a deluded sense of euphoric confidence and endless energy with which the ghosts had a difficult time competing. When I was high, my life seemed back on track; my problems simply vanished. Of course, severe depression always hit me coming down, but that problem was easily remedied with more coke.

At the Cardinal, I quickly discovered my chess game wasn't much of a challenge for most of the regular players. At first, I watched more than I played, but as I started to know the names and faces of the regulars, the urge to play became irresistible, and it wasn't long before I was in front of the board regularly.

I gravitated toward younger, less experienced players who seemed more interested in having fun than establishing their prowess, and it wasn't long before I was a member of an informal gathering of amateurs. I could always find the crew at the Cardinal gathered around a table, laughing, shouting, and chattering. We would play for hours in the afternoons, and then often head to a bar or pub where we would continue the games—and the drinking.

There were seven or eight of us in all, but the one I became closest to was Ellison Clark. Ellison was around twenty-five years old, and always meticulously dressed. He was smart, energetic, and chronically happy—forever laughing and telling jokes. He had a wonderfully infectious smile, and while he was slightly better at chess than I was, he always managed to keep the games light, whether he won or lost.

Ellison always seemed to have girls around him—peeking in on the games, or meeting us for drinks afterward. One girl particularly intrigued me, although she didn't come around very often, and didn't hang around long when she did appear. She had long, straight sandy blonde hair, which she usually wore pulled back, twisted, and stacked loosely on her head. Her eyes were deep green, and light freckles spotted her nose. Something about her made it almost impossible for me to take my eyes off of her. Several times she caught me staring, always returning my gaze with a small smile, which invariably made me look away, embarrassed.

One time, Ellison caught me looking at her. I was mortified, hoping I hadn't offended him, but he just turned up the corner of his mouth in a wry grin. It puzzled me, but I resigned myself at that moment to try to stop watching her.

Almost as soon as I made the decision, however, she left the shop, making my life a little easier. And yet I couldn't help following her with my eyes as she walked out of the Cardinal, my chest tightening slightly.

Ellison had lived in Austin for years. He knew all the best places and had a lot of great friends. The fact that he—a grown man with so many resources—was willing to let a kid like me kick around with him was beyond thrilling, and I all but stopped spending time with anyone my own age. The more I got to know Ellison, the more he provided the kind of comfort I had found in Jack and Pete.

Although we spent time at other places, the Cardinal was our primary hangout, and Ellison generously helped me navigate its surprisingly intricate social framework. Many of the regulars—especially the masters—had been playing in Austin for decades, often for money, and it wasn't uncommon to see two players yelling at each other as a crowd hovered around them to see whether or not a brawl would break out. Surprisingly often, the audience wasn't disappointed. Ellison helped me stay clear of these types of situations—to understand and respect the subtle yet complex politics that drove the chess community, especially at the Cardinal, which was the scene's hub.

"You see those guys over there," he said one day over a game.

I followed his gaze to a table where two men sat hunched over a board. "The black guy's name is Don. He's probably the nicest person you'll ever meet, but nobody knows his last name. And the guy he's playing—the one with the beard and thick glasses—that's John Betty."

The man looked wretched. He wore a stained T-shirt, and his jeans looked as if they hadn't been washed in months. His tennis shoes were filthy and mangled. His hair was greasy and curly, plastered over a balding head, and his beard resembled steel wool.

"He looks like a bum." I said.

"Yeah, well you ought to smell him sometime. Anyway, just a drag worm, right? Wrong." Ellison leaned forward slightly. "Get this: John's folks were killed in a car crash or something like that, five or six years ago, and he inherited about twenty million dollars."

"Really? Why does he look like that?"

"Because he's a fucking weirdo, that's why." Ellison raised his arm and shouted, "John Betty!"

John looked up as though wakened from a deep sleep, blinking rapidly. His thick-rimmed glasses hung halfway down his nose, making his eyes look huge as he scanned the room, searching for the source of the voice.

Ellison snapped his fingers twice and shouted, "Yo, John! Over here!"

John swung his head in our direction and pushed his glasses up. "Ah, yes. Hello, Ellison. Good day." His voice was a nasally monotone, and he pronounced each syllable slowly, with perfect diction. His expression didn't change at all, and as soon as he had greeted Ellison, he returned his attention to the game. His partner—the enigmatic black man with no last name—didn't even look up from the board.

Ellison let out a snort.

"What does he do with all his money?" I asked.

"Who the fuck knows? He may have spent it all by now. One time, just after he inherited it, he and Big Mack—"

"Who?"

Ellison looked surprised. "You've never seen Mack?"

I shook my head.

He chuckled. "He's a big fat prick, but he's also the best chess player in this town. He's from Russia—Ukraine, I think. He doesn't come in here much. He likes to hang out downtown, but you'll meet him. Anyway, after John inherited all that money, Mack challenged him to a game for like a thousand bucks or something. John lost, but they kept playing all afternoon. At the end of the day, John was down fucking *huge*."

"How huge?"

Ellison told me the amount and my mouth fell open. "*Jesus!* You could buy a house for that!

Ellison gave me a knowing smile.

"So what happened?" I asked.

"John refused to pay, and Big Mack went totally fucking nuts. John finally had to be escorted out of the place by friends so Mack wouldn't kick the shit out of him. Now, whenever John sees Mack, he heads for the back door. Mack still rails about it all the time."

I watched the two men playing chess for a moment. The scene could have been a photograph, neither moving a muscle as he stared at the board in front of him. Suddenly the black man's hand shot out so quickly it nearly made me jump. He pushed a piece and then turned his face to me, smiling peacefully, as if he had known I was watching the whole time. I returned a weak smile and slowly pulled my eyes away.

"Are all the chess players in Austin like that?" I asked.

"Yeah, everybody except you and me." Ellison looked at my expression and laughed. "It's not that bad. Don's a strange one. He works at the library in front of a computer all day, typing reference numbers and shit like that. I can't think of a more boring job. I'd probably be a little weird too, if I had to do that."

"What *do* you do, Ellison?"

"I'm an accountant part of the time, but I've been transitioning over the last six months. Now I mostly trade futures."

"What's that?"

"Mmmmm . . . they're like stocks, in a way."

I smiled. "I would guess you probably sit in front of a computer all day too—except that I see you in here so much."

He laughed again. "Yeah, well I do some basic stuff for accounting, but I just don't know enough to use computers for futures research. When it comes to technology, I'm an idiot. I hear the potential is huge, though."

"Your boss must like you a lot if he lets you come in here to play chess on weekday afternoons."

"I don't really have a boss anymore," he said as he picked up a rook. "I do some contract accounting work for a couple firms in town whenever they need extra help, just so I can have some steady income, you know? But mostly now I work with this guy who has been helping me learn to build my futures accounts." He looked at me and grinned. "And I can do that on any schedule I want."

Over the next few weeks, Ellison and I played a lot of chess, and it was during these games that I discovered how passionate he was about trading futures. He gave me a general overview of how the markets work, along with some intriguing commentary on how he planned to tap into the fortunes that resided there. He talked a lot about his partner/mentor—whose name I discovered was Victor Mason—and made several more remarks about how much trouble computers gave them both. "Victor's even worse than I am," he said. "He can barely use a TV remote."

"I could help you sometime, if you want me to." I made the offer casually, thinking he wouldn't be interested.

"Yeah, we might take you up on that," he said, noncommittally.

But as we grew more comfortable with one another, Ellison began to ask me more about my life, and he seemed increasingly interested in my skills with technology.

"I'm at UT right now," I told him. "But I don't like school much, and I may not finish this semester. I inherited some money that should hold me until I figure out what I want to do."

Ellison's eyes lit up. "Would you consider working with me and Victor? If you know as much about computers as you say you do, we could sure use your help. And we could teach you about futures. You'd do great! We'll let you use our resources, and you can trade your own account through our brokers. Victor'll love the idea."

I thought about it for a moment. "Why don't you let me see your office?"

A few days later, my coke dealer invited me to a party in one of Austin's more affluent neighborhoods. I arrived late, got a drink, and began to weave in and out of the crowd gathered around an enormous swimming pool, stopping here and there to socialize a bit with someone I vaguely recognized, or sucking up a spoonful of cocaine.

Sometime after midnight, I met a cute girl with some prominent tattoos. We began flirting, which largely entailed yelling at each other over the deafening music. I managed to learn her name was Amber, and after about a half hour of barely comprehensible small talk, she abruptly grabbed my hand and pulled me through the crowd and into the house, where we shoved our way through still more people, ending up at the front door.

"Where are we going?" I said outside, grateful to be able to speak in a normal tone.

Amber spun around, stood on her toes, and pulled my mouth onto hers. When we separated, I smiled awkwardly, surprised by her aggressiveness. "Let's get out of here," she said.

"Where do you want to go?"

She narrowed her eyes and smiled. "Take me to my place."

I wanted to attribute Amber's interest to my charm and ravishing good looks, but I suspected that the abundant supply of cocaine in my pocket had more to do with it. I shrugged. "My car's this way."

We arrived at Amber's apartment, where she soon learned that I was a student. Shortly thereafter we established that she earned the bulk her income by removing her clothes on stage. And with those formalities out of the way, we decided swimming naked in the pool at her apartment complex was the obvious next step to our budding relationship.

Twenty minutes later, we were back on her sofa, having coke-fueled sex, which we repeated several times. When we were done, we did a couple of lines, commented on the fabulous nature of our respective performances, and exchanged a few pleasantries. Then I put on my clothes and told her I had an appointment, which was true—I was meeting Ellison in a couple of hours to discuss the next possible phase of my career. She gave me her phone number, and I told her I would call.

I returned to my apartment, quickly showered, threw on some relatively clean clothes, and drove to the Cardinal, exhausted, disoriented, and barely on time.

Ellison laughed when he saw me. "You look terrible. Rough night?"

I nodded sheepishly. "Yeah, I didn't get much sleep."

"You don't look like you got *any* sleep." He laughed again. "Well, fuck it. At least you're here. Let's grab a cup of joe and get going."

Ellison drove us to a wealthy neighborhood in south Austin—a country club development built around a golf course. It was a contrived, isolated subdivision, clearly built for the city's nouveau riche.

"Where are we going?" I asked.

"To Victor's house," Ellison said, pulling into the driveway of a two-story ranch house that was neatly, if insipidly, landscaped. "It's cheaper for us to work here than to rent an office." We went inside, where Ellison introduced me to Victor Mason.

Victor was, in size and stature, Ellison's complete opposite. He was an older, short, unhealthy-looking fat man with chapped white lips that seemed not to have adequate circulation. His small, close-set brown eyes gave him a wily look, and he wore a thin mustache which only added to his guileful appearance. Most striking, however, was the way he dressed: he presented himself to me in a bathrobe, under which he wore pajamas. His feet were stuffed into furry slippers.

"It's good to meet you, Douglas," he said, pumping my hand. "Ellison tells me you want to join our venture." He spoke glibly through a slight smile, his lips barely moving.

"Well, I'd like to at least learn what you do."

"Good, good. Why don't you come in and we'll let you ask the questions. I'd like to get started because I want to get in a few rounds of golf this afternoon, if you know what I mean." He winked at me. "You a golfer?" He asked the question as though the answer might affect his assessment of my character.

"No, I've never played."

"Well, that's all right." He winked. "I'm just going to let Ellison here show you around. You let me know if you have any other questions." And with that, Victor walked out of the room, leaving us alone to tour the place.

Victor's appearance had certainly given me reason to question the legitimacy of the operation, but those misgivings all but vanished when I saw the office. For a couple of guys with no computer knowledge, they certainly had a lot of machines, and I instantly saw possibilities—at least from a technological perspective.

"Who runs all these?" I asked.

"We have a guy who comes in a few times a week, or whenever we have an emergency," said Ellison. "And there are a *lot* of emergencies."

His knowledge was cursory, but he was able to go over the basic hardware and show me some of the software they ran. "If I could figure out how to manage all this crap, I'd be able to predict some amazing trends. I've been messing around with it, but I just can't seem to get it."

I toyed with one of the computers for a minute and quickly recognized the basic calculations. "This is a snap." I created a simple formula and ran it. A chart popped up, along with some statistical results.

Ellison brightened. "Wow! You do know your shit, don't you?"

I shrugged. "They took these formulas from basic spreadsheets. I could show you how it works, no problem."

Ellison showed me another monitor that was flashing numbers every few seconds. "This is our live quote feed. Every time a contract trades, the price ticks there." He pointed to the screen. "Here are the commodity ticker symbols, and these arrows show whether the contract is up or down for the day."

He directed my attention to another monitor. "Here's our account, and this is our cost basis." He pointed to a figure, which was impressive. "And this is how much we make or lose every time a price ticks. Here's one that has picked up—the Long Bond. Every time it ticks up, the money we make is calculated in this column." He pointed to a figure, and I watched the number increase rapidly.

My pulse quickened. The allure was immediate. "You've made that much?"

"Yeah, but remember, it can go down by that much too. Look here. That's our position in the Swiss franc. We're short that one, and it's going against us hard."

"How long does it last?"

"As long as you want, or until the contract expires in a couple of months, whichever comes first. But we don't normally hold anything for more than a day, and usually not even more than an hour. I'm about to dump those. You want to see how it works?"

I couldn't take my eyes off the screen. "Uh huh."

"Okay, hold on." He picked up the phone, pressing the first speed-dial button. "Billy? Ellison Clark. Sell the twenty-five December bonds I bought a little while ago, would you? Yeah, thanks." He wrote down some figures. "Okay, got it. Also, would you buy back the seventy-five Swiss francs? Yes, December again. Yeah, thank you." More writing. "Yeah, great." He put down the phone and turned to me. "That's that."

"How much did you make?"

"We did okay. You win some and lose some." He pointed at me and smiled. "The trick is to win more than you lose."

I was hooked. "What makes you decide to buy or sell?"

"We look at a lot of things. But that's why we want you here, to help us test some of our ideas on the computers."

"And you do this for your clients?"

"We don't have any clients," Ellison said. "We only do it for ourselves. Victor used to own a brokerage firm, but when the market crashed a few years ago, he lost a lot of money, so he consolidated his resources and came up with a plan to trade futures. He figured it was the quickest way to get back on top, but he decided not to take on any clients. They're just a pain in the ass."

I was surprised at his candor about Victor's failure, and, for just an instant, I became vaguely aware of a distant thought in my head, picking at me. But it seemed insignificant to my racing mind, and just as quickly as it had appeared, it vanished. I was interested in how much money I could *make*, not how much I stood to lose.

"How did you guys meet?" I asked.

"I handled his books at an accounting firm I used to work for," Ellison said. "We became friends, and when he started doing this a few months ago, he seemed to be making pretty good money, so I asked him if he would teach me. The next thing I knew, I was over here every day."

My eyes scanned the room. I was lost in the possibilities: Ellison and Victor had no idea how much computing power they had at their disposal, but I was ready to show them.

By early afternoon, Ellison had opened and closed several more positions. It was like being in a casino, but with a more prestigious title: the prospect of being called a "futures trader" thrilled me.

"What do you think?" he asked me, finishing the day's entries in his trading journal.

"It looks like a rush."

"It is a rush," said Victor, who had appeared behind us, now dressed in what I presumed were his golfing clothes "So, you think you might be interested in joining us?"

"I think we could help each other out," I said. "How would we work it?"

Suddenly Victor was all business. "You help us with the software and put up a third of the damages for the data feed and the utilities. You'll have full access to our computers, software, and our brokers, but you have to pay your own commissions. We start at seven every weekday morning and stick around until two, unless we decide to call it an early day."

In case you want to play golf, I thought. Yet despite my continuing reservations about Victor, I was certain a great opportunity lay in front of me. Another vague warning appeared in my mind, scratching at me, urging me to ask more questions, but I pushed it aside. Victor added, "Other than that, there's not much to it." His voice was smooth, and his eyes bored into mine. He was a salesman to the core.

"Count me in," I said.

Ellison grinned. "Great!"

Back at the Cardinal, I thanked Ellison and told him I would see him the following morning at seven sharp. Then I got in my car and reached into my pocket for a small vial of coke. I smeared the white powder on my gums with my pinky finger and closed my eyes for a moment. When I opened them, I glanced at myself in the rearview mirror and smiled.

I drove to the administration office at the university and withdrew from all of my classes. Then I went straight to my apartment and slept for about fifteen hours.

———————◆———————

FROM THE FIRST day, I dove into trading with an inexhaustible zeal. I usually got to Victor's house before seven, and for the first couple of weeks, I just tried to absorb as much as I could. Every morning, the three of us would watch the financial networks on two different televisions, waiting for the opening trades at exchanges in Chicago. Suddenly, the computer screens would come alive, blinking in a flurry of activity, at which point Ellison and Victor would each grab a phone, call their brokers, and begin placing trades.

I worked most nights until well after eight or nine, sacrificing huge chunks of my weekends, going over transactions, searching for ways to improve returns, manage risk, and find patterns in the markets. Surprisingly, my drug use actually diminished; I still drank a lot, but never so much that I couldn't wake up and get to work.

"You're like me," Victor commented when he saw me come in one Saturday. "You like the week more than the weekends. I can't wait until Monday."

On the surface, Victor seemed to have a lot of knowledge, but at a deeper level, something just didn't seem quite right. For instance, he loved to talk about how extravagant his lifestyle had once been. In his silky-liquid voice, he would say, "When we were in the brokerage business, we went everywhere in a limousine. Yeah, I even sent my maids to the grocery store in that fuckin' limo. I was going to buy a jet too. You *know* you got it made when you have a jet. You see what I'm sayin'?"

Victor always asked me if I saw what he was saying, but I never quite did.

He could run on about almost anything, but usually it was about money or sex. He frequently spoke of the women he'd "had," describing their physical attributes and talents in meticulous detail.

"Doug," he said one day, "you see that picture over there?"

It was a photograph of Victor standing on a golf course beside a woman. He looked younger, slightly thinner, and wore a shirt made of some shiny black material, unbuttoned to the middle of his chest, out of which exploded a thick mat of hair. Several gold chains seemed almost to slither amidst the curls. He wore a pair of black and white golf shoes and brown polyester pants, two neat creases running down the leg fronts. The hair on his head was longer, parted on the side, and he sported shaggy sideburns, as well as the same thin mustache he had now, if a little less gray.

The woman was almost a foot taller than Victor, and somewhat attractive despite the fashion faux pas she committed; even the era couldn't justify her poor taste. She wore the female counterpart to Victor's outfit—a vinyl-looking, shiny, creamy white one-piece jumpsuit with a huge collar and wide, loud stripes running its length. Protruding from the legs of the suit were a pair of thin red heels strapped to her feet, and I found myself wondering why a woman would want to wear heels on a golf course.

In the photo, Victor had his arm around her, posing like a racecar driver after a critical victory. Their smiles seemed tired and forced.

"You got a girlfriend, Doug? You're not a faggot are you?"

I looked at him hard. "No." Jack sometimes had made similar comments, but somehow they never affected me like this.

"That's my wife," he said proudly, jutting his chin at the photograph. "She's a fuckin' knockout, isn't she?"

"Yeah," I said without looking back at the picture.

He stared at me for a few more long seconds. "Yeah," he repeated.

I held my breath while he looked at me. Finally I said, "So what happened to her?"

"What the fuck are you talkin' about?" He pulled his head back dramatically, chuckling as though I were a fool. "She's downstairs in the living room."

I was confused. I had no idea Victor had a wife, let alone in the house where we were standing.

He continued to stare at me, unblinking. "Listen here," he said in a low tone, licking his lips. "She fucks like a whore."

I nodded slowly. He kept staring at me, presumably waiting for a response. I held my breath again, and when I could stand no more, I blurted, "I believe it."

I could have hit myself in the forehead, and I wanted to retract the statement immediately; I didn't have much respect for Victor, but I didn't want to offend anyone who could teach me how to trade futures.

Victor didn't bat an eye. "Oh, hell, yes she does! She's a beautiful woman! The best I ever had!"

I nodded through another long, awkward pause.

"And I've had a lot of women." He winked at me. "You see what I'm sayin'?"

I never met Victor's wife.

Not long after I began trading, I wrote several rudimentary but powerful software functions designed to analyze decades of historical futures data, and a few of these completed their cycles in only a couple of days, offering results that looked promising. I went over my findings until late into the evening, after which I took the data home. I didn't want to waste any time, so I loaded the functions on my computer, did some coke, and decided to skip dinner, digging yet further into the data.

After several more hours, I began to get excited; I was convinced the system could make us a fortune quickly, but I also knew I should be cautious, so I reset the parameters using some different variables and went to bed.

When I awoke the next morning, the results had generated a strong buy signal. There was no time for breakfast, so I quickly snorted a line before brushing my teeth. Then I drove to the office, where Ellison sat alone in front of one of the television screens, waiting for the market to open.

"Where's Victor?" I said.

Ellison didn't look away from the screen. "He just left. He didn't see anything that made him want to trade today, so he decided to get in a few rounds this morning."

"Well, I have something interesting to tell you."

He turned to look at me.

"I've been testing some data, and I got a buy signal today."

Ellison raised his eyebrows. "How confident are you?"

"I retested it twice last night and it worked like a charm."

"Show me."

I sat down in front of one of the computers and gave him a synopsis of what I had found. When I finished, he smiled, picked up the phone, called his broker and initiated an enormous trade.

Watching him, my heart rate increased and my breathing suddenly seemed more difficult. I reached for another phone and called my broker, instructing him to take an equally sizeable position in my account. I gently replaced the handset in the cradle and looked at Ellison.

He smiled again. "Well I guess we're gonna see how it works."

We both rolled our chairs over to the monitor to watch.

Things went wrong almost immediately. We sat nearly motionless, our eyes glued helplessly to the computer monitor as the prices slowly started moving away from us. My stomach tightened and my throat seemed to swell. I couldn't understand what was going wrong. Finally, after about an hour of watching our losses mount, Ellison reached for the phone. "I'm covering."

I followed his lead, calling the broker to offset my position. When I hung up, I looked at him.

"I guess you need to test that system a little more." He wasn't very happy.

"I don't now what went wrong."

"Don't beat yourself up over it. It's part of the game. Just be more careful next time."

When Victor found out, he exploded. "Goddamn it! You boys don't fuckin' do that again if I'm not here, do you hear me? We can't afford to fuckin' lose that kind of money."

Ellison furrowed his brow. "Your money wasn't at risk, Victor."

"It could have been! You just be more careful." Victor looked worried, and his disquiet resurrected the distant voice of caution in my mind. It was faint, but growing louder every day.

I developed more functions to guide my investments over the next couple of months, but I traded cautiously from then on. Still, no matter how hard I tried to find the perfect system, I couldn't seem to beat the market consistently, and even though I thought I was being careful, I was losing money rapidly. My drinking and drug use had started to pick up again too, and cocaine wasn't a cheap habit, which only further depleted my accounts.

December, Year Eighteen

I HADN'T TOUCHED my cello in a long time. I still heard my pieces in my head, but they were hollow and full of static, like a radio playing in the distance. And while the instrument had once been a distraction for me, these days drinking and snorting away my problems just seemed easier. So when I wasn't in front of my computer, I spent my time at the Cardinal, throwing back beer after beer, playing chess with the usual crew, and hitting on girls. It was the only place I felt even moderately comfortable.

It was mid-December of my eighteenth year, the day the rare snowstorm hit Austin, when I walked out of the bathroom of the Cardinal to find Jefferson Stone sitting at my table, one leg tossed casually over the other as he leafed through my book, staring at the pages through his small round glasses. And so we played our first game of chess together.

Jefferson and I met a few more times in the coming weeks, and soon we were getting together regularly at the Cardinal. As we got to know each other, he took time to help me with my game, and he even gave me a book with some opening strategies. I studied it carefully and my game actually improved, which was surprising, considering my lifestyle. I never beat Jefferson, but the more we played, the more I learned, and our friendship evolved into a kind of student/teacher dynamic. I hung on his every word, heeding his criticism, pushing myself to be a better player.

Jefferson fascinated me. He was exceptionally intelligent, his sense of humor subtle, his timing superb. I sought him out at every opportunity, and I began to look forward to our lessons almost as much as I anticipated my next beer or line of coke. I still spent time with Ellison and the other regulars, but if Jefferson appeared, I would slip away from the crowd to sit with him.

It seemed a little odd to me that I wanted to spend so much time with someone who didn't drink or do drugs—and Jefferson certainly didn't partake, under any circumstances. In fact, he didn't appear to have any habits—bad or good. It was difficult to know much about him; he kept a barrier between us, casually avoiding almost any questions about himself.

He was mysterious enough to be a little frightening, but on the other hand, he was so balanced by moderation, consistency, and equanimity that I found myself trusting him almost unconditionally. He seemed impervious to negative energy, and I got the impression that any emotions he did exhibit appeared only at his bidding. I never saw him angry that I remember, although I detected a bit of sadness at times, but even then he seemed in control. Overall, I don't think anything about Jefferson Stone was uncalculated or unintended.

The one emotion Jefferson did exude in great abundance was happiness. It was a subdued, peaceful sort of joy, but it was also pervasive and infectious. His eyes were kind, self-confident, and always seemed full of mirth—even when he wasn't smiling. More than once, he diffused my frustration with only a look or a slight grin, and I watched him do it to other people, too. He made me feel good about myself, and even optimistic about a future that was dubious at best.

The thing I probably liked best about Jefferson, however, was that he never judged me. The signs of my decline were obvious—the nosebleeds, my appearance, my attitude—but Jefferson never pushed me about any of it. He seemed content just to have a consistent chess partner, and that was fine with me. I didn't need anyone telling me how to live my life.

Late one morning about a month after Jefferson introduced himself to me, I woke up with almost no sense of where I was or what had happened to me for the previous eighteen or so hours. I swung my feet out of bed and put my head in my hands, trying to understand why I felt so horrible. And then I remembered.

I had been to a club the night before, and I had met yet another girl who found me succulently handsome with a bag of coke in my pants. She came back to my apartment with me, and we stayed up all night watching television, drinking incomprehensible amounts of vodka, doing lines, and having sex.

The girl was now gone—along with the rest of my coke, which irritated me to no end. But while my memory of the previous night was still vague, I had no trouble recalling that, the day before, I had agreed to meet Jefferson at the Cardinal today at around noon for some games. I was going to be late if I didn't hurry.

I decided to put my cocaine loss aside. I brushed my teeth, threw on whatever clothes lay close at hand, grabbed my chessboard, and rushed out the door.

When I got to the Cardinal, Jefferson was waiting for me at a table by the windows. "Hey," I said as I approached, setting down my board. "I'm just going to grab a beer before we start."

"I'd rather you didn't," he said.

It had been some time since I had had to go without cocaine. I was quickly becoming irritable, and I had been looking forward to calming my nerves with a beer, or maybe two or three. I stared at him for a moment. "Why would you rather I didn't?"

He smiled so kindly it annoyed me. "You won't offer me much of a challenge if you're numb. If you want to drink beer, we'll just skip our games today."

"I don't offer you much of a challenge anyway," I grumbled, but I wanted to play, so I sat down and set up my board.

After I arranged the pieces, I noticed Barney the ever-present drag worm sitting two tables over, mumbling something about the Dallas Cowboys and CIA agents from the future.

Like many homeless people, Barney had a mental disorder, and while I don't think he was particularly old, his haggard features gave that impression nonetheless. His hair and beard were long and matted, and the few teeth he still possessed were discolored and decayed. Grime smeared his weathered face, and his clothes smelled foul, which guaranteed him a considerable radius of personal space. His trademark uniform was a dirty yellow T-shirt emblazoned by an enormous smiley face, prominently splotched with a dark stain giving it the appearance of having a protruding tooth.

Barney had a habit of pressing his left hand to his ear, twitching and muttering quietly to himself between involuntary shouts. His speech was often unintelligible, but sometimes he could be engaged in broken conversation, which always consisted of a new chapter of his life's work: Barney insisted he was from the future, sent to save the world from some government agency that was plotting to rule the universe. I didn't know Barney's history, and I wasn't sure why he was allowed to loiter at the Cardinal, but he seemed harmless, and I liked him despite his delusions—and his odor. But he could definitely annoy me at times, particularly when I was already irritable. "Barney, forget about it," I said. "There are no men from the future. The terrorists aren't coming."

He narrowed his eyes. "You *know*. You know they're coming, and it's your fucking fault." He twitched slightly and resumed his monologue, glaring at me.

"What are you so pissed off about? I didn't do anything to you, you goddamn freak." I chuckled and looked at Jefferson, but he wasn't laughing.

"Why would you say that to him?" he asked me.

"What?"

"He's obviously having a hard life. I'll bet there are a lot of things about Barney you don't understand. You should think about how bad it must get for him."

The reprimand stung. I suddenly had a vivid image of Barney sitting alone in an alley somewhere, weeping. I tried to put the thought out of my mind, but I couldn't, and it only made my little itch worse. I decided it was time to change the subject. "I don't want to sit through any long games. Let's play with a clock."

"No," said Jefferson.

The abruptness of his reply only further vexed me. "Why not?"

"Because you're impatient, that's why."

"What the fuck does that mean? Why are you being such a fucking prick today?"

"Why do you use the word 'fuck' so much?" Jefferson's eyes glowed.

The question troubled me, setting off some memory I couldn't quite pin down. It niggled at me for a few seconds and then faded.

"Listen to what I'm about to tell you," Jefferson continued. "When you and I play chess, we will never use a clock. It breeds impatience, which you already have plenty of." He paused for a moment and added, "And you can drink beer another time."

I folded my arms and glared at him. "Why do you want to play chess with me at all?"

"Because you could be a great player. And because you're my friend."

I sighed heavily, slumping in my chair, and we began our game.

A half hour later, Jefferson looked up from the board and stared at me. "What?"

He rested his elbows on the table, and steepled his fingers in front of his face, his eyes boring into mine. "You're not seeing it."

"I'm not seeing *what*, Jefferson?"

"The thing absent from your game is nothingness."

I exhaled hard and rolled my eyes. I was in absolutely no mood for his cryptic comments.

A minute later he said, "Listen to what I'm telling you."

I leaned my head back and sighed again. "You know what? You beat the shit out of me whenever we play. You get up and wander around, you read, you look at the art on the walls. You do anything but concentrate on the game. It's like you don't even care!"

"I care," he said. "And if I wasn't concentrating, you'd win, wouldn't you?"

I shifted in my seat. My need for chemicals was making me belligerent. "You can really be a shithead sometimes." The truth was, I didn't know Jefferson well enough to know whether he could really be a shithead or not, but I hoped the accusation would annoy him.

It didn't.

"Nothingness," he repeated.

"Why do you say stuff like that? I just called you a shithead and all you can say is 'nothingness'? What the hell is wrong with you?"

He smiled.

Always the smile, I thought. Then, as much as I didn't want to, I smiled too. "What's so fucking funny?" My grin spread uncontrollably.

"I don't think anything is funny. I just enjoy watching you learn."

"Great! What have I learned?"

"About nothing."

"Jefferson, what in the shit are you talking about, man? Why are you being so goddamn weird?"

"I'm not being weird," he said. "Listen to yourself and think about the difference between your game and mine. I do walk around, and I do read. Sometimes I do nothing at all. It's just like you said: I do anything but play the game with you. And what do you do? What's the difference?"

"I don't know what you're talking about."

"Yes, you do. You're too close to the game."

"What the fuck does that *mean*, Jefferson?"

"You can't see the forest for the trees, to put it in more trite terms for you."

I stopped. Somewhere deep inside, I caught a fleeting glimmer of what he was saying, but I still couldn't quite grasp it.

"It consumes you," he said. "You're too focused on each move—it's everything to you in that moment. You care too much about what *is* instead of what *isn't*. When I play, I step back and watch the game unfold." He moved a piece. "I beat you because I let the game reveal itself—I don't need to control it."

"Whatever, Jefferson. We all know how great a player you are."

A corner of his mouth turned up in a patient grin. "You also have no humility."

"That's bullshit! I just said you were a great player."

"It doesn't have anything to do with me. It's about humbling yourself to everything around you. You're trying so hard to beat me that you've forgotten about the game itself. You can't win if winning is your goal; you only win when the game takes precedence over the outcome." He looked at the board. "You have to find the nothingness."

Something sparked. I remembered Thomas, and the dog that drowned in the creek. Images of Rudy Buck flashed through my mind. I hadn't thought about any of it for a long time, but what Jefferson described was too familiar to ignore.

I looked into his eyes. "A few years ago I went to school with some guys who picked on me; I was like their punching bag or something. They were twice as big as me, and they scared the shit out of me all the time. They really made me hate going to school."

I looked vacantly at the chessboard as the details of the fight returned. "So this one day I was alone in a classroom and these dickheads came in. They started messing with me, and I took it for a while, but I guess I'd just had enough. I can't explain what happened . . . something inside me changed, like I became removed from the scene or something. It was sort of like taking acid . . ." I looked back at Jefferson. "You know what acid is, right?

He smiled and nodded. "I think I've heard of it."

"Yeah, cool. Well, anyway, those guys tried to beat me up, but it didn't work that time. I stopped them, but I don't know how. It was like something snapped inside me. My fear didn't go away, but it just seemed less important, you know? There was a kind of . . . peacefulness or something that came into me." As I paused for breath, I realized I had never really talked to anyone about that fight, and it seemed strange that I would choose to tell Jefferson. "Anyway, I came through it without a scratch, but they were both hurt pretty bad. And you know the weirdest part? They did all the work. I mean, it was like I just let them hurt themselves."

"It was effortless."

"Yeah! That's what it was. I've never felt it again since that day." It occurred to me then how unbelievable my story was, and I suddenly regretted telling Jefferson. I looked down at the table. "I never told anybody about it."

"I've felt it," Jefferson said.

I looked up quickly. "You have?"

"Sure."

"What is it?"

"People call it a lot of things . . . Zen, Tao—"

"Tao? You mean like that Japanese shit?"

"It's not Japanese."

"Yeah, whatever. So it's like Buddha or Nirvana or something."

Jefferson smiled gently. "People have tried to give it names for a long time, but there are no words for this thing." He took a deep breath and exhaled. "You just *were*."

"I was what?"

"Everything, and nothing. It's more than Taoism or Buddhism or quantum physics. All the sciences and philosophies you've read or heard about, they can only begin to explain what it is, because it's part of all of them. And at the same time, it's none of them. That's what you felt that day. You *were*."

"I was *what*?"

His smile broadened. "What you experienced was real and you know it. It was effortless."

The word echoed in my mind: *effortless . . .*

"It's the way everything really works, beyond our limited perception." Jefferson gave a single nod. "Here. Put your hand in the middle of the table—just touch it lightly with your fingertips."

I slowly moved my hand to the middle of the board. "What does all this have to do with chess?" My mood was resuming its downward slide.

His smile widened slightly. "Just do it."

We stared at each other for another moment. "Fine, I'll play your dumb little game."

"Good. Just let your fingertips rest there. Now close your eyes and let your fingers move *through* the board. Don't push on them, just let them become part of it."

I closed my eyes and rested my fingertips as lightly as possible on the chessboard, imagining them melting into its surface.

"Do you feel it?" he said.

I opened my eyes and scowled. "I feel my pulse. Does that count?"

"Look deeper."

I closed my eyes again and waited a few more seconds, but I didn't feel anything out of the ordinary. I was about to blast Jefferson with more sarcasm when I felt something in my fingertips, a subtle feeling, almost a numbness at the point where they touched the chessboard. I opened my eyes and looked at him, unsure whether the sensation was real or imagined. "I feel something."

He nodded. "That's it."

Skepticism took over again. "Oh, come on, Jefferson. I felt a little tingling in my fingers. That doesn't mean anything."

He looked at me over the rims of his glasses. "After all we've learned, we still don't understand that half of progress is simply believing. Just because we can't define something doesn't mean it isn't there . . . sometimes faith alone can be a self-fulfilling prophesy, but if you don't believe, you'll never know what might have been."

"What, are you a Christian now? What the fuck does this have to do with chess?"

He folded his hands in front of his chest. "Have you ever beaten me?" The question seemed insultingly rhetorical to me, so I didn't answer. "Okay," he continued, "have you ever seen anyone else in here beat me?" There was no arrogance in his voice.

"No, I guess I've never seen anyone beat you." But as I looked into his eyes, I was hesitant to point out that there was one person who wanted to face off against him very badly.

I hadn't yet been officially introduced to Big Mack, but I had watched him slaughter a few of the regulars since Ellison told me about him. Big Mack didn't spend a lot of time at the Cardinal, but lately he had been appearing more often, attracted by stories about Jefferson, whose game was gaining a strong reputation.

Mack had been badgering Jefferson for a match, but Jefferson always politely declined. Mack shrugged off the refusals at first, but as the rejections mounted, he had begun resorting to juvenile taunts. If Jefferson heard the insults, they didn't faze him, which only enraged Mack. Still, Jefferson's evasiveness made me wonder if he wasn't a little intimidated.

Jefferson continued to watch me.

Finally I said, "So what? So I've never seen anyone beat you."

"And the reason for that," he said, "is that I am willing to accept notions about reality that most people, including you, do not."

"Yeah, sure—that and knowing about a thousand fucking openings. You probably started playing when you were still shitting in diapers. And what about Big Mack? How come you haven't played him? He's the one guy around here who actually has a chance against you."

"Fair enough," Jefferson said, with a wry grin. "I'm sure Mack and I will play eventually. But leave him out of this for a second. Why hasn't anyone else in here beaten me?"

I was through taking Jefferson's interrogation seriously. "Because you've been touched by the hand of the Lord?"

"Okay, we should quit for today. I'll be back tomorrow at four. I hope I see you then."

"What! Look, you asked me a question and I answered it!"

Jefferson gave me his infuriating smile. "I'll see you tomorrow." He got up and walked out of the coffee shop without another word, leaving me sitting alone in front of my chessboard.

"Fuck this," I said to no one in particular and got up to order a beer. I drained it quickly and headed to my coke dealer's house.

The next day I made sure to be early for our game; I wanted at least one beer before Jefferson got there. Barney sat alone at his table as usual, but now he glowered at me.

As I was drinking my pint, I looked around the shop until my eyes stopped on the gargantuan form of Big Mack, standing over another game, barking criticism. He turned his enormous head, considered me for a moment, and then returned his attention to the match.

Big Mack looked Hawaiian, but he was—as Ellison had said—Ukrainian. The way I understood it, his real name was a polysyllabic nightmare that no one could remember, and so some regular had abbreviated it to "Big Mack"—a particularly appropriate moniker, since he was about six-four and repulsively obese. No one ever explained to me why a Ukrainian looked like a big fat Hawaiian.

Mack had a nasty reputation among the regulars. He was loud, foul-tempered, and never missed an opportunity to let everyone know how good a chess player he was. And yet no one could deny that his game was formidable. He loved to play for money, but his skill made finding a wager difficult, especially considering the fact that he had so decisively defeated John Betty—a solid player in his own right—leaving the astronomical unsettled debt no one could stop talking about.

Of course, Mack's prowess notwithstanding, probably the most significant reason he found it hard to get a game was simply that no one liked him.

Jefferson walked into the Cardinal at three minutes to four and came straight to my table. "Are you ready for a game?" His tone held no tension or animosity.

"Sure," I said.

Mack edged a little closer to watch what was happening at our table.

"Set the board," Jefferson said. "I'll play white." He turned all the way around in his chair so that his back was to the board. He relaxed and crossed his legs.

"What are you doing?" I said.

He ignored my question. "D2 to D4."

"What?"

"D2 to D4," he repeated.

The edge of the chessboard was notated, numbers running up the board's vertical axis from one to eight, and letters running along the horizontal axis from A to H. When the axes were combined, I could identify coordinates. "You want me to move for you?"

"Yes, and after you move for me, I want you to make your move and tell me what it is."

Jefferson had instructed me to move his queen's pawn forward two spaces. "And you aren't going to look at the board?" I said.

"No."

I moved his pawn forward. "Okay, I made your move for you."

"Now what's your move?"

I looked at the coordinates. "D7 to D5." I moved my pawn two spaces forward. Our pieces met in the middle of the board.

"E2 to E3," said Jefferson.

A crowd began to develop around the board, and I moved his piece again. "Okay," I said.

He kept his back turned for the duration, rarely hesitating. I still took my time, but it didn't help; on his twenty-second turn, Jefferson instructed me to move his bishop. "Checkmate," he said.

The crowd began to chatter and there was some scattered applause. Mack stood a few feet away shaking his head and mumbling something to a guy next to him.

Jefferson turned around and said to me, "Okay, now tell me how I beat you—and try to leave the Lord out of it this time." There was no trace of haughtiness in his voice.

"I guess you memorized the board."

"My memory is no better than yours." He paused. "How did you beat up those boys in high school?"

"I tried to tell you, I didn't beat them up. I—"

"Exactly."

"Exactly *what*, Jefferson? It was luck, that's all."

"No it wasn't. It was more than that—you said it yourself." He leaned back. "Now, do you want to play another?"

Before I could answer, in his thick Ukrainian accent Mack said, "Why don't you play with me? You can use any *fockink* peace-hippie-shit you want. I will still *crosh* you."

Jefferson looked up at him. "Do you feel like the profanity is a real selling point? You sound just like my friend Douglas here." He smiled at me and then turned to Mack again. "If you're going to use that filth to express yourself, you should at least learn to pronounce it correctly."

The crowd laughed at the remark.

"I don't want to play you," Jefferson added dismissively.

This infuriated Mack. "Are you frightened to play somebody who will beat you?"

Jefferson chuckled, and in a soft, patronizing tone said, "What would I possibly have to gain?"

"Maybe nobody will think you are poosee anymore."

Jefferson raised his eyebrows. "I don't think that word is an adjective, Mack." He casually ran his finger along one edge of the chessboard, the left corner of his mouth turning up in a characteristic half-smile. "But as long as we've broached the subject, who currently believes I am . . .'*pussy*'?" He didn't ask the question as though the answer meant much to him.

Mack tapped the center of his own chest. "I think you are poosee."

Jefferson looked up, still smiling. "You do, huh?" His calm was almost unbelievable, and Mack grew even angrier. Jefferson seemed almost to be enjoying the exchange, and I wondered if it might turn into a physical brawl. If it did, he would surely be no match for Big Mack.

"Jefferson," I said, "maybe we should just take off."

The smile left his face so suddenly it startled me. He looked at Mack and said, "I'll play you."

"Very good," said Mack. "How do you want to play?"

"Your terms."

"We will play with clock. I will give you ten minutes and I will take five."

It was an obvious and insulting ploy, but Jefferson only smiled again. "We'll play five minutes apiece."

"Very good," Mack repeated.

I got up and Mack took my seat. As I stood, my eyes met Ellison's. I hadn't noticed him in the shop earlier; he must have come in while I was playing Jefferson. He stepped next to me and smiled. "This is going to be good."

Jefferson set his double-faced clock for five minutes each side, and as they prepared the board, more people gathered around the table to watch the long-awaited match.

Jefferson rarely allowed outside games, usually preferring to play only me. One day I asked him why, and he said, "Because these other players are gunslingers, trying to establish a name. You and I are friends." But on the rare occasions Jefferson did play regulars—some of whom were very talented—he destroyed them. The only other person in Austin who held such an impressive reputation was Big Mack, so naturally everyone was very curious to see how the two would match up.

In the draw, Jefferson chose black.

"Are you ready to lose?" Mack asked.

Jefferson smiled, slowly raised his hand, and gently pushed his timer, starting Mack's clock.

Mack moved a pawn and then hit his own side of the clock. They played a standard opening each knew by heart, the moves coming so fast they were hard to follow. Mack contorted his face in strained concentration. Jefferson, however, fixed his eyes on the dark behemoth across the table. He was as calm as I'd ever seen him. The moves continued to come rapidly, each player exhibiting his knowledge of the variation he played.

And then the motion stopped. The shop was silent as Mack studied the board. Jefferson waited patiently, every muscle in his body at rest as he watched Mack. Mack moved, and Jefferson responded immediately.

Mack thought about the newest position. "You move too fast."

Jefferson didn't respond. Nothing.

Mack moved his bishop, and Jefferson reacted quickly, decisively.

Mack glanced up at Jefferson and parted his lips to say something, but no words came. He had finally seen Jefferson's eyes, and the calm there unnerved him. The big Ukrainian tore his gaze from Jefferson's, looking back at the board.

He doesn't know what to do, I thought.

Despite his uncertainty, Mack moved again, this time a pawn. He was trying to buy time.

Jefferson swept up his own knight, taking one of Mack's bishops.

Mack had no reprisal. He was now a piece down.

The crowd groaned; Mack didn't usually go around dropping pieces to his opponents. He stared desperately at the board, and his clock began to show the consequences of his hesitation. He now only had a minute and a half compared to Jefferson's four.

Mack looked alternately from Jefferson's face, to the clock, to the board. His conviction was gone. He reached for a piece, hesitated, then moved.

Jefferson quickly used his rook to threaten Mack's queen, and Mack blocked the threat with a knight. Jefferson castled.

Mack wrung his hands, aware that the last of his time was evaporating.

Jefferson's eyes shifted to the clock and he calmly said, "Your flag has fallen."

The crowd hovered in stunned silence, every eye staring at Mack's clock. Jefferson, with no expression, continued to watch Mack.

The game was over.

There were some chuckles, and then everyone around the table erupted in excited chatter.

"You are locky," Mack said loudly. "We will play another."

"No more," said Jefferson.

"Then you are still *poosee*, yes? Why are you frightened of me?" Mack's face was dark and swollen with rage. Saliva had collected in the corners of his mouth. "We will play again."

Jefferson remained silent, staring calmly at Mack's black eyes.

"Play him again, Jefferson," somebody said. Few, if any, of the people watching had ever seen Mack lose a game, and they wanted more.

Jefferson nodded once at Mack. "Set them up."

He started to get up from the table, but Mack said, "Why don't we make wager this time, just to make it . . . *interestink*." The crowd fell silent, and Mack's fat brown face broke into a pearly white grin.

Jefferson looked at him for a moment. Finally he said, "If I win, John Betty's debt is wiped clean."

Excited chatter broke out again.

"And if I win?" Mack said.

"I'll pay the debt." He removed a leather checkbook from his jacket pocket and tossed it on the table in front of the clock.

The murmuring stopped. Everyone gazed at the checkbook as though it were some ancient talisman, holding the deepest secrets to the universe. I don't think anyone doubted that Jefferson could—and would—pay. Ellison and I looked at each other. His eyes were wide.

Mack nodded, barely able to contain his glee. He had nothing to lose.

The room came alive again and Jefferson rose, walking to the counter to get a glass of water.

I followed him. "Jefferson, are you fucking crazy? Why the hell do you care about John Betty?"

"I don't." His face held no trace of nervousness.

"Then why are you doing this? Let John pay his own goddamn debt! It's not like he doesn't have the money!"

"That's not the point."

"What is the point, Jefferson? Mack's baiting you! He probably dropped that last game just so you'd do something dumb like this!"

"He didn't drop the last game."

"Okay, fine, but what you're doing is still stupid."

He looked at me for a moment and smiled. "It's not stupid if you see clearly."

Before I could argue further, he took his glass and walked back to the table.

Ellison came up to me. "Man, what the fuck is he doing?"

I shrugged, shaking my head. "I have no idea."

We returned to the table just as Jefferson took his seat. The pieces were in place, both clocks set for five minutes.

Mack said, "You *will* pay me." The demand carried an ominous tone.

"If you win," Jefferson said.

With his victory, Jefferson had earned the white pieces. Mack hit his clock to start the game.

As in the first game, the opening moves came rapidly, one after another, an almost calculated rhythm. And once again, Mack caused the first break in play, stopping to consider his position. Jefferson just watched him.

Mack's obese legs began to bounce in agitation, causing the table to shake. He glanced quickly from his clock to the board, and then moved his bishop. I had trouble taking my eyes off Jefferson's checkbook, just lying there in front of the clock, so conspicuous it might have been glowing.

Jefferson also moved a bishop, and suddenly the crowd groaned again. Everyone around the table saw it: Jefferson had exposed his queen. It was lost.

Mack looked like he had just won the lottery. He wasted no time snatching Jefferson's queen from the board, a victorious grin covering his face. "I told you that you move too fast! It will not be so easy for you this time, no? Now you learn, and I will take your *fockink* money!"

Jefferson's expression remained impassive, his eyes bright. He moved a rook.

The Ukrainian bounced his enormous legs even harder now, glancing at his clock. He pushed a pawn.

Jefferson again moved quickly, but with the loss of his queen, I couldn't understand why he wasn't taking more time.

Mack looked nervously between the board and his own clock again, and then moved.

Jefferson didn't hesitate. He picked up his knight and swung it around to find Mack's exposed king. He slammed down the knight with a loud crack, shaking the table with the impact.

The room was chilly in its silence.

Jefferson raised his hand slowly from the board and opened it to reveal Mack's captured king. He lifted it up to his own face, cocked his head, and studied the piece curiously, as though it were an artifact. Then he leveled his eyes with Mack's, and in a low voice said, "Checkmate."

The crowd exploded. Jefferson intentionally sacrificed his queen and Mack had eagerly accepted the artifice. It was brilliant.

Mack's eyes were black with anger. It was the worst kind of defeat, an unforgivable mistake. "You are *locky*," he hissed. "We will play another game!"

"No more games," Jefferson said with finality.

Mack rose from his chair and said loudly, "You are cheater! They saw you! You will play again!"

The crowd hushed at the rash accusation.

Jefferson followed Mack with an unwavering gaze. "There won't be any more games between us, now or ever."

Somebody said, "Let it go, Mack."

"*Fock* you," Mack snarled, his eyes fixed on Jefferson. A chunk of spittle flew from his mouth and landed on the chessboard. "This little man cheats, and I want another game."

"He didn't cheat!" I said with an exasperated laugh.

Mack turned to me. "Do you call me liar?" I felt a hint of fear and Mack yelled, "Do you call me a liar? You are little piece of shit!"

"Let it go, Mack," someone else said.

"Do you call me *liar*?" he demanded, towering over me, his voice rising in anger.

"Yeah, fine . . . I guess I am calling you a liar."

Mack lunged at me, grabbing my shirt, pulling my face close to his. He was about to yell something else when a hand suddenly appeared between us, breaking his hold on my shirt. Another hand came up, taking firm hold of Mack's wrist, folding it forward, the pain driving him powerfully to his knees. I stepped back instinctively.

Jefferson looked small, almost comical standing over the brown bear of a man, twisting his arm behind his back, applying more pressure to the folded hand.

Mack let out a yelp. "Okay, okay, okay!"

"It's time for you to leave." Jefferson's voice was cold and steady. He applied yet more pressure to Mack's hand and wrist, emphasizing the command.

"Okay! Yes! Let me go!"

Jefferson released Mack, who rose slowly to his full height. Next to Jefferson, he was a leviathan. He moved his wrist in a circle, flexing it. Jefferson was perfectly still, never taking his eyes off Mack.

"You are very stupid," Mack spewed, and suddenly I got the impression he didn't intend to leave the shop at all. The crowd backed away, and Mack took a step toward Jefferson with obvious violent intentions.

But then he stopped. He looked at Jefferson, a puzzled, indecisive expression on his face.

Jefferson's head was bowed slightly. His eyes burned under his brows, trained on Mack. There was something dangerous in his expression, and I thought I saw a dark smirk touch his lips, almost as though he were looking forward to what might come next. The sight chilled me, and I knew beyond any doubt at that moment that I would never want to make an enemy of this man.

Half an hour earlier, Jefferson had been just a well-dressed older man who played a good game of chess. Now he had transformed into a predator, and I think everyone in that room knew what he would do to Mack if this continued.

But it didn't continue, because Mack could see Jefferson's eyes as well as the rest of us, and it apparently affected him the same way it did everyone else. His arrogance disintegrated, and he tried to save face: "If you are here tomorrow, you will be sorry." The threat, however, was weak and meaningless.

Jefferson didn't respond, but the smirk was there now—no doubt about it. His eyes almost seemed to be asking Mack to make a move.

Mack pointed at Jefferson, stammering what sounded like the beginning of another insult: "You are . . ." But the sentence died. He lingered in front of Jefferson for a moment longer, his face full of shame, and then he quickly shoved his way through the small crowd, gathered his things, and walked out of the Cardinal.

The crowd was buzzing again. A few people patted Jefferson on the shoulder, offering congratulations and reassurance: "You didn't cheat . . . that guy's fucked up . . . don't worry about it."

Jefferson didn't look too worried.

Ellison was standing with a group of people several feet away, waving his hands in the air, laughing and shouting.

Jefferson sat back down at our table and I joined him. "Jesus!" I laughed nervously.

He was silent, staring pensively at the wall beyond me. "Set up your pieces," he said. "I don't want to talk about this any more today." His tone was firm. He wasn't angry, but I didn't dare defy him.

A few people approached our table to speak to Jefferson, but when he looked at them they reconsidered. The look wasn't threatening; it simply made Jefferson's wishes clear. He wanted to be left alone.

———————◆———————

THE NEXT DAY Mack didn't return to the Cardinal as he had said he would. In fact, it was many months before I saw him again, and when I finally did, he simply ignored me, giving me no trouble at all.

Jefferson and I continued our games with no interference other than an occasional comment from one of the regulars. At one point, John Betty came in the Cardinal, shuffling aimlessly about the shop for a few moments until he saw who he was looking for and joined her for a game.

They set up their board and were just about to start playing when John looked at Jefferson from across the room. Their eyes met, and after several seconds, John nodded once. Jefferson's mouth broke into a slight grin, and he nodded almost imperceptibly in response. Then they both looked away.

"What was that?" I asked.

Jefferson didn't look up from the board. "What?"

"That. Between you and John Betty."

"I think he was thanking me."

I looked at John for a minute, and then back to Jefferson. "That's a fucked-up way to thank someone."

"To you, maybe."

"Why did you do that for him, Jefferson? You could have lost, you know."

"I didn't lose. And I didn't do it for him."

"Then why?"

He didn't answer.

"Fuck it. I'm just glad you put Mack in his place." I snorted and threw my elbow over the back of my chair. "So is everybody else."

"Mack isn't a bad person. You should try to keep that in mind."

"How can you say that? He's such an asshole! He totally had it coming."

Jefferson looked up at me. "The universe doesn't keep a big score card about who has it coming and who doesn't."

"Whatever," I said. "It was karma."

He looked back down at the board. "I suppose a lot of people believe in karma."

I raised my eyebrows. "And you don't? After all that crap you've been telling me?"

"Mmmmm, justice." He took a deep breath and released it. "Everybody's looking for a hero . . . and the universe, it just doesn't care." He moved a rook. "Checkmate."

"Goddamn it!" I said.

"Set up the board again." He rose to get a glass of water, and when he returned, we began our next game.

"I want you to let go," he said.

"Let go of what? You're not going to start that shit again, are you?"

He moved a pawn. "Just let go."

I was about to protest further, but then I thought about Jefferson's eyes the day he played Big Mack. *To hell with it*, I thought, and I moved my own pawn. The game began to unfold slowly in front of me.

Then something interesting happened: instead of losing quickly, as I usually did, I kept up with Jefferson, mentally backing away from the board. I was no longer as concerned with the individual moves—each one seemed less significant than the game as a whole. The flow was easier, more familiar, and the less energy I put into it, the more lucid it seemed to become.

Effortless . . .

I lost no unanswered pieces. Jefferson tried sophisticated assaults but I anticipated them many moves in advance. Adrenaline flowed through my veins, along with a familiar sense of peace, and I leaned back, allowing it in. "I feel it, Jefferson."

"I know."

We continued to play until most of the critical pieces were gone, but finally Jefferson cornered me. "Checkmate," he said softly.

I slouched in my chair, serenity rippling through my body.

"That was the best game you've played against me," he said.

"It was the best game I've *ever* played." I wasn't surprised or overjoyed. It was simply the state of things.

"Yeah," Jefferson said, "I imagine it was."

Late February, Year Eighteen

THERE IS A short period in Austin in the spring when the temperature is perfect. The winter moves on, and the plants and trees seem to announce its passing by throwing out blossoms of every imaginable color, celebrating before the summer Texas sun assumes control—ravaging the landscape, driving everyone into air-conditioned confines. It was just this kind of beautiful afternoon, right before my nineteenth birthday, when I went to the Cardinal and set up my board, hoping Jefferson would show. I waited for about an hour but he didn't appear, and nobody else approached me for a match either.

As I gathered my things to leave, the front door of the shop opened. Ellison walked in, and right behind him was the girl who had so intrigued me before. My heart began to beat a little faster, and I was about to look away, feeling self-conscious, when her eyes met mine. We stared at each other for what seemed like years, and then she smiled a little. My mouth felt sticky.

I looked down and clumsily opened my book, but I could no more have read another word from those pages than I could have stood up and recited the Magna Carta from memory. A few seconds ticked past and I risked a quick glance. They were walking toward me, Ellison carrying a Styrofoam cup of coffee. I looked down again. *Oh fuck. Oh fuck.* I quickly turned the page.

They stopped at the table right in front of mine. "Hey, Douglas," Ellison said.

I looked up. He had an odd smile on his face. "Oh . . . uh, hey Ellison," I said. "What's . . . uh . . . what are you doing?"

"Not much. That was a hell of a chess game the other day, wasn't it?"

I kept my eyes trained on him, trying desperately not to look at the girl. "Game?"

"Yeah! Jefferson and Big Mack!" He cocked his head, and his smile broadened. "You haven't *forgotten*, have you?" There seemed something mischievous about the way he was looking at me.

"Oh, uh, yeah . . . that was good."

Ellison snorted. "That's an understatement. Well, I'm outta here, man—I've got to run to a meeting."

I nodded. "Yeah. That sounds good."

Ellison looked at the girl, who was now sitting at the table facing me, and said, "Call me later, okay?"

She smiled and nodded. "Okay."

He turned and walked out of the shop. The girl reached in her bag, pulled out several large books, opened one, and began leafing through it.

I squinted to see what she was reading, and I could make out from the spines that they were legal books. She continued to read, scribbling notes and pursing her lips with the effort. She tucked a strand of hair behind her ear, and the whole scene made me weak. She was absolutely the most beautiful girl I had ever seen.

I looked down at the table, wondering why I didn't leave immediately. What was I going to do, sit here and drool over Ellison's girlfriend? And yet I was stuck to my chair. I couldn't move.

"So you're Douglas, right?"

My head snapped up. "Me? Oh, yeah. I'm Douglas."

She rose and walked to my table, extending her hand. "I'm Elizabeth Clark."

I jumped out of my seat. "I'm Douglas Cole." Her hand was soft and felt small in mine. "I guess I already told you that—except for the 'Cole' part." My body tensed and I looked down again, not quite certain how I managed to say something so utterly moronic.

She laughed. "Yeah, you told me, except for the 'Cole' part." Her smile was flawless.

Then something clicked. *Elizabeth Clark . . . Elizabeth Clark . . . Clark.* Before I could stop myself, I blurted, "You have the same last name as Ellison." And suddenly I was a worm, wallowing in the dirt, feeding on my humiliation.

Elizabeth pressed her lips together, trying not to laugh. "Yes, we have the same last name."

I was stunned. I had known, and even worked with Ellison for months, and I couldn't believe he wouldn't have shared something like this with me. "Oh. I . . . uh . . . didn't know he was married . . . and all that."

Elizabeth let a small laugh escape, and the realization it hit me like a cement truck. "Oh my God. He's your brother."

She put a hand over her mouth, nodding as she tried to stifle her laughter.

I wanted to crawl under the table and shelter myself from my own pathetic existence, but instead I only shook my head and stared stupidly at the floor, not quite sure what to do. "So, you're a law student?"

She pulled her hand away from her mouth to reveal her smile again, and my lungs decided to stop working. My stomach protested, shrinking to the size of a pea. I awkwardly returned the smile as my mouth turned into a desert wasteland. I was pretty sure my lips were going to stick to my teeth.

"Yes," she said. "Why?"

"Well, I saw your books and . . ." I pointed at her table. "You know?"

She laughed. "If you saw my books, why did you ask? Do you know a lot of people who read environmental law just for fun?"

"No . . . I guess . . . Yeah, no, I don't." Then I quickly added, "But I know some lawyers." I winced and wondered if banging my head against the table would be inappropriate.

She giggled. "You do, huh?"

I looked down again. *Stupid. Stupid. Stupid.*

"You trade futures with Ellison," she said matter-of-factly.

"I guess he told you."

"Yeah." She looked around the room for a few seconds and then back at me. "He tried to explain it to me, but I don't understand it at all."

"They're sort of investments."

"Like stocks?" She tilted her head.

"Kind of, but different. More like contracts."

"Hmmmm . . . it seems boring to me."

Boring? How could anyone think trading futures was boring? I was just about to inform her how wrong she was when she said, "So you play chess? I guess you do since you have a board on the table in front of you, and since you're always here with my brother."

"I play a little," I stammered. "Sometimes."

"Ellison won't teach me."

"I could teach you."

"Would you?"

With as much composure as I could invoke, I said, "Yeah. I'd like that."

Elizabeth and I sat at that table for the next several hours. I tried to teach her the fundamentals of the game, but we didn't get very far. Mostly, we just laughed and watched each other a lot. She told me she was a second-year law student at the university, and that she had done her undergraduate work at Berkeley, where she majored in English. She was originally from San Antonio, so she had decided to return to Texas for law school, to be close to her family.

"You don't have a boyfriend?" I asked.

"No, I dated a guy until about six months ago, but it didn't work out. He graduated and moved to Dallas to practice."

"He's a lawyer?"

"Yes."

"Dallas isn't so far."

"It is for me. Anyway, he didn't really do it for me. And what about you? You don't have a girlfriend?"

"No." I had nothing to add. I had never had a girlfriend, and I didn't think it would be a good idea to tell Elizabeth about some of the girls I had "dated" recently.

"Nobody, huh?"

"Nope," I said.

"That's nice."

Elizabeth's voice was entrancing, slightly raspy, and her pronunciation of some words made me feel as though I was plummeting to Earth at a thousand miles per hour. At times that night I lost track of what she was saying—not because she bored me, but because her voice was so alluring that I drifted in its resonance.

We flirted for hours, but eventually decided to try to be serious about the chess lesson. I was in the middle of a progression when she interrupted me. "What if I do this with the queen?" She touched my hand, gently removing the piece I was holding. Electricity shot up my arm, and my tongue quit working.

She acted as if nothing had happened and waited patiently for my response. But I couldn't focus on the question. After a moment she said, "Douglas? Are you listening to me?"

I looked at the board and regained my bearings. "Uh, yeah, you . . . don't want to do that. I mean you could, but you'd lose your rook."

"I would? Which one is the rook again?"

I pointed to it. "Yeah, you don't want to lose your rook." I gently took the queen from her hand to show her the mistake, and when I touched her again I felt more electricity. It drove the breath from my lungs.

"You seem nervous," she said, smiling. "What's wrong? Do I make you nervous?"

"*No!* I mean, no."

"Ellison thinks I make you nervous. He thinks it's really funny."

And suddenly it was clear to me that Ellison had no small part to play in what was happening here. I sighed, thinking about all his sly grins when he caught me staring at his sister. I didn't know whether to be angry or to thank him with the entirety of my soul.

Elizabeth said, "Why does it make you nervous when I touch you?" She ran her index finger across the top of my hand, again causing my lungs to contract. It was a little vexing that her mere presence was causing my various body parts to fail. She laced her fingers in mine, and I responded slowly, my breathing now shallow and intermittent.

"Do you want to go for a walk?" she asked.

I looked at her. "That would be nice."

We ambled across campus, side by side. I told her about Durango and my work at MacGregor's, about my chess games with Pete and how much pot he smoked. I told her about Jack, and it occurred to me that I hadn't spoken to him in a long time. I talked about him for a while—about his obscene baseball caps and the way he smacked his gum when he told his stupid jokes.

She laughed. "He sounds funny."

"Oh, yeah. Jack's the best! You should meet him—you guys would like each other."

"Is your family still in Durango?" she asked.

"No . . . they don't live there anymore."

"Where do they live?"

I scrambled for an answer. There was no way I was going to ruin what was happening by telling Elizabeth about my dead family—at least not now. "My parents divorced and moved back east." She didn't push the issue, and I was grateful.

We walked across campus, passing under the clock tower and through a maze of buildings until we got to the LBJ library—a beautiful marble edifice with ornate fountains dancing in its courtyard. We stood next to each other, a nearly full moon illuminating the expansive, well-groomed commons stretching below.

The silhouettes of gnarled live oaks broke up the landscape, their branches stretching gracefully outward, often extending for fifteen or twenty feet before landing again to ease their burden. I wondered how many people had sat under their boughs through the years, feeling this same sense of timelessness and awe.

"So what will you do when you get your degree?" I said.

"My dad has a small firm in San Antonio, and I'd like to work for him after I take the bar—at least for a while. I want to be close to Austin. I've made a lot of good friends here, plus I love being near Ellison." She shivered a little and took my arm, pulling herself close, putting her cheek against my shoulder. More electricity ran through my body, and we stayed like that for a few minutes, not saying anything.

Elizabeth turned to face me, and I have no idea how long we gazed at each other. I trembled slightly. She raised her hand and touched my cheek, slowly drawing her face close to mine, putting her lips to my mouth. Her breath smelled sweet, and her soft lips tasted sugary and delicious. It was the most exhilarating thing I had ever experienced.

I walked her home and when we got to her apartment I asked, "Can I call you tomorrow?"

"Of course." She reached in her bag, pulled out a pen and a scrap of paper, and wrote down her number. I kissed her goodnight and walked casually to the street, until I was certain she couldn't see me from a window. Then I sprinted to my apartment.

I took Elizabeth to dinner the next evening. I listened carefully as she spoke, more enraptured than ever by the timbre of her voice. She put her hand on mine whenever she found the opportunity, and dissapointment engulfed me when she removed it to pick up her fork or drink from her glass.

After dinner we decided to go to the Cardinal, where I ordered coffee for Elizabeth and a beer for me. "What do you do for fun besides play chess?" she asked after we sat down.

"I don't know. I really like trading."

"And there's nothing else?"

"I used to play music."

"Really? In a band?"

I laughed. "No, not in a band. I play the cello, but I'm not very good."

She clapped her hands together. "I want to hear you play!"

Suddenly I regretted telling her. I rarely played in front of other people. In fact, I rarely played at all anymore. "Okay, I'll play for you sometime."

She looked disappointed. "No, I want to hear you play now."

I ran my fingers through my hair, biting my lip. "I don't know, Elizabeth—"

"Please?"

Great . . . how the hell am I going to get out of this? "My apartment is a mess—"

"I don't care."

I was trapped. "All right, but only for a little while, and if you don't like it, I'm going to stop."

She rushed me through my beer and we left the Cardinal. When we got to my apartment a few minutes later, Elizabeth walked directly to my cello, propped in a corner.

"It's one of my favorite instruments," she said, running her hand along the finish. "Can we go outside while you play?"

I was getting more nervous. "Okay, but let me make a drink first. Do you want one?"

"Do you have any wine?"

"Sure." I poured us each a glass, grabbed her a blanket, and we walked into the courtyard. She arranged two lawn chairs facing each other, sat, and draped the blanket over her legs. She leaned forward and placed her elbows on her knees, cupping her glass in front of her. The light in the courtyard was soft, but just bright enough that her eyes glowed emerald.

I took the other chair and situated myself. "What do you want to hear?"

"What do you like to play?"

"I know a lot of music by other people, but I enjoy playing my own better."

"You have your own music?"

"Just some stuff I've worked on over the years. It's really nothing."

She leaned forward a little more. "*That's* what I want to hear."

I took a deep breath and closed my eyes. I dragged the bow across one of the strings and allowed my favorite note, the low C, to resonate for a moment. Then I began.

I thought performing for Elizabeth would intimidate me and affect the music, but it didn't. On the contrary, her presence created a passion that surprised me, and the pieces I had played so many times through the years now took on a new level of intensity and meaning, an almost primal ecstasy that I had never known before. Each wave sent smaller undulations of pleasure through my body, and I lost myself in a soothing stillness, as though I were floating in some cool body of water with no thought of the future or the past. I don't know how well I played—I was rusty—but I felt the music more than I had in years.

When I finished, I sat with my eyes closed for a few seconds. I opened them and Elizabeth was staring at me.

"It was perfect." Her choice of words and the roughness of her voice melted me.

"Thank you," I said. The exchange was natural, unforced.

We continued to stare at each other for a long moment before she said, "You know what I like most about you?"

I shook my head.

"Your blue eyes when you look at me like that." Her lips were swollen, her face flushed. Her irises glowed with radiant energy under her eyelids. "More, please."

I played for several hours, and every time I finished a piece she insisted on another. Eventually though, we both got sleepy, and she asked if I would walk her home. When we reached her apartment complex, I kissed her. We probably stood there for half an hour before I finally pulled away. "Goodnight."

"Thank you, Douglas."

I backed away, and she held my hand until the last possible second before letting go. There was no doubt in my mind about what might have happened had I asked to come in, and a huge part of me longed to stay with her. But a stronger, more rational part of me allowed the night to end as it was. Elizabeth and I stood several feet apart, staring at each other for a few more moments.

Then she closed the door and I went home.

Elizabeth and I were nearly inseparable for the next few months together, going to movies, sharing meals, or just hanging out. Sometimes she would come to the coffee shop and study while Ellison and I played chess with the rest of the gang.

About the only time we didn't see each other was when she was in class, and I usually spent that time at the Cardinal.

Soon we began spending nights together, usually at her apartment, which was more comfortable—and cleaner—than mine. But even though we were sleeping together, it was only sleep. Elizabeth was different from any girl I had ever known, and I didn't want to jeopardize what was happening between us with too much, too soon. And while we didn't talk about it specifically, she didn't seem to mind waiting any more than I did.

But two young people falling in love can only spend so much time in the same bed before nature takes its course, and before long, we surrendered. If Elizabeth's touch flooded my body with electricity, our intimacy created a nuclear reaction—easily one of the most wonderful experiences I have ever known. What I shared with her transcended mere physical pleasure; it was immense, and holding her afterward—feeling her drift off in my arms—was the pinnacle of that transcendence.

I had always slept with girls for the same reasons I did drugs—as a distraction. It isn't to say those encounters weren't fun, because they were. But they were also awkward and uncomfortable. With Elizabeth, though, I finally knew what it meant to become part of someone.

The first time I saw Jefferson at the Cardinal after I met Elizabeth, I felt like I was going to explode if I didn't tell him the news, but if he noticed my impatience, he didn't show it.

After we sat down to start our game he said, "You look happy tonight." He might have seemed a little forlorn, but I paid no attention to it.

"I met a girl!"

"Really?" He looked at the board as he spoke, no emotion in his voice. "What's her name?"

"Elizabeth."

"That's wonderful news."

I thought he would want to know more about her, but he didn't say anything else. Finally I said, "I really want you to meet her."

"That would be nice. We should get together sometime." Then he fell silent.

"She comes in here sometimes. Her brother is Ellison."

Jefferson continued to look at the board. "Yes, I might have seen her with him."

I waited a moment and then said, "Well maybe you'll meet her here sometime."

Jefferson looked up, his eyes fixed on mine. "Maybe I will." There was no anger in his voice, yet I felt as though I had been given a warning. I thought about pushing it, but as drawn as I was to Jefferson, something about him still frightened me a little, and what he had done to Big Mack certainly hadn't made him any less intimidating.

I decided to let it go, disappointed he wasn't more excited for me. My elation evaporated, and I mimicked Jefferson's silence. After we finished our game, I muttered something about having some things to do and told him goodnight. He mumbled a perfunctory reply, and I left him there.

Late June, Year Nineteen

I BEGAN TO get depressed on nights when Elizabeth had obligations at school, so I handled the void like all of my other problems—with chemicals. Elizabeth didn't appear to mind at first; we drank together, and even did cocaine a few times. But as our relationship grew, she partook less, and after a while I could see that my use began to trouble her, although she didn't say anything about it for some time. In hindsight, I'm surprised she tolerated the behavior as long as she did.

Other people noticed that cracks were appearing in my life, as well. Ellison had been making little comments for weeks, and he finally confronted me one day in Victor's driveway after a particularly nasty day of trading.

"Hey, I've been meaning to talk to you," he said. "Is everything going okay?"

I had been in the bathroom a few minutes earlier, where I had done a couple of lines to decompress from the day's stress, and I think he could tell. "Yeah, I'm fine. Why?"

"It's just . . . we've been noticing that you come in pretty late these days, and sometimes you don't even show up—"

I furrowed my brow. "I've done everything you've asked me to do, right? Even on days when I stay home."

He shrugged. "Sure. Of course you have."

"So what's the problem? Ellison, if you and Victor don't want me here, just tell me."

He put his hands up in a defensive gesture. "That's not what I'm saying." He gazed hard at me. "Look, it just seems like you spend a lot of late nights at the Cardinal, and you get pretty wasted. I know you're doing a shitload of coke. I'm not trying to judge you or lecture you. I just wanted to talk."

"Fuck you, Ellison! I haven't noticed that you pass up too many tequila shots or bumps in the bathroom."

"Yeah, but I don't do it every night, man!"

"Does this have something to do with Elizabeth?"

He didn't answer at first, but finally he said, "She's my sister, but I don't tell her what to do."

"Has she said something to you?"

There was another pause. "I'm talking to you as your friend. I'm not here to speak for my sister."

I nodded. "Good. Look, you live your life, and I'll live mine, okay?" I got in my car and slammed the door, leaving him standing in the driveway as I sped off.

That night, Elizabeth and I were in bed at her apartment. I had been drinking and doing lines, and as the coke wore off, I laid my head in her lap while she caressed my hair.

"Ellison got mad at me today," I said.

"Really? Why?"

"He said he's worried about me—about how much I drink and stuff."

"And he got *mad* at you?"

"Well . . . I guess he wasn't mad, but—"

Suddenly Elizabeth shuddered. "Douglas!"

"What?" I bolted upright, confused. Small red droplets splattered my T-shirt, and blood streaked the front of Elizabeth's nightgown.

"*Fuck!*" I ran to the bathroom, put a wad of toilet paper against my nose, and leaned my head back. I stayed that way for few moments before I returned to the bedroom to find Elizabeth changing the sheets. The top sheet hung over a chair, stained with a bright burst of crimson. It seemed like a lot of blood, and I wasn't sure how I had managed to get so much on our clothes, as well as the bed.

"I'm sorry," I said. "That doesn't happen very often."

She forced a smile. "It's okay."

"No it's not." I helped her make the bed with the clean sheets, and when we climbed back in, I could tell she was uncomfortable. "I'm sorry," I said again. "Bad timing, huh?"

She looked vacantly at the wall and sighed. "I can see why Ellison's worried about you."

"What do you mean?"

"Why do you do so many drugs, Douglas?"

To kill the fucking ghosts, that's why. Suddenly I had a vivid image of my father lying on his back in a pool of blood, his eyes wide and glassy, his head split open. I shuddered.

Honesty in all things is imperative, and I know now I should have discussed my problems with Elizabeth, because nothing—not even ghosts—could justify what I was doing to myself. Unfortunately, I never found the strength to share with her what I endured in Durango. She asked about my family many times, but I avoided the issue, and the right opportunity to tell her just never seemed to materialize. In truth, I was frightened to open up my past with her; Elizabeth was almost the only bright, stable element left in my otherwise tragic life, and scaring her away with my problems simply wasn't an option. So I kept it all hidden safely away.

My judgment couldn't have been worse.

"I wasn't aware I 'do so many drugs,'" I said defensively.

"But you do. You drink a lot too, and sometimes it scares me. It scares all of us." She glanced at the bloody sheet still draped over the chair.

"Well I'm sorry you're all so goddamn worried about it."

"You should slow down."

I began to get angry. "Why?"

"Because I want you to. Douglas, you use a *lot* of this stuff, and I don't know how long I can deal with it."

"So what are you saying? Are you breaking up with me because I drink a little?"

Elizabeth became irritated. "You know it isn't 'a little,' and it isn't just the drinking." She folded her arms. "And I'm not breaking up with you, so you can quit making this into something it isn't."

There was a tense, awkward silence, and then she said, "I don't want to break up with you, but if you keep going like this, I'll—"

"You'll *what*, Elizabeth?" I got up and started putting on my clothes. I wanted her to stop me, but she didn't. "Here," I said, "I'll make it easy for you. I'll get out of your life. How about that?"

"That's not what I want and you know it."

I put on the rest of my clothes but she still did nothing to stop me. I looked at her for a moment, shaking my head, and then I left the apartment.

At my place, I poured a drink and paced for about an hour, pausing occasionally to do a line. Eventually I tried to sleep, but the anxiety and the coke made it impossible. I expected the phone to ring any moment. It didn't, and in the hours before sunrise I began to get desperate. I paced some more, and soon enough the tears came. I wept for a while, and at some point I finally fell asleep for few hours.

I stayed in my apartment all the next day, drinking and snorting coke. Still the phone didn't ring, and soon grief and loneliness replaced most of my anger. By nightfall I was in a chemical haze, and I began the gradual process of emotional compromise.

I decided to call Elizabeth, but when I found the conviction to pick up the phone and dial her number, I only got her answering machine. "Hey listen," I said. "I thought about last night and I'm still not sure I agree with you, but I'd like to talk about it more if you want to, so give me a call."

I waited a few hours, but still the phone didn't ring, so I called her back. I got the machine again. "It's me. I guess you didn't get my last message. I really want to talk. Call me when you get this."

I waited several more hours. Still nothing.

Soon my imagination—fueled by the cocaine—began to conjure up thoughts of Elizabeth with another man, and then the images took over everything, invading my mind like a virus, consuming any vestige of rationality, polluting my brain with paranoid visions of Elizabeth giving herself to someone else. I wept harder, waiting another long hour before I called her again, sobbing on the answering machine. "*Please* call me . . . I really need to talk to you."

I hung up and dialed Ellison's number. His voice sounded groggy. "Hello?"

"Hey, it's Douglas."

"Mmmm. Hey man. How you holdin' up?"

"Did you hear what happened?"

"Yeah, I heard. Listen, it's late and—"

"Ellison, I really need someone to talk to."

There was a long pause before he said, "All right, come on over."

I made it to his apartment in about ten minutes. He answered the door in his pajamas, holding a mug. His apartment was decorated with sharp, clean, contemporary designs. I was always impressed by how fastidious he was in all aspects of his life—especially for a man in his mid-twenties.

"You want some tea?" he asked.

"No, I'm okay."

He invited me in and sat down.

"I think I fucked up, man," I said.

He nodded slowly. "Everybody's worried about you. You understand that, right?"

"I've been trying to call Elizabeth all night."

"I know. She told me."

"Is she going to break things off?"

He snorted and shook his head. "I don't think she wants to. She's totally in love with you, but she's really upset right now." His expression became sympathetic. "I really don't see how anyone could look at what you're doing to yourself and not be a little freaked out."

I felt tears forming in my eyes. "She's your sister. Tell me what to do."

"Just give her some space. She'll call you when she's ready. But I think you might want to slow down a little with the partying."

We stared at each other for a long moment before I finally said, "Okay. Thanks for letting me come over."

He smiled. "Anytime, my friend."

I didn't hear from Elizabeth that night. I tried to sleep, but it was impossible. I could only imagine where she was, and before long my coke-induced paranoia again resumed control. I sat in a corner of my apartment for the few remaining hours before sunrise, rocking back and forth with my head tucked between my knees, weeping and talking to myself. Finally, I drifted off.

The phone woke me around eleven o'clock the following morning, and I lunged for it. "Hello?"

"Douglas?"

The voice on the other end was as sweet anything I had ever heard. I began to cry again. "Liz, where have you been?"

"I unplugged my phone. I needed some time to think."

"I want to see you," I said.

"I'm not sure that's a good idea."

"Please, Liz. I thought about what you said, and I talked to Ellison. I want to work on it."

"I still need more time."

"Elizabeth, please! Let me talk to you for a little while!"

"I have to study this afternoon, but I'll call you later tonight." She wasn't harsh, but her voice was firm. I began to cry a little harder and she softened slightly. "Douglas? I want to talk, too. Just let me think a little."

I managed to get control of myself. "Okay."

"Will you be all right?"

"I'll be fine. You promise we'll talk later?"

"I promise. I'll call you."

So I spent the afternoon and evening in my apartment, pondering my drug use while I drank scotch and sucked up line after line of cocaine. I held back a little because I wanted to have at least some clarity when I spoke to Elizabeth, but the chemicals still demanded my attention.

In my clouded introspection, I came to the almost inconceivable conclusion that I had no problem. I convinced myself in those hours that I did a fine job of moderating my use, and I could stop whenever I wanted to. And I promised myself I would quit—just as soon as the ghosts went away.

Now my dilemma became perfectly clear: I had to appease Elizabeth if I wanted our relationship to continue. I would have to lie to her, and, apparently, to everyone else around me too.

My life has been characterized by extremes; I have experienced pleasures most human beings could never understand, but I have also known pain so intolerable that I often wonder how I endured it. And yet I did.

But as I look back through the years, I often think about the almost innumerable mistakes I have made, and if I can attribute my survival to anything, it is the fact that I learned not only to understand the universe, but to revise my countless misperceptions quickly in order to match its immutable verdict. Unfortunately, Elizabeth's presence didn't result from this actualization, but rather was one of the tragic consequences that led me to it.

Reality's depiction suffers almost by definition, and yet it cannot be defined. It is simply the *suchness* of all things—the quintessence of impartiality. The universe has no design. It mandates no laws, nor does it possess conscience or compassion. It seeks nothing, yet it is elegantly balanced, poised to correct any excess—to produce order from the very midst of its chaos. Reality has no impetus to affirm hope, and its response to optimistic misjudgment is simple and elegant: change the behavior or prolong the pain.

Hope is nothing more than a human construct—a contentious expression of longing, and when false hope finds the illusory courage to challenge reality, it is always reality that remains intact. Where hope is mere expectation, reality is the outcome—incontrovertible and unaffected by human presumption.

There is only one thing worse for the human psyche than raw hope, and that is a temporary respite from the condition that inspired hope in the first place. Such a pause creates still more fatuous optimism, sometimes in the face of desperate odds, only postponing the necessary pain of the misjudgment. These situations breed dangerous reinforcement of theories that often have no useful value, and when we allow hope to guide our decisions, we set ourselves up for severe or even catastrophic disappointment.

Sometimes the pill, no matter how hard to swallow, is the only remedy.

I don't believe in miracles. Odds are rarely beaten with consistency, and when the odds are poor, hope is the most venomous thing a person can cling to. It is an illusion—the defiance of a reality that cannot be defied.

The rest of the day was hell, but it was nothing compared to the night before. At least now I had hope.

Elizabeth called me that evening. "Hi," she said softly.

"Are you through studying?"

"Yes."

"Can I see you?"

"Yes," she said. "I miss you."

"Me too."

"Can you come over here?" she asked.

I took a shower, brushed my teeth, and ate a package of crackers to soak up the liquor in my stomach. Considering the circumstances, I felt amazingly lucid—more than coherent enough to convince Elizabeth I could change.

I drove to her complex and she let me into her apartment. We sat on the couch, facing each other, knees touching, hands interlaced. Both our faces were swollen and haggard from lack of sleep and hours of tears.

"I love you very much," she said. "You know that?"

Relief flooded me as she spoke those words, and I responded quickly. "I love you too, Liz. I know that now more than ever."

"We have to figure this out. I don't have the stomach for what you're doing to yourself."

I squeezed her hand. "I'll lay off the drugs, okay?" I stared deeply into her eyes as I lied to her, reminding myself that I *would* quit—when the ghosts were gone.

"If you don't slow down, I'll leave—"

"I won't screw it up. I promise."

A tear rolled down her cheek, and she put her arms around me, burying her head in my neck as she cried. I held her for a long time, crying with her.

Then I took Elizabeth by the hand and led her to her bedroom, kissing her face as I removed her clothes. I kissed her arms and neck while she gently pulled off my shirt, running her lips and tongue over my body. We lay on the bed, continuing to caress and kiss each other, and then, with almost no effort, I was inside her. I moved with her until I felt my soul would melt.

I held her as close to my body as I could without hurting her. It would be a long time before I would be as happy as I was that night. Certainly I would never be happier.

Late July, Year Nineteen

As I lost more and more money, I became increasingly disillusioned with trading futures. Ellison and Victor didn't seem to be doing much better than I was, and I didn't even bother to go to the office at all anymore; the atmosphere was just too bleak.

I was determined to continue trading, however, and I have no doubt I owed my persistence mostly to the fact that I was young, arrogant, and chemically deluded—a bad combination by any measure.

I kept up the effort, but the thrill diminished with the value of my account—almost inversely proportional to the number of substances I dumped into my body every day.

The drugs and booze gave me a heightened confidence that caused me to put on bigger trades than I should have. When things went in my favor, I held the positions too long, waiting for the big move that never came, and soon my winnings would evaporate, forcing me to cover at a break-even, or at a loss. On the other hand, when trades went against me, I would wait too long to cover, often losing more than I should have. Invariably, I would fall into deep depression, killing the pain with still more drugs.

I tried to moderate my use enough to make Elizabeth believe my vow to slow down, but she was extremely perceptive, and I have no doubt that she quickly saw through my lies. No matter how much I reassured her, she insisted on having more time to herself. She must have been tremendously disappointed.

I just learned to cope with it, which naturally meant using more drugs. It also meant I now spent almost all my time drinking at the Cardinal.

Ellison also seemed to be more unavailable than ever. I called him a few times to see if he wanted to meet, but I usually got his answering machine or some thin excuse. It barely occurred to me that people were avoiding me.

The only person who still spent time with me with any consistency was Jefferson. He and I continued to meet—usually as I was driving headfirst toward incoherence—but he never mentioned my condition. During our games I would sneak off for a boost in the bathroom, and when I got back to the table, I would chatter mindlessly as I slowly got drunker and more coked up. He had given up trying to help me improve my game—which was disintegrating with the same intensity as everything else in my life—but he was exceedingly patient nonetheless, forever enduring my inane comments and questions.

One day that summer, we sat in the Cardinal playing our fourth or fifth game. I had done enough coke to make my mouth run at a good clip, and I bounced my knees nervously, inundating Jefferson with ceaseless prattle. "You're a pretty strange fucker, you know that?"

He didn't look up from the board. "No, I didn't know that."

"I mean, I don't know anything about you. You're just like . . . this mysterious *guy* I play chess with sometimes. How come you've never told me anything about yourself?"

"You haven't asked the right questions."

I laughed a little too dramatically. "Well, can I ask now?"

He looked up. "If I said no, would that stop you?"

"Where are you from, Jefferson?"

"Here."

"Originally?"

"Sort of." He slouched in his chair, legs crossed, looking back at the board indifferently.

"What do you mean, sort of?"

"I was born in West Texas, but I grew up in Austin. Where were you born, Douglas?"

"In Amarillo, but we moved to Durango when I was young . . ." I eyed him sideways. "Hey . . . you're changing the subject back to me, dude." I jabbed a finger in the air above the chessboard. "But I want to talk about you."

"Colorado's a nice place," he said, ignoring my demand. "And you came directly from Colorado for college?" He didn't seem genuinely interested.

"Yeah. Hey, don't you think it's weird that we hang out all the time but we don't know anything about each other?"

"I suppose it is." He moved a pawn.

I did the same. "Why are you so quiet today?"

"Why are you so loud today?" He took one of my bishops with his rook. "Sometimes nothing needs to be said."

"Maybe I just don't fucking *feel* like being quiet today."

"Yes, and maybe the silence just requires more than you're willing to give."

I snorted. "That doesn't make any fucking sense at all."

"I'm sure it doesn't," he said without looking up. And then, as if to perpetuate my annoyance, he became even more quiet.

Another few minutes passed, and I said, "You know, I haven't felt that . . . that feeling again since that game we played, after you beat Mack."

"I know you haven't."

"Why don't you like to talk about it anymore?"

"What makes you think I don't like to talk about it?"

"It's just that . . . you haven't said anything for a long time."

"What do you want to know?" he said.

"How did you learn about it?"

"I didn't really *learn* about it. It was there all the time; I just had to accept it and let it in." He shifted in his seat. "Michelangelo once said that he didn't create his sculptures—they were already in the stone, and he only helped reveal them. That's the way all things in the universe work; everything is there, all we have to do is discover it."

"Well, how did you figure out how to get to it?"

Jefferson sighed. "You aren't listening to what I'm trying to tell you."

"Yes I am."

He continued to study the board for a moment. "A long time ago, a friend helped me, but I didn't really learn anything new. I just saw something that was already there." He reached down and took another one of my pieces.

"Why do you think it doesn't come to me anymore?"

"Because you shut it out."

"Is it with you all the time?"

"No."

"How often does it come?"

"When I need it."

I bounced my knees almost uncontrollably. "I've been trying to make it come."

"I know you have," he said. "But you can't *make* it come. You have to let go. When you did it before, you experienced more than just a feeling. It was a connection to everything—and nothing."

"Like a connection to the universe or something, right?"

"No, it was more than just the universe. The universe is substance. You were connected to everything. You experienced the *entirety*—all universes in space and time."

I brightened a little. "You mean, like the multiverse?" The instant I said the word, I thought of Jack and Pete, and suddenly I missed them very much.

"Yeah, that's right." Jefferson took my remaining bishop with a rook. "But it's more than that. The entirety transcends everything that can be sensed and known."

"Isn't it part of quantum physics or something like that?"

"Those are just words, Douglas. Science helps some, but our minds are still young in the universe. These things I'm telling you about are much bigger than just perception or understanding, but our arrogance makes it hard to comprehend how little we really know."

I surveyed the board, trying to find a way through his defense. "Well, if we have so much to learn, how do you know all this crap?"

"I have a lot to learn, too."

I advanced a pawn, mainly because I couldn't find another move. "Jefferson, what do you do—I mean, for a living?"

"I'm retired."

"Well, what did you used to do?"

"I was a physicist."

"I fucking *knew* it had to be something like that! Did you work for the government?"

"Yep." He took one of my knights with his queen.

"Like a power plant or something?"

"Something like that. What did you study before you quit school?"

I waggled my finger at him and smiled. "You're changing the subject again, aren't you?"

He looked at me over his glasses.

"Okay, okay, fine," I said. "If I hadn't quit I probably would have done something with computers, I guess."

We played the game for a while longer in silence. I threatened Jefferson's queen with one of my rooks. "Do you think I'll ever feel it again?"

He smiled. "I know you will. That's one thing you shouldn't worry about." He moved his queen again. "Checkmate, Douglas."

AFTER THAT DAY I didn't see Jefferson for a while. Elizabeth was apparently still avoiding me, and Ellison wasn't returning my calls, so I mostly stayed at my apartment, drinking and doing coke to kill the loneliness. The place was filthy—clothes, papers, and books strewn everywhere. Dishes and garbage had piled up in every corner, causing a revolting odor, but I had grown accustomed to it and had neither the interest nor the energy to do anything about it.

The coke kept me from sleeping much, so I killed time by watching television—when the ghosts would let me. The grisly images of Dad, Thomas, and even my mother haunted me almost perpetually now, feeding off my paranoia and insomnia.

I still did some perfunctory research and made a few trades, but almost all of them went against me. I was going broke quickly, but my ego drove me on. *Just a little more time and my systems will turn it all around . . .*

Of course, that assumption was predicated on the idea that I would actually implement and maintain the very systems in question—a notion which seemed more unrealistic each day. The message wasn't sinking in: my calculations were wrong, and I was burning through cash. Only a year before, I had had enough money to see me through a comfortable retirement. Now most of that was gone, yet I continued to ignore the increasing seriousness of the situation. Instead I sat in my apartment, living in squalor, watching hour after hour of mindless television shows, pumping unfathomable quantities of chemicals into my body, struggling to keep my dead family from driving me insane.

One evening, my body surrendered to exhaustion and I fell into a deep sleep. When I awoke the next morning, I discovered that one of my systems had generated a strong sell signal. My brain was foggy, and I was exhausted despite the sleep, so I did some lines to revive myself. I poured a small glass of scotch and sipped it, casually jotting down the system results from my computer monitor. I called the trading desk and told my broker to sell several contracts short.

After my long sleep, the smell of my apartment was finally more than I could tolerate. I needed to get some fresh air, so instead of waiting for my broker's confirmation, I downed the rest of the scotch, threw on some clothes, and headed to the Cardinal.

When I got there, I found Jefferson reading a book. Barney was at the next table, twitching and muttering. He looked horrible, more haggard than usual, mumbling incoherently and following me with exhausted angry eyes as I walked to Jefferson's table.

Jefferson raised his head from his book. There was something strange in his eyes. "What's up?" I said.

"Not too much. How are you?" He cast a fleeting glance at Barney's table. Jefferson was nervous—something I had never seen in him before.

"I came in for a break." I eyed him carefully. "I've been working." He looked apprehensively at Barney's table again, and I turned to look too. "Barney seems weird today," I said. "He looks horrible."

"You don't look so good, yourself," Jefferson said. "You want to play a game?"

I let the comment about my appearance pass. "Sure."

"How's the trading going?" he asked.

"It's okay. My systems are showing promise. I'm going to tweak them a little bit more over the next couple of days, and then I'm going to make some real money." Arrogance laced every word from my lips.

"I'm sure you will." His eyes fixed on me. He wouldn't look away.

Finally I said, "What's going on, Jefferson? You seem weird."

He opened his mouth, hesitated, and then looked at the table. "I have to leave Austin."

I wasn't sure I heard him correctly. "What?"

"I have to go."

"For how long?"

"A long time."

"That's it? Just like that?"

"It's work—"

"What work? I thought you were retired!"

"I was, but I have to return for a while." He raised his eyes to meet mine. "Douglas, I'll be back."

"What the *fuck*? What about our chess games?" As soon as the question left my mouth, I realized how irrational it sounded. I couldn't believe he was leaving, but more than that, I couldn't understand why I was getting so upset. At most, Jefferson and I were casual friends.

"I'll be back," he repeated.

"When are you leaving?"

"Later today."

"What?" My voice grew louder. "What the fuck are you talking about? How long have you known?"

"Not long."

I was getting more upset, and suddenly I realized what Jefferson meant to me—the way I admired him, the way I *depended* on him. It didn't matter how much money I lost or how much I polluted my body, he was a constant—someone I could count on. He was my only beacon in the sea of madness my life had become.

My mind turned into a tornado. Thomas and my father appeared, and I couldn't push their faces from my mind. I thought about how long it had been since Jack and I last spoke. I had been so busy numbing myself that I hadn't bothered to call. *Well, at least I still have Elizabeth*, I thought, but somehow it didn't ease my agitation.

Jefferson and I continued to stare at each other. His face was expressionless, but his eyes betrayed a deep sadness. I wanted to scream at him, to throw something at him, to make him suffer. Instead I said, "What will I do?" It was the most telling question I could have asked.

"I'll be here when you're ready."

"Ready for what? What the fuck are you talking about?"

He shook his head. "I'll be here."

"Then why are you *fucking* leaving?" My voice cracked.

He cast another troubled glance at Barney. "I can't talk about it."

"I have to go," I said, forcing myself from my chair. I expected him to stop me, but he didn't. The scar on his head caught my attention. It seemed more pronounced than ever.

As I turned to leave, Ellison came in the door. He walked directly toward me, his stride purposeful, his eyes burning intensely—half angry, half amused. He wore nice clothes, but they were rumpled and dirty. He was unshaven and his hair was a mess. His eyes were bloodshot, as though he hadn't slept for a while. He came straight to our table and put his face in mine. He smelled awful.

I took a step back and turned to Jefferson. He didn't move, his face impassive.

"How are you today?" Ellison asked, his face breaking into a disturbing smile.

"What's wrong with you?" I said.

"What's wrong with me?" He cackled. "What's wrong with *you?*"

I stared at him, confused. Suddenly he cocked his head, and his expression became demented. I turned to Jefferson, but his face remained neutral, almost as if he weren't witnessing any of it.

Ellison took another step toward me and said, "Watch *this*, Medicine Man."

My eyes seemed to swell in their sockets, and I could feel my pulse in my temples as cold fear raced through my body. "What did you say?"

Just then Barney stood and walked swiftly to our table, his eyes black with anger. He marched directly toward me and Ellison, but then turned to face Jefferson. I searched Barney's eyes, and I knew, unequivocally, he had finally fallen over the edge.

He reached into his coat pocket and removed a small pistol. His face was contorted in an expression of revulsion. He licked his swollen lips angrily, and a thread of spittle oozed into his beard. He looked directly into Jefferson's eyes, and in a raspy voice, he said, "This is *your* fault, you *fucking* asshole! Why couldn't you leave it alone?" He pointed the gun directly at Jefferson's head.

Adrenalin flooded my system and a humming started in my head. Someone screamed. Two people at the next table hit the floor. A chair teetered slowly, then fell.

Barney stood in front of Jefferson, trembling, the pistol protruding from his stiffened arm.

In defiance of the threat to his life, Jefferson simply sat in his chair, and I recognized what I saw in his eyes—the peace that paradoxically boiled like bottled energy. "I know, Barney," he said soothingly. The calm on his face was unnerving. He shook his head slowly and whispered, "I'm sorry."

Barney was undeterred, his eyes rabid. Then his face collapsed into an expression of utter despair. A tear rolled down his cheek. He cocked his head at Jefferson. "Why?"

He turned the pistol toward his own temple and fired. Jefferson flinched, his eyes snapping shut and then open again. Barney's head jerked violently from the impact. Blood and brains splattered the wall.

The body collapsed like a sack of fruit on the floor, the eyes fluttering briefly, then glazing. His tongue hung grotesquely from his mouth and blood immediately pooled under his head.

I took a step to steady myself.

Suddenly Ellison let out a yelp. "Oh my God." He sobbed. "Oh my *God!*" He turned and sprinted from the shop.

I gained partial balance, staring at Jefferson, searching for an answer—any explanation. But when I looked in his eyes, I saw nothing but remorse.

◆

THE POLICE ARRIVED at the Cardinal almost immediately, rushing everyone outside. Television crews buzzed around, trying to get at Jefferson and me, but the police wouldn't let them through. I sat next to Jefferson in shock, unable to process what had happened.

I gave the police my driver's license and told them where I lived. The questions were predictable: "Did you know the suspect?"

"Yeah, we both come in here a lot." *But Barney won't be coming back again,* I thought. "He thought he heard voices in his head," I said as an afterthought. I looked at Jefferson, but he wouldn't make eye contact.

"Mr. Stone," the policeman said, "were you ever threatened by the victim before?"

"No, only today," Jefferson said. "He was always cordial to me."

"There was another man involved. Do either of you know him?"

I looked at Jefferson again, but he made no attempt to answer. "Yeah," I said. "His name is Ellison Clark." I couldn't get Ellison's face out of my mind. *He called me Medicine Man* . . . I felt like I was losing my mind. A fresh wave of chills ran down my spine, and I fought the urge to break into tears.

"Do you know how we can reach Mr. Clark?"

I mumbled Ellison's phone number to the policeman. I tried again to find something in Jefferson's eyes, but it was useless.

Suddenly I had to go to the bathroom, which somehow seemed like a disrespectful interruption to the solemnity of the moment. The Cardinal was, of course, off-limits. *Because Barney's body is in there lying on the floor.* I asked one of the cops if I could go to the restaurant across the street to relieve myself. "Come right back, Mr. Cole," he said. "We still have some questions for you."

I left for about ten minutes. When I returned, Jefferson was gone. I waited for a while, thinking he might have gone to the bathroom, too, but he didn't appear.

A policeman stood next to me, busily writing on a clipboard. "We seem to be unable to reach Mr. Clark. Can you tell us where he lives?"

"Yeah," I said, giving him directions. "Where is Jefferson?"

"Mr. Stone? We finished questioning him and he left."

"Did he say where he was going?" I wanted so badly to talk to him, to make some sense of what was happening.

"No, I don't think so." The policeman continued to write.

When the police finished their questioning, they sealed the Cardinal with bright yellow tape. The crowd broke up, but Jefferson still didn't appear. The police allowed the television people through, and they jumped on me like wolves, grilling me for what seemed like hours. I was unprepared for the onslaught, but I stammered through the questions, wondering how Jefferson had managed to avoid this.

The reporters finally satisfied their curiosity and began to trickle away. I looked for Jefferson one last time, with no success. I was exhausted and emotionally drained, and I decided the best thing I could do was go home and numb myself as much as possible.

When I got there, I poured a drink and did yet more coke. My use had become more than routine, or even ritual; it was now imperative. And yet it barely registered that I felt only slightly better.

I still couldn't get my emotions around what had happened, and the chemicals just made the process harder; not only did the substances cloud my judgment, but they also clawed at me, demanding more attention almost as fast as I could get them into my body. As I made another drink, I could feel the cocaine wearing off. I searched the apartment for more but found none.

Fuck it, I thought, *I can go one night without it.* But I wasn't at all convinced that was true.

I tried to call Jefferson, but I got no answer. Barney's suicide kept playing in my mind, a recorded image looping perpetually. I downed my drink and made another, thinking about Ellison's face, what he had said to me. *I must have misunderstood . . . or maybe I was just hallucinating.* I picked up the phone and tried to call him, but he didn't answer either.

I wanted so badly to talk to Elizabeth, but I knew I was too drunk. I doubted she would tolerate my condition, regardless of the circumstances. I decided I would call her in the morning.

I slipped into semiconsciousness, so many gruesome images sizzling in my mind. The ghosts were with me, teasing me with memories of my childhood, beckoning, reminding me that I would never be able to return. I jolted back to reality and felt a tear rolling down my cheek. I wiped it away and poured more liquor down my throat.

I began to drift again, and now Jack was there, his face clear in my mind, his expression concerned. He was trying to tell me something, but I couldn't hear his voice.

I woke with a start.

The phone was ringing. My head throbbed, and I glanced at the clock. It read 10:47. AM or PM? I noticed a bright rim of light outlining the thick shades on the window. And suddenly the image of Barney's crumpled dead body filled my mind. My stomach tightened. *What day is it?* "Jesus fucking Christ!" I picked up the phone. "Hello?"

"Douglas?"

"Hey, Bill." Bill Matthews was the guy at the brokerage desk who handled my trades.

"We have a problem," he said firmly.

"What's the matter?"

"You don't know?" He sounded shocked.

"No. What's wrong?"

"The S&P went through the roof. The Fed cut rates."

My stomach tightened even further. "Cut rates? I didn't even know they met."

"It was the FOMC meeting, man! Where the fuck have you been?"

"Shit! You should cover my short positions—"

"I did it hours ago," he said. "I just got the return slip. It's been a motherfucker of a day. You'll have to add funds to your account. We need you to wire cash." He lowered his tone. "Right now, Douglas."

Panic began to take over. "Hold on. How did this happen?"

"The contract gapped up at the open, and it's been climbing ever since."

"Oh God," I whispered, running my fingers through my hair. It felt greasy and dirty.

"We need that money."

"I haven't got it." I had transferred almost all of my money to the brokerage, and now Bill was telling me it was gone.

"*Christ*, Douglas! Why did you put on a hundred contracts if you don't have the fucking money?"

One hundred contracts? I don't remember . . . My lungs felt small and tight, filled with ice. I couldn't get a full breath. "I don't know, Bill. I don't think I—"

"Douglas, your account was negative exactly one second after the market opened." I began to tremble as Bill told me how much I owed. It was an enormous figure.

"There must have been a mistake."

"What mistake?" he asked.

"I've never put on that many contracts. Are you sure?"

"If I have to, I'll go back to the record, but I don't think we would make a mistake like that."

"Okay, I need to think a second." I ran my fingers through my hair again. My mind raced, trying to remember.

"I understand," he said, "but we need that money. I mean it. Get your shit together, man, and see what you can do about the money. I'll call you after I've looked into it."

I gently set down the receiver. The only sound I could hear was the pounding of my heart, each beat throbbing against my stinging eyes. I fell hard to the carpet. I was broke.

What the fuck am I going to do? Tears filled my eyes. I lay frozen on the floor, crying. After a while I got up, poured a drink, and downed it quickly. I repeated the procedure several more times.

The phone rang nonstop for the rest of the day, but I didn't answer it. I spent the time drowning my horror, trying to figure out what I was going to do for money.

Should I call Liz? How will I explain all this to her? She'll never understand.

I had some credit cards but they wouldn't last long. I still had a little money left in my checking account. I could write a few checks, but then what? I didn't even have enough to pay rent, which was due in a week. I'd have to get a job. *Yeah right, just what everybody's looking for in an employee.*

Alcohol wasn't doing the trick. I needed cocaine to handle this problem. I opened the drawer in the table beside my bed. No coke. I rifled through the garbage littering the apartment, hoping to find a bag. No coke. I went through every article of clothing I owned. Nothing.

I finally decided to call Elizabeth. I needed her now. The phone rang for what seemed eternity before she picked up. "Hey," I slurred.

"Douglas!" Her voice was choked. There was a small pause, and then she said, "Ellison is dead." She was weeping so hard I didn't think I had understood her.

"What?" I refused to believe her, and suddenly I remembered my mother's face when she had told me about the car crash. *I thought it was some kind of horrible joke.*

"He's *dead!*" She was weeping uncontrollably. "He shot himself . . . in his apartment!"

I leaned against the wall and slid to the floor, listening to her sobs through the phone. *But I just saw him.* How long had it been? *His face . . . his eyes . . . Medicine Man.*

"Where have you been?" she moaned. "I've been trying to call—"

"I'm at my apartment. I've had a bad day. I need to see you."

"*You've* had a bad day? Douglas, did you hear what I said? My brother *killed* himself!" Her voice cracked with a fresh wave of sobs.

Oh, my God . . . Jefferson's gone, Barney just blew his fucking brains out, now Ellison is dead, and . . . I'm bankrupt. It seemed so unbelievable that for an instant I again wondered if it was all just an elaborate joke. Ellison couldn't be dead—not on top of everything else. It wasn't registering. Finally I said, "Can I come over?"

Through her choked breathing she repeated, "I tried to call you."

"Can I please come over? I need to see you." My voice was edgy.

There was a long pause filled with a fresh wave of desperate sobs. Finally she whispered, "Yes."

When I got to Elizabeth's complex, I was so drunk I almost fell out of my car. I stumbled to her apartment.

She cracked the door, her face swollen and streaked with tears. When she registered the shape I was in, she furrowed her brow. "You look *horrible*!" She didn't move.

I put my hand on the door. "Can I come in?"

She resisted. "I saw you on television earlier, Douglas. What the hell is happening?"

I put more pressure on the door, but she still resisted. "I need help," I whined, "That's all. I just want to talk!"

"What's wrong with you?"

"I don't know, everything's crazy! Jefferson left, I lost some money, and now you tell me Ellison is dead . . . I don't know."

She started weeping again. "What do you *mean* you lost some money?" Her voice increased in pitch. "Douglas, I can't talk about this right now!" She pushed the door, trying to close it, but I held it.

"I just need a place to think for a minute!"

"Douglas, I can't *do* this right now!"

"Yes you fucking *can*!" I thrust the door open, and Elizabeth's face changed from despair, to anger, and then to fear.

"Get out of my apartment!"

Searing fury boiled inside me, sudden and uncontrollable. "*Fuck* you! I need help, and you tell me to leave your apartment?" I moved closer, rage surging through my body.

She sensed it and started backing away. "Please leave."

I could hear the fear in her voice, and it felt good—it almost made me hungry. The thought of hurting Elizabeth became alluring. "What the fuck are you gonna do?" A wicked sneer appeared on my lips. "You gonna call the cops?" I laughed.

Elizabeth backed against a wall next to the stairs in the entryway. "Douglas, please leave." She said it with relative composure, but I saw how much effort it took for her to stay calm. She put her hand on a table by the stairs.

"Nah, I don't think I will." I imagined all the ways in which I might make her suffer.

She grabbed a brass lamp from the table, swung, and hit the side of my head, knocking me to the floor.

I recovered quickly and scrambled to my feet, shaking my head. Rage assumed total control now, and my hand moved through space with lightning speed, connecting with her face. She tumbled across the floor and crashed against the stair rail. I laughed as a wave of sadistic joy rushed through my body. I advanced toward her again, smiling and licking my lips. It was the sensation I had felt in the chemistry lab, staring at Mark as he lay trembling before me—a sensation at once revolting and luscious, stronger now than I remembered.

What went through my mind in that moment is something so foreign and repulsive to me now that I have a difficult time recounting it. I almost can't believe I was in that apartment, doing those things to Elizabeth. But I *was* there, and I cannot deny that my desire was to make her suffer as much as I could. I was no longer in control.

But then, as quickly as the rage had taken over, something new appeared. It competed with the anger, forcing in a trickle of rationality. It confused me, and I hesitated. I advanced toward Elizabeth again, but another bolt of reason hit me. Then suddenly, light broke through.

What have I done?

Horror and remorse overshadowed every other emotion. It was the most sadness I have ever felt in a single instant.

I fell to my knees. "Liz?"

She sensed that she was out of danger, and her fear collapsed under the weight of anger. With a remarkable amount of poise she said, "Get out."

"Liz, please—"

"Get out."

"Liz—?"

She screamed, "*Get out!*"

I scrambled to my feet, backing out the door, watching her face as I left. The last memory I have of that afternoon in Elizabeth's apartment is her expression of total repugnance.

◆

I WENT HOME, where I downed several more drinks. After a few hours, the magnitude of what I had done finally began to take firm hold, and I curled into a ball and wept. I tried to call Élizabeth, to attempt an explanation, but only got her machine. At the beep, I sobbed, "Liz, I'm sorry. *Please* pick up!"

Nothing. I hung up and one thought replaced all others: I desperately needed cocaine.

I staggered out to my car and, despite my condition, somehow made it to my dealer's house. I stumbled up his drive, rang the bell, and a few seconds later he opened the door holding a phone to his ear. "I'll call you back," he said, pushing the button to end the call. His face stretched into a broad smile. "Douglas! What's up?"

Then his expression changed to exaggerated concern. "Man, you look like shit!"

"I didn't get much sleep last night. Listen Tony, you got anything for me?"

He scanned the neighborhood furtively. "Sure, how much you want?"

"How about an eight ball?"

"I can do that. Why don't you come in?"

There were several guys sitting around the television in the living room. I recognized a few of them, and we exchanged standoffish nods.

Tony returned with a bag of coke and started to hand it to me, but then he hesitated. A palpable tension formed between us. "Douglas?"

"Yeah?"

He raised his eyebrows. "I need some money." He was obviously surprised I hadn't offered.

"Oh, uh, yeah." I reached in my back pocket and pulled out my wallet, grabbing all the bills I had. I counted them and said, "This is all I've got on me."

He forced a counterfeit smile. "Dude, this isn't even enough to buy a line."

"Can you spot me the rest, just until I get some cash?"

His face became stern, but the smile remained. "You know I can't do that."

An uncomfortable silence ensued, and it was my turn to smile, "Come on, Tony, help me out here."

He didn't say anything. The guys on the couch turned to see what was happening. The silence was almost painful. Finally he said, "I can't—"

"Just give me the fucking coke!"

The smile disintegrated from Tony's face. "You gotta go, dude."

We stared at each other for another awkward moment, and suddenly, without thinking, I grabbed for the bag in his hand. In the same motion, he pulled it out of my reach and hit me hard in the nose with the base of his palm. The blow knocked me to the floor.

Tony and his friends were on me in an instant, the blows coming faster than I could move. I curled into a ball, wincing as they kicked me in the kidneys, shins, and the parts of my face I couldn't cover. Even through the pain I thought, *I deserve this. This is what I did to Elizabeth, and now I'm paying for it.* They picked me up, carried me out the front door, and threw me on the ground. I landed hard, and for a moment couldn't move as I tried to pull air into my lungs. I caught my breath, tasting the blood pouring from my nose and lips.

Tony's friends backed away. He pulled a small pistol from inside his pocket and squatted, pointing it between my eyes. My heart thundered in my chest.

"Douglas, if you ever try any shit like that again," he said, pushing the gun's barrel into my forehead, "I'll put a bullet in your brain. They'll find your body in a garbage can, and nobody will give one-tenth of a fuck. Do you understand me?"

I nodded rapidly.

"Good. Don't show your ugly fucking face here anymore." He walked back to the house with his friends. He turned, grinned, and slowly closed the door.

◆

MY MELTDOWN WAS years in the making, but the ultimate collapse came so quickly that it is difficult for me to recall now the exact order in which everything happened. While I know, roughly, what I did during the next part of my life, the details are only a fragmented series of memories. What is clear is that I made some rash decisions, acting on them with little thought about their long-term implications.

An addict considers any possession he has only for how much it will bring him in cash, and since I was broke, and woefully in need of the substances that would ease my pain, I began to sell almost every object I owned to the highest bidder—usually a pawnshop—for a fraction of its worth, after which I immediately spent the money on any chemical I could get my hands on: pills, coke, booze, or whatever else I could find. The apartment gradually became emptier until I had almost nothing left of value, with one notable exception. I saved it for last, fatuously hoping that my situation might miraculously improve.

But, of course, things didn't improve, and finally I took this last, most precious possession to a pawnshop near my apartment. I rested it against the counter and asked the manager what it was worth. He made an absurdly low offer, which I accepted with no negotiation.

I ran my fingers down the cello's beautiful finish, and for one moment a flicker of sanity shone through, demanding I reconsider this decision. But my dependencies quickly repulsed any rationality, and I took the cash from the counter. I looked at the cello one more time, turned, and walked out of the shop.

My memories become even more mottled after that day. I came home one day to find my key no longer worked, the notice on my door informing me that I had been evicted, signed by Ms. Richmond. I vaguely remember staying with various acquaintances for a little while, but I didn't have too many friends left, and nobody wanted a penniless addict around for long. So I took to the streets. I was officially homeless.

While I do remember selling some things, I have no clear recollection of what happened to a lot of my belongings. One of the biggest mysteries, for instance, was the fate of my car. After my eviction, I slept in it a few times when I had nowhere else to go, but eventually, I decided to sell it for whatever cash I could get.

As absurd as it sounds, I couldn't find it. I searched the neighborhood around my apartment, but it was nowhere. I tried to think where else I might have parked it, but I couldn't remember, so I just forgot about it. It nagged at me for a short time, especially since the little money I did have was rapidly dwindling, but eventually the issue faded into the oblivion my life had become.

When I became destitute, something happened beyond the physical manifestation of my condition. A pall hung over me, obscuring reality and obliterating my self-worth. Lack of money made it hard for me to find even basic nourishment, let alone drugs, and since it was economically impossible to sustain continual chemical intoxication, getting high became a relatively rare diversion—certainly nothing compared to the perpetual state I had enjoyed when I had had money. And even when I did scrape together enough to get what I so desperately needed, the selection was usually limited to cheap pills, crack, or booze.

So the loss of lucidity couldn't be completely attributed to drugs and alcohol. No, when I reached bottom, I subconsciously shut out the world as a form of psychological self-preservation; it wasn't so much that I couldn't think clearly, it was that my mind wouldn't let me. I simply snapped like a circuit breaker to stop the overload.

One of the things I remember clearly is losing a lot of weight. When I did eat, it either came from charity or because I was just so hungry that I would take any meal I could get, including many from dumpsters. As much as I'd like to forget that aspect of my homelessness, it is an irrefutable fact that I drew sustenance from garbage.

Looking back at what my life had become still deeply disturbs me. It seems more like some intangible work of fiction than the vulgar nightmare I actually lived. In less than a year, I went from being a wealthy college student to eating from trashcans, and the road to failure had been much shorter than I ever would have believed possible. I joined the ranks of society's outcasts, whose presence I had always been aware of, but never understood until now. And I was immersed in it—this lawless, sometimes violent collective of displaced human beings whose long-term vision rarely exceeds the next meal or the next drink. I had always been so intent on ignoring the homeless that I simply missed the significance of their numbers.

I began to recognize the individual faces—citizens of a filthy subculture roaming the streets and parks of Austin. They gathered in loose packs like wild dogs, competitive and vicious. Several times I watched men beaten nearly to death over money, drugs, or liquor.

I chose solitude, and I probably avoided a lot of unnecessary conflict and pain by fending for myself. But my isolation and poverty flung the door wide for the ghosts, and if they had been loud before, their cries were earsplitting now. To combat them I spent countless hours digging through dumpsters in alleys behind popular bars, searching for half-empty bottles of beer. During the busiest times of the day, I begged for change around the city. But the downtime was unbearable; dumpsters were often empty, and it took time to gather money. Meanwhile the ghosts mercilessly demanded my attention, driving me to the brink of insanity.

While my wealth had evaporated, my appetite for cocaine had only grown stronger. I've heard people say there's no addiction to rival heroin, and I won't argue that its seduction isn't venomous, but I can't help wonder if the advocates of that theory have any experience with the allure, and ultimate enslavement, of the chemicals I chose.

It's an argument that one can only defend through experience, and I've paid the price for my participation. Heroin's seductiveness may indeed reign supreme, but if that's the case, I can only say that I'm grateful I turned away from it. The path I chose was hell enough for me.

IT WOULD BE unreasonable to suggest that my life was even remotely normal, because it clearly wasn't. Nevertheless, the devastating and even bizarre circumstances defining my path to this point had been at least somewhat explicable, if only marginally so. But that was about to change.

As if my collapse hadn't been enough, in the ensuing months, my mind was invaded. I hate to use that term, because it somehow seems inadequate to explain what happened to me, but I can think of no more appropriate description for what I experienced.

The hottest part of the summer had come when the episodes started—probably August or September. The incursions didn't come slowly, but were sudden and terrifying, and while it seemed easy at the time to chalk it up to my emotional and mental instability—that I was finally slipping off the edge—my psychological state had far less to do with it than I believed.

It felt as though my thoughts were being toyed with—as though I were talking to myself in a rumbling tone over which I had no control. And of all the inexplicable things that had happened in my life, never once had I heard any voices. Those other experiences—from restoring Thomas's breathing, to reviving the dog, to the fight in the chemistry lab—had been more direct, requiring no language, nothing conceptual per se. The incidents seemed to transcend simple human interpretation, and it had been their sheer enormity that had frightened me, but also fascinated me—and even comforted me in a primal way.

But this new voice was different, preternatural, filling my mind with strange words and concepts—*human* concepts—in a voice that was familiar, yet somehow evil, bubbling up from the darkest places in my soul, driving me into a claustrophobic panic as I tried to find some escape from my own mind.

I spent most of my energy that summer trying to find secluded places to sleep— anywhere that could provide at least a little respite—not only from my mental anguish, but also from the sweltering Texas humidity. Early one morning, I passed out under a bush near the university after downing a bottle of cheap whiskey. I had been there only a short while before I felt myself being roused by a policeman. "Come on, you can't stay here." His tone wasn't angry, but he was resolute.

I staggered toward the Drag, but my mind was still foggy and I wasn't paying much attention as I stepped off a curb into the street. I heard a loud screech to my left.

The car hit me and I landed on the hood. My head struck the windshield before I rolled off into the street. Several people rushed to me, gathering in a circle, and I rose to my feet unsteadily.

The alcohol had relaxed me so much that the accident didn't injure me as it might have, but I reeled nevertheless. The world spun, and the crowd grew, chattering, their faces charged, eager to see if I would recover. In that moment, despite my disorientation, I recoiled inwardly at the fact that I was mere fascination to them, like an animal being slaughtered in an ancient Roman arena. I only wanted to get away.

I was about to turn and flee, but my eyes came to an abrupt halt.

Elizabeth was there, her face flushed with horror. Our eyes met and locked. We looked at each other for a long moment before she managed to tear her gaze from mine. Then she melted into the crowd.

I was humiliated beyond measure, and in that moment the defeat was unqualified. I broke through the throng of people and hobbled away as quickly as I could. I made it back to the dumpster where I had been drinking the night before and collapsed, the image of Elizabeth still etched in my mind. I began to cry.

The pain seared my soul. I wanted to find her, to fix everything. The feeling was carnivorous, gnawing at my stomach, sinking into my flesh, ripping me apart. And yet my rational mind was still present enough to remind me that it would bring no relief. The way she had looked at me drove home the fact that she was gone forever, so I wept, certain that nothing could be worse than this moment.

I was woefully mistaken.

"Medicine Man?"

It was nothing more than an echoing whisper. I stopped crying instantly and looked around, not quite able to grasp what I had heard.

"Medicine Man, you know you're already dead."

The old, familiar chill tickled my spine. I swung my eyes in both directions, looking for the source.

"Medicine Man."

I jumped up and backed away from the dumpster, putting my hands over my ears as the voice grew louder. Its insane singsong quality was maddening. My next thought was that it must be the ghosts, but it didn't take long to realize that this was something much different.

It swept through my mind, a low contemptuous growl that rose in pitch from the start of each sentence to the end. "Does *Medicine Man* want to sing a song?" It let out a low snarl. "You're already dead, motherfucker."

I started to cry again. *What the fuck is happening?*

"Medicine Man, Medicine Man, rotting and dead." A revolting sound echoed in my head, something like vomit splashing on concrete. *"Medicine Man, Medicine Man, fucked in the head."*

I sat back down in front of the dumpster, my hands still covering my ears, my head tucked tightly between my knees. I let out a thin moan.

Then it all stopped, as though someone had turned off a switch.

I was in a vacuum, unable to hear anything—not even the sound of my own breath or heartbeat. I lifted my head and looked left and right. I stuck my face around the edge of the dumpster. There was no one there.

Silence.

I brought my head back around and what I saw next drove the air from my lungs.

It was the old man who had been in my mother's room when I found her body. And while the terror of his presence pinned me to the asphalt like a spike through my thigh, something else now demanded my attention—something infinitely more important.

His eyes. He wants me to die.

The black orbs were determined—almost insane, but not quite. He walked silently toward me, his hands behind his back. The only noise was the sound of his shoes hitting the pavement. *Click . . . click . . . click . . .* It echoed in my mind, reverberating through my body.

He was grotesquely thin, his reptilian face wrinkled and leathery. His hair was black, long and greasy, his dark eyes filled with hatred. A smile touched his lips as he searched my eyes.

I mouthed words, but no sound came. *What do you want?*

He stopped walking and stared at me with absolute loathing, squinting, still smiling. "Don't you know?" His words were the only sound now, echoing as though through a tunnel. The rest of the world was gone, melted away. Time had stopped.

I shook my head violently, fear gurgling in my throat, a harsh metallic taste. I tried to scream, but his eyes stopped me.

"Don't you know, *Medicine Man?*" He looked to his right, still grinning maliciously. I followed his gaze and saw a young boy, naked, balled up and shivering on the alley's pavement. I didn't know where he had come from, but it didn't seem to matter.

It's not real. I couldn't see the boy's face, but I could feel his terror.

The old man looked at me, his smile stretching wider across his plastic face. He let his arms fall to his side, and I noticed a thin blade, curved and more than a foot long, dangling from his left hand, glinting in the sun. It was sinister, like a claw. He hovered over the naked child, a storm ready to collapse on the world beneath, yet he hesitated. And then I knew.

The old man turned, his movements swift and surprisingly graceful. He grabbed the boy's hair with his right hand and pulled the head up, exposing the neck.

I stopped breathing, staring in disbelief when I saw the boy's face, staring into eyes that might have been mine. It was Thomas.

I only had enough time to open my mouth, trying to emit a scream that wouldn't come. The blade flashed through the air, found Thomas's throat, and sliced the jugular. Black blood spewed from the throat and mouth, splashing the old man's pants.

Thomas's arms went limp and his body shuddered, heaving as he tried to breathe. His mouth cranked convulsively, gulping for oxygen, but only erupting blood. Finally the eyes glazed and the old man stared at the boy, laughing with delight. I tried to move, but I was still paralyzed.

He dropped Thomas's body to the pavement where it twitched and convulsed in an expanding pool of blood. The old man fixed his eyes on me again, the smile now gone from his face. He resumed his approach, the shoes hitting the pavement in slow motion—*click . . . click . . . click,* like a clock ticking away the last remaining seconds of my life.

"Do you know who you are? Has he told you yet?"

I tried to say something, but still no sound would leave my throat.

The old man walked to where I sat and put his face an inch from mine, raising his lip in a snarl, revealing his sharp, rotten teeth. In a raspy whisper, he said, "I wish *I* could." He breathed slowly in and out, wheezing, his eyes staring into mine unblinking. "Oh . . . the *precious* obligation."

Finally he pulled his head back and stood erect. "You're next, Medicine Man." He raised the blade high in the air and swung it at me.

The vacuum retreated and sound returned—a deluge of reality rushing in, filling the empty space around me. I threw my hands over my head, trying to protect myself from the knife, but it didn't come. I slowly lifted my eyes.

Traffic. Birds. The sounds I took for granted.

The old man was gone. Thomas's body was no longer on the pavement. There was no blood.

It was a hallucination, I thought. *Thomas has been dead for years.*

But deep in my mind, I knew that something was all wrong. It had been too vivid to be a hallucination. I began to shake violently. The thought of becoming like Barney—of losing my capacity to perceive reality—filled me with a crippling fear. My head hurt, and my body ached as the booze wore off, but I didn't dare move.

Finally, despite the terror, I just passed out from sheer exhaustion.

◆

THE OLD MAN stayed away, but as the weeks and months dragged on, I heard the new voice in my head more frequently—vicious and maddening. Sometimes it took on the old man's gravelly voice, but more often it was a twisted version of my own.

It came suddenly at all times of the day and night, always addressing me by that strange name—*Medicine Man*. It taunted me, threatened to kill me, and even encouraged me to kill myself. Sometimes it was aggressive and angry. Other times it was almost calm, nonsensically asking me if I knew who—or *what*—I was. I even responded at times, but it never acknowledged the effort, which was just as well.

The voice was resolute, growling for hours about the death of my brother and father, imposing on me images more horrific even than those I had, in the past, conjured myself—driving the needle slowly into my flesh, through the muscle to the bone. And yet for all its apparent determination to upset me, it never addressed me or any of my family by name.

A dim question began to grow in my mind, perhaps the faintest vestiges of reason: Was it possible that this wretched byproduct of my collapse—this voice that I had been so sure was nothing more than the result of my diminishing sanity—knew too little about me? Could my mind possibly fail to possess the critical details of my own history?

And the answer was clear: no matter how much I had slipped, I still knew who I was, and where I came from. But this voice, while it seemed to understand the basic structure, couldn't quite produce the specifics. It was yet another clue that something wasn't right.

But the more I thought about it, the more I realized that *nothing* made much sense anymore. The dismal truth was that I was going crazy. So what if this voice didn't know my name? If anything, the question only added to the uncertainty of my situation, making things yet bleaker, holding me under, preventing me from getting even one breath. The only question remaining was how long I could persist under these circumstances.

One night, I lay at the dead end of an alley, senseless from cheap whiskey drunk too quickly. I collapsed next to a dumpster, drifting in and out of consciousness, almost catatonic. I slipped away, for how long I don't know, but when I awoke three men stood over me, laughing.

For a moment, I thought it was raining, until I realized one of them was urinating on me. I tried to roll out of the way, but I could barely move. The man finished and zipped his pants. "I'm done," he said. "You can go back to sleep now." They all belched laughter.

I was helpless, wallowing in my own inebriation. Resistance was out of the question, but somehow I still managed a weak insult, spitting on the man's pant leg.

They looked at each other, incapable of believing I could possibly display any defiance. It was just the excuse they needed, and the next thing I felt was the impact of a boot against the side of my head. They landed blows with rapid-fire speed, kicking me wherever I was exposed. I curled into a ball, wrapping my arms around my head, praying the attack would end quickly, but they were beyond return. The violence got worse, and I think they might have killed me had events not taken a very strange turn.

The thrashing simply stopped.

I opened my eyes to see why. About sixty feet from us, at the alley's entrance, stood a lone figure, and the three men had taken their attention from me to consider him. At that distance, the man seemed nothing more than a shadow, completely clad in black.

Silence reigned in the aftermath of the violence. The man at the open end of the alley stood still, his posture relaxed, his face angled downward. In my state, and at that distance, there was no way to see his eyes, and yet, somehow, I could feel them, unwavering, utterly aware. And while he appeared at ease, he also seemed *prepared*—a bird of prey, merely waiting.

An amber streetlight burned behind him, eerily silhouetting his black form. "You'll stop now," he said. The sentence was a mere formality, as if the outcome were a foregone conclusion. His body was still as he spoke, his voice steady—loud enough to be heard but low in pitch.

The three men erupted in laughter. One said, "Why don't you make us stop, *motherfucker?*"

The figure still didn't move. The three men continued their laughter for a moment, and then it faded awkwardly. A strange tension began to grow, and they became more edgy, until one of them screamed, *"Go for it, you fuckin—"*

If I had blinked I would have missed it. The figure covered the distance between us in less than a second, his body shimmering—waves of liquid rippling with every movement. The three stepped back, the confidence draining from their faces, their bodies tense, poised to fight.

He stood directly in front of us. I still couldn't see his face, but somehow I knew any negotiation had ended. With nearly imperceptible speed he threw his arm through the first man's head, and when he withdrew it black liquid erupted from a huge cavity where the man's face had been. The body collapsed to the ground, an abandoned puppet, blood and chunks of meat pouring from the gaping hole.

I buried my face in my arms, but that didn't muffle the sounds of the carnage around me. There were shouts, a few brief, terrifying screams, thuds, crunching, ripping.

Then nothing.

The silence was concussive. My eyes popped open, dancing—bouncing from edge to edge, looking for any beacon of rationality in the night. What I saw gave me no relief.

Blood and meat were everywhere, splattered on the dumpster, coagulating in pools beneath the corpses of the men who had been beating me only a short while before. An arm, neatly severed, lay a few feet from my face. A body lay sprawled on the asphalt, headless. The neck rose up from a blood-soaked shirt and ended in a mass of pink flesh, black liquid spurting from the stump. A little to the left of the corpse, the head faced me, resting against the dumpster, its face contorted in an expression of abject terror, blood leaking from its nose, eyes, and severed neck. It seemed strangely alive, and a new wave of revulsion tore through me as I realized exactly why.

The eyes blinked once, and then again. The mouth opened and closed rhythmically, gasping for air like a freshly landed fish. I used every ounce of energy I possessed to turn my head and vomit.

I looked up, my stomach convulsing. He stood so close to me, but his body still rippled with energy, distorting any details. He surveyed the scene mechanically, but his three victims no longer moved. When he was satisfied, he turned his attention to me.

My heart pumped fast, a low rhythmic thudding in my ears and head, but I was still too drunk and too badly hurt to move. He began to walk toward me, and I tried to back away from him, certain I was about to die.

He moved behind me and I felt arms encircle me, lifting me gently. He threw me over his shoulder and my body relaxed. I knew there was no point in resisting, and I didn't have the energy anyway, so I gave in to what I thought was inevitable.

He carried me several blocks and set me down gently against a wall in another alley, hovering over me, shifting the angle of his head slightly, examining me. For the first time since he appeared, I sensed frustration in his movement. I tried again to find some detail in his face, but it was nothing but a blur.

He put his hands on either side of my face and brought his head close to mine, as though to take a bite out of my neck. I could feel the warmth of his breath against my cheek. "Don't give up."

With my last remaining energy I said, "Who?"

But he was gone. I thought I heard distant voices, maybe footsteps. Then blackness, and nothing more.

MY FIRST THOUGHT was that I had experienced a nightmare. I shot forward in the bed, and pain erupted from every inch of my body. I let out a little cry and then breathed in heavily.

I was in a hospital room, a tube running from my arm to a bag on a stand. I tried to stay calm, to process what had happened, but I started to tremble. I needed a drink.

The door opened and I yanked my head around. A nurse walked into the room. "How are you feeling?" Her smile was plastic.

"How long have I been here?" I said.

"About a day. What's your name?"

"How did I get here?"

"The police brought you in. They have some questions for you, but we aren't going to worry about that right now." She stretched her counterfeit smile a little. "You were lucky. Whoever attacked you killed three other men. Sit tight and I'll get a doctor."

But her eyes told me everything. *She thinks I killed them.*

She pulled her gaze from mine and left the room. I heard voices outside, followed by footsteps fading down the hall.

I turned on the television, surfing the channels until I found a local news broadcast. The anchor spoke with an irritating dramatic tone. "Law enforcement officials continue to search for clues about the mysterious deaths in downtown Austin two nights ago. Police have not commented on the nature of the killings, but they did indicate that they are still working to determine the method used by the assailant or assailants. Investigators refuse to comment on whether this crime is related to last year's Arboretum murders. While police do have a suspect in custody, details of the attack are being withheld."

A wave of heat tore through my body at the newscaster's final statement: *The suspect . . . I'm the fucking suspect!* I turned off the television and looked around the room, taking in as many details as I could. I had to get out.

I reached for the intravenous drip and removed the tape that held it in my arm, slowly pulling it from my vein with trembling fingers. Blood squirted from the hole and I grabbed a tissue from a box on the bed stand, pressing it to the bubbling stream.

I slipped from the bed, barely able to move, and hobbled to the closet where I found my clothing. I fumbled for the buttonholes on my shirt, but when I looked into the mirror for help, I stopped, transfixed by what I saw.

My appearance was repulsive. In the last few months, I had only seen glimpses of my own reflection; the man in front of me now was a total stranger. So many thoughts ran through my mind, a thousand simultaneous voices screaming their indictments, begging for an explanation, demanding to know how much longer I could wage this absurd and futile battle against my own existence.

I ran my fingers over gaunt ribs. My eyes were black, and below them a bandage covered my nose. My curly brown hair had grown long, spilling about my shoulders, matted in places. My cheeks were gaunt under a scraggly beard. My lips were dry and cracked.

I am homeless.

I pulled my eyes away from the mirror. There was no time. I was certain someone would catch me trying to leave. The trembling increased, making it more difficult to dress.

I struggled to the door and opened it a crack. In the hall to my left was a folding plastic chair, an overturned magazine in the seat. I looked farther down the hall and saw a policeman in uniform bending over a water fountain. I looked to my right. The hallway stretched about forty feet before making a sharp left turn.

I slipped through the door and walked away from the cop. I had almost reached the turn in the hallway when I heard a voice behind me: "Sir? Excuse me! *Sir!*"

I bolted around the corner, followed by rapid, pounding footfalls. *"Sir!"*

A set of elevators appeared before me, and beside them a door marked Stairs. I pushed it open, bounding down the treads three at a time, the impact sending pain shooting through my body. I had cleared two-and-a-half floors when I heard the policeman enter the stairwell. He yelled at me again, but I only ran faster, ignoring the pain.

I came to a door labeled Three and ducked through it. Amazingly, one of the elevators stood open and empty, so I got in, pushed the button for the first floor, and held my breath. The elevator stood still for a long moment and then began to move. The light for the third floor went out, and then the second floor light came on. It seemed to hang forever, and I began to wonder if the cop had managed to stop my descent, but just when I was about to panic, the light went dark, and the elevator continued down. Finally, the number *one* illuminated with the dinging of the indicator bell. The elevator stopped with a jolt and the doors slid open.

An old woman sat in front of me in a wheelchair, attended by a man in a white uniform. I stepped out, looked left and then right, but there was no sign of the policeman. A red sign read *EXIT*, under which an arrow pointed down the hall. I walked toward it as quickly as I dared, looking nervously around me. The woman and her attendant stared at me suspiciously, but there was still no sign of the cop.

In front of me, I saw the glow of midafternoon sunshine. I ran the last fifty feet to a door leading out of the hospital. Luckily, it wasn't the main entrance, and I burst through it, nearly sprinting to the parking lot, to the cover of hundreds of automobiles.

I slinked between cars, repeatedly glancing over my shoulder, finally stopping to catch my breath. I looked at the main entrance to the hospital where several police cars and vans had converged, their lights flashing. Uniforms poured out, weapons drawn.

I had to keep moving. I stayed low, almost crawling out of the parking lot into a residential neighborhood just south of the hospital. I straightened up and tried to walk inconspicuously, but after a couple of minutes I heard the sound of a helicopter. I had to get out of sight, so I found a drainpipe, crawled inside, and stayed there for the next few hours.

When night fell, I made my way downtown as quickly as possible. I opened a dumpster behind a pub and saw hundreds of beer bottles amid debris and rotting food. I slipped inside and began to drink and eat whatever I could find to put in my body.

The ghosts floated around me, flitting back and forth—images of Thomas and my dad ripped to pieces by the car crash. Then the new voice appeared, pumping me full of its sickly-sweet venom: "Hello, *Medicine Man!* You want to sing while we watch your fucking family die . . . *again* . . . and *again* . . . and *again*?" It laughed, a gravelly nasty sound, and then began to sing in an off-key, mawkish howl, something like a train's wheels braking—the screech of metal on metal.

I covered my ears, pressing them hard against the side of my head, squeezing my eyes shut. *Please! Not tonight!*

But it ignored my request, crooning and screaming ever louder. The only defense was alcohol, so I drank the tepid stale liquid from discarded bottles for hours, until I finally lost consciousness.

January, Year Nineteen

I AVOIDED THE police even more than usual after my escape from the hospital, but it turned out to be unnecessary. I was only one of innumerable homeless men in Austin, any of whom would fit my description, and I can only assume that I wasn't photographed or fingerprinted while I was unconscious in the hospital.

At first rumors surfaced that police were asking questions on the street, looking for information about the man who had escaped from the hospital. They even offered a reward, which was quickly withdrawn when worms all over the city began snitching on one another.

The police did eventually arrest several men, and the nurse from my hospital room positively identified one of them. When his DNA failed to match any from the alley he was released, and the nurse's credibility as a witness dissolved. There were no more arrests, and eventually the story faded away, as unsolved murders tend to do.

I never spoke a word of it to anyone, and no one bothered me about it after I resumed my life on the streets. But the images from that night in the alley stayed with me for a long time. Perhaps the most troubling aspect was the man who had saved me. His final words echoed in my head, tickling me, driving me mad with their implication.

Don't give up.

And then there was the most nagging question of all: How had he done those things? Ultimately I dismissed the whole episode as a product of my disintegrating relationship with reality, and as with everything else in my life, I used drugs and booze to hide from the questions, along with possible answers. In my mind it was best not to address such issues, no matter how disturbing or inexplicable they might be.

The period I spent on the streets was roughly six months. But while I was there, I had no awareness of the passage of time; one day blurred into the next, weeks melted into months, and seasons changed. I was oblivious to it all. The universe spun around me as I withered, affording me all the consideration of a decomposing animal carcass at the side of the road.

It was the middle of January, and as hot as Austin summers can be, the frigid, damp winters are every bit as brutal to a person with no means. The cold nights took their toll, creating yet another reason for me to numb myself with any drugs I could acquire.

But as the winter wore on I began to see small changes within myself, subtle shifts in my perspective, leading me to look at my life in a new way. It wasn't an epiphany, just a small morsel of perception, a different angle perhaps. It could have been the monstrous image in the mirror that day in the hospital. Or maybe the memories of the people I loved most were simply burning through the fog, driving me to see something different.

I found myself missing Jefferson a lot—our chess games and conversations. I often wondered where he had gone, and if he still remembered me. As I fell further into the abyss, I also thought more and more about Jack. It seemed like forever since we had seen each other, and at the oddest times I broke into quiet laughter, thinking of his crude sense of humor. It was a welcome relief; there wasn't too much worth laughing about anymore.

But any brief happiness always gave way to more pain and guilt. Jefferson had been a good friend and teacher, but I had already set my course by the time I met him, and nothing could change it. Jack, on the other hand, had been the last real beacon of hope in my life, a last chance to avoid the mistakes that would lead me to where I was now, and I had cast aside the opportunity. No one who wasn't related to me had ever loved me the way Jack did, and I had all but discarded our friendship—a fact that haunted me intensely. I missed him so much.

I nearly called him several times, but the thought of letting him see me in this state was inconceivable. What would I say to him? How would he react? The idea of asking him for money was unthinkable, so I squelched any impulse to contact him as quickly as it arose. Still, his memory stayed with me, growing stronger. Something important was happening, but I didn't recognize it yet.

Now, with each substance entering my bloodstream, I began to ache with regret and disappointment, and this was something I hadn't felt in such abundance before. The pain, while intense, had always been distant and separate, merely the fuel for my self-destruction. But now the pain seemed sweeter and less hopeless.

Before, I had always run from reality because I was afraid of what it might hold for me next. There seemed to be no peace in anything but intoxication, so that was where I hid. But now reality was scratching at the glass, beckoning me to revisit my premises. The call was faint, but I was listening. I was beginning to wonder if I had missed something.

I don't know when it came—in a moment, over days, or maybe over weeks, but one day it was there with me. The winter sun felt warmer and a little brighter. Everything around me seemed to have a bit more color. Even the pain seemed more inviting, more real—even friendlier. I had regained something critical to the human condition: for the first time since the death of my brother and father, I wanted to survive.

It was a seed I had to nurture, and while I knew it wouldn't grow overnight, I also had some understanding that if I took care of it, it might eventually blossom into something bigger. I had taken the first and most important step.

Once my conviction emerged, however, I realized it wasn't simply a decision of the mind; I would have to contend with my body and its uncontrollable dependencies. I wasn't sure I could measure up to the task, and with this uncertainty began the inevitable cycle of empty promises to myself. It seemed no matter how firmly I committed to cleaning up, I would slip, putting off sobriety for yet another day. The ghosts—and now the newest voice—wouldn't allow me the peace or strength I needed for the effort. Their constant harassment convinced me that even if I got sober, they would never let me sleep.

And in this haze, I couldn't admit I needed help. I was still determined to tackle my issues on my own, never bothering to notice how badly I had mismanaged the job so far. So I lived another day, not quite sure if I could survive long enough to see the seed take root.

Late one afternoon my hands began to shake, a condition which was now routine. No matter how hard I tried to clean up, I wasn't succeeding, and tonight I decided that if I wanted any peace at all, I would have to find some help.

I scraped together some money and decided I would try to limit myself to booze. I would use the rest of the cash to buy some dinner. I picked up a cheap bottle of wine and downed most of it, but the ghosts screamed louder than ever, joined by the new voice. The clamor was excruciating, like the buzz of a thousand tiny flying insects. I had hoped, at the very least, the wine would alleviate the shaking, but it didn't. Images played in my mind endlessly: my father's bloody face, Barney's and Ellison's suicides, my mother's lifeless eyes staring into eternity.

This was unbearable. I finished the wine and decided to forego dinner, instead taking my remaining cash to a dilapidated area downtown, near Interstate 35, where I could usually find someone selling drugs. The night was frigid, but a handful of people still milled about, conducting their seedy business with furtive glances from dark corners and alleys. I saw several junkies and a couple of prostitutes. A few dealers hung in the shadows.

The first two I approached quickly scampered away. Crack dealers are inherently paranoid, and the substances they put into their bodies only exacerbate this quality. On any given night, I might be required to approach as many as five or six people before I finally scored, and tonight was no exception.

After the first two misses I recognized a man I had done business with a few times in the past. His features were unmistakable—matted shoulder-length hair, kinky and disarrayed, streaked with gray. His beard was equally ratty, the area around his mouth stained, particles of food clinging to the greasy hair. I always recognized him by a scar that ran down the left side of his face, disappearing into the filthy beard. He wore a thin, soiled shirt, buttoned crookedly. Stains riddled his pants, and his weathered shoes had no laces. He kept his hands in the pockets of a torn, faded corduroy coat, the collar flipped up to protect his neck from the cold.

I crossed the street and approached him cautiously.

Without smiling he said, "I ain't seen you in a while." His black eyes flitted here and there, looking for anything out of the ordinary.

"You got anything?" I tried to keep the desperation out of my voice.

"I might have sump'm for you. What you got for me?" His eyes narrowed, sweeping the street around us. He shifted from one leg to the other, trying to warm himself.

"I have this." I moved closer, pulling some bills out of my pocket, discreetly showing them to him.

He shook his head after he saw the amount. "Ain't enough."

"This is what it cost last time, asshole!"

"Well, it ain't enough now." He continued his rhythmic dance. "Prices gone up."

I reached in my other pocket and pulled out a few more bills. "Fine, prick. Take it all."

He looked at me indifferently and shook his head. "Still ain't enough."

"Fuck you," I said in a low harsh voice. "Just take the goddamn money!" I shook the bills at him.

He took a step back. "Fuck you too. I ain't sellin' nothin' at that price." He stopped dancing, his black eyes settling on me. "What else you got?"

"I have cash, motherfucker!"

A smile formed on his lips and then spread across his face. The few remaining teeth in his mouth were dark with decay. "You ever been in jail?"

"What the hell are you talking about?"

"You'd do good in the house," he said. "You got a pretty face." He let out a short cackle.

"Whatever," I said hoarsely. "Do you want the money or not? I haven't got anything else to give you."

"Yeah you do." His smile broadened again, and he started walking slowly backward.

I followed at a safe distance, watching him curiously. Alarm bells began to go off in my head, and I stopped abruptly.

He gestured toward a narrow space between two buildings behind him. "You come on in here with me, and we'll work sump'm out."

The full impact of his suggestion hit me, and I took a step back, growling with disgust. "There's no *fucking* way."

His smile grew wider still and he cackled again. "You got a nasty mouth. I like that."

"I'd rather die, you piece of shit."

He shrugged, "You say what you want, but I ain't got nothin' for you unless you give me somethin'."

"I'll get it somewhere else."

"You'll be back. Ain't nobody else out here tonight." He laughed again.

I walked away, unsure what to do next. I searched the block for another seller, but it was late, the night growing colder every minute. Only two other people were on the street now, one of whom walked away at my approach. The other actually asked *me* for some pills. I ignored her and continued to walk, wondering how I was going to get the sweet chemicals I so needed. The wine had completely worn off, and I now had a splitting headache to go along with the intolerable shaking.

Before I realized it, I had made a full circle of the block, and had come back around to the man who had refused my cash. I felt myself being pulled toward him almost involuntarily.

He watched me through the narrow slits of his eyes, and as I got closer his smile returned. "I guess you need it more than you thought. I told you you'd be back."

I took a deep breath and looked at him for a long moment. "I won't fuck you."

He laughed. "I just want to play a little, that's all. Then I'll give you your rock, and you can go do whatever you want."

I took in another deep breath, unable to believe what I was about to do. He turned and walked toward the space between the buildings, and I followed, dragging my legs forward sluggishly.

When we got to the crevice he walked inside. The passageway was about four feet wide. I moved in behind him, and he turned to face me. I leaned my back against the wall, and he ran his hand down the front of my shirt to my crotch, sucking air between his teeth lustfully. I took several more deep breaths, and suddenly I wanted very much to get out—to run quickly away from this nightmare—but my addiction was stronger, demanding that I submit.

The man unzipped my pants and slipped his hand inside. His other hand remained in his jacket pocket, and he put his face close to mine. I could smell his hot rancid breath, the staleness of his beard. He licked my neck, gripping my penis, rubbing his hand over it.

It was all I could stand. I jerked my head back violently, but before I could bolt, he produced a blade from his coat pocket, pressing the cold steel against my neck. I inhaled sharply and froze.

He grunted. "Where you think you goin', bitch?" He pushed the knife harder into my neck, continuing to touch me through my unzipped pants. His calloused hand was rough and cold, squeezing and massaging me.

Despite the seriousness of the situation, a new development now forcefully consumed my attention: when he had pulled the knife out of his coat pocket, two vials had fallen on the ground. I breathed slowly, trying not to move, my eyes transfixed by the small glass jars containing crack. He continued massaging me, breathing harder as he became aroused. He took his hand from my pants and began to rub his own crotch, and in his excitement he lowered the knife slightly. I knew if I didn't capitalize on his mistake, I would probably die.

I forced my knee into his groin and drove my leg up hard, lifting him off his feet. I grabbed the hand holding the knife, sending my other fist into his nose. The blow forced his head back hard enough that it struck the wall behind him. He fell to the ground unconscious.

I turned my entire focus to the two vials on the ground. I reached down, grabbed them, and started to run. But just as I stepped over the unconscious drug dealer's body, I stopped short and let out a horrified moan, nearly dropping the crack. Another person stood at the entrance to the crevice, blocking my exit.

All sound disappeared.

I stared at the foul, hateful black eyes of the old man, his long, greasy, gray-black hair falling about his shoulders in a tangled mess. He held his long, curved knife, slowly twisting it back and forth as it dangled at his side. "Hello, *Medicine Man.*"

I stepped back, unable to breathe, electric currents shooting through my limbs. I wanted to scream but nothing would come. My mind scrambled for an explanation, for any logical reason why this horrifying specter kept appearing in my life, but my terror precluded any rational thought.

His pale, leathery skin wrinkled grotesquely as his wicked smile stretched across his face. I took another step back, but before I could react any further, he lunged at me, throwing the long knife back above his head, its steel blade glinting in the pale fluorescent street light.

I stumbled backward and tripped over the crack dealer's body, landing hard on the ground. The old man brought the knife down at me in a sweeping arc, and I threw my arms up to block it.

But just before he drove the blade home, he disappeared—his laugh echoing, and then fading in my head.

With a hissing rush, sound returned all around me. I pushed myself shakily to my feet, shuddering violently, my fear merging with frustration. I started to cry. I couldn't understand why my mind would allow these visions to continue. The answer had to be my diminishing sanity, but somehow that explanation still didn't seem good enough. I desperately wished that, if I had to go crazy, my mind would find a gentler way to send me over the edge.

I opened my tightly clenched hand to find the vials of crack intact. If ever I had wanted to escape into the euphoric delirium of chemical intoxication, it was that moment. I watched the entrance to the crevice, wondering what would happen if I dared move.

The crack dealer next to me stirred, mumbling groggily. My breathing was so fast now that I thought I might hyperventilate. I began to feel claustrophobic. I had to get out of the passageway.

I jumped out of the crevice and walked rapidly away, looking back over my shoulder every few seconds to see if anyone was pursuing. I headed to a nearby park, where I ducked into a row of bushes. I reached into my coat pocket with a trembling hand, frantically pulling out a cheap pipe and lighter I kept there. I loaded the pipe with one of the rocks, lit it, and inhaled deeply.

I held the smoke in my lungs, never wanting to release it. The rush was immediate, numbing me, sending the night's events far away, giving me a false sense of optimism and self-confidence. As long as I felt like this, nothing bad could happen.

When I finished the first rock, I smoked the second, lying on the ground for several minutes, praying that the high would last forever, permanently killing reality—the ghosts, the voices, and especially the apparition of the old man. My prayers, however, went unanswered, and within a short time the high began to dissipate. The voices in my mind started creeping back in, clamoring for my attention more loudly with each passing instant.

I got to my feet and made my way to an alley behind some bars on Sixth Street. I crawled into a dumpster and dug through the empty bottles. The crack wore off more quickly now—*too* quickly.

The voice shouted: "You're already dead, *Medicine Man*! You're already fucking dead!" The memory of the old man came back to me, causing me to shudder violently. I thought I detected movement in my peripheral vision and I spun around, expecting to see him, but there was nothing. The lines between reality and insanity were as blurred as ever.

I tried to ignore the voices by talking to my dad and Thomas while I sifted through the bottles, searching for dregs. The now familiar flood of tears began trickling down my face. "I didn't know you were going to *die*!" My voice gurgled with despair. "I would have come with you! I didn't want to stay here by myself!"

I found a bottle, about a quarter full, lipstick streaking the rim, a cigarette butt bobbing in the liquid. I sucked the last drops from the bottle. I closed my eyes and saw my mother's dead body lying on her bed, skin bluish pale, eyes sunken in deep, dark pits. I tried to push the image out, but it wouldn't go.

I trembled harder—both from the cold and from the visions and sounds filling my head. My thoughts turned mercilessly to what I had allowed the vagrant drug dealer to do to me only a short time earlier, and then back to the petrifying memory of the old man lunging at me with his long knife, the black eyes burning above the wicked smile stretching across his face.

My fear and disgust were incalculable; I was at the breaking point. The voice shrieked, laughing maniacally. A wave of rage and fear ran through me, and before I realized what I was doing, I screamed back, "Whoever the *fuck* you are, just get it over with! *I'm waiting!*"

Up to this point, the voice had always been a vague presence, imparting its nasty messages in a general way, never using my name or specifically addressing any details of my life. At most, it seemed only distantly aware of my circumstances, and it had never responded to me.

But now it *did* answer, sending a frigid pulse through my body.

"Soon, *Medicine Man*, soon!" It erupted in laughter, like a hyena teasing its prey. The fact that it had answered me only seemed to confirm my growing fear that I was indeed breaching the limits of sanity.

I couldn't move for a moment, the panic blossoming. My heart felt like a car engine, its pistons pounding in my chest, revving higher and higher. My skin crawled and tingled. "Fuck you! Get away from me!" I fought the urge to jump from the dumpster and run as fast as I could, but then I thought, *Run from what?* The familiar metallic taste of fear rose higher in the back of my throat. *How do I run from my own head?*

The voice screamed again: "You're already dead, Medicine Man! Let's sing a fucking song!"

"Why are you doing this to me?" I sobbed, and I realized how much I sounded like Barney, sitting by himself at the table at the Cardinal, speaking to men from the future. Then, naturally, I had to see Barney blow his brains out again . . . and then *again*. I put my hands over my ears and shook my head. My eyes stretched wide, bulging as though they might pop out of their sockets. "Get out of my fucking head!"

"Oh, I don' think so, Medicine Man! Let's just sing! Cause you're already dead motherfucker!" The voice exploded again in monstrous laughter and then broke into a grinding, screeching melody.

I doubled over, my stomach contracting violently, as though my body wanted to purge itself of every substance I had ever used. Maybe the source of the voice would come out too, landing on the pile of garbage in some corporeal form, writhing, bloody and wet like the aborted fetus of a slug-demon. I could stomp it until its guts squirted out, watching it scream as it died.

The thought nauseated me, and I spewed the foamy contents of my stomach all over the inside of the dumpster. When the wave passed, I started digging through the bottles again. It was imperative I get more alcohol in my system.

The voice continued its assault, and I stopped digging. My breath came in huge sobs, causing my body to heave and shudder. Mucus oozed from my mouth and nose.

I put my hands over my ears again, shaking my head, trying to shut out the noise. I looked at the sky. "Why are you doing this? Please just take me now! I'm ready to go!"

I collapsed against the inside wall of the dumpster, sitting amidst the garbage, my chin resting on my chest. I began mumbling incoherently, and my body went limp with submission. I was more alone than ever in my life, and the decision to commit suicide now seemed better than viable—it actually appealed to me.

The choice was clear. I gave in to the fact that, if I couldn't fix what was broken this instant, I would slip over the edge. And I wasn't going to let that happen. I would rather end my life.

In a final pathetic attempt to find a way to live, barely moving my lips, I whispered, "Somebody . . . please help me."

I leaned my head back, banging it against the cold steel of the dumpster. And something caught my attention. It was a bright red rectangle, lying on top of the trash a few feet away. It looked like a notebook, and it beckoned.

How could I have missed that?, I thought. And yet, I obviously had. I squinted, but I couldn't focus through the tears, so I rubbed my eyes. I stretched forward, reaching for it, missing, reaching again. I took it in my hands and pulled it close, staring at it through my still-blurry vision. My eyes began to focus, and I could finally read the two words on its cover.

I felt as though someone had replaced every drop of my blood with ice water. I moaned, dropping the notebook like a scalding piece of metal. I backed away so quickly that I smashed into the opposite wall of the dumpster, banging my head again, painfully. I forced my eyes to focus, certain I had made a mistake.

But there was no mistake. On the cover of the notebook were the words *Douglas Cole.*

◆

I CONTINUED TO eye the notebook, trying to figure out how to handle this. Finally I jumped across the dumpster and snatched it up, clutching it in my hands, staring at my own name. My mouth hung wide as if I wanted to ask a question but couldn't find the words.

I flung the notebook open and read:

> *Douglas,*
> *What you are about to experience will be the most difficult thing you have ever faced, but if you trust me, you'll get through it.*

You aren't crazy. I know about the voice and the apparition, and you aren't causing them. You can stop all of it if you want to, but you have to have faith in what you're about to read.

What follows are my rules, and if you violate them even once, you'll never hear from me again.

You will never lie to me, you will never tell a soul anything that passes between us, and you will agree never to use drugs or alcohol again. If you can do what I've asked, then get out of the dumpster. Look toward the freeway and you'll see a cab. The driver knows where to take you.

Please leave this notebook where you found it.

Jefferson

My brain simply wouldn't accept what I read.

The voice in my head screamed, "You're a dead cunt!" It howled with wicked laughter again, and I let out another moan. I reread the words in the notebook.

If you trust me, you'll get through it.

The voice screamed, "Let's dance, Medicine Man! You're a dead whore!" It made a wet, slippery noise in my head, the way a human organ might sound it were thrown on a cement floor. I resisted it with every ounce of concentration.

I crawled out of the dumpster and turned my eyes in the direction of the freeway. The cab was there, but I blinked twice to be sure I wasn't imagining it. I began to walk toward it. I picked up my pace, and when I reached it, I got in quickly. The driver didn't say a word, putting the car in gear and driving away. I struggled to maintain consciousness.

I slumped in the back seat, again putting my hands on my ears and shaking my head. We drove for about ten minutes, but I got disoriented as we weaved through several neighborhoods. Finally the cab came to a stop in front of a small house. It took me a moment to register that the ride was over. "Where are we?"

"Rosedale," the driver said.

"Where's that?"

"Near the blind school. You're supposed to go there." He pointed at the small house.

"Who told you to do this?"

"Dispatch sent me instructions to wait for you where I picked you up and take you here. You're supposed to go to the front door." He stared at me, clearly a little disgusted. "You okay, man?"

"I . . . I can't pay you."

"It's already paid for."

I looked at him, confused, and I nodded slowly. I crawled from the car, shut the door, and the cab rounded the corner and disappeared. The voice continued its onslaught, pounding my mind like waves of cannon fire. "It's time to die, you putrid little cunt! Not much time left now!"

I shivered and turned to face the small house, but the night was too dark for me to see many details. A white picket fence skirted the yard, interrupted by an ornate, gated trellis. I went through it and followed the path toward the front door, hesitantly climbing two steps. I knocked softly and waited, but there was no response. I held my finger up to the doorbell, but hesitated. Then I pushed the button. I had no choice.

I heard footsteps and a light came on. The door swung slowly inward and my head lolled, my vision blurring as I tried to maintain my balance. My eyes focused on the person standing in front of me, and for a second I thought it was Jack. I shook my head to make sure I wasn't dreaming. Then I realized it *was* Jack—just another piece of all the mystery surrounding this night.

His eyes grew wide with disbelief. "Oh, Jesus, kid!" He grabbed me, holding me to his chest.

"Jack? How . . .?" I tried to form one of the many questions in my mind, but I couldn't speak.

"What have you done to yourself?" His voice cracked. He rubbed the side of my head as he held me. I had never seen him so distressed, and of all the strange and twisted events that night, Jack's reaction drove home the unequivocal reality of what my life had become.

He put an arm around me, supporting me as he tried to lead me through the door. I took two steps and collapsed.

RESTORATION

I would like to beg you . . . as well as I can, to have patience with every-
thing unresolved in your heart and try to love the questions themselves
as if they were locked rooms or books written in a very foreign language.
Don't search for the answers, which could not be given to you now, because
you would not be able to live them. And the point is, to live everything.
Live the questions now. Perhaps then, someday far in the future, you will
gradually, without even noticing it, live your way into the answer . . .

—RAINER MARIA RILKE

January, Year Nineteen

MY VISION CLEARED. Jack was sitting in a chair across from me in what was obviously a hospital room. He looked up from a book he was reading. "How do you feel, kid?"

Although my head was pounding, for a moment I thought I was back in Durango. My next thought was that I wanted a drink. I sat up and everything came back, a deluge of sewage in my mind—all the putrid memories that shouldn't have been real. And yet somehow I knew they were.

I raised a hand and tried to make it stop trembling, but it was no use.

"Take it easy," Jack said.

Nothing made sense. My stomach heaved, and I gagged a couple of times before I threw up on the floor. It wasn't much; I obviously hadn't eaten for some time.

"Shit. Hold on, I'll get somebody." Jack walked out the only door in the room and came back with two nurses—a man and a woman. The male nurse held an armful of towels and used them to clean the mess on the floor.

The woman came to my side and asked, "How do you feel?"

"Not very good."

"No, I guess you don't," she said, turning to Jack. "He'll be fine. The medicines we gave him might make him nauseous for a while. I'll let you spend some time with him." She gave Jack a look that said, *as we discussed*, and then she turned to me again, "I'll be back in a little while to check on you." She smiled warmly, and both nurses left the room.

"Where am I, Jack?"

"Seton Hospital."

"How long was I asleep?"

"About two days."

I gazed vacantly out the window. "What day is it?"

"Friday."

"No. I mean what's the date?"

He gave me a compassionate expression and told me.

I rubbed my hands up and down my face. "Why are you here?"

"I got a letter that said you might be in trouble—"

"A letter? From who?"

"Jefferson Stone. Who is he?"

I snapped my head around. "Jefferson? Do you know him? Is he here?" The questions forming in my mind seemed infinite.

Jack shook his head. "I just got a letter, that's all."

"Where is it? What did it say?"

"I left it in Durango, but it scared me enough to get on a plane the next morning."

"You came here because of a letter from someone you don't know?"

"Douglas, I haven't heard from you in ages. I tried to call, but your number was disconnected. What the hell happened to you?"

I let a long breath of air hiss between my teeth and looked out the window. I was almost certain I had never told Jefferson anything about Jack. I scoured my memory, scrambling to find some explanation for what might have led Jefferson to Jack.

Jack walked to the bed and sat beside me. "It's okay, kid. Slow down. Let's take this one step at a time."

"How did you know where I was?"

"This guy . . . Jefferson. He sent me the address, with a key."

I began to feel dizzy. *Why is Jefferson doing this? How did he find me? How does he know who Jack is?* I started to cry.

"Are you in trouble, kid?"

"I don't know . . ." I shook my head. "I don't *know*! What's happening to me?"

Jack put his hand on my shoulder and squeezed it gently. "It's all right. I'm here now."

I tried to regain my composure. "Who's going to pay for all this?" I waved my hand around the hospital room. "I can't just let you—"

He shook his head, cutting me off. "Your insurance company. I got your wallet off the kitchen counter."

I looked at Jack, more confused than ever. I hadn't had a wallet in months, and I certainly hadn't been spending my money on health insurance.

He pointed to the table beside the bed. "It's there, with your keys."

"Keys?" I picked them up, examining them. They were mine. "Did you drive me to the hospital?"

"Yeah. I used your car. I didn't think you'd mind."

I picked up my wallet and examined the contents. It contained two credit cards, an insurance card, my driver's license, and a fair sum of cash.

If I had been scared before, now I was petrified. I had known Jefferson less than a year, but I had never been to his house. We had few mutual friends. In fact, when I thought about it, I was surprised by how little I knew about him—and how little he should have known about me. But he obviously knew a lot more than he had ever let on, and now it looked like he was trying to take over my life.

I could think of no real reason why I should trust Jefferson. How could any of this be happening? I felt panic creeping up on me. But then a more rational part of my mind took control and I calmed down enough to consider everything—especially the notebook containing his letter. As implausible as it was—as much as my mind refused to believe he could have known enough about me to make this happen—surely I had to at least consider the benefits of this path, even if the circumstances were disturbing.

I shuddered, indecision tearing at me, and I forced myself to relax a little more. *He's giving me a chance to change my life, even if he's scaring the hell out of me to do it. It would be stupid not to try.* Regardless of Jefferson's motives, he didn't seem to be a bad person—I had a wallet with cash, my car had been returned to me, and I was being well cared for in a hospital.

"I want a drink so bad, Jack," I said.

"Well, you can't have one." He withdrew an envelope from the pocket of his jacket, handed it to me, and sat on the bed. My name was typed on the front. Jack nodded at it. "That was at the house when I got there. It was sealed so I didn't open it."

I looked uncertainly at him, and then at the envelope. And suddenly I wanted to throw it out the window, or to burn it—anything to forget all about it, to return to the streets and continue my journey to self-destruction. But I knew I had no choice; as much as I ached to run, I had made my decision. My course was set. I would have to open the letter to find any clues to Jefferson's motives. I needed to be alone for this.

I said to Jack, "Do you think you could find me something to eat?"

He jumped up from the bed, "Shit, you must be starving! There's a snack bar downstairs. I'll be back in a few minutes." He walked toward the door and turned as he was stepping into the hallway, flashing me the warm smile I had missed so much. "Try not to go anywhere while I'm gone."

I gave him a weak smile in return. "Thanks, Jack."

The door closed, and I turned the envelope for a while. Finally I took a deep breath, broke the seal, and pulled out a typed letter.

> *Douglas,*
>
> *I wish I could be with you now, but that's impossible. I know you're con-fused and I'm sure you have many questions. I can't blame you. But I hope this letter will at least allow me to win some of your trust. If the events of the past few days aren't enough to convince you of my ability to help you, I want to remove any remaining doubt, so I'll get right to the point. What I'm about to suggest will sound strange, but bear with me.*
>
> *Please think of an object that will fit in your pocket. Once you have it in your mind, turn to the next page of this letter.*

I reread the page. *Well, he's right about one thing: all of this is completely fucking strange.* But what did I have to lose? I needed answers, and Jefferson's little game wasn't any more insane than anything else that had happened recently.

The first image that came into my mind was a black pawn, which seemed fit-ting. I slowly flipped to the next page of the letter.

> *Once you've thought of the object, please open the drawer of the bed stand to your left.*

I looked at the drawer, and suddenly it seemed like the only object in the room. My breathing became shallow and my heart beat a little faster. Then I shook my head. "This is stupid." I leaned over and slid the drawer open.

I breathed in sharply and froze, unable even to blink. My mind refused to accept what I saw.

In the center of the drawer stood a solitary black pawn.

I barely suppressed a new wave of nausea. I picked up the pawn with trembling hands and stared at it for a second before it slipped from my fingers and fell to the floor. He couldn't have known. *This isn't happening.*

But it was happening. I picked up Jefferson's letter and tried to hold it steady.

> *It has to be this way, Douglas. This process will require a great deal of trust on your part, but if you are patient, you will have all the answers in*

time. As frightened as you are, it's crucial that you know how much our lives depend on the seriousness with which you take what you've just seen.

I plan to help you through the next few years as much as I can, and in return I want you to help me. The house where the cab dropped you off is mine, and you are welcome to stay there as long as you like. You'll find a library full of books there. I want you to read them. Absorb as much as you can.

I've opened an account for you at the bank across the street from the hospital, and all the relevant information is at the house. I will replenish that account every month. I have covered your debt at the brokerage. Needless to say, I expect you to stay away from futures.

There will be a lot of unanswered questions from here on, but I won't be able to address them, so I encourage you to exploit the resources I'm giving you. The answers are there.

You will find some of our old discussions useful. The doors are open. I want you to use what you've learned.

Good luck, and please know that I am near.

Jefferson

I stared at the trembling pages, uncertain how to react. The absurdity of it might have made me laugh under different circumstances, but there was nothing funny about what was happening to me now.

Why did Jefferson suddenly want to help a junkie whom he knew casually at best? He had my car and my driver's license. *And the pawn . . .*

The only thing that seemed certain was that I was incapable of handling the panic building inside of me, a roiling storm ready to unleash its wrath, destroying everything in its path. My mind had had enough. I needed a drink or some coke—anything.

The door opened and I jumped, letting out a small yelp, dropping the letter in my lap. Jack came in the room, and tears started to roll down my cheeks. He sat down on the bed with me again. "Hey, what happened? It's okay, kid! Take it easy. What did the letter say?"

I pulled the sheets of paper close to my chest and started folding them. "Nothing . . . nothing. He just . . . I don't want to talk about it."

Jack gave me a frustrated, almost angry look and sighed. "Here, I got you these." He unscrewed the cap of an orange juice bottle and handed it to me, along with a doughnut. "Sorry it took so long." He pursed his lips, rolling his eyes. "There was this . . . *nurse* on the elevator, and she sort of decided to give me a lecture about bringing food to patients."

I wiped the tears away and I stared at him, part of me not in the mood for his stupid sense of humor, part of me craving it desperately. "And . . .?"

"*And* I threatened to kick her big fat ass. So she shut up."

I reached for the doughnut and took a bite. "I'm sure it happened just like that," I said, spitting crumbs.

"Don't speak with your mouth full, child." He watched me take another bite and gave me an exasperated look as I finished chewing. "So you want to tell me what the letter says?"

"Nothing. It's just a long speech about how Jefferson wants to help me through this."

Jack eyed me suspiciously. "What do you mean he wants to help you through this?"

"I guess he's going to give me some money and stuff."

"Who is this guy, Douglas?"

"I don't know, just a friend I met at a coffee shop."

"Why does a friend from a coffee shop want to help you?" Jack said. "And how did he find me? How did he find you, for that matter?"

"I don't know!" I felt like I was about to cry again, so I took a deep breath. "Last year, Jefferson and I spent a lot of time together playing chess. I don't know what's going on, but I might be dead now if it wasn't for him."

He nodded slowly, still eyeing me sternly. "When did all this start, kid?"

"July?" I held up my hand, which was still shaking. "I want a drink so bad."

"They told me they have some medicine that will help you with that. They want to move you to their treatment program and I think we should do it."

"We?"

He looked at me sideways, smiling a little. "I didn't come here just to say hello, you little bastard."

"Jack, you don't have to stay—"

"No, no. You aren't going to get rid of me that easily. Hell, I might just move back here! I forgot how much I missed Austin!"

"What about work?"

He let out an exasperated sigh. "I'm on vacation. Why are you asking so many goddamn questions?"

The confluence of so many fateful events in the last few days seemed more than just convenient. Jefferson's sleight of hand demanded an enormous leap of faith, raising uncountable questions about the reliability of my perception of reality itself. Compared to that, Jack's sudden and fortuitous appearance seemed trivial. But in some deep recess of my mind, another vague thought was beginning to germinate, tapping softly on the door to my awareness, whispering that I should yet again look more closely at the things unfolding around me.

Something just wasn't right. Somehow there was more to this than either Jefferson or Jack was letting me see. I searched Jack's eyes for a moment, but despite the sleep I had gotten, I was still deeply exhausted, and I just didn't have the energy to pursue these thoughts. My future seemed like a crapshoot at best, so I forced aside my misgivings, deciding not to look too hard. Jack was here, and that was all that mattered. The questions could wait.

He smiled. "Why don't you tell me what happened?"

I settled in the bed and spent the next hour recounting the last year and a half. I left out the details I couldn't explain: the voice, the apparition of the old man, the red notebook in the dumpster, the murders in the alley. The irrationality of it all weighed heavily enough on me, and I didn't need Jack to think I was crazy on top of everything else.

He waited patiently for me to finish my story and then said, "So the house where I found you, that's Jefferson's place?"

I nodded. "In the letter he said we can stay there for a while."

"And where is he? It didn't look like anyone's lived there for a while."

"Jefferson had to go out of town just before I . . . He didn't say when he'd be back."

Jack looked more wary than ever. "Are you sure this guy is okay?"

"I think so, Jack." I was glad that he was at least trying to accept the story.

He smiled. "Well, the important thing is that you're safe now. If this guy wants to help you, I'll play along."

I nodded and smiled.

Jack started smacking his gum aggressively. "And if he turns out to be a pedophile, then I'll just have to work him over."

———————◆———————

THE NEXT MONTH was the hardest of my life. The clarity was blinding, like walking from a cave into bright sunlight, every moment a staccato burst of anxiety rushing at me from every direction. It had been so long since I had known reality's cold edge. Drugs had been the glue that had held me together through my most formative years, and even my recovery from the deaths of Thomas and Dad paled in comparison to the hell I endured purging the poisonous substances that had controlled my body for so long.

My doctors moved me to a treatment center. They gave me medicines meant to stave off the intense cravings, which helped precious little. My body literally ached for the chemicals it had so suddenly and brutally been deprived of, but my resolve was intact. I never wanted to use again.

The voice stopped bombarding my mind when I started recovery. The gruesome images of the ghosts were still around, but their power was diminishing, and the relief was immeasurable—a bright spot in the blackness. If they had stayed, I don't think I could have made it.

Consciousness meant facing pain, so once sleep finally came I took as much as I could get. But it was always fitful, and when it wouldn't come at all, there were few activities in the hospital able to divert my attention from the dependencies. I asked Jack to bring books from the house, but I could only read so much before I grew restless. Television was more annoying than entertaining, and when there was nothing left to pull me from the pain of withdrawal, I spiraled into hell. I screamed at orderlies, nurses, doctors, or anyone else within range. Loud noises made me jump like a timid cat, sending me into fits of rage. I threw things at the walls or the television.

I wanted to play my cello almost as much as I wanted drugs and booze, and it probably would have made the process easier, but I never mentioned it to anyone—especially not Jack. My remorse was too great. Sometimes, I just rocked back and forth on my bed, usually thinking about Elizabeth, missing her so much. At these moments, I desperately needed to play my music, but there was nothing to be done about it. The thought of trying to replace the cello I had sold to the pawnshop was inconceivable, so I endured the pain without it.

Jack stayed with me almost night and day, tolerating my irritability—even my blackest moods couldn't drive him away. His patience seemed limitless as he took my attacks in stride, allowing me to rant to my heart's content. "We always hurt the ones we love, Douglas, and I'm happy to know you love me."

"I don't love you Jack. You're an asshole."

I told him about the ghosts and he listened closely. When I got to the edge, certain I was going to lose my mind—if I hadn't already—Jack held me as he had when I was boy, the way he did the day the car almost ran me down.

After a month in treatment, I tried to call Jefferson's old number, but I only got a recording: "The number you dialed has been disconnected or is no longer in service . . ." I slammed the phone down and fought the urge to scream. I wanted so badly to see him, mostly so I could yell at him and force some answers. Another part of me, however, ached just to talk to him over a few games. But I heard nothing after his letter, so I progressed without him, sometimes frustrated and angry, other times simply confused, wondering why anyone would go to such lengths to help me.

No matter how determined I was to get through my recovery intact, I had no illusions about the probability of relapse. Statistically, I was almost certain to use again. I trembled constantly, sweat seeping from my emaciated body in defiance of the hospital's cool temperature. The perspiration soaked my long hair, which clung annoyingly to my head. Finally, I asked Jack to cut it.

The next day he arrived with a pair of shears. Holding them up, he said, "I hate to chop those pretty dark curls. They contrast so beautifully with your eyes. Do you really want to look like a goddamn convict?"

"Just do it."

I watched the matted knots fall to the floor in huge clumps, and I felt something shift inside. It was almost as though all the poisons I had pushed into my body had grown out with my hair, and were now drifting harmlessly to the floor. For an instant, I felt light, nearly confident, and for the first time in years, I thought maybe—just maybe—I might have a chance.

Early Spring, Year Nineteen

ONE DAY JACK came into my room carrying a case. His face was a mask of sheer stupidity, and if I hadn't known him, I would have thought he was retarded. He had a stupid expression on his face and looked like some sort of idiotic cartoon character. "I brought you a surprise!" he hooted in a high-pitched voice. He hung on the last syllable, dividing it into two tones, clearly trying to annoy me as much as possible.

It worked.

"There's not much that's going to brighten my day, Jack. Sorry."

"Oh, I think this might help a little," he said with the same vexing tone, giving me a grotesquely goofy grin that further fueled my annoyance. He set the case down on the table across from my bed, opened it, unfurled a chessboard, and removed a clock.

I sighed. "I don't really feel like—"

"Give me a goddamn break. When did you ever not feel like playing chess?"

Not once had I ever seen Jack show an interest in chess. I eyed the board and the clock, both of which looked like they had seen some use. "Where'd you get those?"

"They're mine."

"You don't even know the fucking rules, Jack."

He stuck his hip out dramatically and rested his hand on it. "I've played a few times."

It was obvious he was only trying to cheer me up. "Really, I'm not in the mood. No offense."

"Indulge me, you little prick. I'm not that fucking bad." He stood up and fished around in his front pockets, smacking his gum loudly. Finally he found a quarter and tossed it on the chessboard. "Here. If you win you can have that."

"Oh, well, that just changes everything, doesn't it?" I glared at him for a moment. Finally I slid off my bed with another sigh and sat down at the table. I mixed up two pawns, offering Jack my closed fists.

"What?" he said.

"Choose a hand."

"Oh!" He giggled and pointed at the right one, winning the black pieces.

I pushed his quarter to the side of the board. "Can we play with the clock?"

"Sure."

"And after I beat you, can we quit?"

He scowled. "Fine. One game, you little bastard." He started to set up his pieces, but stopped and looked at me. "You have a crappy attitude, you know that?"

I ignored him and grabbed the clock. "I'll give you ten minutes, and I'll take five."

"Whatever makes you happy."

We arranged the pieces, and Jack looked intently at the board for a moment. "Now remind me again . . . the pawns move . . . forward?"

"Have you ever played before, Jack?"

"Yes! Now just remind me! *God!*"

I gnashed my teeth. "You don't have to do this for me—*really.*"

"Will you just remind me, please?" His mouth hung open in an exaggerated display of stupidity, the worn-out wad of gum hanging between his teeth.

I sighed heavily and explained briefly how pawns move.

"*Thank* you!" His expression became serious. He leaned forward and put one arm on each side of the board, clenching his fists and knitting his brow. He wiggled his butt in his chair and set himself to the task of playing chess. Then he just stared at the board.

After a moment I said, "Jack, I'm white. I move first."

He looked confused. "Right." He nodded his head enthusiastically. "Go ahead and move. I'm waiting for you." He straightened himself and wiggled his butt in the chair again, looking at the board with the same serious expression.

"Goddamn it, Jack! I can't move until you hit your clock."

"Oh!" he said, giggling again. Jack inexpertly hit his side of the double-faced clock and my timer began to tick.

I moved my queen's pawn two spaces and hit the button on my side. He moved a pawn and hit his own button. I moved another pawn.

The game progressed differently than I expected. Jack moved again, quickly taking my bishop. *Too quickly*, I thought. I studied the board, but I had no response. I was stunned to be down a piece. "Jack, you've played a few times, haven't you?" I moved a knight and hit my clock.

"Once. Or maybe twice?" He pushed a pawn.

I moved again, but as soon as I did, I winced, realizing that I had made a costly mistake. Jack's bishop had my king. The game was over.

"Whoops!" he said entirely too dramatically, slowly moving his bishop across the board, knocking down my king. He stopped the clocks. "You lose! Great game!" He snatched the quarter from the side of the board. "You owe me twenty-five cents. And I'll be expecting a reasonable amount of interest with that, thanks." He started to put the pieces in the case.

"What are you doing?"

He looked puzzled. "I'm leaving. You said you only wanted to play one game."

"You're not leaving."

"But I thought . . ." His face held the dullest expression yet.

"Jack, Set them up." I smiled, in spite of myself.

"Okay, but you *said* you only wanted to play one game. And you owe me a quarter. Plus interest."

"I don't have any change. Anyway, Dad taught me never to bet. Just set up the fucking pieces."

"I'll forget the interest today, but next time you better be prepared."

I grabbed the clock to reset it.

"Can I have ten minutes again?" Jack asked.

I ignored the taunt, this time setting both clocks for five minutes.

He beat me even more quickly in the second game. He took the third game, too. I grew increasingly disgusted, but refused to acknowledge that Jack was unleashing some hidden talent on me. I convinced myself it was a combination of my poor condition and Jack's beginner's luck. After his eighth straight victory, however, I had no choice but to reject the theory. "You goddamn liar. I never knew you were any good at chess."

"Neither did I, until today." He scratched his head, looking troubled, slowly chewing his gum. "This is only the second time I ever played. Or is it the third?"

"Bullshit. Why didn't you ever play in Durango?"

Jack shrugged innocently. I tried to look at him with disgust, but the only thing I felt was respect. I shook my head, reached into my wallet, and handed him two dollars.

Jack and I played every day for the rest of my rehabilitation, and even though I never beat him, our games were more therapeutic than anything the doctors gave me. I always made sure to have an ample supply of quarters on hand, and Jack never hesitated to take them away from me. It was a small price to pay; the games were the perfect distraction.

I made strong progress in the hospital and the cravings diminished after about six weeks. But my therapists warned me they would never disappear completely, and I believed it.

After seven weeks, I was released to Jack's care. He helped me pack my things, and a nurse escorted me out of the hospital in a wheelchair. I thought I would be glad to leave, but I felt only fear. Rehab had provided me with a structured environment where I could fight my addictions, but once I left, I was on my own.

Jack and I drove north through Austin, toward the house where we had been reunited, but Jack sped past the turn that led to Jefferson's house, continuing to the next block instead. He turned right, drove another few blocks, and pulled into the driveway of a small house.

"What are you doing?" I said.

"What do you mean?"

"Where are we?"

"This is my house," he said.

"No it's not."

"Yes it is."

"Stop it, Jack. What's going on?"

"I told you, I missed Austin." He leaned toward me and whispered, "The women here make my pants itch."

"This probably isn't the best time to fuck with me."

"I'm not fucking with you."

"Just take me home."

"What? You don't believe me?"

"No I don't, and you're pissing me off, so let's go. We both know you can't move to Austin."

He leaned his head back and stared at the car's ceiling in mock frustration. "Well, first, I can do anything I want. Secondly, I *am* moving to Austin. I grew up here and I probably know ten times more about this place than you do. Thirdly, you're an arrogant little bastard. I'm not moving here because of you. I already told you, it's about the women."

"You're serious."

"I'm always serious about women."

"Jack!"

"Yes, I'm serious, damn it."

I looked at him for another second, scratching my forehead. "What are you going to do here?"

"Work on computers, you moron. What else would I do?"

"But you have to find a job—"

"I've already got one, and they're paying me twice what I made in Durango. Do you think you can ask me some tough questions now?"

"But . . . Why are you doing this?"

"What do you mean? I already told you."

"Jack, really!"

Jack leaned his forehead against the steering wheel for a moment and then looked at me, smiling. "Because I'm going to help you get through this."

Nothing could have made me happier. For the first time in months, I didn't feel alone. But in spite of my excitement I still couldn't escape the nagging thought in the back of my mind. As hard as I tried to push it aside, it reminded me again that things seemed too convenient.

Summer, Year Twenty

I SPENT MOST of the next few months reading and playing chess with Jack, distracting myself as much as possible from the cravings that tore at me. I was less anxious about the circumstances of my salvation, but I still ached to understand my role in Jefferson's game. I simply couldn't figure out why he had chosen me as the beneficiary of such a comfortable lifestyle.

My skepticism gnawed at me. Without offering any clues, Jefferson had asked for my help, which seemed ridiculous. After all, the man could read minds—or so it seemed. What could I possibly do for him? It made me uncomfortable, even angry at times, and more than once I fought the urge to run as far away as I could, to return to my life on the streets. The cravings exacerbated my uncertainty, snapping at me like animals competing for the last vestiges of meat on a carcass.

But even at the worst of times, reason eventually returned, reminding me that this was going to be a difficult journey, and that I needed all the help I could get if I really wanted to stay straight. As long as Jefferson's generosity continued with no uncomfortable demands or repercussions, I saw no reason not to stay. Anyway, Jack wasn't going to let me far out of his sight, and I knew I could always turn to him if things got out of control.

The first time I saw the thousands of books lining the shelves in Jefferson's small house, my mouth nearly fell open. They covered almost every available square foot of wall space, with a range of material more vast than I would have thought possible: Eastern and Western philosophies, drugs and psychology, quantum mechanics, economics, mathematics—a staggering array of disciplines. Even the task of where to begin seemed daunting, and I wasn't sure how Jefferson expected me to scratch the surface.

Once I finally did get started, however, I couldn't stop, the hours tearing by as I slipped from subject to subject, drawn seductively to each new discovery. The books seemed to melt together, one leading to another, the connections elegant and illuminating. Reading had always been dear to me, and now Jefferson had provided me with a house full of books so engrossing that the authors might have written them just for me.

It comforted me each morning to wake up knowing I had the entire day to prowl the shelves from floor to ceiling, climbing ladders or standing on chairs and tables, stretching my limbs in search of the next discovery, immersed in an intellectual sea. I stacked books in every room, on every table, making notes on scraps of paper, which soon littered the tiny house.

I was especially drawn to books on finance and economics, which I suppose was not surprising, considering my love affair with futures. Part of me wanted to understand where I had gone wrong, but at first, the material only confused and frustrated me.

The theories were alien; the authors condemned any type of short-term speculation and trading—most notably, futures trading. I disagreed vehemently with their assumptions, and more than once I put the books down in frustration, only to return to them after I reminded myself I had gone broke clinging to the ideas these men and women were warning against. Maybe it was time to reconsider my perspective.

My frustration soon gave way to the first rays of understanding. My failure had resulted from my singular focus on the movements of futures contracts, rather than understanding the meaning of the underlying instruments and assets they actually represented. Trading commodities had been like playing video games, and while it jibed with getting high, I now began to realize that what I had been doing was nothing more than a technological foray into the mystery of human action. But predicting the chaotic whims of human beings is as fruitless as trying to predict the precise path of a hurricane.

Now I slowly began to perceive the distinction between true wealth creation and the folly of speculation. I started seeing companies as whole entities rather than merely as sheets of paper called "stocks." Once the concept took hold it was natural, and I realized that I had been relying on mere surface-level knowledge when I was trading.

These ideas started to remind me of the lessons my father—and later Jefferson—had taught me about successful chess strategies: if a player focuses too much, his game will suffer and he will lose. But if he understands the game as a whole, it becomes effortless. I had always focused on the minutia in everything I did, but the few times in my life when I had been able to step back, I had been able to achieve, however briefly, a new level of understanding of the whole of the relationships *among* the minutiae. This was the type of awareness I needed to pursue.

I began to realize that my mistakes might not be as catastrophic as I had believed. I started to find value in my failures—not merely as a trader, but as a human being—deriving a new understanding of my life, realizing that my naïveté and capriciousness hadn't been wholly bad. From the ashes of my humiliation, I discovered a blessing: my ruin was a beacon, guiding me away from future errors. The issue was no longer what I should do with my knowledge. Instead I now saw that any future success I might have would hinge on what I *shouldn't* do.

I soaked up everything I could about successful investors. I recognized that their achievements came not from compulsive management, but from passivity and nonintervention—the balance and equanimity with which they almost universally lived their entire lives. This was the lesson I needed to learn, although it seemed a strange context to discover it in.

I began to embrace the idea that successful wealth creation requires a strong foundation and hard work, but likewise I saw that there is also a time when the foundation is completed, and growth must begin. Once the garden is planted, it must be given the opportunity to flourish unhindered.

Esoterica and complexity had given way to consistency and simplicity, luring me back. But this time I had a new strategy. I saved every dime I could. I stopped eating out and bought my clothes at secondhand stores. I budgeted in every possible way, and soon I had saved enough money from Jefferson's stipend to open a brokerage account.

Then I hesitated. The new philosophies I had adopted were as different from speculation as night is from day, but I wanted to make sure I wasn't violating Jefferson's faith. He had, of course, implicitly pointed me to the books that had brought me to this juncture, so I wasn't too worried about it, but I still wanted to be careful.

My defeat as a speculator had smashed my self-confidence. I had a deep new respect for markets and their ability to annihilate wealth. But there was another factor behind my hesitation: I couldn't find any bargains. Stock prices were too high, and if I had learned anything from my mistakes, it was that success resulted from patience and caution, not from blindly jumping at the first opportunity. If I resisted the imperative to act prematurely, the time to strike would be obvious. Until then, I would hold on to my accumulating cash. I could wait.

I still thought about Elizabeth a lot. Her face haunted me, the pain clawing fiercely at my heart. I missed her so much, and I wondered where she was, what she was doing, and if she was happy. More than anything, I wondered if she had met someone new, but I knew I couldn't pursue that knowledge; it wasn't my business. She had no reason to forgive me for the things I had done, and I would never ask that from her. So I endured the ache, distracting myself with the world of discoveries at my fingertips, comforted by the fact that the pain became less severe with each new day.

One afternoon, almost a year after my release from the hospital, I sat in the backyard reading quietly when something caused me to raise my eyes. I looked around for a moment, and then leaned my head back, taking a deep breath, suddenly aware that I wanted nothing—not drugs, liquor, or any other of the distractions that had conspired to destroy me. I basked in a state of serenity, cognizant of a new thought brightening in my mind the way the darkness slowly melts into dawn.

For the first time in my life, I finally understood the true meaning of patience. The adjustment had been so subtle I hadn't been conscious of it until this moment, but I recognized it nonetheless. This was the serenity that Jefferson had tried so hard to make me understand.

I smiled a little. Things had finally begun to change.

Early Spring, Year Twenty

I STILL THOUGHT about Jefferson a lot, and beyond the immediate and most troubling questions there was something subtler—something about how he had brought Jack back into my life—that still ate at me. The niggling suspicion persisted that I had missed something important, and while I didn't ignore the feeling completely, neither did I yet feel comfortable confronting Jack.

Sometimes I discreetly tried to move our conversations in a direction that might lead to a few answers, but Jack always became evasive, usually turning into a total clown. I just let it pass; the more I thought about it, the more ridiculous a conspiracy seemed. I knew I was being paranoid—I had more important things on my mind than trying to uncover something that might not even exist in the first place. And after all, regardless of my misgivings, I *was* elated to have Jack with me in Austin.

He seemed genuinely interested not only in my recovery, but also in the subjects I studied. He asked pointed questions about everything, which often led to heated discussions in the middle of chess games, during which he delicately—and sometimes not so delicately—led me to even more discoveries.

Like any great mentor, he pushed me harder than I would have pushed myself. He helped me find strength I didn't know I had, as well as the courage to do the one thing I never believed would have been possible.

"Why don't you go with me to that goddamn coffee shop?" he said one day over a chess game at his house. "Hell, you talk about the place all the time. I know you miss it."

"I don't want to go back. Forget it."

"You know what they say. When you fall off a horse…" He raised his eyebrows.

"Could you use a more tired cliché, please?"

"You really have a shitty attitude." He glanced at the board. "Hey, looky here! Checkmate!" he said, snatching my quarter from the table.

Jack, of course, chiseled away at me, and eventually I relented, agreeing to go back to the Cardinal, if only once, to face some of the demons that had fought so long to bring me down. He reminded me he would be with me for support, and he assured me that, if I couldn't handle it, we would just leave.

When we walked in the door, my eyes moved immediately to the spot where Barney had shot himself. A painting hung over the place where his brains had hit the wall, and I wondered if the stain was still there. The whole scene went through my mind again and I winced, turning away. "Can we leave?"

Jack looked at me sympathetically. "This place is part of you, kid. I guarantee you can put it behind you, if you want to."

I looked at him for a long moment and then reluctantly agreed to stay and play a few games.

Once I sat down and got into a game, I felt a little less anxious, and over the next couple of hours, a few of the regulars said hello to me, commenting that they hadn't seen me for a while, asking how I had been. It was good to see them.

Jack convinced me to come back the next night, and the next few nights after that too. Each time was a little easier, and within about a week I was relatively comfortable. Barney's ghost never completely left me, but I learned to live with it.

The Cardinal was important to me. It was home.

———————◆———————

ONE NIGHT WE were at the coffee shop, in the middle of our fifth game—the previous four of which I had lost—again. I might have had more success if Jack hadn't been grinding at my nerves all night with his nonstop prattle.

Finally I had had enough. "If you don't stop acting like a jackass, I'm going home."

"Am I annoying you?" he asked.

"Just quit running your fucking mouth."

He looked confused. "I don't know if that's possible."

"It's not, but why don't you try anyway."

"What say we talk about you for a while?" he said.

"Look, just shut up."

"Hmmmmm . . . let's see. What facet of Douglas's complex life should we talk about? Oh, I know! How are things going with this . . . *Jefferson* person?"

"Jack, what's your fucking problem?"

"I've seen some of the crap in that library at your house, and I think this weirdo has a master plan for you. I think he's trying to induct you into a sex ring."

"You don't know shit. Jefferson has ten times the integrity you'll ever have. If you knew anything about him, you wouldn't say that, so just leave it alone."

"Whatever. I think he's a pedophile. He probably just wants to tickle your mud flap." He casually moved his rook and said, "By the way, checkmate." He took my quarter from the board and leaned close, narrowing his eyes and whispering, "Has he ever touched you?"

I felt a burst of anger, but I choked it back, refusing steadfastly to satisfy Jack's primary mission in life, which was to get a reaction from me whenever possible. There was no way I was going to dignify his insinuation with an argument. "That's it. I'm going home."

"Okay, okay. I'm sorry." He laughed a little. "I'm just giving you a little shit. Don't be so goddamn sensitive."

"It's hard enough to do this without you fucking with me all the time, Jack."

"Well, I don't know why you're reading all that stuff anyway."

I still didn't want to tell Jack about Jefferson's letter so I said, "I just need to focus—it helps me stay strong." I hunched in my chair. "But I've read so much of the stuff in that house, and it seems like the more I learn the harder it is."

"That's the way everything is, kid: it gets harder before it gets easier. Look, let me buy you some dinner. How does that sound?"

I looked at him doubtfully. "You promise not to run your goddamn mouth?"

He put his hand over his heart. "I give you my solemn oath."

As we were leaving, my eyes were drawn to two men in front of me right outside the Cardinal. I stopped walking. One of the men was a drag worm, sitting against a piece of railing on the sidewalk, his head hanging low. The other was a well-dressed, balding man in his thirties, standing over the worm, speaking harshly. "If you don't want to hear it, then don't sit out here and beg for goddamn money."

"Fuck off, asshole." The worm's tone was pathetic and meek.

"Why'd you ask, huh?" the balding man said. He started nudging the worm with his foot. "Why'd you ask, huh? Just answer the question, you fucking rat."

A few people had gathered now, and while a couple of them looked concerned, others began laughing a little. The man raised his hand as if to strike the worm, who covered his head with his arms. The man suspended the blow in midair, and the onlookers laughed harder.

Something familiar rushed through me—not overwhelming, as it had been in the past, but still piercing. It had been a long time since I felt its presence this strongly. "Stop," I said. I felt no animosity or anger. I felt almost nothing.

The balding man turned and our gazes collided like a train wreck. Anger boiled in his eyes. He opened his mouth to say something, but then stopped, glancing at the worm and then back at me, trying to understand why I had interfered. The anger melted from his eyes, but a bitterness remained.

He wanted to respond to me, but something wouldn't let him. It couldn't have been fear, because I gave him nothing to be scared of, yet something definitely quelled his anger.

This is what Jefferson does . . .

The man said to the worm, "You piece of shit," but his voice now lacked conviction. He turned to me again, looking again as though he wanted to say something, but still holding back. He gave me a disgusted look and walked away.

Soon the rest of the crowd disbursed too, uncomfortable, muttering. No one looked me in the eye, their faces now troubled, as if they wished they could disappear entirely. I angled my head, staring at the worm in front of me, and a burst of insight hit me.

I knew what it meant to fall as far as possible without dying, to live at the bottom of the deepest pit of filth, and yet I disapproved of this creature sitting in front of me—not for what he was, but for what he allowed himself to be. It wasn't that I disliked him. I felt nothing for him—he was merely the product of a society that wouldn't accept him, and yet he refused to adopt, and defend, a higher standard. To this man, surrender was simply more convenient than challenging a collective self-appointed authority whose judgments were almost universally inaccurate. His complicity, in that sense, disgusted me.

Society, however, was equally culpable—ceaselessly pointing its proverbial finger at someone, or something, in blame. I disdained any part of a culture so stringent and dogmatic that it could readily destroy a man simply for his refusal to embrace the status quo. But more than anything, I detested a society that so fatuously sought to impose immutable notions of virtue on a universe that neither invited nor necessarily accepted those ideas. And I marveled at the self-righteous persistence, despite how rarely the effort succeeds.

Manipulation and control are such iniquitous barricades to progress—and the man in front of me was a living testament to the soundness of that notion. He didn't want to grow; he simply wanted to survive, with as little effort as possible. It was a cruel cycle: society's myopic and intransigent standards had inspired his indifference, yet his prolonged stagnation was every bit as attributable to his own detachment.

I had never understood the depth of this disease so clearly, and in that moment I condemned human apathy unequivocally. But I did it with the full realization that the condemnation extended to me, for it had been my own apathy that had permitted and tolerated the fear that had, for so long, governed me. Now, the only remaining dilemma was whether it was my strength, or Jefferson's strange generosity that had snatched me from the brink of self-destruction.

This homeless man was a gift to society, representing a series of mistakes, all of which were available for scrutiny. If he failed it would probably be by choice, and the sacrifice would add to the growth of knowledge. His life, and possibly his death, would be a model, forcing us to question our premises and conclusions about living.

And if he survived, or even prospered? That legacy too, would be a gift. His success could be measured against his failures, and perhaps used for inspiration and guidance. Regardless of the outcome, knowledge would result, facilitating and defining progress.

The worst thing society could do was to manipulate the outcome of this man's destiny. The seeds for his salvation were already planted, resources readily available to him at every turn—infinite opportunities. But if he were going to be saved, he would have to do it himself. The clarity of it ran through my veins, incontrovertible, and from this understanding came a wave of optimism and repose. I was glad to feel its warmth, its irrefutable balance.

This man made me realize that what I had been searching for had always been with me. I finally understood why I had endured the things I had, and for an instant I saw the entire picture. This thing inside me—this wonderful and mysterious energy—had never left me. I had only shut it out.

I could have done it alone, I thought. And maybe I should have tried. I certainly didn't regret the help I had received, but now I understood that no amount of aid could ever be enough if the recipient cannot—or will not—strive for something more. I had made the commitment and succeeded; I was grateful for what Jefferson and Jack had done for me, but it was incidental. They would have given up had I not been willing to struggle for a better life. And whether or not I would have, I certainly *could* have done it without them. I undoubtedly could have found other resources to help me find my way, but ultimately, no matter what path I had chosen, the change would have had to come from me.

I searched the man's eyes. He didn't deserve this life, nor did he *not* deserve it. He had beaten his path, and now he walked on it. That was punishment enough. Suddenly I was back on the streets, if only for an instant, living in the filth and killing myself in the slowest, most agonizing way. The awareness only made it clearer how far I had come in such a short time.

His eyes glowed as he smiled at me, and he seized what he perceived to be an excellent opportunity. "You got any change, dude?"

"No, I don't."

He looked at Jack, standing next to me, and opened his mouth to try his luck again. But before he could speak, Jack put a finger to his own lips and smiled. The worm sighed and shrugged.

"Come on," Jack said to me. He grabbed my arm and squeezed it gently. "Let's get some dinner."

I expected to hear the word "kid," but it never came.

Summer, Year Twenty-Two

I WORRIED THAT I would become too reliant on Jack and I worked hard to distract myself enough to avoid just such a dependence. I spent most of my time deep in Jefferson's library or in front of my computer analyzing financial statements. We spent many evenings playing chess, but most of the time, Jack kept a watchful distance, giving me plenty of space. Still, I had this odd feeling that he was always near, even when I knew he wasn't.

When Jack wasn't working, he seemed to occupy most of his free time dating as many women as possible. But as much as he undoubtedly wanted the world to think him a philanderer, I suspected that most of his relationships were platonic.

His girlfriends were always intelligent, and he was too honest and compassionate to use anyone for his own hedonistic pleasure. I don't think he had the constitution for casual promiscuity—or for the emotional and psychological baggage that nearly always came with it. I'm sure he enjoyed female companionship, but I never believed he would find a partner to whom he would commit forever.

One night soon after my twenty-second birthday, we were at the Cardinal, engrossed in a series of games. Jack was taking entirely too long to make his moves. "Why have you never settled down?" I said, to break the montomy.

He pulled his eyes away from the board and blinked a few times. "Because the suicide rate among single women in North America would go through the roof."

"Yes, I'm sure it would, Jackson."

He scowled. "Don't call me Jackson. And while we're on the subject, why don't *you* ever date anyone, Douglas?"

"Lots of reasons, I guess."

Jack's eyes narrowed. "I think we all know what's going on here." He leaned forward. "It's okay to be . . . you know . . . *gay*."

"What if I am? Is there anything wrong with that? Are you a homophobe, Jackson?"

"No!"

"Are you coming on to me?"

"*Certainly* not!" He looked furtively from side to side. "I'm just trying to facilitate your desire to express your homosexuality."

"I think you're coming on to me."

"I think my record speaks for itself."

"Uh huh."

"Okay, why *don't* you date anyone, Douglas?"

"Are you changing the subject?"

Jack rolled his eyes. "I'm just asking the same question you asked me."

I thought about it for a second. "I guess I haven't met anyone who does it for me—at least not for a long time." I had never told Jack about Elizabeth, but now I added, "There was someone, before you came to Austin. She was special. If I found something like that again, I'd put a lot of energy into it."

"Then you answered your own question."

"What question?"

"I knew someone once, but she—" He didn't seem to know how to finish the sentence. "Well, anyway . . ." For an instant his eyes seemed to be far away.

"She what?"

Jack shook his head. "I'll tell you about it sometime."

Somehow I knew I shouldn't push the issue. He looked at the board for a minute longer and moved a piece. "You think you'll ever start dating again? I'd hate to think of you broadcasting this image of being queer for the rest of your life."

I shook my head and smiled. "I don't know. I haven't thought about it much."

"You don't have to get married, you know."

"Well you've certainly been a good role model in that regard, haven't you, Jackson?"

I looked back at the board and then I saw it; it seemed too obvious to be real. I hesitated, checking all the options to make sure I hadn't made a mistake.

Then Jack saw it too and pulled his head back, his eyes flitting about the board. Finally he said, "Well?"

"Well what?"

"Well, are you going to do it or not, you little bastard?"

I took my rook and moved it across the board. "Checkmate." It was the first time I had ever beaten Jack.

He shook his head. "I can't goddamn believe it. You finally won a game. I guess you aren't a retard after all."

I stood up, snatched his quarter from the table, and put it in my pocket. "Fuck you, Jack."

"Fuck *you*."

"No, fuck you."

After my conversation with Jack, I started allowing myself to think about Elizabeth more often, and I realized that, in part, I had chosen seclusion after my release from the hospital for fear of seeing her. My situation had been precarious enough; my heart might not have withstood that torment. But I had grown strong in the last couple of years, and I couldn't avoid human contact forever, so I strted going to the Cardinal again—without Jack.

Yet despite my courage, I tried to stay relatively hidden when I was there alone—choosing corner tables, always ready to slink out if she should come in the door. Some of the regulars tried to lure me into games, but I usually declined politely, preferring to watch from a safe distance. So far, however, Elizabeth hadn't appeared, and I started to think maybe she wouldn't; she had been planning to return to San Antonio after law school and that was probably exactly what she had done. Further, the memories this place held for her were undoubtedly crippling.

One late afternoon, not long after my victory over Jack, I sat in a corner of the Cardinal under a lamp, next to a window where I could watch people passing. I slouched in an easy chair, one leg over the arm. I leaned my face against the soft overstuffed back of the chair, reading a paperback.

Suddenly I had the distinct impression someone was watching me. I looked over the top of my book at a girl sitting at a table several feet away, staring at me. She had straight dark hair, pulled back and piled loosely behind her head, small strands falling in her face. Her eyes were narrow slits of green and her skin looked soft, with an olive tint. Her lips were full and parted slightly. When our eyes met, she smiled, and then looked quickly down at a magazine she was reading.

Although I was no match for Jack's good looks, I'd never had much trouble meeting girls when I wanted to. But since Elizabeth, I hadn't had much interest; her memory kept me from letting anyone else in. I had grown in every imaginable way in recent years, and I had begun to imagine that she would appreciate the changes in me. I still toyed with the idea that she could somehow forgive me— that we could be happy again—but every time the thought entered my mind, I quickly dismissed it.

Losing Elizabeth was part of me—part of the balance. What we shared, however brief, was now history and reviving it would be wrong. Somewhere inside me, I knew our past together couldn't be imported into the new life I was creating for myself.

But the idea of being with other women seemed equally out of the question. So I withdrew, choosing instead to concentrate on my recovery—becoming stronger and more whole. Unfortunately, with my returning strength came an uncomfortable restlessness I couldn't ignore. I began to realize I wouldn't be able to shut out intimacy forever.

I settled more comfortably into my chair and continued to read my book, but a few minutes later I got the same feeling I was being watched. I looked at the girl again. She smiled, and this time I realized just how pretty she was. For the first time in years, my stomach began to tighten at the thought of meeting a woman.

I raised my book and tried to read again but something wouldn't let go. I took a deep breath and closed my eyes. I missed Elizabeth so much, and the image in my mind of her beautiful smile made my heart ache. I could still smell her, and even taste her lips.

I opened my eyes and looked up over the top of my book, partly wishing the girl would be gone. But there she was—still watching, still smiling, and now I caught myself smiling back. I quickly raised my book again, embarrassed.

The conflict raged in my mind, keeping me from concentrating on anything but the presence of the girl a few feet away. And just when I thought I couldn't stand it anymore—that I was going to have to leave the coffee shop—something inside me changed. I closed my eyes and exhaled slowly, serenity replacing indecision.

Maybe it had been my conversation with Jack, but in that instant, almost effortlessly, I released the memory of Elizabeth, the way a parent might say goodbye to a child leaving for college—not gone forever, but somehow no longer there either.

Now I understood: if losing Elizabeth had been part of my growth, then completing the process required that I move on. I made the decision almost involuntarily. It was time.

I closed my book and rose from my chair, walking over to the girl's table. To my surprise, I wasn't nervous at all. I stood over her. "Hi."

"Hi," she said.

I extended my hand. "I'm Douglas."

She took it, shaking it gently. She glanced at the tattered paperback in my other hand. "I've read it twice," she said. "It's the best thing she ever wrote."

I nodded and smiled.

THE STRANGE SERENITY to which Jefferson had opened my eyes came more often now, but ironically, it only appeared when I did nothing to invoke it. It was like a frightened animal, only allowing me to approach slowly, bolting at any sudden movements.

My perception seemed to grow stronger each day, and I sensed things with more clarity than ever before. I'm not saying I could read minds, but when I looked into someone's eyes, I could feel even the most carefully veiled subtleties, like sadness, guilt, or even deception.

I began to devour literature on various modern philosophies of science, and while I didn't understand why I was so drawn to these schools, the more I learned, the more fascinated I became by the connections between critical rationalism and Taoism—the elegance and balance of an open interpretation of the universe.

These connections spurred me to delve in earnest into Taoism, and this new perspective brought Jefferson's delicate lessons rushing back, as though awakened from hibernation. In my mind, I could almost hear his soft raspy voice across the chessboard, gently, almost poetically urging me toward new intellectual and spiritual frontiers.

When we find balance, that fragile equilibrium, what do we do with it? Do we share it? Is that even possible?

And then I would recall my insufferable hubris, and I would recoil in humiliation, unable to believe I could have been that impudent. Yet he had been so tolerant, so forgiving.

Why?

And that question—a single word containing only three letters—now dominated my life.

One day as I searched the bookshelves at the house, I came across an old copy of *Tao Te Ching*. I was surprised to find it; I had bought my own copy some time earlier and I thought I had seen all the books in the house. How could I have missed it?

I opened it to the first page, blank but for one sentence:

The Tao that can be expressed is not the eternal Tao.

I chuckled. "That didn't stop you, did it?"

Leafing through the book, I came across some scraps of paper tucked in the pages—a magazine clipping, stapled to a note, both yellowed with time. The handwriting on the note seemed familiar, yet I couldn't place it. The long, thin strokes conveyed a casual confidence that made me think of Jack, although I couldn't have said why; it certainly wasn't his handwriting. In any case, both the clipping and the note appeared to be decades old.

The note read:

> *This is a passage from that Chinese manuscript I told you about. A British academic made the translation, but he's been dead for about 35 years. The manuscript was written anonymously. At first they thought it was from the Tao Te Ching, but it isn't related. There are a lot of problems with its authenticity, and nobody knows where the original is. It allegedly disappeared soon after the translation was made. Nobody I've talked to will even confirm it ever existed. Sorry.*
>
> *Per our discussion, the last paragraph is the one that got those physicists excited, but everyone I know leans toward the conclusion that it's a hoax, and in the absence of the original, I tend to agree.*
>
> *If there's anything else I can do for you, let me know.*
> *PL*

The top of the magazine page had been torn off. I turned it over looking for a date or a publisher, but found neither. I read what remained of the article.

> *. . . we use the process to pass time, but we use it sparingly, for its use often brings death to the practitioner. The apothecaries have known of the process for lifetimes, but have been reticent in revealing its secret. I have used the process only twice, and after the second time I came close to death. I lost feeling in one hand for many months. The apothecaries tell us how to use the potion they give us, and they tell us we must know the Way. It is only a short span to pass time, but it tires the body and makes one weak.*
>
> *We cannot pass much time. We only pass forward. We cannot go back.*
>
> *It puts great fear in me to think what might happen if we went too far, for no man has moved more than two days forward and lived to tell of it. Those who die do so before they pass. Their corpses remain.*
>
> *The potion contains components I do not understand. It has been years since I passed time, and if I ever knew the ingredients, I have long since forgotten them. But I do remember what the apothecary said to me: "Passing is difficult, for it tears you at the lowest level, at the level of the Way. That place is the smallest, where the foundation begins and ends. It is as empty as the vast spaces, yet the universe exists most significantly at its depths. It is the Way, and any man who does not know it will certainly die passing time."*

I read the passage several times. I couldn't imagine that anyone, especially Jefferson, would take it seriously. And suddenly all the old nagging questions poured forth. I started to get angry—and even a little scared. *Why am I even doing this?* I thought. *What's the fucking point?* I wondered whether Jefferson would ever give me any answers at all, and I stared at the passage again. And then, all at once, my anger passed and something entered me that eclipsed my frustration—I was suddenly flooded with peace.

Why is this coming to me now? And for some reason, at that instant I understood that I was meant to see the passage I held in my hands, and that my anger was pointless—insignificant compared to the meaning of this moment, however hidden from me. I accepted the certainty of it. I knew that to fight this feeling would have been more than futile—it would have been damaging. I had no choice but to let my curiosity go, along with my irritation, and the last of it melted away like rainwater evaporating from asphalt on a sweltering day.

I read the passage one last time and then folded the papers, returning them to the book, and sliding it back into place on the shelf. I breathed deeply, contentment creeping in where the resentment had been only moments before. *This is the way it is supposed to be.*

Without a trace of doubt, I now knew the answers were coming. I didn't know how, and I didn't know when, but I did know one thing with almost absolute certainty: all I had to do was wait.

Late April, Year Twenty-Three

SINCE MY CHILDHOOD in Durango, I had known that Jack meditated and engaged in other Eastern practices, but I had never bothered to find out much about it from him for two reasons. First, I knew my chances of getting a serious answer were infinitesimally small. Second, I didn't really care. I thought such things were weird—especially if Jack was doing them. But my ideas about Eastern philosophies were changing, and I was becoming more and more curious about Jack's involvement in them.

I also had another reason to be curious: cocaine destroys a user's appetite, and when I cleaned up, I began to eat a lot—partly to stave off my cravings for drugs and booze, and partly because I was just hungry all the time. I ate when and what I wanted to and didn't exercise at all.

So I got fat.

I wasn't exactly obese, but I certainly wasn't thin anymore. Jack naturally thought this was the funniest thing that had ever happened in the history of the entire universe, and he let me know it whenever he could.

I began to realize the only way I would ever truly balance my life was to be as efficient with my body as I was becoming with my mind, so I decided to get in shape. And since Jack seemed so eager to abuse me about my weight, I also decided he could help me shed it.

One afternoon we met for a chess game over lunch at a Thai restaurant near his office downtown. As we were setting up the board I said, "I want to ask you a question."

He raised his eyebrows.

"I've thought about it a lot, and I feel kind of silly, so I really want you to try to answer me without being a clown, okay?"

"I can do that." He nodded enthusiastically, his eyes wide with innocent curiosity.

I let go of a long breath and began cautiously. "It's about martial arts."

"Yeah?"

"Okay, well I'm not talking about all that crap in the movies. I'm talking about something beyond that. Martial arts are based on Taoism, right?"

"Yeah, most of them—at least to some degree," he said.

"Have you studied Taoism?"

"I've read some books, if that's what you mean."

"Like how many?"

"I don't know," he said. "A lot. Where are you going with this?"

"You do a lot of that stuff, don't you? I mean meditating and stuff."

"I don't know if I would categorize the activity as 'doing it,' but yes."

"Well, I want to start. Will you help me?"

"Why?"

"I don't know. I just kind of want to get back . . . in shape, I guess."

He stared at me with one of his predictable idiotic expressions. Finally he said, "Are you sure you don't want to start with badminton or croquet or something like that? You're pretty fat."

"You know what, Jack? Why don't you just shut up? At least I'm trying to do something about it."

"It doesn't look like it. I'm amazed you can even still move those two meat cakes you used to call legs."

"Look, asshole, are you going to help me or not?"

"No."

Just then a beautiful woman crossed the room, and Jack's eyes drifted to her butt. "Oh my Lord . . ." His mouth hung open as he followed her with his head.

I snapped my fingers at him. "Hey! Jack!"

"What?" he said without looking away from the woman's rear end.

"Answer my question."

"I did."

"Well, could you at least tell me *why* you won't help me?"

He pulled his eyes away, clearly annoyed. "Yeah, I'll tell you." He slouched in his chair. "Do you take fart classes, Douglas?"

"*Please* don't be a jackass. Please?"

"Just answer my question."

I cocked my head and folded my arms in front of my chest. "What in the hell are you talking about?"

"Do you have to take lessons to pass gas properly?" His face was completely serious.

"No, Jack, I don't go to fart school."

"Why not?"

I sighed. "Jesus, just forget it."

"Do you want me to explain this or not?"

I just stared at him.

"Okay, let's try again. Why don't you attend poot class?"

"Why do you have to be so goddamn gross all the time? And why are you so fascinated with gas?"

He ignored my questions, holding his arms out like a coach explaining a big play. "Okay, here's the answer: You don't go to fart school because you know how to do it instinctively. When you have to rip burlap, you just lift your cheek and push. It's natural." He scratched his head. "Taoism is like that too."

"I can't believe you just compared Taoism to farting."

"Why not?" He folded his arms.

"Look Jack, forget it. I was just trying to see if you wanted to help me."

He leaned forward, his eyes sparkling. Something in his voice changed—it became more serious, more direct. "I am helping you, but you just don't want to see it."

"How? By comparing Taoism to farting?

He shook his head. "The Tao is part of you. You don't need lessons."

"Why not?"

"I can't help you now. Take my word for it. You won't learn anything from books or lessons; it will come from your relationship with the universe. All that other crap—tai chi and yoga—it's just words. The real thing has to come from experience."

I paused, something tugging at my thoughts. "Don't you think it's weird that we've never talked about this before?"

"You know, I never thought about that! Come to think of it, we've also never discussed the thin film of grease between a duck's balls and its sphincter. How very odd."

"Ducks don't have balls, Jack."

"Yes they do."

I glared at him.

"What the hell is there to talk about?" he said, finally. "Anybody who tries to tell you he understands it is probably full of shit."

"And you don't find it odd that I just happen to be reading about some ancient philosophy that you know a lot about, but we've never discussed it?"

"I think you're making a big deal out of nothing." After a moment he added, "Speaking of the books you're reading, have you heard anything from your friend Jefferson?"

"Not a word."

"And he's still paying all your bills and all that?"

"Yep."

"What a fucking weirdo. Have you even tried to find him?"

"Yeah, but there's no trace. It's like he doesn't exist."

"Man, I like his style!" Jack hooted. "Just *gives* you his goddamn house! I would love to meet this crazy bastard."

"It might pain you to know this, but I actually think you two would get along, Jack."

He snorted. "I doubt it."

I opened my mouth to let him know exactly how much his very existence in the universe annoyed me, but something stopped me. I straightened in my chair, inhaling deeply. A wave hit me and I scanned the restaurant carefully. *Something is wrong . . .*

Jack leaned across the table, his eyes bright and intense, as though he were responsible for what was happening. In a low voice he said, "It's effortless. I can't teach it to you."

I grew calmer, my breathing and heart rate slowing. *Someone is making this happen now.* There was no doubt in my mind.

I looked at Jack, and he nodded slowly.

A few people were paying at the cash register. *It's not them.* Another group was leaving the restaurant, but somehow I knew they weren't involved either. *What is this . . .?*

A man entered almost in slow motion, and somehow I knew beyond any doubt that he was the one. He was clean and neat, one arm tucked inside a beige trench coat he wore over a well-tailored suit. His eyes swept the restaurant wildly. "Hello, everyone!" he called out. "How are *you* today?"

A woman at the table next to ours jumped, startled. Other people exchanged puzzled expressions.

"I'm looking for the *Medicine Man*! Has anyone seen him?" The words fell on me like a block of ice, the hairs on the nape of my neck rising. The man let out a barrage of insane laughter.

Jack's eyes were as alive as I had ever seen them, and my own senses pulsed with heightened awareness. Something compelled me to move, and my self-control surprised me. Without a word Jack and I rose from our seats and walked toward the bar.

I couldn't see what the man was doing, yet I was still somehow aware of his every move. I sensed that turning around would be a mistake, so I just kept walking forward with Jack.

"Has anyone seen the *Medicine Man?*" He cackled again, and with all the giddy excitement of a game show host he howled, "Well, there he is!"

Screams erupted in the restaurant, and I turned my head, watching the man with my peripheral vision. He had drawn a sawed-off shotgun from his coat, leveling it at us. In unison, Jack and I dove over the bar, hitting the floor hard, taking cover just before two blasts thundered.

The spray of buckshot destroyed bottles and a mirror behind the bar. The bartender huddled in the corner, wide-eyed and trembling. I gently smiled at her, trying to ease her terror. And then something occurred to me: *Where am I finding the strength to reassure her?* But I felt no fear at all.

Everything seemed to slow down again, and I watched Jack crawl to the end of the bar. I remained crouched where I had landed, and in the reflection of a shard of broken mirror, I watched the man with the shotgun move through the restaurant.

Whimpers and stifled screams came from every direction, broken suddenly by the man's insane, sickly-sweet voice, rhythmically emphasizing each word: *"You . . . are . . . already . . . dead, Medicine Man!"*

He walked slowly across the room, stopped, and turned to look at a woman crouched beside him. He cracked open the gun, ejected two empty shells, reached in his pocket and put two fresh ones in the chambers. He snapped the gun closed.

The woman whimpered, her body convulsing with fear.

He said, "How are *you* today? Do you know the *Medicine Man*?" He smiled maniacally at her, cocking his head. "Do you think he'd feel sorry for you if I did something bad?" A look of mock pity replaced his insidious smile.

I screamed, "*No!*"

He pointed the shotgun at the woman's face and pulled the trigger. Her head disappeared in an explosion of red mist. Chunks of bloody meat and brains splattered against a nearby table, and her headless body collapsed to the floor, blood pulsing from the neck.

He howled with pleasure. "That's right! You're next, Medicine Man!"

My equanimity returned like water rushing in, replacing rage and fear with detached numbness. My mind wanted to register the horror of the act, but something bigger wouldn't allow it. I struggled to explain my apathy. I wanted to feel something—*anything.*

A new thought displaced the conflict: *He did it to provoke me . . . he wants me to come out.* I pushed the thought of the woman's death from my mind and waited.

Timing is everything now. The thought came out of nowhere, like a voice, but there was no time to think about the source; somehow I knew the next few seconds would determine whether I lived or died.

The man leaned his upper body over the bar. Our eyes met and a smile touched his lips. The shotgun was coming down fast.

Neither of us expected my sudden speed and fluidity. In one hand, I caught the barrel and used it to pull myself up, twisting his arm, turning the gun upside down. His elbow now faced outward, bent slightly.

I pointed his arm, along with the shotgun, at the wall behind the bar. I found his finger over the trigger and pulled it. The shotgun fired just as I let go of the barrel, allowing the odd angle of his arm to bear the weapon's full kick. The blast snapped the arm, ripping it from its socket, tearing the muscles from the bone in his shoulder.

The gun fell to the floor, and his arm flopped limply to his side, giving him the look of a deranged rag doll. He opened his mouth to scream, but I hit him hard in the throat and felt something shatter. I thrust my fingers into his eyes.

Jack appeared at his feet and I removed my hand, blood gushing from the eye sockets. Before the man had a chance to react, I shoved him backward and Jack took his lower legs, bringing him down hard, rolling him onto his stomach and pulling his left arm behind him.

The man attempted a scream—a gravelly liquid sound, which clearly annoyed Jack. He hit the man in the side of his head, knocking him unconscious. The motion was calculated and quick, so efficient that I found myself staring at Jack in dismay, wondering how he had obtained such a skill. Then I realized I didn't even understand what *I* had done.

I surveyed the destruction and carnage, unable to process what I was seeing— people huddled together, crouched behind anything that might give them protection, staring at me with wide, terrified eyes. And suddenly reality snapped back into focus, cold and vivid, as if in that instant some numbing agent in my system had simply vanished.

I began to tremble, looking at Jack. He stared back at me for what seemed like hours, his eyes full of something powerful—remorse, or maybe sorrow.

He pulled his gaze away from mine, walked to the phone at the counter, and called the police.

◆

WE SAT OUTSIDE on the hood of a patrol car while police swarmed the scene. Television camera crews lined up beyond a barricade, the reporters pacing like wolves, waiting to pounce. It was Barney's suicide all over again.

Whatever had kept me from reacting to the woman's gruesome death was no longer insulating me from the reality of what had just happened. I began to panic.

Jack put a hand on my shoulder. "Are you okay?"

"I don't know . . ." My eyes were everywhere, darting from face to face. "What *happened*?"

"It's okay. Everything's fine now. Everything is going to be fine."

I was almost hysterical. I pushed his arm away. "He blew that woman's head off! *How could anyone do that?*" Jack just looked at the ground.

The police interrogated everyone from the restaurant, the questions standard— as they had been after Barney killed himself. Many of the other witnesses were as shaken as I was, and I could see them pointing to Jack and me animatedly as they described what happened.

"Did you know the suspect?" The question came suddenly, from a policeman in plain clothes. I looked up at him, but he didn't offer his name.

"No." I stared blankly at the ground trying to remember if I had seen the man with the shotgun somewhere before, but I was certain I hadn't.

The policeman scribbled something on a notepad. "Other witnesses have told us the suspect kept referring to 'the Medicine Man.' Do you know what that phrase means?"

I put my hand on my forehead. "No." *But I'd very much like to.*

"Okay," he said, scribbling again. "And two shots were fired at you as you fled from the man. Is that correct?"

Jack answered for me. "Yes, that's right."

The policeman turned to him. "The question is for Mr. Cole." He stared icily at Jack, trying to intimidate him. Jack just looked away. The policeman returned his attention to me.

"Yes, he shot at us," I said.

"Do you know why?"

"I have no idea."

"Uh huh," he said, scribbling again. "Mr. Cole, one of my colleagues believes he recognizes you from another, similar . . . *incident*. Is that correct?"

I felt dizzy and steadied myself. "I was at the coffee shop a few years ago and a man committed suicide in front of me."

The detective's eyebrows rose instantly. "Really? Do you think these two events are related?"

I looked at the ground again. "I don't see how they could be." I shook my head, sighing deeply. "I'm as confused as anybody else. I wish I had some answers for you, Officer."

"Detective," he said without looking up.

Jack and I both looked at him, unable to believe this display of ego in the face of what had just happened. *He thinks I'm lying. He is trying to fluster me.*

The detective continued, "And you were with someone at the time of the other incident, is that correct?"

"Yes."

"Who was that person?"

"His name is Jefferson Stone."

"And where is Mr. Stone now?" His eyes narrowed.

"I don't know. He left town and I haven't seen him."

"Uh huh. And when exactly did he leave town?"

"After the suicide sometime. I don't know the exact date. I don't even know where he went—we've lost touch." *Except that I'm living in his house, and he's supporting me financially.* And as the thought formed in my mind, I remembered the three men killed in the alley. *I was the suspect.* The police would make these connections. Things were about to get complicated.

Suddenly I was scared. I thought about the black pawn in the hospital room, and the notebook in the dumpster. Jefferson had known about the voice in my mind; in fact, he seemed to know just about everything, and regardless of what I had told the detective, there was no doubt in my mind Barney's suicide *was* somehow related to this shooting. *And Ellison, the man who had everything, who was so happy all the time . . . These aren't coincidences.*

But as much as the police needed answers about Jefferson, I needed them even more. And beyond that, I needed to buy time, because none of this was going to look very innocent when the pieces finally did come together. No, I wasn't going to give this detective anything more than I had to.

"Did Mr. Stone know either of these men, to your knowledge?" he asked.

I put my hand on my forehead. "I don't think so."

"And did *you* know either of them, Mr. Cole?" He continued to eye me suspiciously. My mounting discomfort was undoubtedly starting to show.

"I already told you I don't know the guy with the shotgun," I snapped. "I only casually knew the guy who killed himself—his name was Barney. He was homeless and hung out at the coffee shop where I spent a lot of time. Everybody knew him."

"The same coffee shop where he killed himself?"

"Yes, the same one—the Cardinal. Look, Barney was a good guy, and I didn't enjoy watching him put a bullet in his brain. Jefferson and I didn't have anything to do with it, if that's what you're getting at." I felt like I was going insane. Reality was slipping.

Jack put his hand on my shoulder again and said to the policeman, "Why don't you give him a few minutes to get himself together?"

The response was acid: "I don't think it's up to you to tell me—"

The detective stopped midsentence, and I looked up to see why. His face took on a perplexed expression as he stared at Jack.

In a husky whisper, Jack said, "I told you to let my friend have a few minutes. I don't think he's a suspect, but even if he is, you're going to rule him out right away, isn't that correct?"

The detective seemed uncertain, almost groggy. "Uh . . . yeah. Yes, of course. I'll be back in a minute to ask him more questions." He turned to me, his face blank and humbled, like that of a child dismissed for bed. "Is that okay with you, Mr. Cole?"

I nodded slowly, my mouth hanging open. He walked away and I turned to Jack. "What the *hell*?" The old nagging thoughts in the back of my mind were back, full force. "What was *that*?" Jack wouldn't look at me. "What did you just do to him?" I demanded.

"I told him to leave you alone."

Several minutes later, as promised, the detective returned to ask me a few more questions about Jefferson—politely this time. But I had nothing to add. He smiled warmly. "Well that's all I have for you Mr. Cole. I'm sorry to have put you through this. You're free to go."

I stared at him in disbelief. *That's it? Just like that?*

He led us to a barricade far away from the crowd of reporters. "If you go through here, you should be able to avoid that mob."

"Thank you, Detective," Jack said. I stared at the two of them in disbelief. Jack still wouldn't make eye contact with me. I followed him to his car in a stupor.

When we got in, he started the engine, and I turned to him. "Jack . . .?"

He hung over the steering wheel for a moment, staring vacantly out the windshield. Finally, he looked at me. His eyes were heavy with exhaustion and despair—almost pleading with me to leave it alone.

I knew the confrontation was imminent, but I was too numb to push it. For now I was content just to lean my head back, close my eyes, and let him drive me home in silence.

The police had more questions about Jefferson, and I spoke to them several times in the next week. The inquiries, however, carried no hint of suspicion or accusation.

In the days after the shooting I spoke to Jack by phone several times, but I avoided seeing him. I wanted time to think about what had happened, because I knew I would have to confront him soon. I wanted to understand his behavior, both during and after the shooting: the calmness in his eyes—how he seemed to understand what was happening as it happened.

I also wanted to know how he had so easily changed that detective's attitude with only a few words. The policeman's curiosity was certainly understandable. After all, I had been present for two shootings. *And three other murders, as yet unsolved . . .*

But the detective *wasn't* suspicious. In fact, the entire Austin Police Department now seemed content to overlook the possibility of a relationship between the two events. And on top of everything else, no one seemed to have made the connection that I was currently residing in Jefferson's house—an oversight which seemed absurdly improbable. None of it made any sense. Even *I* suspected that something was terribly amiss, and the sudden lack of interest from the police raised more concerns than it alleviated in my mind.

A few days later, I sat in the living room, restlessly reading, trying to find a little peace. But no matter what I did, I was tormented for answers that simply wouldn't come.

The phone rang and I picked it up. "Hello?"

"This is Detective Roberts with the Austin Police Department, Mr. Cole."

I recognized his voice from the interview outside the restaurant. "Hello, Detective," I said coolly, remembering his initial arrogance. But his tone remained pleasant and polite.

"I have more information about the man you and Mr. Alexander apprehended the other day."

Apprehended, I thought. *What a nice way of putting it.*

"The suspect seems to have some sort of psychological disorder," he continued.

"I'm not trying to be cheeky, Detective Roberts, but his mental instability isn't a new development to me."

He chuckled. "I know what you mean. The doctors have diagnosed it as delusional schizophrenia—or something like that anyway. I don't think they really know what they're dealing with. They all seem pretty confused by his state of mind."

I ran my fingers through my hair. "Detective, the man was well-dressed. Can you tell me how a delusional schizophrenic finds the presence of mind to look so good before he goes on a killing spree?"

"We wondered that ourselves. The man's name is Aaron Lambert, and he is—or was—an attorney. He and his wife recently filed for divorce, and apparently there are some questions about the division of assets and custody of their children. My understanding is that the wife has been having an affair for some time. Mr. Lambert's colleagues described him as severely depressed, but he just doesn't fit the profile of a killer at all, and we were hoping you might be able to shed some light on this now that things have cooled down a bit." Hastily he added, "I don't want to pressure you, because you're no longer under suspicion. Do you understand that?" The statement seemed totally incongruent with the conversation—almost mechanical, like a recording.

No, I don't understand at all, I thought. "Thank you, Detective. I wish I could help you, but I'd never seen him before that day in the restaurant. What does he say about killing that woman?"

"He doesn't seem to remember it," Roberts said. "You know . . . the doctors say he'll never see again."

The words reminded me how easily I had disarmed the man, blinding him with almost no effort, as though I had rehearsed the act thousands of times. Somehow I'd known what to do, and I had simply done it. Nothing made sense—nothing at all.

"He just babbles," Roberts continued. "He keeps talking about *the Medicine Man* and people from the future. Crazy stuff."

My vision blurred. My face suddenly felt hot and swollen, tingly. I couldn't seem to get enough oxygen in my lungs. "I'm sorry, what did you say?" Chills stabbed my entire body.

"About what? About Lambert? He's crazy. He talks gibberish—"

"No, no. Did you say something about people from the future?"

"Yeah, he says there are voices in his head. Does that mean something to you?"

I rubbed the bridge of my nose, taking several deep breaths before answering. "No . . . it just seems strange that a man who has everything going for him would go on a shooting rampage, that's all." I kept my speech as even and controlled as possible, but my mind was panicking, racing uncontrollably. *What have I missed? Think!*

"Yeah, strange," Roberts said. "Well, I thought it might help to talk to you about Lambert's condition. If anything else comes up on our end, we'll call you. Thanks again for your time, Mr. Cole."

"Thank you, Detective." I put the receiver back in its cradle.

There are no coincidences.

I looked out the window into the park across the street, racking my brain. After the shooting, I had hesitated, yet again, to ask Jack the questions that had burned in my mind too long—fearful of the answers I might receive, choosing instead to take my time, examining the circumstances carefully. But now, no matter how frightening the implications, I could no longer hide from the fact that all the evidence pointed in one direction. Jack was part of this.

I picked up the phone and dialed his number. He answered on the first ring.

"Can you come over here?" I said. "I need to talk to you."

"Yeah, I'll be right there."

When Jack arrived, we stood awkwardly in the living room for a few moments. I wasn't quite sure how to begin.

He fidgeted. "What is it?"

"A lot of shit has been bothering me in the last week." I let out a short laugh. "Actually, it's been bothering me since you came to Austin. Why do you think all of this has happened?"

"I don't know . . . what do you mean? The guy with the shotgun?"

"Everything! Other people don't feel what I felt in that goddamn restaurant. But you know what? I think you know exactly what I'm talking about! I think you felt it too!"

"Yeah, I felt pretty weird in there."

"You felt more than just *weird*, Jack!" I started pacing. "How did I stop that guy with the shotgun? I knew *precisely* what to do! How is that possible?"

He shrugged, lookng even more uncomfortable. "I don't know—"

"No, Jack, I think you *do* know!

What the *fuck* is going on, man? I saw your eyes in that restaurant, and I know you felt it! How is it that you and I both experienced that same feeling? What are the odds, huh?"

"I didn't really do anything—"

"Jefferson refuses to give it a name. What do you call it, Jack?" My eyes bored into his.

He looked at one of the bookshelves, absently rubbing his hands together. "I don't know, I guess it's like we talked about, Taoism and stuff—"

"No, it's not just 'Taoism and stuff.' It's a hell of a lot more than that, and you know it!" My mind cranked faster. "You know who just called me?"

He shook his head slowly.

"Well, I'll tell you. It was that fuckhead detective who questioned me outside the restaurant. But the funny thing is that he wasn't being a fuckhead anymore— he was being polite! I saw what you did to him, Jack, and now he says I'm no longer a suspect! Don't you think that's a little strange? I've now witnessed two shootings, but I'm no longer a suspect! Funny, huh?"

He shrugged again.

"He told me the guy with the shotgun is talking about men from the future."

"You mean he's crazy? Wow, I wouldn't have guessed *that* in a million years—"

I pointed at him. "You fucking *stop* it! That woman's dead, and I'm not in any mood for your goddamn jokes!"

Jack just looked at the floor, his face expressionless.

"You know that guy Barney, the one who killed himself in front of me and Jefferson? He talked about men from the future too. Did you know that?"

Jack put his hands in his pockets. "I guess lots of people hear voices from the future." The statement carried no conviction.

"I had a good friend named Ellison, Jack. He had everything. He was young, successful—everyone loved him! Did you know he shot himself the same day as Barney?"

He didn't respond.

"No more bullshit, Jack! What do you think the odds are I'd be involved in two episodes with gun-toting psychotic schizophrenics who claim to be in contact with men from the future? Why don't you tell me about that?"

"I . . . don't know."

I looked out the window again for a moment. Then I turned to the bookshelves, and there it was—the Tao Te Ching, with the clipping tucked in its pages. I walked to the bookshelf and thumbed through it until I found the two pieces of paper. *What am I missing here?*

I thought about the day Thomas and Dad were killed—the day Jack introduced me to subatomic physics at the diner in Pagosa Springs. *Multiple universes . . . passing time. . .* I looked at Jack, then at the papers in my hands again. *Am I going crazy?*

I waved the sheets of paper at him.

"Do you know what these are?"

Jack lifted his eyes, staring painfully at me.

"I found them in Jefferson's bookcase a while back. They're about some ancient manuscript."

He still said nothing.

"That's right, Jack, some old Chinese bastard was talking about passing through time. *Passing through time!* Now why would Jefferson be interested in something like that?"

I waited for a moment. Still nothing.

"Jack!" I yelled. "Give me some answers! I'm afraid even to suggest what's in my head because it sounds so fucking crazy!"

"I—"

I gritted my teeth. "You've known me my whole life."

He nodded.

"It wasn't just chance, was it, Jack? You came to Durango for me." I closed my eyes and my childhood rushed through my mind, images of Jack at every turn. "You were always there. When I needed you, you were always . . ." I caught my breath. "You saved me from that car. I stepped off the curb, and you were there . . ."

He stood perfectly still.

"I was supposed to be with Dad and Thomas, but we broke down in Pagosa."

"Douglas, I can't—"

"Goddamn it, why are you doing this to me? What the hell is happening? You're acting like Jefferson—"

The dam broke. It was absolutely clear, and I felt like a fool for not accepting it sooner. "You know him. You know about *everything*."

Jack gazed at the floor like a child being castigated by an angry parent, his face full of remorse, eyes exhausted. Even through my anger I could see how hard this was for him.

"How could I have been so stupid?"

"You aren't stupid."

"You *know* him! How long, Jack?" I began to pace through the living room again. "I suspected it the whole time, but I just thought I was being paranoid, or just fucking crazy! What is it with you two? Who the fuck are you? *What* are you? Are you with the CIA? Am I an experiment, Jack?" I stopped pacing and looked at him. "I've known you my whole life and it's all been a fucking *lie!*"

"Don't say it like that."

I pointed at the door. "Get out. When you're ready to help me, you let me know."

Jack left, closing the door behind him.

I sat down on the sofa, trembling.

I spent the rest of the day trying to quell my anger. I meditated and read, but those things couldn't distract me. I tried to reconcile the events of my life, searching for connections between Jack and Jefferson. It seemed too unbelievable to be real. I imagined them sitting together, maybe in front of a chessboard, quietly discussing my life. *My life!*

I almost quaked with indignation, wondering how many of my experiences were by their design, and I fought the urge to call Jack and scream at him. Yet in spite of everything, I was disappointed in myself for dismissing him the way I had.

Finally, very late that night, I went to my room, but sleeping was impossible. I tossed and turned, thinking about how my two closest friends had manipulated my life. What had they manufactured and why? I ached to know where they had come from, even though the answers looming before me only filled me with fear. More than anything, I was now aware of something new in my perspective—a form of imminence hanging menacingly over everything, quietly murmuring that nothing would ever be the same again.

The next day, I stayed in the house for most of the morning, pacing, drinking tea, trying to read, but I still couldn't concentrate. I needed Jack's friendship desperately right now, and despite the fact that he was a major source of everything that was wrong, I wanted nothing more than to play chess with him, to talk through it all.

Finally I got tired of being cooped up in the house, so I headed to the Cardinal, hoping to find distraction in a few games. When I got there, I set up my chess pieces slowly, meticulously. I took out a book, slouched in my chair, and waited for a game, hoping my fear and confusion would disappear. Suddenly the old craving hit me, and I wanted a drink more than at any time since the beginning of my recovery. I pushed it aside, surprised by the urge.

I tried to read for about an hour, but the words on the page only looked like a swarm of tiny insects. No one seemed interested in a game, and eventually I decided I could endure this frustration as easily at the house as here. I was about to start putting my things in my bag when it hit me—a ripple of peace rushing in, spilling over me in waves.

I remembered that the last time this feeling had come, it had brought with it the man with the shotgun. But then I felt a subtle change, a melodic whisper, and somehow I knew there was no danger in this . . .

I closed my eyes, leaned back, and let serenity fill my veins like a sweet drug. Light pulsed in my head, tension melting from my body, and I breathed deeply and easily as my heart rate slowed.

"I thought I might find you here."

There was no mistaking the sound of the voice. I opened my eyes, and there he stood, arms crossed, the knowing smile on his face.

In spite of it all, I found myself returning the smile. "Hello, Jefferson."

CONFLUENCE

It is somewhere between death and recovery that one finds that inscrutable succor—a nearly absolute sense of relief, derived solely from the ecstasy of his own restoration. This is also the place from which he will vow never to betray himself again. And yet, almost universally, the pact is violated as quickly as it is made.

Once in a while, however, you will find that person who not only respects his promise to himself, but devotes himself to it, nurturing it with all his being. These are the people who change history.

We are obligated to guide the boy, but we cannot live for him. He has to find his own path. You must never forget your imperative.

—JEFFERSON STONE, FROM A LETTER
TO JACK ALEXANDER, DATE UNDISCLOSED

Late April, Year Twenty-Three

WE LOOKED AT each other for a long time in silence.

The reunion was bittersweet. On one hand I could barely contain my excitement at finally seeing him again, and on the other, I was furious with him for lying to me and manipulating my life. I breathed deeply, forcing myself to be patient. "I guess I should ask what you're doing here."

"Do you mind if I sit down?"

I gestured toward the other chair. He sat and immediately pushed his queen's pawn two spaces. I imitated him.

"I see you aren't using a clock," he said.

"Somebody once advised me against it—said I was impatient or something like that."

"You probably were."

"Yeah, I probably was."

We played in silence, and I kept up with him for a long time. Eventually he cornered my king, ending the game. "You've improved," he said.

"A friend of yours taught me."

He smiled again, looking down. "Jack."

Anger began to seep back in but I controlled my urge to lash out.

He looked up at me and the smile dissolved. "There's a bigger picture here, Douglas. You'll understand someday. Jack cares about you more than you know. He wouldn't do anything to hurt you, and neither would I."

I picked up my king and toyed with it. "I can't fathom the big picture, Jefferson. I don't even know what the small picture is."

"I'll explain as much as I can."

I stared at him for a moment. "Jesus *Christ*, Jefferson. I've played this crazy fucking game for a long time, doing everything you asked. But I'm freaking the fuck out here! You owe me some goddamn answers."

"It seems you haven't improved your vocabulary in my absence."

"Whatever." I rubbed my temples. "I'm not in any mood to censor my language."

"You'll understand a lot more by the time you go to sleep tonight."

I stared at him for another moment. "How have you been? You look like you've been taking care of yourself."

"I'm doing well."

"Where are you staying?" I asked.

"At my house."

"What house?"

"The one you've been living in for the last few years."

"Yeah . . ." I said, nodding. "Listen, Jefferson, the police are going to want to talk to you. There was a shooting. Jack and I—"

"I know about it."

I chuckled. "Of course you do." He smiled again with me and I added, "Barney, Ellison and now this guy—"

He lifted his hand to stop me. "We should go to the house. It's going to be a long night."

When we got home I noticed Jefferson had already unloaded a couple of suitcases in the guest bedroom. It reminded me that I was only a guest here, and for a second I felt like a teenager again, my eyes involuntarily wandering through the house to see if anything was out of place or broken on my account. Suddenly I was glad I had kept the place neat. I went into the kitchen and started heating a kettle of water. "You want some tea?"

"That sounds good." He walked to the living room, and after I put the water on the stove, I joined him. He stood in front of a set of bookshelves, leafing through one of the countless titles. "Did you read them all?"

"You're joking, right?" I scanned the thousands of spines in this room alone and looked back at him. "I did the best I could."

He smiled gently, his voice was as calm and soothing as ever. "I'm sure you did fine." He walked to the couch and sat down.

"I'm not sure I'm ready for this," I said.

He looked at me over his glasses. "You are."

I sat in a chair across from him and put my elbows on my knees, resting my chin in my hands. I took a deep breath. "I'm listening."

Jefferson scratched his face. His speech was slow and easy. "Where to start?"

"How about the beginning?"

"The beginning . . . I'm afraid it may not be that easy." He held his breath and looked directly into my eyes. He intertwined his fingers and asked, "How old do you think I am?"

The question took me off guard. "I don't know . . . probably in your middle sixties. The way you move sometimes makes me think you might be younger. What does that—?"

"I'm much older than that."

"Like how old?"

He just stared at me.

"What, like in your seventies or—"

Jefferson shook his head slowly, never taking his eyes off me. "*Much* older, Douglas."

I watched him, waiting for him to tell me it was a joke—an icebreaker just to cut the tension between us. But the sobering look on his face told me exactly how serious he was. "Come on! What am I supposed to say to that?" We were silent for long seconds while I absorbed the gravity of the moment. "How?"

"You'll be the same way someday."

"What, am I going to live *forever*?" Sarcasm laced my words.

"Not forever, but a very long time."

A small chill fell on me. "How much longer?"

"That will depend on a lot of things."

A million questions formed in my mind. My heart thumped loudly in my chest. "And you know this because you're . . ." I couldn't complete the sentence. It was just too implausible—too *crazy* to utter.

Jefferson finished for me. "Because I came here from the future."

I let out a short involuntary bark of laughter. The words wouldn't process. This was science fiction, not reality. To a lesser degree, it was how I felt the moment I heard Thomas and Dad had been killed.

Do I just call him a liar? Is this the price I pay for his generosity? Then another paralyzing thought hit me. *What if Jefferson is insane? And what about Jack? This really isn't possible, is it?* I pushed back the panic, grasping for any thread of rationality.

The kettle of water erupted in a scream and I jumped in my seat. "*Fuck!*" I exhaled hard and pointed toward the kitchen. "I'll just get that." I walked quickly out of the room, looking over my shoulder at the strange man sitting on the couch in my house.

Correction, I thought. *Sitting on the couch in* his *house.*

I made us each a cup of tea, hands trembling, the motions mechanical and forced. *This isn't real. It's a stupid joke.*

But I knew it wasn't a joke. Reality had spoken loudly, with finality, and the truth was inescapable. Jefferson's revelation explained too much to be a lie, and besides, I had seen it coming for a long time—whether or not I had chosen to acknowledge it.

I walked back into the room, gave Jefferson his tea, and sat down.

"Do you believe me?" he asked.

I thought again about the black pawn in the hospital room. "I don't know." I bounced my knees nervously and then forced myself to stop. I looked hard at him, carefully articulating each of the next words from my mouth. "Jefferson, I need you to explain why you are doing this to me."

He rubbed his hands together slowly. "I came to help you."

"It doesn't feel like you're helping me. It feels like you've been manipulating me. It feels like you've torn my life apart."

"Am I mistaken," he said, furrowing his brow, "or did you not beg for mercy, sitting alone one winter night, sprawled in filth?" He made a sweeping gesture around the room. "I gave you that mercy."

"And why, exactly, would you do that?"

"Because I have to teach you."

"Teach me *what?*"

"That's why we're here tonight."

I ground my teeth. "None of this makes any fucking sense—"

He raised his hands. "It will. Just be patient."

A long heavy silence hung between us. Finally, exasperated, I said, "Fine. How did you do it?"

He stood and walked to the bookshelf, scanning the spines again. "When I was younger I became curious about our connection to the universe as it relates to the effects of psychotropic drugs, so I began to do research. Part of the reason I'm here with you now is because I know you've felt that connection, too."

"Yes," I said tentatively.

"Well, you've only scratched the surface. I spent a good part of my life looking for people like you, but in all that time, I found no more than a handful of potential candidates. Of those, only a few exhibited the characteristics this thing requires."

"What thing?"

"Moving through time." He pulled a book, looking vacantly at the title page for a moment, then replaced it and returned to the couch.

"Who are these other people?" I asked.

"Most of them aren't important to this story, but you already know one of them."

"Jack."

He nodded.

"How long have you two known each other?"

"A long time."

"And he's from . . .?" The concept seemed so ludicrous, so utterly irrational, that I almost couldn't say it. "He's from the future, too?"

Jefferson looked at me sympathetically.

"Why didn't he just tell me? Why do you two have to be so fucking secretive about everything?"

He leaned forward and clasped his hands together. "Experience is so important. You had to learn from your mistakes; we couldn't just give everything to you."

"*Give* everything to me? I don't even know why this is happening! How did you even *find* me, Jefferson?"

"There are some things I can't tell you. You understand that, right?"

"No, I *don't* understand!"

"Well, try, because it has to be that way."

I tensed my jaw. "Where is Jack?"

"He'll be here."

I drummed my fingers on the arm of my chair. "Okay, just tell me whatever it is you have to tell me."

"It's not that simple, Douglas." He settled more comfortably on the couch. "As I dug deeper into the effects drugs have on our perception of the universe, I began to make some startling discoveries—some things almost no one else has ever seen. This was when I first began to understand the depth of the *entirety*. Do you remember what that is?"

I nodded. "Yeah, the theory—all the universes, together in space and time."

"Well, it's real. And what I saw scared the hell out of me."

"And what was that?" I asked cautiously. I thought about the clipping from the manuscript on the shelves only a few feet away from me, and I held my breath.

"You already know the answer," he said. "I discovered what happens when we give ourselves over to the entirety. I discovered that there have been a small number of people in history who have learned to transcend the fabric of space and time. These people learned not only how to span vast distances in our universe, but how to move through *all* universes—*across* time itself."

"And how did you come by this information? This doesn't exactly sound like the sort of research you'd find at the library, Jefferson."

"It wasn't just information—it was a matter of perception, and it took me years to understand what I had discovered. But when I finally did, the possibilities became endless. Do you remember when Jack described the multiverse to you when you were younger?"

My mouth fell open. "How did you know about—?"

He gazed at me patiently, his expression almost ashamed, and I thought, *Of course he fucking knows—he knows everything about my whole goddamn life. He could probably tell me how many times I've gotten laid.* And with that thought I cringed, suddenly feeling like a rape victim. I choked back my indignation, and forced myself back to his question. "You *aren't* about to tell me that on top of everything else, you and Jack are from a different universe."

"It's less preposterous than you're making it sound, Douglas. The universe Jack and I came from is nearly identical in every detail to the one we're in now. But the multiverse is more than multiple universes—that's an incomplete description. We know that space and time are one and the same—that each universe in the entirety is made up, independently, of both components. An outcome in one universe might not affect what happens in another."

"So if you aren't coming to affect the future, why did you come back at all?"

"Let me finish. I said the outcome in one universe *might* not affect what happens in another, and therein lies the incompleteness of multiverse theory. I exist in an infinite number of universes—including this one—only as a complex combination of probabilities that make up a complete picture in the entirety. It's true that what happens here might not affect my life in my original universe, but I have to try because the probability is high that if I didn't, the outcome could cost us our lives, in almost every universe in which we exist."

"So this conversation is happening in an infinite number of universes?"

"Not this exact conversation," Jefferson said, "but variations of it. In the multiverse an uncountable number of probabilistic versions of me have traveled to other universes, to teach an army of probabilistic Douglas Coles. Some will fail in their task, but most won't. It's a complicated relationship that you will understand more as you grow; each instant of time is another universe existing with this one as a part of a vast network of probabilities, and these universes run together seamlessly—or at least we perceive them to be seamless. This is what we call *time*, and we believe it is linear, that it flows."

He took off his glasses and rubbed his eyes. "But no matter what our senses tell us, time is *not* linear. Space and time are infinite and curved, with no beginning and no end. We can move from universe to universe, staying in each one as long as we like—but only if we understand the way it all works. And that requires a great deal more than simply what our senses show us."

"How can time not be linear?"

He slipped his spectacles back on his face. "Time doesn't flow. It doesn't *cause* us to age—that's absurd. Our bodies are machines, unable to inhibit their own disintegration, and time is just a concept we use to explain what happens as things change around us. But it doesn't move at all, forward or backward. All things exist—in all universes, and at all times—simultaneously."

"You're saying everything that has ever happened—or that will happen—exists right now?"

"Yes. Somewhere in the entirety every historical and future event is happening as we speak."

"And why are you telling *me* all this?"

"Because you're critical to this story."

I rubbed my face with my palms and then ran my fingers through my hair. "So what does all this have to do with drugs?"

"They weren't just any drugs—they were psychotropics. But that was only the beginning; later in my life, someone introduced me to another, more powerful chemical, and it was the key to moving through time."

"What *chemical*?"

"It's not important right now."

"Well, it sounds pretty fucking important, Jefferson."

"It hasn't been invented yet. The technology isn't even available."

"How convenient for you."

Jefferson ignored the barb. "Have you heard of Project Bluebird?"

"No, but it sounds just stupid enough to fit into this story."

He gave me a tepid smile. "In the nineteen fifties and sixties, the government did some experiments, looking for ways to induce telepathy in humans. The project was controversial, not to mention unsuccessful, so they scrapped it.

"But a few years after it was shut down, another project rose from its ashes. A new group of scientists believed that some psychotropic substances cause users to move through time—if only very slightly. They were convinced that the hallucinations associated with these drugs are the result of such minor temporal shifts, which they called *bursting*. These scientists were the ones who laid the groundwork for the new drug."

I folded my arms. "And now you're going to tell me this super-top-secret drug proves that this . . . *bursting* is possible."

He sighed at my skepticism, and continued. "Yes. It causes temporal transformations, forcing the human body to move into different universes at the subatomic level. The transformations allow us to see these multiple universes distinctly, and they also allow us to physically exist in these other universes—at least temporarily—*if* we can master the entirety at a new level."

"Well, it's funny, I've never heard anything about *that* project either."

"Its existence was never revealed to the public. I tried for years with no luck to find information about it."

"Then how *did* you know about it?"

"A friend told me."

"What friend?"

"Just a friend. You have to be patient, Douglas."

I was becoming more irascible by the second. "So you somehow found some of this drug?"

"I don't know if I would say I found it, so much as it found me. A friend gave me a little bit when I was much younger."

"Is this the same friend who told you about the project?"

He nodded.

"And where did he . . . or *she* get it?"

"I don't know where *he* got it. We only used it a few times."

"Do you have any left?"

"None of that batch, but I do have a small amount that I stole from the organization that synthesized it."

"You *stole* it? What organization?"

Jefferson looked hard at me and exhaled. "I can't completely answer that."

I slumped in my chair and rolled my eyes. "Jesus Christ. Is there anything you *can* answer?"

"The people who ran it had a lot of resources at their disposal, so I have to believe they were related to the government, but nobody knew much about it. It was hard for me to get information because I didn't want to draw too much attention to myself. There was someone in the organization I had to steal the drug from. He was the only person who knew how to synthesize the chemical, but he kept the secret well hidden, and he was extremely protective of the small supply he had."

"And who was *he*?"

"He was the organization's head. I only knew him as Groeden. I don't know whether that was his first name or his last."

"So you're telling me that you didn't know this *Groeden* guy's full name, and you can't—or won't—tell me where he worked?"

"That's right."

I let out a sharp laugh. "Give me a break, Jefferson! This is hard enough without all the secret agent bullshit!" I glared at him peevishly. "So you just marched in and . . . *misappropriated* this drug?"

Jefferson sighed again. "I joined the organization for a little while."

"Oh? And how, exactly, did you do that? Did you just fill out an application?"

"I go where I want to go. You'll understand eventually."

"I'm sure I will," I sneered. I rubbed my eyes again. "So why didn't he just give you the drug? Or why didn't he sell it to you or something?"

"Because he wants to kill me."

I threw up my hands. "Do you *know* how this all sounds?"

"I know *exactly* how it sounds."

I exhaled slowly. "So you say Groeden was the only person who could make the drug?"

"That's what I was told. I never heard of anyone else who could synthesize it, although I looked very hard."

"Did he take it? Can he travel through time too?"

"In a way, yes."

"Oh, really?" I folded my arms. "Well, if that's the case, then why doesn't he just come back and kill you?"

"Because he has a very difficult time finding me—finding any of us."

My face was a picture of confusion and frustration.

"Douglas, this story doesn't have a beginning and an end—it's much more complex. You're going to have to let me fill in the blanks slowly. For now, just accept that Groeden *has* been here—in any number of forms."

"What does that mean?"

His eyes drilled into mine. "When he appeared to you—" He caught himself.

My mouth went dry, a cold tingle rippling across the back of my head and neck, and suddenly I knew. "He's the old man."

Jefferson nodded. "He was an apparition generated by your own mind. It's how he most often appears. And he's not actually an old man—everything about his appearance is carefully designed to terrify you."

I shook my head slowly. "It worked." And all at once I was back in my destitution. "He tried to kill me."

"No, Douglas. He wanted you to believe those things, but they were only images. He found you when you were weakest, and he tried to manipulate you the only way he could—with fear and anger. He wanted you to submit to him."

I thought about those cold black eyes. "How did he get in my head?"

"Again, I'm going to get to that in time. Right now there are other, more crucial things you need to understand."

"No, Jefferson. I want to know why he did that to me? What does he want?"

"You're a part of this, and he wants to stop you—to stop us."

"A part of what?"

He gave me an exasperated look, and I knew that I was pushing too hard. As vexing as this was, I could see the strain it was putting on Jefferson. "I'm doing this the best way I know how, Douglas."

We gazed at each other for a few seconds before I reluctantly said, "Okay. I'm sorry."

"Look, for now, the most critical part of all this is Groeden. There's something you have to understand about him. He's consumed with an absolute rage, and he enjoys it. He perceives it as power, and it drives him. He'll do anything to stop us. He understands true transcendence, but he's impure—he doesn't have the strength to master it. He lacks proper training and discipline, and he knows that trying to physically travel between universes will kill him if he isn't meticulously careful."

Jefferson's story had begun to take on a little more plausibility. I thought about the rage he described in Groeden—it was something I understood intimately, and my heart suddenly felt cold. I saw Elizabeth's face in my mind, and I remembered the day I hit her—her repugnance as she threw me out of her apartment. "I've felt that anger. It was *intoxicating*." I looked at the floor, ashamed.

He nodded. "But you didn't let it win. You walked away."

I lifted my head. "And Groeden didn't walk away?"

"He wasn't strong enough. His anger controls him so much that he can't admit he's impure. He's like an addict, dogmatic to a fault, and that's probably the biggest factor in the inconsistency of his ability to come back physically."

"What do you mean *inconsistency*?" I asked. "Can he come back or not?"

"Look, there's something you need to understand: like you said earlier, you can't just go to a library and check out a book about these concepts. A lot of them haven't even been discovered yet. We don't really know exactly what Groeden can or can't do, or when he may appear physically. And that's what makes him so dangerous.

"When you were younger, he almost never appeared. We have to believe there's some explanation for that, but we don't know what it is. What we *are* fairly certain of is that, as our universes converge temporally, conditions make bursting less difficult. So the older you get, the more likely it is that Groeden will appear."

"So it's easier for you and Jack?"

He nodded.

"Why? Do you use the drug?"

"No. We used to have to use it, but we learned to burst without it a long time ago. We don't know the formula, so we can't make more, and that means we wouldn't be able to sustain ourselves in this universe if we relied on it—we'd revert as soon as the drug wore off."

"Is that what happens to Groeden when he tries to burst?"

"We think so. He doesn't understand how to perceive the entirety properly. He's like us—it exists within him, but his anger takes over."

"How did you know to go to him for this drug? I mean, if everything was so secretive, how did you find his organization?"

Jefferson seemed to choose his words carefully. "I read a book a long time ago, and it confirmed the things my friend had told me."

"I guess this is the same mysterious friend who introduced you to this drug?"

"Yes, the same one."

"Can we just dispense with the mystery bullshit now?" I was beyond caring how flippant I sounded at this point. I was frustrated and I wanted Jefferson to know it. "Who was this friend? Was it Jack? Or was it some other nut?"

Jefferson's face darkened. "Douglas, that's enough. You had better understand that anything I leave out of this explanation is for your protection. I'm not forcing you to participate in this—or even to believe my story—but I'm tired of your impatience. I've offered you a lot of goodwill and good faith to earn your trust, and I'm not going to tolerate any more of your childish comments, so you'll just have to accept the answers I give you. Otherwise, you're free to leave anytime you like."

I had never heard Jefferson speak so harshly, and it drove the hubris out of me. It wasn't that I didn't believe him; as hard as the story was to accept, and as

much as I would have liked to dismiss it, there was too much evidence supporting his claims. And, above all else, I had simply been through too much not to
believe him.

Of course, I *was* angry that Jack and Jefferson had forced me into this game
without my knowledge, but after the reprimand, I felt ashamed about the way I
was acting. Deep down, I knew neither of them would have pulled me into this
unless it was unavoidable. "I'm sorry," I said. "You're right."

His voice became gentle. "I know how hard this is for you, but I want you to
try not to be frustrated. It isn't easy for any of us."

I nodded.

"Now where were we?"

I held my head up, and took a deep breath. "Your friend gave you a book . . ."

"Yes." He pursed his lips and laced his fingers in front of his chest. He seemed
again to be trying to find the right words. "I'm going to wait to tell you about the
book. I know you have a lot of questions, but like I said, there's no way we can do
all of this in one night. And there's some of it I won't be able to talk about at all."

Jefferson sounded tired. He blinked slowly, his eyelids drooping. "Look, for
now it's important that you understand Groeden's intent, because we have to stop
him." He seemed to slump a little, but he didn't take his eyes off me.

"What do you mean 'stop him'?"

Jefferson's eyes hardened into something like frustrated resignation, and his
silence told me everything. "You're going to kill him," I said.

"Yes."

"And that's why he's coming after you?"

He nodded and then looked at the floor. "If I don't do this, I'm not sure exactly
what will happen. So many people will die . . . an *incomprehensible* number—bil-
lions of people in each of an infinite number of universes." He lifted his head suddenly, his eyes desperate now. "Can you even fathom that?"

For a moment, I thought I might, but the look in his eyes forced the full magnitude on me. I shook my head slowly, not knowing how to respond. My mind was
swimming . . . the entirety, multiple universes, the drug . . . And somehow I was
supposed to help stop something I could barely conceptualize. It was too much.
Finally I asked the only question that seemed to matter. "Do you know where he
is? How do you find him?"

"I can always find him."

"Then why don't you kill him now and get it over with? Or better yet, why not
just find his parents and stop them from meeting—stop him from being born?"

Jefferson smiled gently. "That's a convenient science fiction cliché, but unfortunately it won't work for us. Look, I'm almost positive Groeden is going to die, so I have to be patient. If I kill him now, or if I tamper with his past in any way, I might also change history in some way that would harm us—not to mention a lot of other people as well.

"But besides all that, there's nothing simple about this game. I've watched a lot of people die because they underestimated Groeden, and trying to kill him now would expose us to a lot of unnecessary risk. For all his anger and hatred, he's one of the shrewdest people I've ever known. There's a precision to everything he does. He is one of the few people in my adult life who ever frightened me."

Jefferson saw the way his words were affecting me and paused. "I'm just trying to prepare you. I want you to understand that Groeden has no inhibitions—he'll do anything to save himself, and if we make any mistakes, he'll find us and kill us." He hesitated, and then said, "And that's just the beginning."

"What if he finds you first?"

"He won't."

"How do you know for sure?"

"I don't know anything for sure, Douglas, but I have a lot of confidence in the outcome."

"Okay, I'm going to ask this again: Why me? What do I have to do with this?"

"Without you, we will fail. And I hope I've been clear about what failure means."

"But I haven't done anything! I'm a drug addict with no means. How on earth can I be that important?"

"You have more potential than you give yourself credit for. I know it, Jack knows it, and, unfortunately, Groeden knows it too."

"And he wants to kill me too?"

Jefferson nodded.

"Am I going to get hurt?"

He looked at me gravely. "I'm not going to lie to you. There's a chance it could happen, but Jack and I are here to do everything we can to make sure you stay safe."

"And how will you do that?" An image of Groeden popped into my mind, smiling gluttonously, his long blade dangling from his hand, blood running down the shiny surface. I closed my eyes and forced the image out of my head.

Jefferson said, "We'll teach you everything we can."

"To travel through time?"

"That's the plan."

"Has it ever occurred to you I might not want to? And what if I'm not capable of it?"

"Oh, you're capable of it, no need to worry about that. And I already know how much the idea appeals to you, so don't act like it doesn't." He chuckled. "If anything, my job will be to keep you from doing it too soon."

In spite of all my apprehension in that moment, the thought of moving through universes was compelling. I sat still and considered this new turn in my life. Finally everything was beginning to make sense—the events and circumstances I had never been able to explain. I replayed the last few years in my mind, trying to reconcile the memories with what I was learning from Jefferson, and suddenly my mind halted at the image of the three men who had beaten me so badly in the alley, and who had, in turn, been so brutally murdered. "Jefferson, one night some men tried to hurt me, but—"

He nodded. "Yes, I know."

"It was you . . . "

He was already shaking his head. "No."

"Then who?" And almost before I could finish the sentence, I knew. "Jack."

Jefferson smiled a little.

"But he was in Durango."

"No, he was here. You were never out of his sight. It's ironic, but you may have been safer during your homelessness than at any other point in your life. Those men paid dearly to find out how much you mean to him. So many other times, I had to restrain him."

I gazed through the window. "How did he do those things?"

"There are no words to describe Jack," Jefferson said flatly.

"Those men would have killed me."

"Yes, they might have."

"Why did he have to . . .?" I winced, remembering the carnage. "It was horrible."

Jefferson's eyes glowed. "If he's protecting something he cherishes, he has trouble holding back."

It's intoxicating, I repeated in my mind, remembering the rage. I couldn't comprehend the mental and physical strength it must have required to take lives so quickly and easily—so *methodically*. As much as I loved Jack and as long as he'd been a part of my life, I realized in that instant how little I really knew about him.

Another moment passed and I said, "Did those men attack me because of Groeden?"

"We don't think so. It was just bad luck—mostly for them, whoever they were."

I shook my head, trying to clear my mind, unable to reconcile how Jack could have hidden so much from me through the years. And suddenly I remembered something. "He introduced me to LSD. He was there when I did it the first time."

Jefferson nodded almost imperceptibly. "He hated getting you involved with the drug at that age, but he had no choice. You had to feel the connection to the entirety."

"And he was here with me, in Austin, the whole time?"

"After I left, yes," Jefferson said.

"Why *did* you leave?"

"I had some other things to take care of."

"For four years?"

"I won't be able to stay long this time either."

I looked at him incredulously, about to protest, but I stopped. I knew those eyes; discussion was futile.

The door opened, and we both turned. Jack walked tentatively into the living room. He looked at me sheepishly. "Hey."

"Hi," I said. He looked almost like a stranger to me.

He approached the couch and Jefferson rose.

"How are you?" Jack said as he and Jefferson clasped hands.

Watching them, I had the impression they had been through a lot together and that they cared for each other very much. More than anything I saw the nearly unconditional respect Jack had for Jefferson; his loyalty was indisputable.

Jack almost wants to call him Sir, I thought.

They both turned to me, and in that instant I was aware of every painful thing I had ever endured. I just couldn't seem to accept that these two men had manipulated my life without my awareness. The magnitude of the revelation exhausted me.

Jefferson had told me things to me that until a short time earlier I had believed impossible—that I *still* believed impossible. In fact the details of his story were so implausible they were almost comical, and yet I found no amusement in the explanations. My life had taken an inexorable and irreversible turn—within hours my perception of reality had disintegrated in the face of a cold new perspective. Only my faith in Jefferson's integrity had preserved my ability to participate in the discussion, but that faith was slipping. "How long have you been planning all this?"

"It wasn't planned," Jefferson said. "I would hope you'd understand that by now."

"Don't *patronize* me!" I nearly snarled the words. "How *long*?"

He gazed at me for a moment, and then his eyes capitulated. "Your whole life."

I was getting angry again. "This is too fucking much! How could you just sit by and watch me destroy myself?"

Jack's eyes were sympathetic but I found no comfort in them. It disturbed me that a man could kill so easily and efficiently yet be so compassionate.

"What if we had been truthful with you years ago?" Jefferson said. "Would you have believed us? Even after everything you've experienced, you've had trouble accepting the things I've told you." He sat back down on the sofa and added, "If you burned your hand on a stove, would you touch it twice? You suffered, and you rose above your adversity. No one could have told you how to do that."

I shook my head rapidly. "No. there must have been another way."

"Only arrogant people think they can find true humility," he said. "But humility descends on us when we aren't aware of it. Knowledge means nothing without experience. You can read a thousand-page book about how to ride a bicycle, but until you actually get on the seat, the information is almost meaningless."

My expression was twisted with sadness and frustration. "You say I'm so critical to the future . . .?"

He nodded.

"If that's true, why'd you give me a choice the night I found the note from you—when I was in that garbage can? What made you so sure I would decide to take your advice? I mean, I was *so* close to killing myself."

Jefferson took a long breath. "We knew you might reject the letter, but there was no other choice. If you hadn't chosen to change your life, you would have been worthless to the future anyway. If we had tried to force it on you, you would have resented it."

His voice grew quieter, more intense. "You have no way of knowing just how much was at risk. Through everything, my instincts begged me to save you, but reason told me I couldn't—that you would have to make the decision yourself. Someday you'll be faced with critical decisions like these, and I hope you will meet them with the understanding that the best reaction is almost always no reaction at all. No matter how much we try to rearrange the universe to suit our needs, it will always revert in the end."

I didn't know what else I could say. I was drained almost to the point of shutting down.

"You're free to walk away whenever you want to," Jefferson said. "But if you do, more people than you can fathom will almost certainly die."

"That's not much of a choice, is it? I don't think I can do this."

"Yes, you can," Jack said. "You know what exists within you, now it's up to you to allow it in."

Almost at Jack's suggestion, my breathing slowed and I felt my body relax. "I still have so many questions."

"You'll never be alone," Jefferson said.

No one spoke for several minutes until Jefferson broke the silence. "I have some things to attend to, so I'll let you two talk." He headed toward the door. "I'll see you both soon."

"Where are you going?" I asked.

"To the police station," he said, reaching for his coat. "I think they have some questions for me." He opened the door.

"Jefferson?"

He turned, framed by the doorway.

"Groeden . . . he was responsible for Barney and Ellison, wasn't he?" *And my mom and Rudy Buck, and who knows how many other people . . .*

His face was solemn. "Yes."

We looked at each other another moment, and I said, "What are you going to tell the police?"

He smiled. "Only what they need to hear." He turned and closed the door behind him.

Jack gave me a weak smile. "Are you still mad at me?"

I considered the question for a moment. "No, I suppose not."

"So we're friends again?"

I managed to push my fear and anger aside. "We were never friends, Jack. You're an asshole. Do you want some tea?"

"I'm fine, thanks."

I refilled my cup and when I came back, he was staring at a book of chess openings. "So how old are *you*?" I said.

He looked up. "I've been around for a while."

"Jack, I'm just about at the end of my rope right now, so be straight with me. Okay?"

"I'm *very* old. That's all you need to know."

"Why don't you look it?"

He smiled at the question. "This isn't about taking vitamins and eating right. We exist *with* our bodies, not in spite of them. The idea that we have to die—that our cells have to stop dividing and that our immune systems have to decline—that's all bullshit. We've learned to affect our existence at the most basic level. We can change anything we want to."

"Then why does Jefferson look older?"

Jack shrugged. "It's just the way it has to be."

"And the scar on his head? Why doesn't he change that?"

He smiled again. "He keeps it to remember . . . Look, it's not important."

"It *is* important, goddamn it! Right now everything is important!"

He laughed gently. "No it's not, Douglas. Let it go."

I tensed my jaw again, releasing a long stream of breath. "How long will it be before I can . . . do what you do?"

"It'll happen when you're ready."

I looked at the floor, trying to accept what Jack was telling me—or rather, what he *wasn't* telling me. "I want to talk about my dad."

"Sure."

"How did you meet him?"

"I met him and your mom at a party."

"You didn't plan it?"

"I'm sure Jefferson told you that we don't really control anything. If we try to force it, to *make* it the way we think it's supposed to be, we'll screw it up. You'll learn as you go that it's best just to flow with it, to move in the general direction you think you're supposed to."

I rubbed my right temple with my index finger. "So . . . you and Dad were close, right? You weren't friends with him just because—?"

Jack laughed. "*Jesus*, no! I could've found a trillion different ways to get to you. I didn't need to use Max." He leaned closer. "Your dad was my friend. Please don't think anything different, okay?"

I nodded. "Jack—" I paused. I didn't know how to ask the next question. "You knew what was going to happen the night we broke down in Pagosa—before Dad and Thomas died."

He avoided my eyes. "I had to keep you out of Durango, man. I couldn't allow you to be in that car."

"How could you have let it happen?" My throat tightened a little.

"I had a long time to think about it. I had known it was coming for years." Jack averted his eyes, and suddenly I got the definite impression he was leaving something out.

"That's it?" I said. "You just accepted their deaths?"

He raised his hands in a gesture of helplessness. "What do you want me to do, Douglas? Huh? You think it was easy for me?"

Anger was assuming control again. "You could have *stopped* it!"

He leveled his gaze at me. "Listen to me. I have been around for a *very* long time, and with the knowledge I possess, I could have prevented more tragedies than you will ever be able to comprehend. My objective is to preserve history, not to defy it. Do you understand that?"

I stared at him without responding.

"Look, if I had been responsible for their deaths, I could understand your anger. But I wasn't. I just did what I had to do." He looked down. "If it helps, I miss them terribly." He lifted his head, his eyes suddenly full of anguish. "*Terribly.*"

I took a deep breath and held it.

"Don't go to war with us," he said. "We're on your side." He pointed to the chessboard in the living room. "Let's play a game."

I looked at him for a few more seconds and let the anger slip away. I walked to the chessboard. "There's a lot you're not telling me."

"Yeah, well, there's a lot we're not going to tell you, so you better get used to it. I know how hard this is for you, but it will be easier for all of us if you don't push me and Jefferson too hard. Do you get that?"

"I'm trying."

I sat down in front of the board and we each put out a quarter. We set up our pieces, and I moved a pawn. "Jefferson says there have only been a few people who could experience what you've seen."

"That's true."

"You knew the other ones, didn't you?"

"I knew one, but she died."

"What happened to her?"

"She just *died.* Let's not talk about that, okay? It was a long time ago."

I looked at his eyes, and I thought, *She was the one you were telling me about.*

We played in silence for a while longer, and then I said, "You and Jefferson are close."

Jack nodded. "Yeah, he taught me everything."

"So that's why you look at him like that."

"Like what?" He pulled his head back, genuinely surprised.

"You're loyal to him."

He shrugged. "I don't know what you're talking about."

"Jefferson says there are no words to describe you."

He snorted. "Whatever I am, it's only because he recognized and nurtured it. Without him I'd be nothing."

"He makes it sound like you're stronger than he is."

"Yeah, well, he's full of shit, and you can tell him I said so." Jack's eyes took on a frightening sharpness. "You listen to what I'm about to tell you: there may be things Jefferson won't do, but there's nothing he *can't* do. There's never been anyone like him."

We spent the rest of the night mostly in silence. We played five games, of which I took two.

"You know I can't beat Jefferson," Jack said during our last game. "I've never won a game against him."

"Me either. I don't even know if it's possible."

"Oh, no," he said, slowly crossing his arms. A confident grin touched his lips and his eyes sparkled. "It's possible."

When Jack went home, I straightened up a bit and decided to go to bed. I hadn't been so psychologically devastated since my destitution. My mind felt like the aftermath of a tropical storm; tomorrow I would start picking up the pieces, rearranging my new perspective. But now I needed sleep.

I crawled into bed and drifted, wondering what confluence of events was necessary to create men like Jefferson and Jack. I thought about Jack's description of Jefferson: *There's never been anyone like him.*

That was my last thought before I collapsed into the welcome oblivion of sleep.

Summer, Year Twenty-Three

Jefferson's continuing absences startled me at first, despite his warning that he wouldn't be around much. I would wake up or come home, and he would just be gone—nothing to indicate where. He would stay away for a week, sometimes longer, only to return as abruptly and mysteriously as he had left. And even when he was in town, we saw each other only briefly, never finding much of a chance to have any meaningful conversations.

I asked Jack about it, but he wasn't much help. "That old jackass does just about whatever the fuck he wants to, and there's nothing you can do about it. God knows how long I've been trying to figure him out, but I've never had any luck. You just have to trust that he's doing what needs to be done."

"Jack, I still have so many questions."

He stuck out his lips and raised his brow so high it looked like his eyes were going to explode from their sockets.

"What's that face, Jack? What is that?"

"That's my baboon face."

"You're such a prick."

"Yes, I am. I'm a prick who's not going to tell you anything." Then in a high-pitched, singsong voice he added, "That's Jefferson's job!"

"You know what, Jack?"

He raised his brow again.

"Fuck it. Never mind. Where has he been going?"

"How the hell should I know? He doesn't tell me anything. But I promise you, he's always close, so don't you worry about it."

About a week later, Jack called me. "What are you doing tonight?"

"I had a date but she bailed."

"Doesn't surprise me much."

"That makes me feel so much better. Thanks, Jack."

"How about we get some dinner and play a few games?"

When I got to Jack's house, I let myself in and found him standing in the living room with no shirt on. "Why aren't you dressed?"

"I'll be ready in a minute! Don't be in such a rush, you impatient little bastard!" He glared at me and went into his bedroom, where I could hear him shuffling around. "Hey," he yelled. "I want you to have a look at something I got a few years ago."

"What is it?" I said suspiciously.

"Oh, it's just something I picked up at a junk shop, but I thought you might be interested in it."

I walked cautiously into his bedroom where he was sitting on a loveseat. He pretended to examine the object in question resting next to him, his brow wrinkled in an absurd expression of feigned perplexity.

I stopped breathing. There was no mistaking what I saw: the rich finish, the age of the wood. It was as beautiful as I remembered.

"Jack . . ." I caught myself.

"What? You think it's worth something?"

"Shut up, Jack . . ." I could barely speak.

"What the hell is wrong with you, Douglas? Sometimes you really act like a pussy, you know that?"

"Shut *up*!" I repeated, hoarsely.

"Well, are you going to play the goddamn thing or just stare at it like a porn addict?"

For years my regret over the loss of my cello had been almost intolerable, and now Jack had repaired yet another part of my seemingly irreparable life. I walked slowly to the instrument and sat behind it, running my fingers along the finish. I picked up the bow and pulled it across the low C, resting my hand on its top, allowing the vibration to run up my arm.

I closed my eyes and played for the first time in years. My lack of practice was apparent, the notes stuttering and slipping, but after a few minutes, I relaxed and let go. My music, pent up for so long, now came rushing out in a deluge. Images of Dad and Thomas swam through my mind. I thought about my destitution and all the substances I had dumped into my body with such abandon—the drugs that had created dependencies so powerful I had given up my most precious possession to feed them. I relived the moment I sold the cello to the pawnshop, and yet here

I was, holding it again—the years of regret melting away under the richness of its tones, trickling through my body. My mind shifted again to thoughts of Elizabeth. I imagined this was what it would be like to hold her again.

I don't know how long I played, but when I opened my eyes Jack was gone. I went into the living room where he sat reading a book. "It sounds like you haven't lost your touch," he said.

"Where did you—?"

"I just picked it up somewhere." He flapped his hand dismissively.

"Thank you, Jack."

"*Jesus,*" he said. "Quit being so goddamn emotional. You're making me nervous."

"I'm sorry I didn't talk to you about it sooner."

"Didn't I tell you to quit being emotional?"

"I never forgave myself for selling it. It was the best thing anyone ever gave me—"

Jack grinned mischievously and folded his arms in front of his chest.

"What?" I asked.

"I didn't give it to you."

"I thought—"

"Are you listening? I didn't give it to you."

"But I called you that night . . . when I found it at the house."

He shook his head.

"Who then?" My eyes danced around the room, and then suddenly it came to me. "Jefferson?"

His smile broadened.

"And you just let me think it was you all those years?"

"Well . . . *yeah.*"

"*Jefferson?*"

Jack nodded.

And the next question seemed inevitable. "How old is it?"

"Mmmmm . . . sometimes it's better not to know too much."

My face slowly stretched into a smile. I turned, walked back into his bedroom, picked up the cello, and pulled the bow across the strings.

———◆———

IN THE FALL of my twenty-third year, the stock market began to unravel as it reacted to a slowing economy. Companies across the globe laid off huge percentages of their workforces, and the U.S. central bank responded several times, manipulating financial and economic components to stimulate growth. Theoretically, this manipulation was meant to create more spending and production. And more production, in turn, meant more jobs, and eventually, economic expansion. But not this time.

After the Fed acted, markets rallied for a short while, but then the slide resumed. I held the savings I had accumulated in cash, which left it almost totally immune to the devastation. But I had a lot empathy for unwary investors who saw their net worths destroyed over the ensuing months.

Gradually, the downturn slowed. It seemed like the economy had stabilized and might even soon be on its way back to health. Analysts and economists became optimistic; everyone was ready for a recovery. But then a series of unexpected misfortunes fell on the United States, causing even more instability.

A new round of poor financial results shook investor and consumer confidence yet again, and the economy returned to stagnation. Stocks resumed their downward charge, and no one seemed willing to predict when the pain might end. Unfortunately, neither could anyone predict that the problems had only begun.

For years, Washington politicians had campaigned against smaller foreign powers to bolster their own popularity, and with every new act of aggression, the salivating American public devoured the violence with a tidal wave of nationalistic furor. People cleared store shelves of cheap plastic American flags, waving them on cue, while regurgitating the dramatic propaganda doled out like candy by politicians and the media.

Nothing in the universe goes unanswered. At the very moment when it appeared the economy was poised to recover, several major cities around the world were attacked by unseen soldiers—wasps reacting to the disruption of their nests, stinging, retreating, ready to reform and sting again. Buildings were blown up, communication lines were destroyed, and massive amounts of data were lost. Terror was having its day, and global markets collapsed as confidence in governments' abilities to control security waned.

When the bottom fell out, everything went—good and bad companies alike. I watched the stock prices of the best firms in the world lose three-quarters or more of their value as investors responded to the drama surrounding the banking and credit industry. In a slow economy, there's often some justification for a decline in stock prices; reductions in productivity and employment certainly impair a firm's ability to create wealth for shareholders, and a stock's price should reflect these changes. Humans, though, are extreme by nature, and when danger appears, we behave irrationally—and erratically.

With the money I had saved, I began to buy shares of my favorite companies, and some of the discounts absolutely shocked me. As things got worse, I bought more, snapping up cheap shares and holding them. And when I had no more cash, I simply stopped.

I didn't watch the market obsessively, nor did I succumb to overly dramatized media reports. I knew it might be a while before rationality ruled again, but I was prepared to wait decades for the inevitable returns. And if I had confidence in anything, it was that the returns *were* inevitable.

One day I sat in the living room leafing through a newspaper, when I suddenly began to think about Jefferson—the image of his face appearing vividly in my mind. He had disappeared yet again, suddenly and without explanation, about a week earlier, and I had been wondering during this absence if we would ever get around to discussing my numerous questions. The gaps in his story were generating near maddening frustration and anger, severely testing the limits of my patience.

The phone interrupted my thoughts, startling me. "Hello?"

"Douglas."

It took me a moment to respond. "Jefferson? Where are you?"

He ignored my inquiry. "I have some questions for you."

I felt the familiar anger return and I scoffed. "*You've* got questions?"

There was silence on the other end of the line.

"Look, Jefferson, fuck this cloak and dagger shit. *I'm* the one with all the fucking questions! You informed me that my whole goddamn life has been one big goddamn science fiction story, and then you just disappear? When are you going to be back? And when are we going to talk about this shit?"

He chuckled softly.

"I'm serious. What the fuck are you laughing at?"

"You sound so . . . *tough.*"

I took a deep breath, his laughter disarming me as it always did. "You and Jack are making this really hard." My anger began to slip away, and I sighed.

"Patience," he said.

I could almost feel the mirth in his eyes through the phone, and I said, "Fine. Ask."

"You've been buying some stock, haven't you?"

The question caught me off guard, and suddenly I was nervous. "Yeah, I've bought a little."

"Good."

"You're not angry?"

"I believe, if I'm not mistaken, I warned you not to fool around with futures anymore. Buying stocks is hardly the same thing, wouldn't you agree?"

"Well, yes, but I just didn't—"

He cut me off. "I've opened a brokerage account in your name. It contains a fairly large sum of money. You should get all the information in the mail soon."

"What the hell are you talking about? I can't take any more handouts from you."

"What I've given you isn't a handout, it's a loan. I expect you to pay me back in full, plus a fair rate of interest."

"Fair *interest*? This is crazy! I appreciate your offer, but I didn't agree to any loans."

He ignored my resistance. "You'll pay me what's fair when the time comes."

"How do you know that?"

The question was absurd, but before I could retract it, Jefferson laughed again. "I'm investing in you because I have faith in you. And I also feel very confident you'll repay me."

I didn't know what to say. I could certainly use the money to buy undervalued stocks, but I didn't want to live off Jefferson any longer. As though he had read my mind, he said, "Douglas, life is a difficult struggle; when opportunities arise you should take them. Honest money is green no matter where it comes from. If you squander my investment, it will be my poor judgment, not yours."

And how, exactly, could I argue with that? Jefferson had offered me yet another opportunity, and I knew I had to pursue it.

He changed the subject. "I want to hear your thoughts on what's happening in the world right now."

"You called me for a news update?"

"No, I want to know what you think," he said flatly.

I hesitated, and suddenly I was nervous again. "Okay, I, uh . . . I think this stuff is probably going to keep happening for a long time, but I also think it's overblown. It's creating a lot of unrecognized value in the market."

"I suspected you would say something like that." He paused, then asked my opinion about several companies, most of which I already owned shares in. But he seemed especially interested in one particular business, and he asked me more about it than all the others.

I told him everything I knew about the company's management and strategies—why I thought it could be a sound investment. "The stock is expensive, so I haven't bought any. I wish the price would fall a little." I paused, waiting for his response.

"I'm proud of you," he said finally, exhaling audibly, as though relieved by what I had told him. He continued: "In two weeks the Fed is going to meet. Everybody is expecting another rate-cut, but that won't happen. Investors are going to be disappointed, and the market is going to take another hit. About four days after that, you'll get your chance to buy some of that stock; the company is going to miss its number for the first time in a string of good quarters, and the stock is going to get pounded again. When that happens, I want you to load up."

"You want me to use the cash you put in my account."

"Yes, but I want you to set about a third of the funds aside."

"Why?"

He hesitated. "There will be opportunities you'll want to capitalize on later."

"What opportunities?"

"You'll have to make those decisions yourself."

"Jefferson, if you're so sure about this, why don't you buy the stock?"

"You have to do this thing," he said.

"What the fuck does that *mean*? I'm beginning to feel like I'm not making *any* of these decisions! I'm basically doing what you tell me—like I'm your goddamn puppet, or something! Just give me some straight answers!"

He laughed again, and I thought I was going to throw the phone against the wall. Then he said, "Douglas, wholeness isn't the same as perfection. You're looking for the wrong thing. The answers won't seem as important if you stop letting the questions consume you."

"*See*? That's exactly what I'm talking about! That doesn't even *mean* anything! Tell me what that means, Jefferson!"

"It's the way things are." His voice was firm. "I have to go. I'll see you in a few weeks."

I started to respond, but the phone clicked and Jefferson was gone again. I set down the handset, leaned back, and stared at the ceiling, shaking my head. "This is so fucked up," I whispered to nobody.

A few days later, I received access to the account, and I was stunned when I found out how much was there. It was far more than I had received from my father's estate.

Two weeks after our phone conversation, the Federal Open Market Committee met, and, just as Jefferson had predicted, their decision disappointed investors. The market tanked, and the stock we had discussed began to decline with the averages. Trusting Jefferson's insight more than ever, I didn't buy right away.

Four days later, the company missed its earnings estimate—again as Jefferson had predicted—and the stock went into a tailspin. For the first time in several years, the company sold at a tremendous discount to what I knew to be its intrinsic value. I bought as much as I could with the money Jefferson had provided, leaving—as he had instructed—a third in cash.

While I didn't yet know it, this was the foundation on which so much of the future would be built.

Fall, Year Twenty-Three

JEFFERSON RETURNED SEVERAL weeks after our phone conversation, and although he remained in Austin for a while this time, I still didn't see much of him. He was distant, coming in and out of the house like a specter, smiling and nodding as he went about whatever it was he did, never saying much of anything to me.

In contrast, Jack and I spent a considerable amount of time together, and while he actually *did* talk to me—incessantly and without respite—the conversations were even more vexing than Jefferson's evasiveness. Jack would run on at the mouth about anything and everything meaningless in the universe, stuffing every sentence with incomprehensible quantities of profanity, while still somehow maintaining an intelligible rhetorical framework. It was truly remarkable. Of course, I just tolerated it, because telling Jack to be quiet was like telling gravity to go away.

The whole situation was positively infuriating, but I finally resigned myself to the fact that I was decidedly *not* in control of the rate at which I would be given information about all of the events that had shattered my previous understanding of my very existence in the universe. And why should *I* care about such things? This was, after all, nothing more significant than my perception of reality. Of *course* Jefferson and Jack had every right to keep me in the dark.

This was precisely my state of mind one autumn evening as I sat in the kitchen, eating a bowl of soup and reading some piece of fiction that didn't interest me a whole lot. I decided it was time to replace it with something more engaging, so I started to get up.

Jefferson was standing in the doorway, watching me. I kept my seat, and we stared at each other.

"What?" I asked finally.

"Do you want to talk?"

I raised my eyebrows. "Yeah," I snorted. "I think I could be persuaded to do that."

He smiled and walked into the living room.

I put my dishes in the sink and followed him.

Jefferson sat in the same spot on the sofa where he had been a few months earlier—when we had started this process. The night was chilly, so I lit the gas fireplace and sat in the chair next to it.

He looked at me for a moment and then said, "Okay."

"Okay what?"

He chuckled. "You're the one with all the questions, if I'm not mistaken."

Here I was, finally getting the very thing I had been demanding for months, and I barely knew where to start. I folded my hands in front of me. "Okay, I guess we should start where we left off . . . with Groeden." I shifted in my chair. "You said he was involved with Barney and Ellison."

Jefferson nodded gently. "Right."

I hesitated, not sure I even wanted to ask the next question. "And my mother?"

He continued to nod.

"And there were others too—"

"Yes, all of them."

"There's this thing they always say . . ." I looked absently at one of the bookshelves, remembering my mother's face the night before she died, remembering the insanity in Rudy Buck's eyes.

Jefferson finished the sentence for me. "Medicine Man."

I met his gaze. "Why?"

He looked as if he was about to speak, but then he stopped, pursed his lips, and shook his head slowly. "Soon enough."

I looked back down at the floor in resignation. "How does Groeden get to them like that?"

Jefferson let out a long breath. "This part is going to take some time."

"Well, I have plenty."

He looked at me over his glasses. "You remember I told you that Groeden is very interested in bursting."

I nodded.

"He walks that proverbial fine line between insanity and genius, and I imagine the idea of manipulating history is particularly alluring to someone as egomaniacal as he is. At some point, through the work of the organization I told you about, he saw the potential of the drug, and he began to run tests." Jefferson took a breath and released it. "When I say that, you probably imagine mice and rats—and I'm sure there was some of that . . ." Jefferson's face took on a hard expression as his voice trailed off.

"What are you saying? He used people?"

Jefferson nodded solemnly.

"But you said it's dangerous. Why would anyone agree—?"

"Most of them didn't," he said. "Groeden abducted them—at least in the beginning."

"You have to be joking."

"I'm not. Remember we're talking about the government here, and since when does a clandestine agency care how many lives it destroys? At first, only 'undesirables' were nabbed—homeless people mostly. The organization also ran a lot of operations in small, poor countries around the world, and I think that's where many of the subjects came from. But when the experiments failed—"

"What do you mean 'failed'?"

Jefferson looked up at me, his expression bleak. "All the subjects died. Using the drug without understanding transcendence is a death sentence—it will kill anyone who tries to burst without comprehension and experience. But Groeden didn't care about any of that. He was frantic to find anyone who could burst. He finally decided the homeless and poor were just too weak to be of any use, so he started getting desperate, and he ordered his agents to grab stronger, healthier subjects. Now they were snatching people who would be missed.

"He tore them from their lives, their families, and stuck them in labs where technicians administered the drug. But this group obviously didn't understand transcendence any better than the homeless subjects, and they all died too."

"You talk about it like you saw it."

Jefferson looked at the floor. "I did." He stayed with that thought for a moment, and when he looked up, his eyes were filled with horror. "They were terrified. They had no idea what was happening to them. They struggled—screaming, crying, reaching out to the technicians, pleading for their lives. They urinated on themselves . . . it was reprehensible."

He let go of a long breath, looking vacantly out the window, and I knew he was back there in his mind, experiencing some hell I could never imagine. As if to no one, he said, "The panic in their eyes . . ."

He shook his head slowly a few times and then turned back to me. "Groeden ripped their dignity from them. They were strapped to a table and slowly executed.

"It took all the self-control I possessed to stay quiet. At times it was almost impossible to see how important the bigger picture is—that we have to do everything we can to preserve history, to make sure our destinies aren't derailed. The only reason I put myself there in the first place was to steal the drug, and I had no choice but to stay quiet, because stopping Groeden is more important than anything."

He took another deep breath. "I want you to think about what it would mean if someone like him controlled every single aspect of reality, the past *and* the future, not just of this world, but all universes that exist in space and time—the entirety itself. Try to imagine Hitler with the kind of resources I've been describing to you. The burden we carry is almost too big to comprehend." Jefferson's jaw was clenched, his eyes on fire. He looked at me for another moment, allowing the gravity of his expression to find its way into my soul.

Finally he said, "If you only hear one thing I say about Groeden, let it be this: he wants to be God, and he knows he has a reasonable shot at achieving exactly that. He'll stop at nothing to reach his goal."

He held another breath for a few seconds. "You listen to what I'm telling you, Douglas. I don't want you to be scared. I want you to be absolutely terrified."

Then Jefferson's shoulders slumped and he looked down at his hands. "You may think I should have done something to save those people, but someday you're going to see some things—" He stopped himself. "Look, if you let your emotions win, you'll die. We'll all die."

I nodded, carefully noting his tone, his posture, the distress that seemed to emanate from this man who had always displayed so much poise and control. And I found myself suddenly quite content not to find out anything more about what I might see later. Another moment passed, and I said, "How many times did you have to go through that?"

Jefferson looked utterly defeated. "Too many." He looked away for a moment, and then seemed satisfied with the answer and resumed. "After enough failures, Groeden finally stopped killing innocent people. Instead he put together a new team of agents. They continued the experiments on themselves."

"Them*selves*? They agreed to it?"

"Oh, they were *eager* to do it. They even jokingly called themselves the Volunteers. He paid them obscene amounts of money and promised them the keys to the universe. They were quintessential soldiers, unstoppable machines—very loyal to their leader and his promise of the future."

"Where did they come from?"

Jefferson shrugged. "Who knows. Military probably. While all this was happening, Groeden had more backing than I could begin to fathom. I tried to root out his sources but he kept them well concealed, and in spite of my abilities, I never discovered anything substantive about his connections."

"Were any of these Volunteers successful?"

"No, they died like everyone else."

"Then why did they keep doing it? Didn't they know what was going to happen?"

"Why do people crash airplanes into skyscrapers? Why do people strap dynamite to their chests and blow themselves up in crowded markets?" He scoffed. "If I hadn't seen it myself, over and over . . ." Jefferson shook his head, his eyes grim. "Groeden convinced the Volunteers that if they were strong enough, they could transcend the vastness of space and time—which might actually have been true in some cases, had they been prepared correctly. They were driven by their egos— by the promise of immortality and unimaginable power. Each of the Volunteers believed he would be the one to survive."

"So, how did the experiments work?"

Jefferson winced and leaned his head back, staring at the ceiling. If nothing else, he had achieved one goal: I was now absolutely terrified. *If it's affecting* him *like this, what am* I *going to have to face . . .?*

"Volunteers or not," he said, "the scientists just strapped them down—to hold them in place—and hooked up wires and sensors all over their bodies. Then the drug was pumped into their veins. In all the cases, the subjects began to convulse after a short time. Their fingers would curl up, and their muscles atrophied. If I hadn't seen them before the tests, I wouldn't have believed they had once been actual people. They disintegrated right in front of our eyes." Jefferson leaned forward. "It still disturbs me to think about how fast the human body can degenerate if it isn't prepared to burst."

"So they really were basically just lab rats?"

"It was all very clinical. Do you remember I told you about the book?"

I nodded.

"Well, Groeden has seen it too—he read it during the first round of experiments. In fact, it was the content of the book that made him put together the Volunteers." Jefferson sucked air between his teeth. "This made it all the more inhuman because the book specifically said Groeden's experiments would fail. The moment he read it, he knew the critical ingredient to success was the transcendence of human perception, and he also knew that almost no one is capable of achieving that. But he kept going anyway."

"Tell me about this book. Where did it come from?"

Jefferson considered that, but then slowly shook his head. "No, it's not time yet."

I scanned the room, my eyes not really seeing anything at all, my mind mired in escalating fear. "Maybe the formula for the drug was wrong. Maybe that's why the experiments failed."

"If that were true, Jack and I wouldn't be here. Anyway, Groeden knew he was on the right path because the monitoring equipment in the lab made it clear that *something* had happened to the subjects at a subatomic level. Plus, some of the Volunteers were able to burst to a small degree before their bodies gave out.

"The book discussed what components were necessary to burst, so in his recruitment of subjects, Groeden concentrated on people who exhibited qualities that should have led to success—like unusually strong reflexes or uncanny abilities of perception. The Volunteers went through rigorous training, studying martial arts and meditating for hours every day. Groeden even had them read books about Taoism and other philosophies that should have contributed to transcendence, but unfortunately it wasn't enough."

Jefferson let out a sigh. "The Volunteers couldn't really accept what they were learning. Most of them laughed about the metaphysical part of their training—

they just didn't believe in it. This was the crux of their downfall, because words can't describe what it takes to move beyond human perception. It doesn't matter how many books you read or how many hours you meditate; those things can't replace the most important step, which is total submission to the entirety.

"But even in the face of doubt, the intense level of training must have made it possible for a few of them to transcend slightly, because before they died, they described seeing multiple universes—the *multiverse*. One of the subjects even disappeared briefly, and then returned to the laboratory before he died."

"How long was it before you got access to the drug?" I asked.

"Groeden was the only person with the formula and, like I said, he hid it carefully. It took a long time, but he finally made a mistake, and that was when I found and stole a vial."

"How much is left?"

"Not much at all."

"Can't you reverse engineer it or something?"

Jefferson shook his head. "I hired some talented chemists, but they couldn't completely identify the compound. They understood the composition, but not how the molecules were assembled; something crucial changes in the process—when the components come together—and without that knowledge, it can't be synthesized."

"What does it feel like—I mean, if it doesn't *kill* you?"

Jefferson smiled. "It's like LSD, only about a thousand times more powerful. You have more control when you burst—or even if you just split time."

"What's the difference?"

"When you burst, you physically move to another universe. But what we call splitting time is only the awareness of those universes, divided and separated. It's more like hovering and watching."

I clasped my hands together and squeezed them. "And what's it like to travel through time?"

"The first few times I took the drug, when I was younger, I only split time—I saw the different universes but I didn't enter them. It was hard, both physically and psychologically. I felt like the drug was shredding the fabric of my soul, like my sanity was slipping away."

"I've been there," I said, remembering the first time I took acid.

Jefferson nodded in understanding. "Years later when Jack and I took it, the transcendence was easier for both of us. We had studied and practiced for years, and we understood it with a more mature clarity. It was still physically and psychologically difficult, but we maintained our discipline, and neither of us was hurt too badly. After several times, we became much better at it."

"And Groeden just let you go with the drug?"

"Let's just say he didn't have much of a choice. But believe me, he has never given up looking for us."

Jefferson leaned back and collected his thoughts for a moment. "There's another aspect to all this I need to tell you about. Do you remember I told you that Groeden has difficulty moving through the multiverse?"

"You said he's not as strong as you are, and that his anger takes over."

"Yes, and I also told you that we don't know much about what he can and can't do—that he is unpredictable, and he could appear at any time."

I nodded, and Jefferson said, "Well, what we do know is, because of all that, Groeden needed to find a more predictable and consistent way to reach through time, to manipulate the outcome. He put a lot of money into developing a technology that would help him do that. It's called the Bell, and it allows for the transmission of data through space and time—across universes. It lets Groeden and his team reach into the past and monitor people, and even affect their minds." Jefferson paused and looked at me, as if waiting for something.

And then I understood. "That's how he got into my head when I was on the streets." I looked at the floor, shaking my head slowly. "Barney and Ellison . . . my mother . . ."

Jefferson nodded. "Yes, probably."

"What do you mean, *probably*?"

"He may be using a combination of all of it—the Bell, splitting time, or even bursting. Like I said, we just don't know what he can do, or when he can do it."

Bumps raised on my arms as I remembered Groeden's face, his sharp black teeth. "I thought I was crazy. I kept hearing him, *seeing* him." I closed my eyes, recalling how close to the edge that voice had taken me.

"The power to transcend is inherent in you," Jefferson said. "But Groeden knows that, and he used it to his advantage. He was able to create illusions that no one else could have perceived the way you did."

Jefferson gave me a moment and then continued. "Anyway, I'm almost certain he uses the Bell to track us. You can think of it like a kind of radar, although that's not the best analogy. Essentially Groeden and his team devised a way to transmit particles to different universes at the subatomic level. They can identify small holes in the quantum fabric through which they send these particles, and when the particles return, the technicians can detect what's happening in different universes.

"But for all its promise, the Bell is a crude technology and its scope is limited. The scientists use it to identify something called an energy print, which is a unique pattern we all carry in our bodies at the subatomic level. Then they broadcast particles encoded with information to that person. It comes through as a manifestation of the subject's own voice."

"And they can use this thing to get to anyone?"

"Well, yes and no. When Groeden's technicians find someone's energy print in another universe, they create a data stream at the quantum level. Any signal they create—like someone speaking into a microphone, for instance—converts to what is called particle code. It broadcasts as both waves and particles, like light. Only it's not light—it's pure energy at the quantum level.

"The signal is then broadcast over a large area, and when the transmission finds a target, the particle code creates a chain reaction in the subject's body at the subatomic level. The data converts from a quantum stream to an analog signal at the cellular level, and the body of the individual who is receiving the signal becomes a kind of a self-contained soundboard. Unfortunately I can't get too much more specific for you—like I said, it's all been so well hidden. Groeden knows I'm watching him, and he's not taking any chances. He has found ways to hide a lot of things from me, and that troubles me deeply, because it shouldn't be possible."

"Why not?"

"I told you, I always know where he is. He shouldn't be able to keep anything from me, yet he does, and I don't know how. It's just another part of this process I have to accept, and unfortunately, you're going to have to approach a lot of it on faith too. I wish it were different, but there's nothing we can do about it."

I grimaced at the thought of the voice that tormented me for so long, thinking about Rudy Buck and my mother, Barney and Ellison. "How many people have been affected?"

"Not as many as you might think. The Bell is undependable—Groeden's team has no way to target any specific person, so the victims are usually random and difficult to isolate. Like I told you, they use a sort of a shotgun effect—broadcasting over a large area. And even when they are able to lock onto a target, the return signal is usually weak—although that isn't always the case, and I don't know why. I think it may have something to do with the proximity of each time period—the closer together they are, the clearer the signal.

"I also know that a person's energy print changes and distorts over time, which only adds to the scientists' problems. But once they lock on to a print, they can usually track their subject indefinitely, adjusting for the shifts."

Jefferson inhaled deeply. "The biggest problem is that, even when they isolate an energy print, they rarely understand anything about the person they've hit—the technicians know they've made a connection, but the details are unclear. Mostly it's a one-way transmission. For instance, to my knowledge, they've almost certainly never been able to concretely identify a person, or to obtain someone's precise location. I know for sure they've never been able to get any of our names, or any details about us.

"And there's another big problem with the Bell. I think I mentioned that the subject's mind translates the transmission in a distorted version of his own inner voice. Because of that, the broadcasters have to use suggestion to affect the person they target—"

"What, like hypnosis?"

"Something like that. Groeden brought some brilliant psychologists into the program, but none of them could find a way to dictate orders to a victim—so the sender is forced to manipulate the target's mind very carefully. That's why you thought you were going crazy."

"It was intolerable," I said. "I couldn't get away."

"You were an exceptional case, Douglas. Most of the time the broadcasts are a total crapshoot, which makes the Bell highly impractical. In fact, most of the time, the targets just ignore the broadcasts altogether."

"How can they possibly ignore it?"

"Most people are impervious to suggestion. A target has to be extremely vulnerable, psychologically, for the broadcasts to have any effect. Even then, a lot of the intended victims resist what they're being told—like Barney and Ellison did."

I thought about Barney and his incessant muttering. Then I recalled the day he killed himself. I could still see his brains sliding down the wall. I squeezed shut my eyes and Ellison's face appeared in my mind. *He was my friend . . .* I remembered the day I met Elizabeth, when Ellison left us alone in the Cardinal—that mischievous little smile on his face. *That* wonderful *smile . . .*

I opened my eyes. "You knew they had Barney, and you knew that Ellison was going to—"

"There was nothing I could do."

I considered everything for a moment. "I know how weak I was, and there's no question about Barney. But Ellison didn't seem vulnerable."

Jefferson pursed his lips. "He had lost a lot more money than you thought, Douglas. He had even gone into debt. He was completely broke."

I put my hand on my forehead and laced my fingers through my hair. *He never said a word, and he never stopped laughing through it all. If I had only known . . .* And then I thought about the weight of my own problems at that time. *What could I have done to help him anyway?* If anything, my trading systems had been responsible for his downfall, and with that thought a wave of guilt and remorse pounded my soul like a maelstrom. I managed to fight back tears. "Look, let's just get on with this," I said.

Jefferson stared at me compassionately. He continued, "Another big problem Groeden has with the broadcasts is that most of the victims eventually go insane. You're the only person I've known to endure it without losing his mind."

"Well, it was *fucking* close, believe me." My voice nearly cracked, and I pushed myself up from my chair, desperately trying to suppress my emotions. My eyes bounced around the room, and I clenched my teeth. I started pacing in front of the fire as another thought trickled in. "Groeden doesn't go breaking into peoples' heads just to observe what's going on, does he?" I stopped pacing and looked at Jefferson.

"No."

I pressed my temples with the heels of my hands, and suddenly I had a vivid memory of Barney pointing his pistol at Jefferson's head. I felt as if a brick had landed on me. I whispered, "They were supposed to *kill* us."

Jefferson nodded gently.

"And that kid, Rudy? And my *mother*?"

Jefferson only continued to watch me.

I closed my eyes tightly for a moment, and then returned to my chair. "So, why didn't they do it?"

"I don't know that either Ellison or Barney was capable of killing. They resisted the suggestions, which probably took every ounce of their strength. They were good people."

I tightened my jaw further. "Yes, they were."

Jefferson added, "For whatever reason, I don't think Groeden had much control over your mother and that kid who tormented you. It may have something to do with the time differential."

I sat still for a moment. Finally I said, "If Groeden wants to kill me so bad, why didn't he try to find other people?"

"He probably did." Jefferson looked at me uncertainly. "This is complicated. There are basically two reasons why I think they might not have found you when you were younger. The first we've already discussed: we're just not sure what Groeden can or can't do. Our best guess is what I just said—the time differential; maybe he just wasn't capable of going back that far.

"The second possible explanation is equally ambiguous, and I can't provide you with any evidence for my conclusion." He hesitated. "I think the other reason they couldn't find you when you were younger may be because they didn't have your energy print."

"Well, they obviously knew where to find me! They got to my mother and Rudy!"

"That's true," he said.

"But if they didn't have my sig—"

"They got to your mom and that kid because of me."

I stared at him, not believing what I had heard. "You were in Durango?"

He nodded. "I was when those things happened, yes."

"What the fuck? You were there before I *met* you?"

Jefferson's face was impassive. "I was in Durango several times when you were young."

I remembered the cello. *Jefferson gave it to me . . . Did he come into my house . . . ?* Suddenly I felt naked and dirty. "Were you . . . *watching* me?"

"Don't ask that question. I won't tell you anything else about this. I can't."

I put my hands behind my head and pulled my chin against my chest. "*Jesus,* this is just too much!" I let air hiss between my teeth. "Why is this happening to me? It seems like these people—" I pointed at Jefferson, "—*you* people can get to anybody!"

Jefferson looked hurt and angry. "Douglas, we're on your side. Don't forget that."

I was nearly unable to contain my anger. "Well, if they don't have my energy print, then how did they find me when I was older? You left Austin—or at least you *told* me you did. How did they find me then?"

"I *did* leave Austin. That's the part we're not sure about. There's only one set of conditions that allows them to actually direct the signal, and that requires them to have a predetermined energy print; when those conditions are ideal, they can then pick out a target with less difficulty, although the process is still problematic."

He shrugged. "They may have gotten your print at some point, although we can't be sure. Jack and I have spent a lot of time trying to figure that out, but we've never found the answer."

I looked at him sideways. "If they have my energy print, they can find me without you."

"Look, we don't know that they have it for sure. I can't be certain of anything except that they've found us in the past, and they'll probably find us again. Like I told you, they'll have a hard time tracking us—even if they do have our prints—but they're out there, and I won't take any risks I don't have to. That's why I left."

I began to feel like I was missing some critical components to the story. Jefferson was holding back too much. "But they still managed to broadcast those terrible things into my head," I said. "And Groeden found me too. That leads me to believe they do have my print."

"That may be true."

"Then why would you have left me?" I said, stunned.

"If they did have your print, Jack would protect you in my absence—which he did anyway. If they didn't have your print, then I distracted them by leaving—they had to use a lot of their resources to track me. So let's say they do have it . . . picture what it might have been like if I *hadn't* left—if they could have tracked both of us. Either way, my decision to leave was better for you."

Jefferson shifted his body. "And besides all that, the book said I would leave, so that's what I did. We have to do what our destiny requires, Douglas. That's perhaps the most important lesson I can give you."

I furrowed my brow, scratching my forehead as I looked vacantly at the Persian rug at my feet. "I thought you said an energy print distorts over time. Even if they have ours, how can they still find us?"

"Because they've tracked us perpetually since they got our prints, always adjusting for any distortions."

"And how did they get your energy print to begin with?"

"They got it when I stole the drug from Groeden. But by then it was too late to catch me—I was already gone."

"Then why didn't he just broadcast your print back in time, to himself—before you left?"

"It wouldn't have done any good. I told you, location can't be accurately pinpointed using the Bell. The technicians can track us in a general sense—maybe, for instance, they know we're in Austin right now. But they would never be able to track us to this house—or even to this neighborhood, for that matter. They might get details from other sources, like the book, but not from the Bell. Also, they never knew my identity. They never saw me—I'm a ghost to them; even if they had broadcast the print back, they had no way of specifically identifying me. The organization had who *knows* how many thousands of employees, and matching energy signatures isn't an exact science. Believe me, Groeden has been trying to find my real identity for as long as this loop has been repeating, and so far he has been unsuccessful."

"But they'll know where we are from now on—"

"They'll have a general idea. But I told you, the Bell is unreliable. They're still shooting in the dark."

"Well, it seems like giving them your print was a pretty serious mistake, Jefferson."

"I had to give it to them."

"*What*? If these people are as dangerous as you say they are, it doesn't seem like you should give them *any* information about us."

He smiled slightly. "Security around the drug was tight, and when I stole it, I had to expose myself temporarily. It was the only way."

"But that's not the whole story, is it?"

He gazed at me for a few seconds, unsure how much to tell me. Finally he said, "No, but it's enough for now."

"And what about Jack? Why haven't they tracked him?"

"Because they never had his print. He never associated with Groeden or his team—we were careful about that."

"But he's been close to you, right? Shouldn't they be able to find him?"

"There *have* been times they found him because of me." He held a breath, his face full of uncertainty, and then added, "We're almost positive they don't have his print. Look, I don't have all the answers, Douglas. I don't exactly know why they've never identified Jack, just like I don't know how Groeden can appear sometimes, but not others. The book doesn't answer those questions so we can only speculate."

I considered everything for a moment. "If they have my print, why aren't they broadcasting to me now?"

"They probably are, but you've grown strong again. Your mind no longer accepts what they send."

I got up and paced around the living room again, still trying to make all the connections. Then I stopped and turned to face him. "What am I supposed to do now?"

His expression became sympathetic. "Not *you*, Douglas, *we*. *We* will teach you what we know, and we'll be patient."

"And what about the Bell? We should do something to get it away from them." I took a few deep breaths trying to calm myself. "You should, I don't know—" I flapped my hand in the air. "—do your time-travel thing and get it away from them!"

"No. We don't need to do that, and anyway I'm not sure we could if we wanted to."

"But it should be destroyed! That's part of why you're here, isn't it? To stop them?"

"Yes and no," he said. "Look, I'm supposed to kill Groeden, and I intend to. But I am not here to interfere in any other way, and destroying the Bell just isn't part of the plan."

"What are you talking about? It could be catastrophic in the wrong hands!"

"It's already in the wrong hands, and they haven't done anything seriously destructive with it."

"They killed Barney and Ellison! *That's* destructive! I watched a woman's head explode from a shotgun blast! Does that qualify as destructive?" I started pacing again.

"I'm not defending them, but it has cost them a fortune to do what they've done. Despite Groeden's desperation and his willingness to spend ludicrous sums of money on this, the Bell has been a huge failure—believe me, I was there."

"Yeah, and you saw all those people die! It doesn't seem like a failure to me!"

Jefferson persisted. "The technology is imperfect and hard to keep up. Maintaining a connection tracking signatures is often nearly impossible. The odds of them finding us are demonstrably low."

We stared defiantly at each other. After a moment, his expression softened. "I understand your concerns, and I'm not going to lie to you. It *is* important you understand the magnitude of our dilemma. No matter how problematic and difficult the technology is for them, you have to be cautious every moment, because they could find us again at any time—no matter how slim the odds. But that doesn't mean we're going to attempt to destroy a technology we don't know anything about. The book mentions nothing along those lines, and the risk therefore far outweighs any potential reward. The consequences of defying our paths in this loop could be absolutely horrific. Don't you understand that yet?"

I stopped pacing again and looked at him. "You know something, don't you? That wasn't the last attack."

He didn't answer.

"Jefferson, you're scaring the hell out of me. This man is dangerous! Christ, how many times has he tried to kill me? Is he going to attack us again?"

"There's a strong possibility it will happen again."

"When?"

His face was somber. "Just because I can find Groeden doesn't mean I know what he's thinking or what he's doing."

"Then let's just destroy the Bell, Jefferson! *Fuck*, let's just end it! I don't want to live my life like this—always waiting for the next crazy fucking jackass to blow me away!"

"And you think it would be that easy." He chuckled softly.

"Why are you laughing at me?"

"I'm laughing at your reaction."

I was becoming more indignant by the second. "What's that supposed to mean?"

"You didn't hear a word I said. I don't think I could stop it if I wanted to. And the truth is I *don't* want to. We don't know where it came from, or even when it was invented for that matter, so I can't begin to guess who's responsible. But I *am* sure that whoever created it protects the investment very carefully. And even if I did find when and where it was invented, what am I supposed to do about it? Your idea to destroy it is the Law of Parsimony run amuck."

"The *what*?"

"The Law of Parsimony," he said. "Ockham's Razor."

"I don't even know what that is, and what the fuck does it have to do with us dodging bullets for the rest of our lives?"

"It's the idea that the simpler of two solutions is most likely the best one. But the problem with that is, sometimes the simplest solution *isn't* the best one."

"I thought you liked simplicity, Jefferson!"

"I'm all about simplicity, but that doesn't mean the entirety isn't complex. Acting with incorrect premises—using some principle like Ockham's Razor as justification—isn't the best answer. Do you remember when I played chess against that guy Mack several years ago at the Cardinal—when I gave him my queen?"

"Yeah, so?"

"Mack saw a simple solution to his problem—it was obvious to him. But it turned out to be the death of his king, didn't it?"

"But—"

Jefferson crossed his legs. "Everything in the universe is either knowledge or potential knowledge. Every decision we make is the manifestation of ideas—progress is generally defined as the growth of knowledge. And while knowledge can be both helpful and deadly, once it exists the only way to control it is *not* to control it.

That's true simplicity. If you try to swim up a river, eventually the river will win. The more we try to defy reality, the more dramatic the repercussions will be."

I continued to glare at him. "You know how much I respect you, Jefferson, but you're wrong. We should do something."

He smiled gently and shook his head. "We can't protect ourselves from our mistakes—assuming the Bell even *is* a mistake. We can be aware of them. We can respect them. We can certainly study them. We can even prevent ourselves from repeating them. But we *cannot* defy the universe; we can only move with it. Reality is *not* negotiable."

I looked at him in disbelief. "So you think that just anyone should be able to broadcast into different times using the Bell?"

"It doesn't matter what I think, it's already the state of things. The Bell is going to exist. We can try to conceal it, but its existence is a foregone conclusion because no matter what we do, ideas—including the technology behind the Bell—are going to proliferate."

I folded my arms defiantly. "I don't believe that. We can stop anything we want to."

"You think so? Name one idea, substance, or technology that was ever successfully eliminated from the library of human knowledge."

"If it's been eliminated, then I wouldn't know about it, would I?"

Jefferson nodded and gave me an almost devious smile. "But I would." He let me sit with that thought for a few seconds and then said, "Institutions have been trying to suppress knowledge since the dawn of rational thought. It never works. We can waste as many resources as we like trying to prevent the outcome, but the truth will always win—no matter how long it takes."

"Well, you already know the outcome, don't you?" I said. "How widespread is the Bell in the future?"

"Does it matter? If people want to destroy themselves then it's inevitable; any attempt to stop knowledge is futile. Regardless, I think the Bell will continue to exist—although I don't think it will ever be a reliable technology."

I thought about that for a moment. "All technologies improve."

"Not that it would change my argument, but I don't think this one will. The Bell's function—to send a signal through holes in the fabric of space-time—is inherently limited in its capacity to improve. To truly capitalize on the principles behind the Bell would require people to move beyond current mechanistic thinking. If that happens humanity will likely have lost any desire to manipulate the past—or so it would seem, because otherwise I don't think we'd be having this conversation."

"No," I said, shaking my head, remembering all the horrible things I endured because of this machine. "No, because even if you're right, how do you know people won't destroy themselves with it? It seems to me that you've been given a huge responsibility. I mean, you have the opportunity to stop what may be the most dangerous human invention ever, and you've chosen not to."

A corner of Jefferson's mouth turned up in a half grin. "This isn't my responsibility. Just because I'm aware of the Bell's existence doesn't make it my job to stop it—as if I *could* stop it." He hesitated and then said, "How many people are killed in car crashes every year? Should we go back and prevent the invention of the combustion engine?"

I sat down and folded my hands between my knees. My stomach was in knots.

Jefferson continued, "We can't allow any lack of faith in humanity to stop the growth of knowledge, because knowledge is the very core of our existence—from technology to genetics to atomic structure. Short of destroying every sentient being in the universe, any attempt to manipulate discoveries about our existence—about knowledge and potential knowledge—is a losing battle."

He steepled his hands in front of his face. "There's something else potentially important about the Bell I want to mention." He leaned back, inhaling deeply. "I want you to think about some of the greatest innovations in human history. It's easy to comprehend discoveries and advances after the fact, but think about how revolutionary many accomplishments must have been in the moment."

I furrowed my brow and shrugged. "Okay?"

"How is it that new technologies and ideas often appear almost simultaneously in different parts of the globe? That seems fortuitous and coincidental to me; it's one thing to see new ideas evolve, but quite another when they spontaneously appear with little or no precedent."

"You think it has something to do with the Bell? I thought you said details couldn't be transmitted."

"They can't. But I already told you—there are so many things about this technology I don't understand. Who's to say that general notions of plausibility can't turn into specific moments of clarity and inspiration? And to think that two people might come to the same revolutionary, abstract conclusion at precisely the same moment . . . well . . ."

I was getting more irritated with every second. "And you think that justifies your unwillingness to act?"

Jefferson's eyes looked tired. "My unwillingness to act isn't some whimsical decision, Douglas. And, in any case—as I've told you repeatedly tonight—it may be more of an *inability* to act, so you're arguing what very well could be a moot point." He stood up slowly. "Anyway, I'm not convinced the Bell is responsible for *anything* in human history. I'm just trying to illustrate to you that the implications of this technology *could* run far deeper into the fabric of our past than we can fathom. And that alone is a strong argument for letting things be."

He stretched and yawned. "I've told you enough for tonight. I'm going to sleep." He started to walk out of the room.

I looked at him incredulously. "Wait. Where are you going?"

He stopped and turned. "I told you. To sleep."

"That's it? The conversation's just . . . over?"

He seemed to consider my question for a moment. Then he simply said, "Yes."

"How in the fuck am I supposed to handle all this?"

His eyes glowed like pools of blue water behind his spectacles. "Gently, I suppose . . . and with great skepticism."

"*What?* You can't just keep fucking cutting me off like this!"

He shook his head disapprovingly. "Always the profanity . . ."

I stared at him, my mouth hanging open. I didn't have a response.

He smiled. "A little at a time." Then he turned again and walked toward his bedroom.

I sat staring at the bookshelf, fuming. "*Fuck!*" I said to no one.

I awoke the next morning and jumped out of bed, determined to catch Jefferson and force more conversation. I went into the kitchen only to find Jack sitting at the table. I glared at him. "What the fuck are you doing here?"

He pulled his head back in a mock display of concern. "You're not happy to see me?"

"Where's Jefferson?"

"Oh, him? He left early this morning."

"Where'd he go?"

"He said he was going on a *looooooong* trip." Jack clapped his hands together. "*Oh!* And he said he was going to bring you a T-shirt!"

I pounded my fist against the wall. "God*damn* it!"

Jack's eyes widened. "Are you upset about something, Douglas?"

I pointed at him, waggling my finger. "Go fuck yourself, Jack." I turned and stormed back to my bedroom, slamming the door.

Late Spring, Year Twenty-Four

TRUE TO JACK's declaration, Jefferson stayed away for months, leaving me more frustrated than ever. Jack was essentially useless, as usual, but he was a great chess partner, and every once in a while he would give me some piece of information that helped clarify things—at least to some small degree. So I continued to tolerate him.

One evening that spring, shortly after my twenty-fourth birthday, he and I met at the Cardinal for a few games of chess. When I got there, I saw a microphone set up in one corner where a small crowd had gathered. Jack sat at a nearby table, a quarter resting on his side of the chessboard. I sat down and put my quarter next to his, eyeing the crowd near the microphone. "What's going on over there?"

"Poetry night."

"Shit. I forgot. Can we go somewhere else to play?"

"You don't like poetry?"

"Come on, Jack, let's get out of here."

He scowled. "You're uncultured."

"So I guess we're staying?"

"Can we just stay for a *little* while? My *God!*"

Reacting to Jack's dramatic outbursts was like encouraging a screaming brat, so I started the game. We played for a few minutes before a small woman with long gray hair stood, walked to the microphone, and began her recitation. She had a quiet, mousy voice, and at first I had trouble hearing her. She soon alleviated that problem, however, by screaming and shaking her head so violently that I jumped in my seat. Her hair flew everywhere, finally settling in a tangled mass in front of her face. She pulled the dense mane aside and her eyes rolled back in her head. She began to moan.

"She's dying, Jack."

"I find that her poetry soothes," he said. "It's gentle. Don't you find it soothing and gentle?"

"I find it annoying."

"That's because you're an uncivilized cretin."

"You know, you've become something of an asshole in your retirement."

"You're uncivilized," he repeated.

"No, wait! You were always an asshole! Now you're just a *bigger* asshole. Maybe you shouldn't have quit your job." Jack had made a good show of working during my recovery, but when Jefferson returned and the revelations began, he saw no reason to continue the façade, and he quit his job immediately.

"I deserve a nice retirement after everything you've put me through," he said. "And now that I don't have to lie to you anymore, why *should* I work?" He collapsed back in his chair like an impatient child.

"Don't ask me for any money when you go broke."

He made a twisted, arrogant face. "Well, since I know every success story in the stock market for, like, at *least* the next hundred years, I guess you don't have a lot to worry about, do you?"

"I didn't know you were interested in the market, Jack."

"I'm not, you stupid little bastard. How interested do I have to be to pick up the phone and call a goddamn broker? It's not like I had to do a bunch of math and shit. Don't be retarded."

Another poet now took the stage, unleashing a lyrical tragedy about a girl who had recently broken up with him. Halfway through the poem, he started to cry.

Jack turned his head to the poet and suddenly looked devastated. "That poor, poor man."

The poet was sobbing so hard now that his words were unintelligible. As he tried to speak, he shuddered and heaved, saliva and mucus stretching from his upper to lower lip, tears streaming down his reddened face. Finally, when he was too upset to finish his poem, one of his friends helped him away from the microphone.

After a prolonged round of applause and several consolatory hugs, the heartbroken rhymester was replaced by a new poet, who began a tirade against automobiles and fossil fuels.

Jack and I concentrated on our game. "What's it like in the future?" I said.

"That's a stupid question. What's *what* like in the future?"

"Austin?"

"It'll be about the same as it is now—after the Republic is formed."

I lifted my head suddenly. "The Republic?"

"Yeah, the Republic of Texas."

"Do you just make this shit up as you go along?" I stared hard at him. I was testing him and he knew it.

He looked at me blankly. "Texas is going to secede, along with most of the rest of the states in the union."

"Right." But my mind was racing. Jack never gave me anything. *This is calculated . . . pay attention.*

He shrugged. "Look, you asked and I answered."

I scowled at him. "That's not possible Jack."

"I'm sure the average Soviet citizen said the same thing the day before the Wall came down."

"Come on. It's not the same thing."

"Oh? So I guess you know more about the future than I do?"

I watched every movement of his face. "You aren't joking."

"No, I'm not. And if you aren't going to believe my answers then don't ask me questions." He returned to listening to the ranting poet, who was now attacking modern conveniences.

". . . *Microwaves and VCRs and computers fill our lives,*
Maybe in the next decade, we'll have robotic wives.
We poison ourselves with our technological drugs . . ."

"And maybe we should get rid of indoor plumbing and vision correction too." I sighed, still eyeing Jack. "This is ridiculous. Can we leave now?"

Jack continued to watch the poet with exaggerated interest. "I think he makes sense. I'd like to have a robot for a wife."

I steered the conversation carefully. "So the country just fell apart one day—as simple as that?"

Jack turned around. "Huh?"

"You said the states seceded—"

"It didn't just *fall apart* one day. Things changed."

"How could things change that much, that fast?"

"Who said it was fast, you little smart-ass bastard? God you think you're clever, don't you?"

"Well, how'd it happen then?"

"Do you really want to know, or are you just trying to argue with me?"

"I really want to know." My façade had crumbled; I looked like a salivating dog. Jack had me exactly where he wanted me.

His eyelids drooped in a vulgar display of stupidity, his lips twisted grotesquely. "You help."

"What?"

"You help make it happen. That's part of the reason Jefferson and I came back."

"You know me in the future?"

"Oh, yeah . . . I know you all right." He rolled his eyes.

Jack now had my complete attention. "So what am I going to do?"

"Can't tell you. Sorry. Maybe Jefferson will tell you, but I doubt it." He giggled.

"What's so goddamn funny?"

"I *love* secrets!" He shrugged and put his palms together in front of his chest. "They make me feel silly!"

"I hate you."

"I don't care. Lots of people hate me."

"Tell me what happens, Jack."

"Nope, I'm a vault. Experience is everything."

"Jesus fucking Christ." I sighed. "Well at least tell me what my life's going to be like."

He slouched in his chair again, pinching the bridge of his nose, blowing a long stream of air between his lips. "No, I don't think we want to talk about that. You don't want to know."

"Oh, stop it, Jack. Just *tell* me."

He scanned the room carefully, as if to ensure no one could hear what he was about to say, his movements more exaggerated—and annoying—than ever. He whispered, "You have a little . . . *problem.*"

I crossed my arms and leaned back. I could see where this was heading. "What problem?"

"You know, you have a *thing.*"

"What *thing*? Just get to the fucking point."

He checked the room again. "Are you *sure* you want to know?"

"*Jack!*"

"*Okay, okay!* Just calm down!" He leaned closer and whispered, "You have a rodent fetish."

"Goddamn it, Jack!" Some of the poets turned their heads.

"*What!*" He leaned back again and shrugged defensively.

"Why can't you ever be serious?"

"I am serious!" He looked hurt. "Why don't you think I'm serious? Why should I tell you anything about the future if you won't believe me anyway? It's not my fault you live in denial. Do you want to hear about your rodent problem or not?"

"No, I guess I don't want to hear about that."

He shrugged again, and then moved a bishop. "Checkmate." He took both of our quarters from the board.

"Hey, put one of those back. We're not finished."

Jack put a finger to his lips and turned to the microphone just as the Luddite poet ended his rhapsodic invective against technology and convenience. The small crowd erupted in applause, and when the clapping ended the host took the microphone and scanned the clipboard in her hand.

"Okay! Thank you, Jim! That was a very enlightening reading!" She beamed at her fellow poets, who smiled back warmly. "Next we'll hear from a newcomer. Would you please give a warm welcome to—" she looked at her clipboard and then scanned the room, "Mr. Jack Alexander!"

I looked down and shook my head. "Oh, my *God*."

Jack rose from his seat, reached into the pocket of his coat, pulled out a baseball cap, and put it on his head. It bore the slogan, "My Savior was a Carpenter."

"Jack, *no!*"

He walked to the microphone, grinning at the collection of poets, and thumped the head of the microphone inexpertly. "Testing?"

There was a groan of feedback.

"Okay, I'd like to thank you all for allowing me this opportunity to express myself." His smile was ridiculous, but the other poets grinned back dutifully. A few applauded briefly.

Jack clapped his hands together once. "I'd like to dedicate this to my friend Douglas." He waved at me. "Douglas, will you stand up?"

"No," I said, folding my arms, appalled that he had the temerity to include me in his stupid game.

"Well, anyway, this is for Douglas." The poets all turned toward me and applauded. I smiled weakly.

"Okay. I'll now recite my poem." Jack cleared his throat entirely too enthusiastically. His face became serious, and in a rich, thespian voice he said, "*My Sphincter*, by Jack Alexander."

My sphincter is a duck call,
Quack, quack, quack.
When I air out my corn pipe,

The ducks come to visit me in droves."

The poets looked at each other uneasily, and Jack shrugged sheepishly. "I couldn't think of nothing that rhymed with 'quack'." He furrowed his brow and extended his arms, looking regally at the ceiling. He resumed his recitation in the same spectacular voice:

"My anus is a speaker,
The volume I control,
If you cannot hear it,
I shall turn up my butthole.

My sphincter can blow steady,
Or in short reports,
Sometimes my faith runs very deep,
And I soil my shorts . . .

I blow air out my buttlips,
I can play a tune,
Sometimes I blow so much foul air
I could fill up a balloon."

He nodded, grinning excitedly. "Okay, here's the grand finale." He hitched up his pants and grabbed the microphone stand.

"My rectum is ebullient,
It goes and goes and goes,
But the vapor from my sphincter bag
Might cauterize your nose."

He looked at his audience triumphantly and grinned again, chewing his gum enthusiastically.

Everyone was silent.

"The end," he proclaimed, nodding proudly and folding his arms.

Still no response.

Finally someone said, "That's so immature."

I left the Cardinal.

———————◆———————

Despite the fact that Jack had emphatically refused to instruct me in any of the disciplines we discussed the day the man attacked us with the shotgun, there was one physical outlet he didn't mind sharing with me at all, and that was running. Jack had been a runner for as long as I could remember—as far back as my childhood in Durango—and when I told him I was interested in starting, he was happy to let me train with him, mainly because it gave him yet one more context in which he could ridicule me to his heart's content. So, for months now, we had been rising early several days a week and hitting the trails.

From the beginning, I found it nearly impossible to keep up with him. The most difficult part for me had always been the beginning of a run—building up to a steady pace. My body and mind resisted the effort, but when I found my tempo, my breathing always became more controlled and even. The endorphins brought me peace, shutting out pain and making my vision of the world sharper and clearer.

One morning during a particularly long run, Jack said, "Do you remember I told you I wouldn't study tai chi with you?"

"Yeah," I said. "Something about fart lessons, if I remember correctly."

"Right. Well anyway, we can study it together now."

I stopped running. "But you said—"

"I know what I told you, but it's time now."

"Time for what?"

"You need to learn how to move correctly."

"And tai chi can teach me?" I asked skeptically, waiting for one of his annoying punch lines, but Jack, for once, remained serious, and I found myself paying attention to the response.

"No, no, no. Tai chi is a concept invented by people. I'm going to show you something a little different—but it's closer to tai chi than anything else."

And so, Jack removed the furniture from one room in his house, and it was here I learned to move properly.

As usual, he was less than explicit about his intentions. He encouraged me to focus, and even to experiment, but he also ended the lessons quickly. I felt as though we had only barely begun when he invariably announced we were finished, and it frustrated me, because Jack made it seem as though he wasn't interested in showing me anything at all.

After one particularly short lesson I said, "Jack, if you don't want to help me learn, I don't want to take up your time."

"What's *your* problem?"

"This was your idea, remember? We don't even *do* anything here. You just show me a couple of stupid stretches and then we're done."

He fell forward, planting his hands and feet firmly, his butt up in the air.

"What the hell are you doing?"

"Downward dog." His face began to turn purple and in a strained voice, he said, "I have nothing to teach you. Why are you so goddamn impatient?"

"If you have nothing to teach me, then why are we here?"

"So you'll learn." Jack moved to his feet, stretching his arms toward the ceiling and leaning back.

"Well, that just makes all the fucking sense in the world. You're just wasting my goddamn time! I'm not learning anything."

He relaxed and stood erect, his face stretching into an annoying smile. "Yes, you are."

"No, I'm not."

"Yes, you *are*."

"Okay, tell me what I'm learning. I can't wait to hear this."

His smile softened. "You're learning how to teach yourself. I'm just showing you where to look."

"Do you know how stupid that sounds?"

Jack fell to a sitting position, landing on his butt with a loud thud.

I folded my arms and smiled with satisfaction. "Did that hurt, Jack?"

"No," he said, wincing and crossing his legs. "Douglas, the concepts can't convey experience." He leaned forward and put his face on the floor in front of his crossed legs. "If I tried to teach you in human terms, you'd only understand in human terms." His face started turning purple again. "Look, we could sign you up for a yoga class at some health club full of fat, middle-aged housewives, but that's not really yoga—it's a room full of fat, middle-aged housewives. These things can't be learned, they have to be experienced. That's why I don't teach you."

"This is such bullshit."

Then Jack was on his feet, just a blur of light. I stepped back, startled. He was in front of me, his face in mine, his hand wrapped around my throat. His eyes were wild. "You think this is bullshit? Let me tell you something: when they come after you, you'll have less than one second to react before they rip your *fucking* throat out."

"What are you doing?" I said shakily. "*Stop* it, Jack!" His body shimmered like liquid, almost glowing. I tried to grab his wrist but my hand went through it. My eyes widened with shock.

Jack's eyes were still wild and he grinned slightly, almost maliciously. "Sometimes I can't believe who you are . . ."

"Jack, you're hurting me."

"Why don't you stop talking and show me some humility." He released my throat and stepped back about five feet. He made a quick downward gesture with his fingers, as though telling a dog to sit.

A tremendous force drove me to my knees.

"That's right," he said. "Now, head down."

My head bent forward involuntarily.

"Normally I'd say it's probably good that you seem to question every goddamn thing in the universe," he said. "But not in here. Do you understand me?"

My head snapped back as he released me from whatever he had used to drive me into submission. I blinked hard several times. "How did you—?"

"Just shut up." His eyes were calm now and he smiled arrogantly. "You're going to listen to what I say, and you're going to learn to move. Got it? And don't talk so goddamn much."

I massaged the back of my neck, glaring at him. "You talk more than anybody I know, you *ass*hole."

Jack folded his arms, looking thoughtfully at the ceiling. "No, I don't."

"Yes, you do."

"No, I *don't*."

I moved my head in a circle, trying to ease the pain. "You're a fucking weirdo."

He squinted his eyes. "Yeah, but I'm a weirdo who can whip your ass, you little bastard. Try not to forget that."

Fall, Year Twenty-Four

JEFFERSON AND JACK had certainly given me ample reason to respect what they could do, but if I had any remaining doubts at all, the incident at Jack's house squelched them for good. It seemed pointless to resist the evidence, even if it did happen to defy the very principles of physics—along with just about everything else I had ever known. So I finally accepted that this was the way my life was going to be. But that didn't mean I had to like it.

Jefferson had been absent for some time, so Jack was the only person I could hound with my questions, but he still refused to give me any substantive answers. "You know exactly what we can do," he said, pointing at me one afternoon, "and if you really want to understand it, you just keep doing what I tell you."

I glared at him. "Yeah, I think you may have already said that once or twice."

So I followed Jack's instructions, mostly keeping my mouth shut. What choice did I have?

One crisp morning that fall, Jack and I went for a run, each of us consumed by our own thoughts. Our runs were becoming one of the most peaceful parts of my day. On these mornings I invariably fell into an endorphin-driven trance, lost in the details of my life, only vaguely aware of the world around me. And today was no different—my mind wandered, almost oblivious to everything.

Suddenly, about thirty minutes into it, a wave shattered my serenity, bringing me back into the immediacy of the moment. I didn't understand what was happening at first, but then another current shook me. Something was very wrong.

I instinctively slowed my pace, shaking off the last vestiges of the trance. I turned to say something to Jack, but he was no longer beside me. He had stopped about ten feet back.

He feels it too, I thought.

Jack's eyes were drawn into narrow slits, slowly sweeping the scene, looking for the source of the disturbance. I became still more aware of everything around me, and I imitated him—searching the street and the park beside the river for any sign of danger, ready to act in an instant. All I could think about was the man with the shotgun. *Not again. Please, not again . . .*

At first, I noticed nothing unusual, but something compelled me to look straight ahead. I absorbed every detail, searching for even the slightest warning signal. A woman pushing a carriage approached the intersection ahead, accompanied by a little girl—no more than four years old. The child had fine blonde hair tied up in a white ribbon. She wore a blue and white plaid dress, white stockings, and red shoes. Her innocence was beatific—like a subject in a Norman Rockwell painting; the image struck me as incongruously humorous for an instant, until the seriousness of my awareness took over again.

Her mother called her back, but the little girl paid no attention, running ahead. Something about the scene wasn't at all right. My heart began to race as yet another wave of premonition swept over me.

The girl stepped into the intersection, oblivious to a car that barreled through a red light. It would hit her; nothing could stop it. The scene rolled in front of me, a movie in slow motion. I wanted to cry out, but it was too late.

The mother screamed as the car struck her daughter. Her small frame folded almost in half then rolled and bounced over the top of the car. Her body hit the ground behind the car, tumbling grotesquely for perhaps forty feet. I could almost feel her bones shattering each time she impacted with the ground. Her tiny form bounced onto the sidewalk, hit the railing hard, and finally lay motionless in a twisted bundle.

The car's brakes screeched sending out smoke. The driver lost control, plowing into the railing on the other side of the street, the front end compacting like an accordion with a loud crunch of metal. The horn erupted in a steady, persistent note.

My breathing and heart rate slowed, but my senses heightened further. The mother sprinted toward her daughter, and suddenly I was running too. I reached the girl first, kneeling over the small broken body to see if anything could be done, but it was over. She was dead.

Jack caught the mother who was by now hysterical. *She knows,* I thought. *She has to know her little girl is gone.*

Time slowed further and I turned the body over. The girl's eyes were glazed in a fixed, lifeless stare. Her whole body was gashed and scraped; blood saturated my arms and chest. Her mouth hung open, her tongue protruding slightly. A line of saliva stretched from her lips to her chin, and her head hung limply. She was a rag doll in my arms.

For a moment, I thought the mother had stopped screaming. *And the car's horn . . .?* But then realized it was only my perception; all sound had vanished.

In my mind, I heard Jack's voice: *What are you going to do?* It was only a whisper, rough and soothing, echoing. I turned my head, and our eyes met as he struggled to keep the woman from breaking free. His eyes were serene, and slight smile touched his lips, as if to defy the magnitude of the situation.

Jack, what's happening? My hands grew warm. The feeling spread to my arms, and then further through my body, wrapping around me with as much gentle care as I now offered this small creature in my own arms.

A memory flashed in my mind—Thomas in his bed, suffocating . . . and then the dog in the river. *It was dead.*

I watched the girl's eyes, not quite sure what I was looking for. My body began to tingle with the strange energy, a benevolent disease conquering my extremities. The areas where the little girl's body made contact with mine felt almost electric.

I looked at Jack, still restraining the weeping mother. I begged for understanding with my eyes, but he only continued to smile, nodding once. I looked back to the girl. Time resumed all around us—the wailing mother, the screeching horn.

Her eyes fluttered.

This can't be happening . . .

She convulsed in my arms, and then she opened her mouth, gulping air, coughing violently as she exhaled. Her small body trembled and grew warmer.

"That's right," I whispered. "Come back." I pulled her to my chest and felt her heart beating, her chest rising and falling. She was with me, moving with me. She was alive.

I pulled her away from my chest, looking at her small face, and I caught my breath. The wounds were gone. The blood remained, but that was all.

Suddenly I was aware of someone standing over us and I looked up to see a man staring at me. I had no idea how long he had been there. His lips hung apart in disbelief. "There's no way. What did you—?"

I had no time to answer his questions. "Do you have a phone?"

His face twisted with confusion.

"*Listen* to me!" I said harshly. "Do you have a phone?"

The tone of my voice brought him back to reality, and he sputtered, "Yeah, right here." He fumbled in his pockets.

"Call an ambulance," I said with more calmness than I would have believed possible.

The mother screamed. "*My baby! Let me go!*" She tore at Jack's arms, her voice a gravelly moan of desperation and hopelessness.

"She's alive," Jack said.

Something in Jack's voice made the woman look at his face, and she saw his smile, her expression turned blank. She looked at me, and then at Jack again. "How?" She was confused, incapable of processing the conflicting information her mind was receiving. "Really?" she whispered.

He nodded slowly.

"*Really?*" In her eyes, hope replaced disbelief, followed at last by relief and acceptance. She began to laugh and cry at the same time, covering her mouth with her hands.

Her eyes melted with gratitude. As long as I live, I will never forget the look she gave me. She knew what I had done. She may not have understood, but somehow she knew.

A crowd was gathering. I felt Jack's hand on my shoulder. He whispered in my ear, "We have to go."

And then we ran.

We didn't speak on the run home. I had so many questions in my head, I didn't know how to formulate them. Silence seemed best for now.

When we got to my house, Jack turned on the television, flipping through stations until he found a live local news broadcast. The man whom I had instructed to call the ambulance had a microphone thrust in his face. ". . . came over to the girl and he was crouched over her, but she was dead." He shook his head. "I don't know, maybe I'm wrong." He ran his fingers through his hair. "There's no way . . . the way the car hit her . . . and blood everywhere . . ." He blew out a long breath of air, still shaking his head. "There's no *way* that girl was alive! But then she just started . . . *breathing*, you know?"

The man was almost hysterical as he continued to speak, and then a female reporter appeared on the screen, standing near the scene of the accident. "That's a clip from an interview taken a few minutes ago with an eyewitness." The correspondent spoke slowly with characteristic exaggerated emphasis.

A male anchor spoke. "Paula, could you update the viewers who are just joining us? What do you know at this time?" The television screen divided into two panes, one containing the anchor, the other framing the reporter.

"Sure, Ted." Paula looked down at a notepad in her hand. "At approximately 8:15 AM, four-year-old Rachael Guidry was run down by an automobile in the intersection behind me." The camera panned to the street, now clogged with ambulances, fire trucks, and police cars. "Witnesses say the girl flew over the car, rolling sixty or seventy feet before her body finally came to rest."

"And what is the little girl's condition?"

"She is listed in good condition at Brackenridge Hospital."

"You say she's in *good* condition?"

"That's right, Ted. Everything we're hearing suggests that the little girl was miraculously unhurt by the accident."

"And do we know anything about the driver?" The anchor asked.

"Well, the Austin Police Department has told me that the driver *was* drunk and may have a history of alcohol-related offenses. He was injured when his car collided with the railing in the intersection, and he was rushed to Brackenridge Hospital, where he is listed as being stable. His identity hasn't been released."

"And witnesses say two men might be responsible for saving the little girl's life? Is that right, Paula?"

"That's correct, Ted. Bystanders say two men were the first on the scene, and several witnesses claim that one of the men . . ." Paula was choosing her words carefully. ". . . *revived* the girl."

"By CPR, or some other means?"

"Ted, it's very difficult to get a clear picture from authorities and witnesses as to exactly how the girl was revived."

"And where are these men now?"

"Apparently, the two men left the scene immediately after the girl was revived." Paula hesitated briefly. "I think it's important to add something here, Ted: we have no medical confirmation that the girl was indeed revived by either of the two men."

Jack chuckled at the television. "Yeah, cover your ass, sweetheart . . ."

The anchor said, "Thank you for that update. That was News Eight's Paula Conrad live at the Congress Street—"

Jack turned off the television and looked at me for a moment. He seemed proud.

"What happened to that little girl?" I asked.

"She's alive, isn't she? This isn't the first time you've done this."

I thought about the dog in the river again. "How?"

"I don't know. But *you* do, don't you?"

"Jack," I said, my breath becoming shallow. "What exactly is it that I'm supposed to know?"

"Now you know where they came up with that stupid goddamn name."

"What name?"

He smiled. "Like it or not, Douglas, you're the *Medicine Man*."

◆

IF JACK AND I kept low profiles before the incident with the little girl, we became virtually invisible afterward. Jefferson, not surprisingly, remained absent—and probably with good reason: our respective presences at Barney's suicide and the shotgun rampage had already made us too visible; there was no way to calculate what damage might ensue if we were associated with the little girl's recovery as well. While I was still awed by Jefferson's and Jack's mysterious ability to manipulate people psychologically, I was pretty certain that eventually the police would catch on. And, of course, there was Groeden to think about too.

I stayed in a semistupor for days. Over the years I had many times brushed with the memories of the dog in the creek and Thomas's miraculous recovery. For the most part, however, I had tried to keep them carefully tucked away, content not to try to explain what had happened. But now, with the little girl's revival, those memories were back in force, commanding me to take responsibility for this thing inside me. And to me, that's exactly what it was: some *thing*, over which I had no control.

Finally one morning a few days later, my uneasiness became completely intolerable and I decided to call Jack. After about ten rings he finally picked up.

"Hello?" His voice was nasal and gravelly. He sounded like he was dying.

"What the hell is wrong with you?"

"I . . . had kind of a late one."

I heard a woman giggle, and then muffled voices as Jack quickly covered the mouthpiece.

"I need to see you, Jack."

He took his hand off the phone. "Uh huh. Can we do it later?"

"No. I really need to talk to you."

He covered the mouthpiece again and there was a long pause, during which I heard more muffled conversation. Finally he said, "Okay. Give me half an hour."

When I got to his house, he answered the door in a dark blue bathrobe and fuzzy pink slippers. He looked like he hadn't shaved in days, and he squinted his eyes against the bright light outside. "Come on in." He turned around and I saw

FBI printed in big yellow letters across his back. "I made some tea," he said, shuffling into the kitchen.

I sat on the couch in his living room and he returned with two cups. He handed me one and took the chair across from me, crossing his legs, looking reasonably unconcerned about anything I might have to say.

"Did you have a big night?" I asked.

"As a matter of fact I did—not that it's any of your business."

"Where's your friend?"

"I don't have any friends," he said, reaching inside the robe and scratching his armpit.

"You look like shit."

His expression became mortified. "God, I *do*, don't I? You want me to just run in there and put on some makeup or something?" He lifted his right butt cheek and let out a tremendous fart.

I was losing patience quickly. "I'm glad you feel comfortable enough to stay out all night partying, Jack. But in the meantime, I'm really having a hard time with this."

"What do you want me to do about it?" he asked, taking a sip of tea.

I stood up and pointed at him. "Is this just a big fucking joke to you?"

He looked at the ceiling and sighed. "I know you've had to deal with a lot lately, but I think maybe you should be getting used to the idea that you're just a *little* different than other people."

"Why don't you go fuck yourself? You're not off the hook, you know."

He raised his eyebrows. "Says who?"

"There's still a *lot* you and Jefferson haven't told me."

"That's nothing new."

I sat back down, trying to regain a little calm. "I wasn't ready for the other day."

"Yes, you were, or it wouldn't have happened."

I clenched my jaw and glared at him. "Jack, I recognize how much pleasure you get from playing the role of the enigmatic mentor, but I have no idea what I did and I'm scared to death. So do me a favor and help me out a little, okay?"

"It might surprise you to learn that I don't know what you did either," he said. "It's not like I can look it up in a book or something."

"Yeah, Jefferson's used that little aphorism on me once or twice too. It's not good enough."

"Jefferson and I aren't your personal soothsayers, Douglas. You don't have to like it, but this is the way it is, do you understand? There are some things I just *can't* tell you—you *have* to make the discoveries on your own. I'll help you with what I can, but that's all I can do." He sighed again. "How many times do we have to tell you that, exactly?"

"What am I supposed to say to that? You're asking me to blindly accept something I can't even *begin* to comprehend! If people find out I can do this, I'm fucked."

"That's true," he said, chuckling. "And you think that if you don't do something with it, you'll feel guilty."

"I *will* feel guilty if I don't figure out what I'm supposed to do."

"Well, don't."

"Don't what?"

"Don't feel guilty!"

"You just expect me to turn off my feelings?"

"You act like you're a victim! Look, guilt is a worthless emotion, Douglas. You're not *supposed* to do anything." He rose and walked to a large window overlooking his backyard. "What you did for that little girl isn't a gift from God, can we agree on that?"

"I don't know what it is!"

He turned and smiled again. "Man, I'm trying to help, but you're making this harder than it has to be." He took another sip of tea and looked at the sky, still squinting against the light. "You're not about to go all Jesus on me are you?"

"I don't know what my responsibility is!"

"*Responsibility?*" He leaned his head back and laughed. "*What* responsibility? Your *purpose* in life falls within the context of your own goals and desires—not some predestined bullshit from the Bible. There's no ultimate goal! The entirety doesn't give a *fuck* what you do! This thing that happened to you is nothing more than an extremely sophisticated accident. And whether you like it or not, it's yours, and it's going to define who you are for the rest of your life."

"You knew it was coming. You could have—"

"I could have *what?* You keep saying that!" He laughed again. "I'm not telling you fucking *anything*. Got it?"

"Oh, you've made that abundantly clear."

"Good."

I glared at him. He gave me a wry grin and said, "You can't go back now anyway, so instead of yelling at me and Jefferson, why don't focus on what's really important? What are you going to do with this?"

I looked vacantly at the rug under the coffee table. "I want to use it to help people."

"You don't even know what 'it' is! What if there's more to it than what you've seen?"

I raised my head. "You tell me, Jack."

"If you think you were only put here to raise the dead, then you're very narrow-minded. This goes much deeper than that; what you did for that little girl was only a taste."

"And I *liked* it! It felt as good as any drug I ever took! Why shouldn't I keep going? Why shouldn't I try to help people?"

"When did I ever say you shouldn't help people? The question is *how* you're going to help them." He paused for a moment. "Look, I hate to tell you this, but that little girl is still going to die someday. You didn't make her immortal, you just postponed her departure."

"So?"

He shrugged. "I'm just trying to give you some perspective."

"You aren't answering my questions."

"Yes I am. You just don't want to hear the answers. What's the goal, Douglas? Do you want to save every human being on earth?"

"If I could."

"And what would you save them *from*? From death? Maybe you want to end their suffering? Whose suffering, and for how long?"

I glared at him again, frustrated by my inability to answer.

"It seems to me there are a lot of important questions you haven't asked yourself," he said.

"Just tell me why it happened. Why me?"

"Why *not* you? You had to save her, Douglas, so that you could see more clearly."

"See what?"

"That no matter how hard you try, you can't save every little girl. When you come to terms with that, you'll understand that no matter how important life and death are to us, those conditions have no real meaning in the universe. And *that's* the biggest part of all of it."

Jack looked out the window again. "This conflict you're feeling was meant to be, and it isn't going to go away tomorrow. The guilt will tear at you for a long time, but it's what you do with it that will determine everything. Check your premises, and when you understand them clearly, you'll find what you're looking for."

I put my forehead in my hands. "*I don't understand!*"

"Yes, you do." He put his cup to his lips. "You know where the easy path leads. You also know that the difficult path would mean helping a far greater number of people. And that path requires vision and humility—two qualities most people don't possess in great abundance."

I looked at him pleadingly. "Was it a test, Jack?"

He laughed again. "The entirety doesn't test us! You are what you are. This has much less to do with that little girl than you think." He tapped his temple with his index finger. "It has to do with your mind."

I thought about the girl lying in a small heap, her lifeless face. "I can't just walk away from this."

"You don't have to. But if you focus too much on each move, you'll neglect the game as a whole." He pointed his finger at me. "And you'll lose."

The way he used the final word sent a small ripple of fear through me. I chewed my lip nervously.

He crossed the room and sat down next to me on the couch. "Look, we'll figure it out, just like we always do."

"It's not always going to be this hard, is it? I mean, it's all going to make sense someday, right?"

"Yeah, I think so." He smiled again. "Now, if you're through with your little temper tantrum, can you go home so I can get some sleep?"

Summer, Year Twenty-Eight

JEFFERSON AND JACK continued to make it emphatically clear they would give me no more information than they considered absolutely necessary, and for the next several years, that meant I learned almost nothing new about my situation. For a while, it was maddening, but soon enough I resigned myself to finding at least some patience—mainly because I didn't have any choice in the matter.

It was a quiet time for all of us; there were no more attacks, and life was fairly easy. I continued to learn as much as I could from every available resource, concentrating more than anything else on building as much wealth as I could from the money Jefferson had so generously provided. For about a year after he opened the brokerage account for me, my investments grew prodigiously—exceeding even my greatest expectations. The surge I enjoyed, however, was by no means limited only to my shares; stocks across the spectrum rose with astronomical velocity that I knew couldn't possibly represent true underlying value. Still, economic and financial pundits proclaimed this to be a new era of unprecedented growth—indefinitely sustainable—and the public responded by sending share prices even higher. I watched it all with great skepticism, shaking my head, waiting for the inevitable to come.

And then it did: just when the optimism had reached a fevered pitch, the economy collapsed, suddenly and without mercy, into the worst recession in decades. Despite numerous efforts by U.S. Central Bank to mitigate the situation, markets shed, over a period of mere months, a nearly unfathomable quantity of wealth. No recovery seemed in sight.

Occasionally the averages swung up in a false rally, only to be crushed again shortly after, and the disappointment that followed the temporary upswings further quelled investor confidence. On most days I didn't even look at the market. I was invested for the long term, and I didn't care about the minutia. Occasionally I saw news reports, the tones of which might have suggested the world was ending. Still I did nothing.

The media is a strange animal; its audience is its lifeblood, and nothing captivates an audience more than fear. The random acts of violence continued—and even escalated—not only in the United States, but in cities all around the world, and the media dutifully played its role in keeping its audiences petrified, blaming the terrorist acts on everything from energy prices to religious fanaticism. But something about those explanations didn't feel quite right. The events were most often painted as chaotic, but in the back of my mind I thought I began to sense a subtle pattern. Ultimately, though, I dismissed my suspicions; I had more important things to do than to pursue a list of conspiracy theories. The acts *were*, after all, sporadic.

Unfortunately, when buildings weren't conveniently exploding in front of the cameras, people nonetheless demanded to be horrified by their news sources, and the effects of the recession most readily filled the gaps—providing the public with the dire outlook it so desperately craved. On any given day, I could find any number of heart-rending stories about investors who had lost their entire life savings to the collapsing market. Pitiful narratives about lay-off victims and their near-starving families abounded. The world was ending yet again, and still I didn't react.

Report after report suggested it might be time to sell everything. The experts now advised the wise investor to sell stocks and wait out the bear market with hard cash, but I just ignored the sensationalism. I had worked diligently to understand the companies I followed, and I had faith in my ability to succeed—if I could just be patient. So my purchases languished and I continued to ignore them.

Just prior to the bear market's second year, a rally appeared. It wasn't as spectacular as previous moves, but it was real, nonetheless. I glimpsed headlines or heard stories on television proclaiming this the next false upturn, but the news meant nothing to me.

As it happened, there was nothing false about this move, and it marked the beginning of one of the strongest bull markets in history as valuations returned to normal. Poverty still existed in the world, but the new level of economic growth was unprecedented. To almost everyone's surprise, the world hadn't ended after all, and it was business as usual, with one exception: I was now part of it. My biggest holding was the company Jefferson and I had discussed on the phone. In just a few years, the stock increased ninefold.

Jefferson had also asked me to keep a considerable amount of money in cash, and somehow I knew current conditions were ideal for putting it to use. This was what he had wanted me to see. After the market collapse, I had found out about a privately held insurance company in Kansas City, Missouri, that had been unprofitable for years. Despite its problems, it was for sale at an absurdly low price, so I bought the whole company and converted many of the its assets to cash, with which I began purchasing undervalued stocks. In the languishing aftermath of the collapse, I was able to pick up some incomprehensible bargains, and when the market started to rise again, my new investments rose along with it.

Within another year, I bought a large majority of a struggling publicly traded technology business in Austin. After the purchase, I had a controlling interest, so I took the company's idle cash and began to buy still more undervalued securities. I sold the remainder of the company's assets and discontinued operations, then changed the firm's name and turned it into an umbrella corporation under which I placed all my holdings.

Within a few more years, the holding company owned seven other businesses outright. We also held considerable interests in several of the world's biggest corporations. Because of Jefferson's kindness and generosity, I wasn't yet thirty and I had gone from the depths of poverty to financial success in under ten years.

Suddenly I could live wherever I wanted to; I could buy any house, drive any car, and travel wherever I wished, because I had more money than I ever dreamed I would. And yet, in spite of my new wealth, I didn't change anything about my lifestyle. I continued to live in Jefferson's small comfortable house. I traded in my old car for a cheap reliable import. Something in my perspective had shifted: money was no longer the goal, it was simply part of the business of life, and I didn't need much of it to be content.

Still, my quality of life did matter and I tried to keep things balanced. Never was I in any danger of becoming a miser, hoarding every penny I made to no apparent end. But while some people need to possess objects to enjoy life, I didn't require such things in order to find happiness. Life is an end unto itself, and the experience was now my objective.

Despite the burgeoning global economy, social upheaval persisted, and even continued to intensify, in major cities everywhere, and this only caused my mind to return to the idea that something was amiss. Technology and innovation had lowered commodity costs dramatically in recent decades, universally raising standards of living, as well as increasing life expectancy. How could terrorism be proliferating?

In the years I had been building what was now becoming something of a financial empire, I had naturally gravitated toward books on economic philosophies—

from every point on the spectrum. I found myself comparing tenets from the different schools, and I quickly recognized how toxic some of the ideas were to the openness and growth of society—killing alternatives, destroying innovation, attempting to suppress knowledge.

A bigger picture was forming in my mind; the disciplines I had studied in the last several years now melted elegantly with one another, as though each were an inextricable component of a bigger whole—like a jigsaw puzzle coming together in front of my eyes. The complex underlying roots of the financial and social crises plaguing the globe were becoming clear: bureaucratic manipulation never works. And without my understanding why, Groeden began to appear in my thoughts more frequently. Somehow I knew he had to be connected to all this.

I was surprised it had taken me so long to suspect a link. People, in order to be productive, must be free, and freedom demands balance and honesty toward the growth of knowledge. Society had allowed corrupt institutions to manipulate it—to restrict freedom for too long—and now everyone was paying the price.

It jibed. This was the picture Jefferson had so meticulously tried to paint since his return. I certainly no longer had any doubt our fates were tied to Groeden, but as I spent more time considering his intentions, one thing became abundantly clear: the source of his entire plight had begun with his organization, which, in turn, was doubtlessly spawned from and nurtured by these very institutions so bent on the destruction of freedom. The resources at his disposal had to be incalculable, and the budding realization that he might be, in some way, driving the turmoil afflicting the world made me feel cold. If I was right, the next inevitable question was obvious: who would have the power to sanction his involvement? Or, worse still, what if he didn't *need* sanction?

I tried to engage Jack and Jefferson—to confirm my suspicions—but they offered no enlightenment at all. So the theories remained unanswered, burning in my mind, threatening to drive me mad. And yet, it was these paths of thought that led me to even more connections. Strangely, it was the examination of these precarious relationships between society and the largely corrupt minority of men who govern it that now caused me to explore my relationship with myself—especially during my collapse.

Curiosity has always been the fuel that drives me, and I have spent my life seeking answers—trying to find new ways to view the world. At the beginning of my recovery, however, I had punished myself for allowing my addictions to control me, and as strange as it might sound, I actually condemned my need for constant change—for new ideas and fresh perspectives—much the way society has often castigated those who explore unfamiliar theories.

I came to the ridiculous conclusion that I had turned to recreational drugs—at least in part—as relief from the tedious day-to-day churn of society's mediocrity. I decided that the real solution was simply to accept the halting pace of humanity's progress; surely then I wouldn't be bored, and therefore wouldn't need to use drugs.

But as I became more familiar with the nebulous themes emerging from Jefferson's library, I realized that, while I had pursued my craving for fresh ideas in many of the worst ways, the desire itself was an asset, not a weakness. It wasn't something to fight, but rather, was something to embrace and encourage. It was true—my pursuit of the cutting edge had harmed me, but it had also been the critical component motivating me to grow intellectually and spiritually.

Blisters before calluses.

If I dismissed my ability to consider new perspectives, I would join the ranks of the mediocrity surrounding me; dogmatism and myopia are crippling diseases, and they, more than anything, had the power to kill my progress. That just wasn't something I was going to allow.

IN THE PAST few years, Jefferson had continued to appear in Austin only sporadically, but one day during one of his stays, he and I met for lunch at an outdoor café near the house. It was often hard to pin him down—even for an hour—so I was always happy when he wanted to spend time with me. I used the opportunities to pick his brain as much as he would allow, and while he and Jack were both still reluctant to tell me too much, somehow I knew the rest of the answers were coming—one way or another.

"Where have you been going all this time, Jefferson?" I asked as we ate, not really expecting an answer.

"Near Durango. Lake Vallecito."

His response was so quick and direct that I became silent for a moment. It occurred to me that his interest in the place where I grew up was probably more than mere coincidence. I chose my next words stategically. "Vallecito is a nice place."

"I bought a house there years ago—when you were young."

"And I guess you bought it because of me?"

"That was part of it."

"Why do you go there now?"

He laughed. "Why wouldn't I? It's peaceful. I like to go there to watch what's happening elsewhere."

"Groeden?"

"Yes."

I shifted in my seat. "Jefferson, I want to talk more about the future."

He leaned back and folded his hands behind his head smiling. "What's new about that?"

"I want to know about the book."

He considered that for a moment, narrowing his eyes. "Okay."

I held my breath, unable to believe after so long I was finally going to get more. I kept the air in my lungs for a moment and then released it. "So, has it already been written?"

He pushed his chair back from the table and crossed his legs. "Yes."

"And it describes the concepts we've talked about—bursting, splitting time, and all that?"

"Yes."

"But I thought you said those things hadn't been discovered yet."

"They haven't. The book was published as fiction."

"Fiction? Then how—"

Jefferson held up a finger. "It tells about three men who devote their lives to killing another man, and that character strongly resembles Groeden. In fact, the similarities are unmistakable. At the end, one of the men succeeds." He hesitated. "I don't have to tell you that the book isn't fiction, Douglas. It's about you and Jack, too—you are the ones who will help me stop Groeden."

In that instant, I could again feel the magnitude of the burden he was carrying. I waited, letting my thoughts catch up, staring wistfully at the table. I whispered, "The book is about us . . ." I brought my eyes up to meet Jefferson's. "But our identities . . . didn't you say—?"

"The names in the book are all false, and many of the details aren't accurate."

I ran my fingers through my hair and closed my eyes. I caught my lower lip between my teeth for a moment. "How in the hell did this happen, Jefferson?"

"At some point, Groeden decided to try to burst, but regardless of his reasons, as soon as he made that decision, he created some kind of instability in the multi-verse. I don't know how to define that instability, because it goes beyond any labels we can put on it, but whatever it is, when Groeden chose to manipulate space and time, an equal and opposite reaction immediately followed. The entirety always balances."

"And you think you're that reaction."

"Yes."

"Why you?"

He looked at the sky and narrowed his eyes. "I don't know, but I have to stop Groeden, because if he prevents it—if he breaks out of the loop—he'll be able to carry on with whatever he's been working on. None of us wants that to happen."

I nodded slowly.

He leveled his eyes with mine. "Anyway, for some reason that I don't understand, my existence is the only barrier to his success."

"How certain are you about all of this?"

"I always have misgivings, but I think I'm probably close, even if I have some of the details wrong. I've never known exactly how the loop originated, but no matter what caused it, I think it has been happening repeatedly ever since the first iteration. Groeden is locked in a self-fulfilling prophecy that he created when he decided to experiment with the drug. Somehow I got dragged into it, and here we are."

I considered that for a moment. "So . . . when did all this start?"

"That question isn't so easy to answer. The concept of *when* doesn't really apply. The important thing is that, in some universe, somewhere in the entirety, the loop did begin. Now we dutifully play our roles over and over—all of us existing as probabilities in an infinite number of universes. But the outcome is by no means certain."

"How many times?" I gestured around the cafe with my arm. "How many times have we met? How many times have you killed Groeden?"

"There's no way to know the answer to those questions. It may be infinite."

I put my elbows on the table, looking absently at the plate in front of me, rubbing my temples slowly. "Who wrote it? Who could have known?"

"I never knew the author, but either he or someone close to him knows all of us very well."

"Does Jack know him?"

"No."

"Maybe I know him."

"I doubt it."

"Well, how then? There must be a connection."

"I'm fairly certain the author got the story—or at least part of it—from the Bell." Jefferson touched the scar running the length of his scalp. "I can't give you any concrete proof of that. I don't know any more details than what I'm telling you now."

"Surely other people know the book wasn't fiction."

"I'm sure a few people do. But most people don't. How could they?" Jefferson paused. "Think about it like this: I've waited four years to explain this piece of the puzzle to you. I knew you would need pretty indisputable evidence to understand it, to accept it. More than anything, I wanted you to be ready. And yet you *still* find yourself doubting what I'm telling you, don't you?"

I nodded slowly. "I struggle with it, yes."

"So how do you think the average person would react to this story?"

"I suppose it would be a hard leap to make. Why didn't the author just put it out as nonfiction? Why not try to convince the world of its truth? Wouldn't that be better for us all?"

He lifted one eyebrow. "Who would believe this? Anyway, he needed to protect us."

"Then why write the book at all? Why put us at risk?"

"Because we have to have it. It's a map of the loop, and without it we'd be lost."

"So why didn't Groeden just kill the author?"

"He tried, unsuccessfully, several times. But in the end, it doesn't really matter if he kills the author or not—that wouldn't have stopped me. Someone else would have been given the story to write, and I would have gotten a copy of it."

I closed my eyes for a few moments, shifting gears, trying to put everything together. Finally I looked at Jefferson and asked, "Did you know Groeden when you worked for his . . . organization? I mean, did you spend time with him?"

"Yes." Jefferson smiled wryly. "We even played chess together a couple of times."

"You were close to him?"

He chuckled. "I wouldn't say that." He hesitated, choosing his words carefully. "After Groeden read the book, he encouraged his employees and colleagues to play him. He thought I might reveal myself that way. He knew someone was trying to get the drug, and he knew chess might be a good way to flush me out."

"Who won?"

"He did, of course. Groeden is a strong player and not too many people can challenge him. If I had beaten him, he would have known who I was immediately."

"But you could have beaten him, right?"

Jefferson only continued to smile.

I sighed heavily. "Does he know what you look like?"

"No, I've . . . changed a little since then. There's no chance he would recognize me."

"Jefferson, could the book be about somebody else? Has anyone besides you and Jack been able to burst?"

"I told you before there were others." He hesitated, furrowing his brow, as though he had committed some error. Finally he said, "Centuries ago there was a handful of people who could do it briefly."

"I read an old magazine article about it," I said. "It was in one of your bookshelves."

He nodded. "By using the drug, Jack and I were the first people to make real time travel feasible—without it, we would never have been able to hold our place in another universe." Jefferson paused and thought again for a moment. "For hundreds of years, the knowledge was lost, but then this all started. Since then, I've known of some other people who succeeded—besides me and Jack."

"Who?"

"They're almost all gone." His eyes filled with anguish.

"*Almost?*"

His expression became stern. "There are things about this I won't tell you, and you know that."

Cautiously, I said, "Well . . . what do you mean 'gone'?"

"They're dead. Groeden murdered them."

I caught my breath. "I'm sorry. I didn't mean to—"

He smiled gently. "Don't apologize. It's important."

I hesitated and then said, "How is Groeden able to make any of this happen? Don't you and Jack know in advance about the attacks? Can't you do something to prepare for them?"

"Douglas, *all* we do is prepare for them. We don't know exactly where or when anything is going to happen—we only know that the attacks *will* occur. But most of the details in the book are inaccurate—to protect us."

"But I thought the book told you everything."

"It only gives us general information. Each time this loop completes another iteration, the details change a little, so we don't know exactly what is going to happen or when. Groeden is brilliant, and I told you he's very careful about what he does. Whether you like it or not, we are in an intricate chess game—only the stakes are higher than any of us can even imagine. Every single word we speak might change the outcome. We have to see everything—every single move, long before it happens. What seems obvious to you might be the very thing that kills us all."

I shook my head slowly, staring at the table, wishing yet again that I could rid myself of this burden. "How can we ever be careful enough?"

"I don't know that we can. But the book helps us stay on our path."

"Did you ever try to contact the author?"

"I've seen him several times."

I looked up. "But you said you don't know him."

"That doesn't mean I've never seen him."

"Did you speak to him?"

Jefferson seemed to consider that. "No."

I was incredulous. "Did he know who you were?"

"We both knew."

"Why didn't you talk to him about it?"

"Because it's not supposed to be that way. It took a lot of strength to resist, but we knew it would be best to avoid each other. Any contact could violate the integrity of the loop."

"Will I ever see him?"

Jefferson smiled and shrugged. "I don't know." His face told me he wasn't going to offer me any more on the subject, so we sat in silence for another moment.

Finally I said, "Did you ever go forward in time?"

"No. I'm not sure what damage it might cause. Plus, the book said I would only return to the past." He paused. "Besides that, I don't want to know."

"Why not?"

"Would you want to know your future, Douglas? Maybe . . . how you're going to die?"

I thought about that. "No, I guess not . . . but still, wouldn't it cause more damage to come back than to go forward?"

"I had the book to guide me through the past, but I had nothing to help me if I had gone forward. I would have risked disrupting the loop, and that's the most dangerous thing I can think of." Jefferson clasped his hands around his crossed knee. "The more I move through different universes, the bigger the risk that several instances of *me* might end up together in the same universe, at the same time. If one version recognized another without understanding the process, it would irrevocably alter the future's course, so I've only burst a few times, and only once over a large time span—when I came back here."

"How many instances of a person can exist in one universe?"

"I don't think there's a limit, but I wouldn't want to test that theory."

"So is there another version of you alive here, now?"

"Yes."

"Have you met him?"

"No, that wouldn't be smart."

"Why?"

"Well, physically it's no more dangerous for the same person to meet himself than it would be for twins to shake hands. In every new instant, a new universe comes into being and we actually *become* different people. You're not the same person you were five minutes ago—that person now exists as a probability in another universe.

"Imagine that your life is a river, moving through space and time. And imagine that, in each passing instant of time, a new river comes into being, and these rivers are parallel universes running next to each other—in a manner of speaking. In each river, another Douglas Cole is created, and each version exists only as a probability. Each version of Douglas Cole has an infinite number of choices, and each one will probably choose a slightly different path than the others."

"So if it's not dangerous, why wouldn't you want to meet yourself?"

"It's not *physically* dangerous," he said, "but it can still be very harmful. There are an infinite number of universes, simultaneously coexisting. Any number of members of these universes might at some point visit any other members. So if I were to meet myself now, it wouldn't just make my future dependent on my past, it could potentially make many of my futures dependent on many of my pasts. It is a complex problem, creating an obligatory infinite loop that would have to be satisfied by each subsequent generation. If I remembered meeting an older version of myself when I was younger, then I would have an obligation to meet myself again now. But since I don't recall any such meeting, I shouldn't take the risk. I have to preserve history, as much as I am able to."

"But aren't you scared you'll change history even if you don't meet yourself?"

"Of course. In fact, we've already changed the course of events, but only slightly. The copy of the book I read when I was young was subtly different from the one I read years later. With every repetition of the loop, a new version is published, changing a little each time. We try hard to preserve the past, but we always unknowingly make a few small changes."

"Like what?"

Jefferson thought about the question for a moment. "Hmmmm. Take Jack's stupid sense of humor. I don't think he's capable of using the same line twice. He just makes everything up as he goes along, although his wit—if you want to call it that—never seems to get any less childish.

"When two different universes overlap, creating the loop, it's impossible for one to be precisely the same as the other, so small details change a little with each iteration. Because of all these factors, some things in the book happened differently than I remembered them in reality. Along the same lines, I expected other events to happen, but they never did. There are no dates in the book either, so the timing of everything we do is guesswork."

"How many versions of this book have you seen?"

"I can't be certain. There's no way of knowing how or when we might do something that changes the story."

I considered that for a moment and then said, "So what does the book say about me? When can I see it?"

"Not anytime soon. You're not even close to being ready yet."

I felt myself flush. "Why not?"

"Why not? Are you serious?"

"Yes, Jefferson, I *am* serious. When are you guys going to quit treating me like a fucking child?"

He didn't seem very concerned about my indignation. "The fact that you're angry right now is all the explanation I really owe you. But if you must have something more concrete, please try to remember that our duty is to preserve history. If you were to read the book now, there's a strong possibility you wouldn't be able to resist creating elaborate plans to change things that are, frankly, horrific almost beyond description.

"And there's another, more subtle risk: just because something has happened over and over again doesn't mean that we have a right to force that event to happen in a subsequent iteration. In other words, we know the way things are supposed to happen, but it doesn't mean we can manipulate events just to ensure an outcome we expect. If the loop changes because of our mistakes, we will simply have to do our best with the new choices we're given. And despite everything you've learned, you're just not ready to handle a responsibility like that."

"Whatever, Jefferson. I've done everything you've asked, and I've endured this bullshit for years. I don't need you to tell me what I can and can't handle anymore."

Jefferson leaned forward so suddenly that I reflexively moved back in my chair. His blue eyes were piercing in the sunlight, almost reaching into my soul. "You are absolutely forbidden to ever seek out that book," he said. "If you do, we'll all die. Even if you stumble across a copy, which is highly improbable, you'll just walk away. It's not open for debate."

I caught my breath, my eyes wide.

"You listen to me," he continued, "Groeden is here, right now—in one form or another—and he's doing everything he can to kill us. Do you understand that? Who do you think is responsible for the economic collapse that you so handsomely profited from? Who do you think is causing all this social upheaval?"

My heart was racing now, and I stared at Jefferson with wide eyes. "I was beginning to wonder . . ."

He leaned a little closer. "It's only going to get worse."

"But why would he—?"

"Because he knows we will try to stop him, and he knows that the more involved we get, the more potential we have to make mistakes. That's what he wants."

"What are you going to do about it?"

In the years I had known Jefferson, I had never failed to appreciate the intensity of his eyes, and while I had certainly seen them on fire, never were they more frightening to me than in this moment. His voice nearly dripped with disapproval. "What am *I* going to do about it?" He angled his head slightly. "No, Douglas, what are *you* going to do about it?"

"What are you talking about?"

"Pay attention. This is your role."

"*No!* I'm not—"

"Yes."

I sat in front of him, frozen. *It's what Jack said. The country is going to disintegrate.* I had achieved so much in the last several years, and yet none of my experiences had prepared me for what I saw in Jefferson's eyes. "What am I supposed to do?"

He said nothing.

All my hubris had evaporated like smoke. Suddenly I had absolutely no interest in ever seeing a copy of this mysterious book. "I'm not ready. I can't do this." I could barely hold his gaze, and yet neither could I find the strength to pull my eyes away.

Finally he said, "Oh, yes, you *can*." And then for the first time in minutes, he allowed a small, terrifying smile. He drew his face even closer to mine. Almost in a whisper, he said, "And you *will*."

PREPARATION

Fall, Year Twenty-Nine

OVER THE FOLLOWING year, the holding company I had created continued to do well. Unfortunately, while I was becoming more adept at making the business decisions that repeatedly benefited my shareholders, I had also been informed by my mentors and closest friends that the proliferating global acts of terrorism—along with the economic catastrophe which had ended only a few years earlier—had been engineered by a power-hungry madman whose sole objective was to become a deity, thereby ruling the entirety of space and time. And if this revelation wasn't enough to shatter my faith in reason, there was one other detail: somehow I was going to be instrumental in stopping this lunatic, although I had no idea how.

Had I not been nearly coerced to participate in this comic book fantasy, I might have more aggressively pursued my role as the leader of the capital group I had created. As things stood, however, it was clear I needed to distance myself from the public eye—and Groeden—in any way possible. So I left the day-to-day operations to a team of executives I had grown to trust over the past several years. I still consulted with them when they needed me, offering ideas when no others seemed appropriate. But mostly, I spent my time researching and studying at a more furious pace than ever—seeking a solution to a problem I couldn't even yet define.

I still spent a lot of time playing my cello, and I also continued to practice the disciplines behind the art of movement with Jack. I felt like I was making progress, but I couldn't really define what that progress was; I just felt more aware of my body—of my physical actions and reactions.

Jefferson, as usual, appeared only so often, and while I continued to press him and Jack at every opportunity, it seemed as though the conversation at the café surrounding the book would be the last insight I would receive for some time. Still, even without their help, I was making headway on my own.

In fact, an idea was growing in my mind, a concept that bloomed out of my limited knowledge of what would happen in the future, as it related to the whole of all my experiences so far—especially what I had seen happening in the world for the past few years.

At first, the idea seemed absurd, and I didn't consider it seriously. But as time passed, it continued to resurface, nagging at me, growing in plausibility with each new horrific news story. And the more I tried to reject it, the more it persisted. Eventually I felt I had no choice but to present it to Jefferson—if for no other reason to have him annihilate it forever.

One day that September, I walked out of my bedroom to find him sitting in his usual spot on the sofa, leafing through some documents. I had no idea he was in town, but I had ceased being amazed at his sudden appearances or disappearances long ago. Still, I needed to speak to him, and from past experience, I knew he was unlikely to stay in that spot for very long, so I realized I better pin him down while I could—*if* I could.

"You got a minute?"

He looked up at me over his glasses but didn't say anything.

"Okay, let's cut to the chase," I said. "I want to talk about something Jack told me."

Jefferson's expression turned to a look of confusion, and possibly slight annoyance. "What, exactly, did Jack tell you?"

"The United States falls apart," I was trying to be nonchalant, but my entire body was vibrating with nervous energy.

"And?"

"Tell me what happens, Jefferson."

He shook his head and looked back at the documents in his hands. "When a crisis appears, people begin to think differently. Nobody ever really trusts the government—they just tolerate it. And when things get bad enough, they start looking for safety in new ideas."

"Well, I've been studying some of the ways countries and even empires have collapsed, historically."

"Right?"

"It's almost always economic."

"But the economy is doing fine." He continued gazing at the documents in his hands.

"It's not going to last." I tensed. "The dollar's going to fail."

Jefferson looked up at me again, his eyebrows raised. "That's quite a leap. What would make you say that?"

I told him about what I had been reading—the economic philosophies, the history, even Tao Te Ching. He listened patiently. "The dollar is vulnerable," I said. "We moved away from the gold standard years ago, and it has been losing value for a long time. The violence is getting so much worse, and I'm starting to see new signs of economic weakness." I hesitated, collecting my thoughts. "Look, it was what you said about this being a big chess game and all that. If Groeden is as smart as you say he is—if he attacked the economy before, and he's causing all this terrorism—his logical next move is to attack the dollar. It only makes sense."

Jefferson's eyes narrowed.

"There's another aspect to it, though," I said.

He stared at me, silently urging me to continue.

I rubbed my hands together. "I feel it. I *know* it's going to happen. It's like I know what he's thinking."

Jefferson remained quiet, eyeing me carefully. Finally he said, "You're anticipating his moves so far in advance." He narrowed his eyes further, and just when I didn't think I was going to be able to endure another second of gaze, he smiled gently. "Let's just say you're right for a second."

That sentence was all I needed, and I couldn't resist smiling. I sat in the chair across from him, clasping my hands in front of me. "Okay, when the dollar fails, people are going to need some form of currency to fill the void."

His eyes were bright. "*If* it were to fail, that would be true, yes."

"I've been thinking about this a lot, Jefferson, and it seems to me that a group of investors could form a currency backed by gold, or some other form of assets. When the dollar starts its real decline, these investors would stand to make a fortune. It would be the perfect solution to a liquidity crisis."

Jefferson rubbed his chin. "What about legal tender laws? Governments would be upset by that sort of competition."

"I thought about that. Why couldn't it be started offshore? It doesn't even really have to be called a currency. Jefferson, this idea would have been impossible a few decades ago, but moving capital around is easy now. And a currency pegged to gold would be a huge success when the dollar collapses."

"And how would this group provide money to the average person after the collapse?"

I started to get more excited. "We could make contingency deals with banks— people who need cash will only have to have a credit or cash card, which almost everyone already has. We could offer banks a conditional partnership. If they ever need quick liquidity, what could be better than a currency backed by precious assets? We could provide an instant conversion at the first sign of danger, and, in return, banks would have to guarantee us exclusive use of their cash machine networks for distribution of the currency after the collapse. Think about it: no bank would have to commit until the dollar actually fails, but when it *does* fail, credit and cash cardholders would automatically have access to this new currency. Everyone would win."

"A group of investors might have to wait a long time to get a return on their investment," he said.

"I've gotten used to waiting. If I'm right, don't you think it's worth a shot?"

He was quiet again for a moment, watching me carefully, clearly deep in thought. Finally he said, "It's a good idea."

I worked on the plan for several weeks, bouncing ideas off Jefferson whenever I could. But because neither he nor Jack would tell me exactly when—or even *if*—the dollar's collapse was going to happen, it was impossible to calculate with any degree of precision the opportunity costs investors would have to sustain. And no one was going to consider a plan without some sort of a tangible timetable or estimated rate of return—neither of which I could provide. On top of that, very few investors were likely to bet against the United States dollar over the long term anyway.

I carefully screened lists of wealthy people to whom I had access through my businesses, choosing as candidates only those I thought could be both serious and discreet. The list was a short one, and I was reluctant to approach anyone in any case; I was all too aware that, with each new person I let in on the plan, the risk of exposure increased dramatically, and the idea of alerting Groeden was simply unthinkable.

My own asset base, while impressive by any standard, would never be enough to start a stable liquid currency, and the fact that I had so meticulously shielded myself from the public eye would make raising capital all the more difficult. I was beginning to lose faith in the plan; no matter how good it appeared on paper, it would never work without a very large amount of money behind it.

One afternoon, I was going over projections in my office when Jefferson walked in and stared at me for a moment. He obviously had something to say, but didn't seem to know how to start.

"What is it?" I finally said.

"You've run into some problems with your new idea, haven't you?"

I gave him a puzzled look. "Well, actually, yes. I don't think I can raise enough money to make it work."

He extended a couple of folded sheets of paper. "This is for you."

I took the sheets and scanned them. They were bank statements of some sort. Then I saw the individual account balances and my eyes bulged—the sums were astronomical, stated in both Swiss francs and U.S. dollars. "What the hell is this, Jefferson?"

"Numbered accounts in Switzerland. You're the only person who can access them."

"*What?*" I looked at him incredulously. "Where did you get this much fucking money?"

"I've been saving."

"For how long? *Jesus*! it would take ten thousand years to save this much money!"

He shrugged.

"I can't take this from you! I'll never be able to repay it! King Midas couldn't repay this!"

"You can, and you will."

"I've never seen this much money!" I exhaled sharply. "Now that I think about it, most *governments* have never even seen this much money! What am I supposed to do with this?" I checked to see that I had correctly counted the number of digits to the left of the decimal point.

I had.

Jefferson smiled. "So, you said something about creating a currency?"

"Holy *shit*! Are you serious? Who . . . oh, *whoa!* Jefferson, this means I don't need outside investors! Who knows about this? What about the IRS?"

"No one knows except the bank, and they won't tell a soul. The money has been accumulating for some time."

"This is complicated! How can I move this much money without someone getting nosy?"

"Why would you move it? Just keep it simple."

I nodded slowly. "Will you help me?"

He shook his head. "You have to do—"

"Of course I have to do this thing." I ran my hand through my hair. "Who do I talk to? How do I—?"

"There's a man at the bank. You can trust him."

"What's his name?"

"Ask for Klaus Junger."

"So how——?"

"Let it go, Douglas. Klaus will be the one to help you. That's all you need to know."

I started to push it further, but Jefferson had that indomitable look in his eyes. I knew he wouldn't say anything more.

I smiled, "So I guess we can get started?"

"It would seem so."

May, Year Thirty, Austin, Texas
and Durango, Colorado

"PACK YOUR BAGS, you little bastard," Jack said over the phone.

"Why?"

"Why are you a little bastard?"

"Jack, I'm not in the mood. I have a lot of work to do." I didn't know how much I had slept in the months since Jefferson had funded my plans, but it wasn't a whole lot. I worked from the minute I got out of bed in the morning to the minute I went to sleep at night, researching and preparing for the task in front of me. I had barely made time for eating and training, and I didn't know how long it had been since I played chess. The last thing I needed right now was Jack's silliness.

"Well, you can do your work from Durango for a while," he said. "Because Jefferson requests the pleasure of our company."

"Colorado? Why?"

"You'll find out soon enough."

"How long will we be there?"

"Just pack enough to stay a while. The old man does have a washer and dryer, you know."

We landed in Colorado two days later and Jefferson met us at the airport. "How was the trip?" he asked as we walked down the small concourse to the baggage claim.

"Not bad considering the short notice," I said. "What's this all about?"

"Let's get you and Jack settled first, and then we'll talk."

We gathered our bags, loaded up Jefferson's car, and started the journey northeast. We left the high desert near the Durango airport and started our climb into the mountains, and I began to feel a familiar serenity trickling through me. It was good to be back again.

About forty-five minutes later, we reached Lake Vallecito—a nondescript, peaceful town surrounded by national forest, far enough away from everything to be largely ignored by tourists. Austin had been unusually hot and sticky that spring, and the cool, dry Colorado mountain air was a welcome respite. But there was more to my serenity than the mere change in climate. The land seemed to be welcoming me, whispering softly that I was supposed to be here now. No matter how much I loved Austin, I was born and raised in these woods, and they would always be a home to me.

When we arrived, Jefferson showed me around his tastefully decorated house. The vaulted living room was the focal point, flooded with natural light from enormous windows, overlooking the lake. Bookcases stretched along almost every wall, and contained nearly as many titles as the library in Austin. Overstuffed chairs and couches rested atop rich, textured Persian rugs cast at angles, which in turn seemed to melt into the warm, dark polished pine floors, giving the room a feeling of old, well-worn comfort. Jack started a fire in a double-sided brick fireplace dividing the kitchen and living room.

My quarters were on the second floor. A large four-poster bed stood at an angle in the corner, taking up a third of the room. It was covered with down bedding piled chest-high, making it seem like a nest. A ceiling fan spun lazily high overhead.

I unpacked my things and went back down to the kitchen, which I found to be the most inviting room yet. Cookbooks and plants lined granite countertops, and recessed lights spotted the ceiling. Various cooking instruments dangled from the hooks of a copper pot rack above the island in the middle of the room. Huge windows on each wall offered still more magnificent views of the lake and mountains. Jefferson slouched on a loveseat in the corner, under two converging windows, reading a newspaper, one leg thrown casually over the other.

"This is where you've been hiding from us," I said.

"Mostly, yes." He didn't look up from his paper.

"So why did you bring us here?" The question was a formality. I was almost certain I knew the answer, and suddenly I found I was nervous.

"It's time."

My heart skipped a beat. "I don't know if I'm ready. I've—"

"You're ready," he said, looking over the newspaper.

"You're sure? I wish you had given me some warning."

He pulled the newspaper back up. "You'll be fine. Now I know you have a lot of work to do with your project, so I'll give you the better part of your days to do that. But I need at least three hours a day from you, because I want you to become acclimated to the altitude before we do anything. So, in the mornings you'll continue your routine with Jack. I'll be joining you for your runs."

"You will?"

He pulled the newspaper down again, looking at me over his glasses. "Why wouldn't I?"

"I just thought—"

He raised his eyebrows.

"Never mind," I added. If Jefferson thought he could keep up with Jack and me, then he had every right to try.

After another moment, I said, "Will it be possible for me to visit friends while I'm here?"

"No, we can't risk that. I don't want Groeden to use our prints to hurt anyone else."

Since my recovery, Jack and I had kept in touch with Pete, and he had even visited us in Austin a few times over the years. But we hadn't seen him in a while, and I had been looking forward to a reunion. I was disappointed to know we wouldn't be able to get together.

Jack walked into the kitchen.

Jefferson said, "Jack will be going into town for the things we need. That way you and I won't attract any unwanted attention."

"I'll be seeing Pete a lot," Jack said. "He doesn't know you're here, so he won't be upset."

I managed a smile. "It's probably better that way."

The next morning we rose before the sun and I spent a half-hour alone on Jefferson's pier, stretching my body slowly, allowing serenity to govern the flow of my movements. Despite my resistance to Jack's crude methodology, he had been right—my understanding of the ancient arts now transcended traditional translations, and I had become deeply attuned to my body and its connection to the universe.

The disciplines had become most powerful in me because of my ability to reject the rigidity of the conventional definitions, teaching myself instead to experiment outside the confines of the customary interpretation and structure. They were part of me now in a way that I could never have discovered from any human explanations.

Jefferson and Jack joined me on the pier just as I finished stretching, and we began our run. "Let's take it slow," Jefferson said.

Jack gave him a condescending look. "Who the hell are you talking to, you old worn-out sack of beans? You just take care of yourself and don't worry too much about us younger folk." Jack took off, leaving Jefferson and me behind.

Jefferson gave me a puzzled look and shook his head.

Although we started more slowly than I was accustomed to, it wasn't long before we caught up to Jack. He was breathing harder than normal, and I was having difficulty too; we seemed to have grossly underestimated the effects of the altitude. Jefferson, however, appeared completely unaffected, his rhythm flawless. Jack and I started lagging behind, and gradually Jefferson disappeared in the distance in front of us.

When we finally caught up to him, he was sitting on a large boulder in the middle of the path. "This is far enough for today. Let's head back."

Jack, for once, didn't have much to say.

"I wonder," I said to him between breaths, after Jefferson had taken off, "how you can do so many seemingly impossible things with your body, yet you can't even keep up with an old man on a morning run."

Jack was bent over panting, his hands on his knees. "You don't pull your bone out at just any old dog show."

"Great answer, Jack."

We continued this routine for the next two weeks, increasing the distance each day, and after the first week, Jack and I stayed with Jefferson for most of the run. I was sure that Jack and I would eventually have to slow down for him, but each day he kept a solid pace.

One morning after our run, we congregated in the kitchen. I was stretching and I noticed Jack and Jefferson looking at each other almost nervously.

I stopped stretching. "What is it?"

"How do you feel?" Jack said.

"I feel fine. What are you talking about?"

"No, I mean how does your body feel—do you feel strong?"

I thought about it for a second. "Yeah, I think I've beaten the altitude."

"I do, too. It might be time."

He looked at Jefferson, who nodded agreement and said to me, "You're ready."

I felt a tinge of fear, but I nodded.

I didn't have breakfast; Jefferson and Jack wanted me to fast for the day. After they finished eating, Jack drove into town for some things while Jefferson and I spent the late morning and early afternoon sitting quietly by the lake. I found it difficult not to be anxious; I wanted to discuss so many different things, and our meditation seemed contradictory to my mindset.

"I really may not be ready for this," I said. "I'm nervous."

"You should be—that's part of the balance. It's your body's way of preparing you."

"Jefferson, I've wanted to ask you some more questions."

"What's on your mind?"

I hesitated and then said, "Why don't you just start the currency? I've learned a lot in the last ten years, but you probably know a lot more about all this than I do."

"No, it's your role. Experience is—"

I smiled. "Right, right—I get it." I looked vacantly across the water. "Why do I even bother asking anymore?"

"It may test your patience, Douglas, but it's the most important part of your existence."

We talked for a long time, the feeling between us easy and relaxed. Despite my age, I often still felt like a child around Jack and Jefferson. Maybe that perception owed to the fact that I had so much less experience and knowledge than they did, but today, I felt different. Watching Jefferson, I realized for the first time in our relationship that my respect for him wasn't one-way—that he had put an incalculable amount of time, energy, and faith into helping me grow. He was proud of me and considered me more than his student. I was his friend.

During our conversation that afternoon, I suddenly had the odd feeling I was with my father again. Without thinking, I said, "Thank you."

"For what?"

I shook my head trying to ignore a strange awkwardness spreading inside me. "I . . . don't know exactly. For everything, I guess."

"You'd have done the same for me."

"Would I have?"

"Yes."

I thought about that for a moment. "I know I would now, but considering some of the selfish things I've done, I'm not so sure—"

"I'm sure." Jefferson's statement held enough conviction to make me believe that he was probably right; no matter how low I had gone, I would have somehow found the strength to help him had he needed me.

The sound of an engine distracted us, and we both turned to see Jack pulling into the driveway. He stopped the truck and yelled, "I don't want to interrupt your alone time, but I've got some groceries that need to be carried inside."

We unloaded the bags in silence and a strange feeling pervaded the kitchen—a nervous expectation between the three of us. Considering the amount of preparation that had gone into what we would do tonight, it was no wonder that we were all a bit anxious. I felt like an Olympic athlete, merely hours away from the event that would test years of commitment and training.

Only this test wasn't a mere sporting event. Our lives and futures would depend on the outcome, and that thought alone would have been powerful enough to terrify me, were it not for the state of tranquility I had worked so hard to master. It seeped into my soul, eclipsing the fear as quickly as it appeared, reminding me of my place in the entirety.

Finally Jefferson said, "We'll start in about two hours, so do whatever you need to do to prepare yourself."

Jefferson and Jack ate a small meal, but I maintained my fast. Jack was eating a bowl of fruit and said, "*Man*, this just tastes *so* goddamn good!" He held a spoonful out to me. "Do you want some, Douglas?" Then his face became pitiful. "Oh, *no*! You can't, can you? I'm so sorry."

"I'm sure he's nervous enough without having to listen to your nonsense," Jefferson said. "Why don't you leave the boy alone?"

He caught himself and looked at me, "But then, I suppose you aren't a boy anymore, are you?"

"No," I said. "I guess it's been a little over a decade now, Jefferson."

Jack laughed and pointed his thumb at Jefferson. "Compared to this old bastard, you're a goddamn embryo."

Jefferson ignored Jack and said to me, "How do you feel?"

"I'm not as nervous as I thought I'd be."

"Do you feel it running through you?"

"A little."

"Just let it in." He seemed to brighten and he angled his head, watching me carefully.

Warm colors streamed in the windows as the sun set. I began to feel familiar chills all over my body, and I trembled a little.

Jefferson went into his room and returned with a small vial. He moved directly in front of me and gently grabbed the back of my neck with a swift motion. I felt a pinprick in the side of my neck and winced, instinctively trying to recoil, but he held me firmly in place. A warm sensation spread through my neck, and my throat began to feel numb, swollen.

"That's it?" I asked.

Jefferson gave me a slight smile. "Did you expect a ceremony?"

I turned to Jack, his eyes demanding every ounce of my focus. His self-confidence and control riveted me; I couldn't pull my gaze away. He grinned and narrowed his eyes; tiny crow's feet appeared at their edges.

I felt a deep rumbling, shadows moving in every direction.

Now I was falling . . . as though someone had pushed me out of an airplane. And then I was still again. Sound evaporated and I closed my eyes. A fraction of a second later, I opened them, taking in everything around me. Space stuttered like the frames of an old film.

Silence.

What is this?

My head felt swollen and my jaw tensed. I moaned, but no sound came. My body expanded . . . inches, or maybe even feet, filling the space in every direction—from end to end, side to side.

I tried to relax but my head swam, reality shaking around me, porcelain teetering on the edge of an abyss. Motion alternated between fast-forward and absolute stillness.

Then blackness.

"You've crossed." The statement came as pure thought. It was Jefferson.

"Where are you?" My lips didn't move, but my voice came nonetheless.

"Here, with you."

I tried to move again, but I couldn't. There was nowhere to go. Panic started to overtake me.

"Douglas, you're going to be fine," he said, but the fear increased its hold.

"I don't want to do this," I said. "I want to stop. Take me back."

"You can't go back," he said. "Don't fight it. Humble yourself."

"*No*, I don't want to *do* this!"

"Face your weakness, Douglas. I can't do this for you—you have to discover it your own way."

The threat of insanity loomed over me. I was in the blackest void, unable to move, certain I was about to die. "Jefferson, *help me!*"

"Listen to me. If you trust me, you'll be fine. Just relax and have faith that you will get through this. You have to believe."

And with that sentence, something shifted—Jefferson was right. I had never known a place so lonely—so utterly dark—but I had to let go, to find faith in the benevolence of the abyss . . .

. . . I was falling again, deliberate and with immutable confidence, galvanized by my faith in the outcome.

Glorious . . .

Now I was still again.

I could see, but it wasn't with vision as I had always known it—I perceived everything with a simpler, more direct understanding. My senses were no longer limited to the area around my body; I was aware of everything. I could feel neither my breathing nor my heartbeat. I was frozen in space and time, and yet I had transcended their limitations.

I had done what so many had failed to do. I had conquered the drug.

My eyes found Jefferson. The details of his presence filled my mind with cognition that went beyond mere sight—he was nobler; almost a deity. I was experiencing him in his purest form. Jack was there, too, and he also looked different to me, taller—the way he had appeared to me in my childhood.

We stood in a rolling meadow full of wildflowers and tall grasses, mountains rising around us in the distance. The sky was a deep blue, spotted with clouds, and the sun hovered just above the horizon, creating streaks of mixed colors, pink, orange, and red.

The scent of this place reminded me of the freshness of spring, but the experience went beyond just smelling; the fragrances were pure and seemed to fill my soul. I perceived them much the same way I felt—rather than heard or saw—Jefferson and Jack.

The air was eider against my skin, a gentle anesthetic prohibiting any pain. But my faculties remained sharp. Everything was almost too perfect—better than reality itself.

"Where are we?"

"Wherever you want us to be." Jefferson said. "We're still physically in the living room at the lake house, but consciously, we have transcended. For lack of a better way of saying it, we're *everywhere*. This is the way space and time really are. This is the entirety. You create your perception here."

"Can you see it?"

"Not the same way you do."

I tried to move, but couldn't.

"You have to let go," Jack said. He walked a few steps, his movement slow and halting. Physical echoes of his image flowed behind him, and when he stopped, they melted into his body.

I tried to move again, but still couldn't.

Jefferson touched my forehead and more contentment rippled through my body. "When you're here, it's effortless. If you don't think too much about it, it will fall into place automatically."

My arm rose, stuttering through space, trails following. "I did it!"

"Good," Jefferson said. "You have it now."

Jack raised his arm. "Hold up your hand." I did, and he pushed his own hand through mine, as though he were pushing it into a thick liquid. My hand rippled, spreading apart as his fingers melted into my palm. I felt a tingling sensation, like low levels of electricity. I instinctively tried to pull my arm away, but our hands were fused.

Jack gently pulled his hand out of mine. "Our bodies were connected at the quantum level. You try it now."

I moved my hand toward Jack's shoulder and touched it. "Now just let it flow through me," he said. My hand wouldn't penetrate his skin. "Relax, Douglas."

I tried again, this time not pushing or forcing anything, and my hand slowly melted into his shoulder. "Oh my *God*!"

"That's it," Jack said. "Now you've got it."

I pulled my hand out. "I don't want to hurt you."

"Don't be arrogant. I've faced a lot worse shit than your hand." He started to walk. "Come over here with me."

I tried to walk, but again I couldn't move. Jack said, "It's like trying to pee in front of an audience—the harder you try, the more it won't happen."

"That really helps, Jack. Thanks." I tried to allow myself to relax, and suddenly I took a step, and then another—my echoes falling into line behind me, staggered, imitating whatever I did. When I stopped, they melted into me again. "Are those the other universes?"

"Yes, that's right," Jack said. "The probabilities. Those are the new instances of you."

"Watch me," said Jefferson. He took several steps and five tracers appeared. But this time, they didn't melt into him when he stopped. He turned to face me and his tracers followed suit—a total of six Jeffersons now standing before me. "This is the multiplicity, the overlapping of multiple universes," he said, his tracers echoing the words, each an interval later than the one before it.

"Which one are you?"

"We're all the same—all different parts of the same probability, existing in different universes."

"But you can't be all of them."

He smiled and his tracers followed suit. "Remember what I told you? Time and space aren't linear. We simply *are*. We're all just probabilities making up the whole in the entirety." As Jefferson spoke, his tracers each echoed his words in turn like a distant staccato burst of gunfire. "Every instance of me you are seeing is a different component of the probability that comprises who I am—all of us exist simultaneously in different universes. This place is like the hub—a central station, to and from which we can see into the infinite universes in the multiverse. This is the origin."

I watched the tracers in awe. "Are they dependent on you?"

The first Jefferson remained silent, looking at the tracer beside him, and the second Jefferson said, "No, we aren't dependent on each other. You've just watched me manipulate history."

"How?"

"Because this instance of me is speaking to you, and the first one is not."

Each subsequent version repeated his words.

Then the first Jefferson said, "I changed the past in a small context this time, to show you that it can be done, but it's dangerous and we won't try it again." Then all the different versions of Jefferson melted into one.

"I want to try it."

"You can if you like. Walk to your right," Jefferson said. I did what he told me, and then he said, "Now look at the other versions of you."

I turned, and several different instances of me also turned, subsequently. It was like standing in a room full of mirrors. After a second, they all melted back into me.

"Let them have independence."

I moved to my right again, and three of *me* fell in line. I let go, just as I had earlier, allowing all my misgivings and apprehension slide away. My echoes remained separated, each fixed in space, maintaining its own integrity. "That's me?"

"Yes," said Jefferson. "They're autonomous, but they're still you."

I felt them all. We existed together in the entirety. I looked at the echoes, each one in turn looking at his subsequent version, like dominos moving one after another. "Could I talk to one?"

"No, Douglas," Jefferson said in a warning tone. "I showed you it can be done, but I don't want you to try it."

"How do I get back to being only one?"

"Just let it happen," Jack said. "Each will return to its respective universe and you'll perceive yourself as one person again."

"Which universe will I be in?"

"You'll revert to the one where you started," Jefferson said.

As I thought about returning to my universe, all of my versions slowly merged into me. "Can I see into the other universes from here?"

As though in response to my question, an image appeared in front of me. I saw myself at ten years old riding my bicycle. Then I was sitting at a table, playing chess at the Cardinal. I was younger—around the time I met Jefferson.

"You're seeing other universes," Jefferson said. "You're splitting time." Then suddenly his voice became apprehensive. "Jack, he's going too far." Then to me: "Douglas, come back. You aren't ready for this."

Now Thomas was walking with me, so close I could almost touch him. I turned and smiled, and my little brother smiled back at me.

For the first time in so long.

Now Dad was with us. *So real.* "Dad?" He looked at me curiously, but then turned and started walking away.

"Come back, Douglas." Jefferson's voice was distant, less important.

Thomas and I were walking to the creek, the summer sun dancing through the rippling shadows of the Aspen trees.

But there was something important.

Jack's voice burst through from somewhere. "*Stop,* Douglas! You'll change history. You have to come back now, okay, kid?"

"Come to the creek with us, Jack!"

"No. You have to come with me."

He was in front of me now, so tall. I looked around. "Where'd Thomas go?"

"Just come with me. That's it, that's good." He took my tiny hand in his.

"Where'd he go?" I started to cry. "Where's Thomas?"

"Hell, kid, they're around here somewhere." He picked up my small body, holding me close to his chest. "I'm sorry."

"Jack?" I couldn't breathe.

Sound and light rushed in, and I gasped for air. "Jack? *Jack!*" I opened my eyes. Jack, Jefferson, and I were back in the house at Lake Vallecito. Tears streamed down my face.

They opened their eyes, blinking several times.

My vision blurred and my legs felt weak. I fell to my knees, weeping, calling out for my little brother and my father.

Jack and Jefferson gently picked me up, helping me to my bed like a drunk on the verge of blacking out. They stayed with me, whispering to each other and to me.

I plummeted into the void, fitful, dreaming of my dad and Thomas.

◆

I WOKE UP to a gentle shaking. "Douglas." Jack was leaning over me. "Wake up."

"Where am I?"

"We're still at the lake."

I sat up abruptly, my eyes snapping open and shut. "I saw Dad and Thomas. I was there."

"I was there too."

"How long have I been asleep?"

"For two days."

Thomas's face was still fresh in my mind, close enough to reach out and take his hand. "I want to go back! I could stop the crash—"

Jack put his hand on my shoulder. "You can't do that, Douglas. Their lives would affect the future. You have to let it go."

"They were right with me." I stared vacantly out the window, reason slowly replacing the intensity of the experience, forcing me to release the bittersweet visions. I looked into Jack's eyes. "I know you're right." I squeezed my eyes shut. "Goddamn it, this is so hard."

He smiled gently. "I'm sorry. But at least now you know what you're capable of." He gently put the back of his hand on my forehead. "You must be starving."

I looked absently around the room and nodded hesitantly. "Yeah, I could use some food." I swung my legs around and tried to stand, grabbing him for support. I took one shaky step, then another. "I never thought about how hard it would be, Jack. I never thought about seeing Dad and Thomas again."

"I know," he said, taking my weight as I hobbled into the hallway. "The first time is always the hardest, but we did it and that's all that matters."

When we got downstairs, Jefferson was sitting on the couch in the living room reading a book. "How do you feel?"

"I'm dizzy," I said, collapsing on the sofa. "My legs are weak."

"It'll go away in a few days."

"Do you always feel like this afterward?"

"Jefferson does, because he's so fucking old." Jack screwed his face into a standard moronic expression, smacking his gum more audibly than usual, and I smiled a little through the nagging ache.

Jefferson set his book in his lap and looked at Jack impassively. Jack stopped chewing his gum for a moment, trying to hold Jefferson's gaze, as well as the dumb expression on his face, but finally gave in to a boyish grin. "What?" he said, chewing again. He glanced quickly at the ceiling, and then back at Jefferson, his grin spreading. "*What*? Quit staring at me like that."

Jefferson's face remained neutral but his eyes were radiant. After a moment his gaze drifted to me. "No, we don't feel like that. Once you're able to burst without the drug, you won't feel those side effects anymore."

"How long before I won't have to use the drug?"

He smiled. "You still have a lot of things to learn before it's time to ask that question."

I don't know if I can attribute it to the drug, but despite the sadness that lingered from my brief reunion with Thomas and Dad, the days after my first experience were some of the most peaceful and carefree of my life. The weather was unusually warm for the time of year, and I spent the majority of the daylight hours outside by the lake, working on the details of the currency we would create through the bank in Switzerland—making phone calls, and running models and mock allocations.

Jack left almost every day to get us the things we needed from town, and when he was gone, I used the time to talk to Jefferson. He seemed to take a great interest in my thoughts—encouraging me, gently correcting me when he thought I was missing something important. Our conversations were warm, almost intimate, but totally unforced; it had never been easier to talk to Jefferson, and never before had I felt so close to him.

At night after dinner, the three of us alternately played chess for hours, always laughing, talking about anything and everything. I almost enjoyed watching the games between Jack and Jefferson more than I enjoyed playing. Jack ribbed

Jefferson constantly, but Jefferson never seemed affected by the sarcasm, usually responding with gentle laughter. But his eyes told me he loved Jack absolutely, and there was no doubt the feeling was mutual.

I never saw Jack win a game against Jefferson. He made endless ludicrous excuses for his defeats, but over time I began to get the impression that Jack didn't really want to beat Jefferson—that it might somehow disrupt what he considered to be the order of things.

One night after a particularly nasty loss, Jack came up with an idea: "Jefferson, why don't you let me and Douglas here play you as a team. I'll bet you can't beat us both at the same time."

"Okay," Jefferson said.

Jack seemed suspicious of the quick reply and decided to negotiate more favorable terms. "Okay. And why don't we play with a clock. We'll take fifteen minutes and you can have five. How does that sound?"

"Fine by me."

Jack looked at him even more suspiciously. "And maybe you could play blindfolded?"

Jefferson gave him a sardonic expression. "And maybe I could drink a bottle of scotch, too?"

Jack scratched his chin. "Okay."

We started the game, but only after Jack changed his mind about the clock. "Now that I think about it, I don't want to give the arrogant old bastard an excuse," he said.

Jefferson gave us white, so we moved first. I let Jack handle the opening. After the standard moves, he stopped play for a while to consider our position. We discussed our options and decided on each subsequent move.

The game lasted about an hour and a half, with Jefferson unable to obtain any advantage. The board dwindled down to our kings, along with three pawns and a knight apiece. Jack and I played well, but ultimately Jefferson saved a pawn and ended the game after he marched it to the end of its file, turning it into a queen.

"God*damn* it!" Jack bellowed. "You cheated, you old fucking rooster! Nobody's that good!"

Jefferson ignored him, resetting his side of the board.

Jack folded his arms. "Cheaters never *really* win, you know."

I rose from my chair. "Well, I'd love to sit here and listen to Jack whine all night, but I'm tired, so I'm going to bed."

"Hold on a second," Jefferson said. "I want to play one more game." His seriousness caught me off guard.

Jack gave him a curious smile and then went into the kitchen.

I watched Jack as he walked away, puzzled by his expression. I shrugged. "Okay."

Jefferson finished setting the white pieces on his side. I waited for him to open, but he didn't move. He only stared at me.

"What?" I said nervously.

"Are you ready?"

"I guess."

"'I guess' isn't an answer. Put your hand here, in the middle of the board."

I hesitated and then slowly placed it palm down between us.

I was unprepared for the speed with which Jefferson grabbed my wrist. Temperature, sound, and light ceased to exist. Time stopped like a train grinding to a standstill, and I floated in the massive void. *What the hell is he doing?*

"I want you to see something." His thoughts became mine, intermingled in the entirety. I understood them clearly.

"Do you know where you are?" he said.

I hesitated, and then it came to me. "Yes, it's like it has always been here."

"It always has been."

All around me I saw the familiar openings, all the variations I had used—from the childhood games with my father to the present. But they were clearer now. Then I saw more—I went to the next level, and the openings became part of me, fusing with my existing understanding of the game, as well as the universe as a whole. "This is your world?"

"Part of it," he said.

"What do you want me to do?"

"You are the game, and the game is you, so you should understand it the same way you understand yourself."

"Yes, I see it . . ." The combinations in front of me became an almost infinite number of probabilities.

"That's good," he said.

Suddenly I was back in the living room. My senses scrambled to process the onslaught of reality resuming around me, and I opened my eyes wide, blinking hard. Jefferson was in front of me, the chessboard between us, my hand still in the middle of the table. I sat in my chair, frozen, breathing slowly.

"So now you know." He pushed his king's pawn two spaces.

I saw the infinite probabilities, most of them unviable. But the good ones were there too, easier to comprehend now. "How—?" I felt like a piece of software had been installed in my mind.

"I told you—it was always there."

I pushed my queen's pawn one space, and the possibilities changed instantly. Things progressed rapidly as we swept through the standard opening, and when we had exhausted the common responses, we settled to the probabilities—to the game as it should be played.

I didn't simply absorb Jefferson's knowledge when he took me into his mind. What he showed me wasn't just a massive collection of standard chess procedures; he opened my perception to the probabilities that make the game flow. My game before had been nothing more than a series of reactions, but now I saw everything in a new way.

A chess game, when played properly, consists of no reactions at all. It is more than the sum of its moves—it is a beautiful and elegant flow of strategies, all inter-twined within one another. But when the game is played poorly, the opportunities never materialize at all, and frustration obstructs fluidity.

Chess no more depends on the player than the player depends on the game, and when it is played at its most synergistic level, it almost plays itself—good moves materializing effortlessly, opening up highly probable winning paths, cre-ating endless opportunities. It is, for lack of a better description, the absence of dogmatism. It is transcendence.

Our game progressed slowly, and after two hours we each still had a knight, a rook, and our kings. Jefferson had four pawns to my five. It was the first time I had ever been up a piece against him.

I thought I'd be nervous but I wasn't; the game came easily to me. I felt the familiar tranquility and control, but it didn't overwhelm me as it had other times. It was comfortable now, like an old friend. The game's outcome was no longer significant, and yet, ironically, it was so important at another level. This is the paradoxical nature of the entirety—the duality that is so elusive, and yet, once found, so startlingly simple.

Jefferson moved. I captured his knight and he took mine in response. We had anticipated the exchange for many moves, and now he began slowly to advance his pawns. Before long, I took another one from him.

He's letting me win, I thought.

I lifted my arms to stretch, looking to my right, and was surprised to see Jack standing next to me. "I thought you left. How long have you been there?"

"About an hour and a half." He was looking at Jefferson. I followed his gaze, and what I saw completely unnerved me.

Jefferson's eyes blazed, just as they had the day he beat Big Mack. And suddenly I knew: *He isn't giving it to me. He's losing and he knows it.*

Jack smiled and a new feeling of repose wrapped around me. The game now stood at a rook apiece, along with our kings. Jefferson had three pawns to my five. He took my rook and I responded by taking his. We had both, once again, long anticipated the exchange of pieces.

It was the last move of the game. Two of Jefferson's pawns were together, but the other was staggered several files over. It was lost. My pawns, however, all stood together—two protecting my king on one side of the board, three others protecting each other on the opposite side. My positions were solid.

Jefferson's eyes induced in me a familiar fear, but my mind quickly suppressed it.

He studied the board for a few more minutes and then our eyes met. "It can't be done," he said. "Against someone more foolish maybe, but not against you."

I had seen Jefferson play countless games of chess, but even until the last move that night, I nearly refused to believe that he could be defeated. Then something happened I will never forget.

He nodded at me once. He picked up his king and held it in front of his face for a moment, looking at me respectfully. Then he laid the king on its side in a gesture of gentle surrender.

I had done what I had never seen anyone else do. I had beaten Jefferson Stone.

◆

STRANGELY, DESPITE EVERYTHING it meant, my victory against Jefferson seemed like nothing more than a natural part of the progression of our relationship. The next day, I woke up before everyone else, started coffee, and went out to the lake to stretch as the sun rose. The water was still—a crystalline plane in the morning serenity. The first rays of sunlight burst over the mountains and cut across the water like blades, ricocheting every direction in sharp prismatic flashes.

I mulled over the game with Jefferson, replaying every move in my head, still not quite able to believe I had beaten him. After about twenty minutes, I heard a sound and turned to see Jack walking toward the pier. He handed me a cup of coffee and sat down, but neither of us spoke for some time.

"What you did last night was incredible," he said finally.

"I didn't do anything."

"Whatever."

"You could beat him, Jack."

"No. You still don't understand."

"I understand enough. If you took him to the end, you could beat him."

"No, I couldn't," he said, taking a sip of his coffee and then lowering the cup. "You two see more than I do."

"I don't really believe that."

"Believe what you want. I've never beaten Jefferson—at least not like that."

I turned to him. "What do you mean, 'not like that'? You told me you've never beaten him at all."

He looked across the lake, his eyes squinting against a gentle breeze. Then he smiled knowingly. "No, I never have beaten Jefferson."

Over the next few days, when I wasn't glued to my laptop working on plans for the construction of the new currency, I played chess with Jefferson whenever I could find a break. And while the games were fierce, always taken to the very end, I didn't beat him again.

One night, after several long hours of chipping away at him, I retired to my room where I worked on my computer for about an hour. I grew weary of staring at numbers, but I wasn't sleepy, so I decided to go downstairs to the library and find something to read. I got out of bed and opened my closet to get a sweater, but as I reached for it something made me look up. A box rested on the shelf above my clothes. I stared at it for a moment, curious why it held my attention.

A wave shattered time and space, blurring my vision. My senses heightened and I felt something pulling me. I pinched the bridge of my nose and squeezed my eyes, trying to understand what was happening.

There is something in there I have to see. The urge now turned into an irresistible, aching desire. Uncomfortable spikes of electricity ran down my neck and spine like the onset of a fever. I was frightened, but the pressing need to get into that box overshadowed every other thought or emotion.

With the last bit of reason I possessed, it occurred to me that even my addictions had never affected me with this power. Time stopped briefly, then resumed, moving back and forth like a jittery carnival ride.

I thought I heard distant maniacal laughter and I turned my head toward the window, but there was nothing there. I pulled the box down from the shelf and dropped it hard on the bed, throwing open the top.

A stack of photographs caught my eye, and I reached for them. The pictures were of me, Thomas, Jack, and Dad. There were some trinkets that meant nothing to me, and at the bottom was a newspaper, yellowed with age.

I snatched it up. It was a Durango Herald, printed when I was in high school. On the cover was a photograph of an old Native American man and the headline above his picture read:

"Tribal Leader Dead at 84"

I stared at the newspaper. *What the hell does that mean?* I read part of the article, but I only became more confused. At the bottom of the page, I saw a smaller article. The fear was back now, holding its ground. The caption read:

"Durango Man and Son Killed in Car Crash"

I closed my eyes and took a deep breath. Vague unexplored memories flashed in my mind, the pieces of a shattered mosaic trying to find their way home. I looked back at the paper:

"A Durango man and his son were killed last night when a car ran a red light, hitting their vehicle. Maximilian Cole and his son Thomas were returning home when the accident occurred."

The article gave the driver's name and some small details, but I had seen it all before. And yet I felt as though I were missing something.

And then I saw it:

"Police suggest the suspect might be mentally unstable and cited a recent history of psychiatric observation . . . "

The confusion was crippling. *How could I have missed it?*

"He killed your father and brother."

I wheeled at the sound of the raspy voice. Groeden leaned against the wall near the bedroom door, his head tilted forward, his hair hiding his face.

"How did you—?"

"Doesn't matter," he said. "I'm showing you the truth."

"You're an illusion."

He looked up suddenly. "Is that what he told you?" He let out a gravelly chuckle. "*He* killed them, you ignorant fool. You saw the newspaper." He smiled confidently, sucking air through his teeth.

"No. He wouldn't—"

"He was here. He came to make sure they died."

"*What?*" I looked at the paper trembling in my clenched fist.

"You know what you have to do," he said.

Anger ripped through me.

"That's right . . ." His smiled broadened.

I looked at him, confused, but then it all became clear. The old broken man in front of me saw the change in my eyes, and his smile stretched still wider across his wrinkled face. Then his image simply dissolved into nothingness.

Rage churned in my arteries, liquid hate. I had one clear purpose: I was going to choke the life out of Jefferson—to watch him suffer the way I had after Thomas and Dad died. I dropped the newspaper and threw myself at the door, nearly tearing it off its hinges. But when I opened it, I lost all my momentum, taking a step back, surprised. Jack blocked my path.

"Get out of my way," I said.

"He's beating you."

"Get the *fuck* out of my way!"

"*Stop it!*"

The fury became acid in my mind, a muddled mixture of elation and cancerous rot. Time slowed, but it wasn't the entirety—it was some darker, distorted element of it.

"You can't stop me now," I spewed, with a sneer on my lips. "If you don't get out of my way, I'll rip your fucking head off."

"Don't overestimate what you can do." Jack's eyes were steady, his body firmly planted. "This isn't who you are."

The engine that drove reality seized, bringing time to a halt.

"Don't do it." Jack's voice was unnervingly calm, echoing through my mind. He still blocked my way, his expression neutral, his eyes brilliant.

I met his gaze, and suddenly I felt cold. I closed my eyes and swung at him. My hand entered his body and I reached for his heart, pushing through what felt like a thick warm liquid.

I opened my eyes again and saw my father staring at me, inches away, his face blank. Brains hung from a wound on his scalp, and his disfigured arm dangled limply at his side. My arm was buried deep in his chest.

I screamed and hauled myself backward. A sharp pain filled my own chest and something sucked me backward. I had no strength to resist, the wind forced from my lungs. My body went limp.

Now I floated in a black sea, waiting for the answer to some unasked question—detached, utterly indifferent about my existence in the universe—my present, my past. I saw myself in Jefferson's living room lying on the floor, and while I was part of the scene, I was also strangely separated from it. I tried to inhale and found that I couldn't, but it didn't matter; the silence was beautiful, so peaceful.

I watched with unconcerned curiosity as Jack leaned over my still body. "Douglas, breathe for me." He pushed my chest and I felt another sharp pain.

Even hovering so far away . . .

"Open up," he said. "I'm here. Let it back in . . . let it come." His voice was steady, and yet it seemed on the verge of hysteria.

I hung suspended in the universe, drifting through the endless void. I began to laugh but no sound came.

"Open up, Douglas."

I could still see Jack, but he seemed even more distant and hazy, leaning over my body, his face an inch from mine. I was simultaneously above and below him. "You come back right *now,* goddamn it! Do you hear me? It isn't supposed to happen like this!" A tear fell down his nose and hit my face, but I didn't feel it.

Something is wrong. I laughed harder and still no sound came.

"You're dying, Douglas." Jefferson's voice echoed through my being—distant cannon fire, its rhythm calculated and cold.

Where are you?

"I'm here with you, where I've always been."

Jefferson? My laughter began to fall away.

"You have to control this or you'll die," he said. "Do it for me and Jack or it's all over."

I was alone, standing before the entirety. I saw nothing, and yet I saw everything. The distances were unfathomable, so peaceful and alluring.

Then the entirety itself spoke, its presence magnificent, leaving me with no doubt as to its origin. There were no words. The concepts were whole and instantaneous: *Are you ready to join me?* It tugged at me irresistibly.

Yes, I want to . . .

"If you go, I can't help you. I'm not allowed to. We'll all die," Jefferson interrupted.

I don't want you to die.

"Then come back to me and Jack."

You killed Thomas and Dad.

"I didn't kill them. I only did what was required."

Required? They died *because of you.*

"I didn't kill them. Someday you'll see that."

The entirety resonated in my mind again: *Do you want to join me?*

"It doesn't want you, Douglas," Jefferson said. "You're listening to the appeal of your own death. If you go, we all go together."

I don't want you to die.

"Come back."

I inhaled violently, my lungs filling to capacity with air. My chest heaved upward and I felt Jack's arms wrap around me, holding me tightly. He pulled away for a moment, and we stared at each other. Terror filled his eyes, and his expression froze in my mind.

Then nothing.

———————◆———————

I HAD SOME concept of time, but it was vague at best. Visions came and went throughout my sleep; Jack and Jefferson were with me, sometimes singly and sometimes together, watching me with concerned expressions, speaking gently to me.

At times, I dreamt fitfully, vivid images of Groeden descending on me with his blade raised high. I tried to scream, but nothing would come, and at the last possible moment, he simply vanished, his wicked cackles echoing into space.

At other times, I was in the void again, floating, peaceful. Sometimes Dad and Thomas were there moving slowly with me, reaching out to me.

At other times I was alone, simply waiting.

"Douglas?"

I blinked a few times. Jefferson stood over me, his face anxious.

I bolted upright. "What happened? Where—?"

Jack sat in a chair next to the bed. "Douglas, just relax."

I shook my head to clear it, pressing my palm against my throbbing forehead. I looked acidly at Jack. "Don't say that to me again. I'm fucking sick of you talking to me like a child." I tried to move, but my chest hurt and I winced. "What the *fuck* happened?"

"Take it easy," Jack said.

"No, *you* fucking take it easy! I saw the goddamn newspaper!"

"I know—" Jefferson began.

I snapped my head around. "You tell me everything, Jefferson. Right now. Tell me about the man who drove the car that killed Thomas and Dad."

He looked at the floor. "He committed suicide. You already knew that."

"You *fucking* tell me what happened right now! Did Groeden send him?"

Neither of them responded.

"*Tell* me, goddamn it!" My voice began to quaver.

Jefferson's expression was emotionless, but his eyes showed complete honesty. "Groeden . . ." He breathed deeply. "Groeden influenced the driver—"

"And you came to Durango, knowing what that meant?"

"Yes," he said uncomfortably. "I've always been honest with you about my presence in Durango, and that it allowed Groeden to influence some people—"

"Yeah, sure! My mother—and that kid Rudy! But it never occurred to me that Groeden might have gotten to the guy driving that car! How could I have been so *stupid*?"

I looked back and forth from Jefferson to Jack. "It was hard enough knowing that you didn't warn them, that neither of you tried to stop it. And somehow I even accepted that as part of this *stupid* fucking duty you keep talking about." I felt my throat tighten. "But now I know it was more than that." I glared at Jefferson. "You came here on purpose. You knew what would happen. You *wanted* it to happen."

Jefferson only continued to stare at the floor. "I know how it seems."

The pitch of my voice increased. "Groeden murdered my father and my brother, and you were *fucking* complicit!" I pulled my hair hard, squeezing my eyes shut. "*Why*?"

I turned to Jack, but he wouldn't meet my gaze. Tears filled my eyes. "That was my dad. He was my *dad*! Do you know how much I loved him? Do you know how much I loved my little brother? *Can* you fucking know? Did you lead those bastards to my dad and my little Thomas?"

Jack rose suddenly. "You mind your *fucking* tongue! You don't know anything about—"

"That's enough," Jefferson said.

"No, it's *not*!" Jack glared at Jefferson. He was about to say something else, but the stillness in Jefferson's eyes stopped him.

Jefferson said to him, "Need I remind you of your own vulnerability?" A look of caution passed over his face as he spoke. "You would do well to take a deep breath and sit down."

Jack stared at Jefferson for a moment longer and then sat, glowering at me. He closed his eyes and began to breathe deeply.

Jefferson's face remained impassive, and he said to me, "You're right, it was my fault your father and brother were killed, and it hurts me as much as anything I've ever known. Even though you don't understand that now, you will someday, and I hope you'll forgive me." Then he turned and left the room.

"Jefferson—" I said. But he was gone.

"He's not mad at you," Jack said, his eyes still closed. "If you could just see—"

"It's too much."

"I know." He looked at me compassionately. "I thought I could handle this, but I can't. It's killing me to watch it unfold."

I furrowed my brow. "You once told me you'd be able to understand my anger if you had actually been responsible for their deaths. Do you remember saying that, Jack?"

He nodded, looking at the floor, ashamed.

"Well, Jefferson *was* responsible!"

"He had no choice. God*damn* it! There's so much you don't understand!"

"Then fucking tell me!"

"Do you think we *wanted* to see your dad and Thomas die?"

We stared at each other for a moment, and then I exhaled deeply, lacing my fingers in my hair. "I don't even know who I am anymore. I didn't ask for any of this."

"None of us asked for it, but here we are."

Jack walked to the window, gazing at the lake as I collected my thoughts for a long moment. Finally I said, "What happened, Jack?" I shook my head, looking at the quilt covering my legs. "Groeden—he was in my room. He told me what to do." I looked back up at him, pleading. "I let him win."

Jack sighed. "This may be the part I've dreaded most." He took a deep breath, staring vacantly out the window. "Fear was the only thing you'd respond to, but your heart stopped—" He closed his eyes. "I didn't expect that. You almost died."

"I saw it all happen. I'm sorry—"

"This isn't your fault, Douglas. We're all doing the best we can. I'm just glad it's over." He tightened his jaw and he said, "Just get some more rest." He turned and walked toward the door. "I'll check on you in a little while."

I spent the rest of the day trying to forgive Jefferson for his involvement in Thomas's and my father's deaths, but it was nearly impossible. Still, if it hadn't been clear before, one thing was now irrefutable: transcendence is least effective, and most dangerous, in the face of rage. I would have to find a way to get past this; any other path would create risks that I was incapable of calculating.

After hours of anguish, I was exhausted again. I finally let go, closing my eyes. I was on the verge of sleep when I heard a noise. Jefferson stood beside my bed. "How are you doing?"

I sat up. "Better." I hesitated. "I'm sorry—"

"No, Douglas, *I'm* sorry—more than you can know. But it's done, and words won't change it." He tried to smile through his obvious despair, but it was awkward. "We have the power to manipulate anything we want to, but we won't. We have to leave things the way they are."

He looked at me expectantly, and I said, "It's hard, that's all."

"Well, our lives depend on your ability to comprehend how important this is, so the sooner you accept it, the better it will be for all of us." He took a breath and caught it. "You are going to face some decisions in your life that will contradict every ounce of rationality and reason you possess, and you will have to make those decisions with no hesitation. Do you understand what I'm saying?"

I nodded.

He looked sternly at me for a moment and said. "Get some sleep. We'll talk more later."

◆

ON THE MORNING after my fifth day of rest, I woke up early and took a walk by the lake. The sun was shining, and the smell of the trees only enhanced the crispness of the pristine air. I walked about a mile, and when I got back to the house, I felt surprisingly strong.

Jefferson and Jack were in the kitchen, reading the paper as they ate breakfast. "Are you ready to try it again?" Jefferson said without preamble.

"Yeah, I'm ready." There was no question in my mind.

He nodded. "We'll do it in a few days, after you're fully rested. This time it will be easier."

"I'm not scared."

Jefferson raised his eyebrows.

"I feel almost like a different person," I said. "Does that sound strange?"

He smiled. "Not at all."

Three days later, I took the drug again, and while it was powerful, it couldn't approach the intensity of the first time. I don't mean to say that the experience was mundane; I simply knew what to expect, and that familiarity allowed me to make discoveries I couldn't make the first time.

I stopped trying to understand the complexity of the multiplicity in traditional terms; instead I temporarily put reason aside, and I began to feel—in a way that could never be explained in logical or mathematical terms—our probabilistic existence in separate universes. It no longer needed to make sense; any connection with the entirety derives from direct experience, transcending mere interpretation and theory. Now every preconceived notion I ever had regarding reality—or at least what I had always thought was reality—lived in the shadow of that connection.

I didn't sleep as long after the second experience; I went to bed when I was ready and awoke about fifteen hours later. I was surprised at the resilience of my body and mind—that they had both grown stronger in spite of the trauma of recent weeks.

It was midafternoon when I opened my eyes, and I found Jefferson and Jack downstairs engaged in a game of chess.

"Hello, Douglas," Jack said in an off-handed tone. "Did you sleep well?"

"I did, Jackson, thank you for asking." I noticed that Jefferson was ahead of Jack by a bishop and two pawns. "And I see you're having a little trouble, as usual."

Jack scowled at me. "You know, there are intricate facets to Jefferson that you simply don't understand. He's a sensitive old man, and if I were to descend upon him with my full capability, there's no way to comprehend what the psychological implications might be. He has a very fragile emotional makeup."

"Checkmate," Jefferson said.

Jack didn't even bother to look at the board, staring at me instead with a clownish sincerity. "You see? Do you see how utterly considerate and compassionate I am?"

Jefferson said to me, "Do you feel okay?"

"Better than ever."

"Good, because you're going to Switzerland."

"Switzerland? Now?"

"It's time," he said.

There was no point arguing with a man who knew the future. "Are you coming?"

"No, I'm not supposed to be there."

"But I am," Jack said, folding his arms. "Cause somebody's got to take care of you, you little bastard."

June, Year Thirty, Zürich, Switzerland

JACK AND I touched down in Zürich after almost two days of traveling. We went straight to our hotel, where Jack immediately passed out and began snoring like a satiated hog. I didn't sleep well at all, plagued both by jet lag and the fearful anticipation of our undertaking. For all my experience as an investor and a speculator, I was now attempting to put together a project of greater scope than I had ever dreamed possible. I wasn't at all sure I was up to the task.

The next morning, we rose early, ran several miles, ate breakfast, and returned to our room to get ready for our meeting at the bank. As I stood in front of the mirror Jack said, "You know, you really aren't all that ugly in a suit. Hell, when you clean up you're almost as good-looking as I am." He furrowed his brow, scratching his head as if to consider his statement with deep intensity. Then he said, "No, actually that's not possible."

Jack had always played the role of my surrogate father, but while I had aged normally, his appearance had changed very little since my childhood. His thick, dark curls showed no signs of gray, and even considering my receding hairline—which he brought up at every available opportunity—we could easily have passed for brothers.

Just before we left the room, he looked thoughtfully at me and furrowed his brow. "You know, you're really getting old, Douglas. At some point, I'm going to have to start introducing you as my father."

I reached for my briefcase without bothering to look at him. "I don't think that would be at all inappropriate, Jackson, considering how fucking immature you are."

At the bank, we approached a woman sitting behind an information desk. She smiled, and I said, "We're here to see Klaus Junger."

"Do you have an appointment?" she said in an accent I couldn't place.

I doubt we're going to need one, I thought, presenting the account documents Jefferson had given me. She looked at them for a few seconds and said, "Will you give me a moment?"

In the previous decade, I had stood in countless boardrooms, addressing everyone from shareholders, to managers, to investment bankers; to say I was familiar with the corporate environment was like saying geese are familiar with flight. And yet, at this moment, I was terrified. I looked at Jack, but he seemed as calm as I had ever seen him, and he smiled at me knowingly.

A minute later, a well-dressed middle-aged man approached us, and the first thing I noticed was how gracefully he carried himself; he seemed prepared for anything. He was tall and fit, with striking features—a strong jaw, wavy blonde hair, and deep green eyes. The instant he walked into the room, I felt the command of his presence, and I knew unequivocally he was the man we had come to see.

He spoke slowly, extending his hand. "I'm Klaus Junger. I understand you would like to access an account?" His English was flawless through a heavy German accent. His smile was warm.

"Yes," I said, taking his hand and shaking it. "My name is Douglas Cole, and this is my colleague, Jack Alexander. It's nice to meet you."

"Please, call me Klaus," he said as he and Jack shook hands. He turned back to me. "You are the account holder, Mr. Cole?"

"Douglas, please—and yes, I'm the account holder."

"Very good. Then, we will only need two things from you: a signature and a fingerprint scan—after which you may conduct your business as you need to."

"That will be fine." I tensed, hoping desperately that Jefferson knew what he was doing. I also hoped my apprehension wasn't written all over my face.

Klaus led us into a room filled with computer equipment. He directed me to a small pad with a stylus attached. "If you could just sign here."

I scribbled my signature, trying to maintain a calm demeanor that belied my inner turmoil. We stared at the monitor on which some German words appeared. Then the monitor flashed, and another German phrase popped up in green letters, along with the figure 96%.

"Very good," Klaus said. "One more verification and we can proceed."

I looked at Jack. He smiled slightly and raised one eyebrow.

Klaus led me to a scanner. "Please place your hand on this pad. Your palms should not touch the pad—only your fingertips."

The signature had been a surprisingly easy obstacle to surmount, but I suddenly doubted Jefferson's ability to falsify my fingerprints, and my nervousness increased as I followed Klaus's instructions.

He touched a button and light pulsed across the pad. Klaus glanced at another monitor. The screen read, in English this time, *Identification in progress. Please wait.* After what seemed like hours it flashed, *Identity confirmed: 97.45% match. Douglas Cole.*

I realized that I had been holding my breath, and I slowly released it. *Oh, Jefferson, how did you manage that?*

"Thank you," Klaus said. "That is all."

Klaus led us to a door near the security center. He opened it, and in the middle of the room stood an enormous rectangular oak table surrounded by leather chairs. He directed us toward the near end of the table and motioned for us to sit. "How can we help you?"

"Klaus," I said. "I should start by asking, how many people know we're here?"

"Our security staff is aware that I am with clients, and they are monitoring us, but they do not know your identities. That information was purged from our computers the instant your identity was confirmed."

"Can you erase any video record of our presence here today?" I asked. "Also, I wonder if you might refrain from capturing our images whenever we meet in the future? Please forgive my belaboring the point, but trust and anonymity are crucial. To help facilitate the process, I'd like to know if you can meet us outside of the bank whenever possible?"

"So I can assume you are here for more than just a simple counter transaction?"

"Klaus," I said, "we're here to find out if your bank can help us with a rather unorthodox list of requests."

He nodded. "Our bank is accustomed to . . . *unusual* requests. I will do what you've asked to ensure your anonymity."

I looked hard at him for a moment. Something in his eyes told me that he understood the seriousness of our visit. I said, "Okay, let's just get right into it then. First, we'll require a team of lawyers who specialize in international law, as well as the services of your accountants. We need to form at least two international corporations in countries that recognize no tax treaties with the United States; we don't want any American agencies to have jurisdiction or legal authority."

"That should not be a problem."

"Once this team is assembled I want to know if it's feasible for you—and only you—to act as our agent. It's imperative that our names be mentioned in as few documents as possible." I paused. "Klaus, no one can ever learn who we are."

His eyes never strayed from mine. "And I must ask you something candidly: would these companies be associated with anything considered illegal by the Swiss government?"

"Absolutely not. Neither is the money in this account."

"Well then, anonymity is our specialty, as I'm sure you are no doubt aware. I think we can create the companies according to your guidelines, and I would be honored to serve as your exclusive agent, provided the activities remain legal."

"Thank you, Klaus. We have no intention of violating Swiss law at any time. Nevertheless, if our identities are discovered, the consequences will be . . . dire, to say the least."

His expression told me he understood.

I moved on to the next question, "How hard would it be for you to convert the majority of this account to gold ingot and other precious assets?"

For the first time since our introduction, Klaus looked uncomfortable. "That would be a difficult task, even if anonymity were not an issue. This is an unusually large sum of money." He leaned back and put his hands together. "It might take some time to buy that many hard assets quietly, but we can probably do it if you are patient."

"How long?"

"I can't be certain—perhaps as long as three to five years, again considering your request for anonymity."

I looked at Jack, and he nodded. "That will be fine," I said. "In the interim, I'd like you to continue to denominate our cash in Swiss francs until it can be converted."

"That *certainly* won't be a problem."

"Good. Obviously you will need strong relationships with the large mining firms and dealers of precious assets around the globe."

"Those relationships are already in place. In addition, we have dealers employed exclusively by our bank in every country that exports significant amounts of precious assets—including gems, metals, and other commodities."

"Can you negotiate contingency agreements with these people to give you exclusive rights to a flow of hard assets during a global financial crisis?"

"On what terms?" he asked.

"We'll pay up to two percent above prevailing market prices in that event."

"And what would you require in return?"

"We want absolute first right of refusal when the time comes. In exchange, we'll also offer the firms guaranteed minimum orders, and we'll index payment against the assets and cash you hold in our names. It would be nearly risk-free to them."

"I am sure we could negotiate such an arrangement," he said. "I may even be able to obtain more favorable terms than those you have requested."

At that moment, I knew I was going to like working with Klaus very much. I relaxed a little. "Good."

"What else?"

"Do you have a strong relationship with the major credit card companies in the United States?"

"Naturally." He turned his palms up and shrugged. "We are, after all, a Swiss bank."

"Yes, of course," I said, chuckling. "I need to know if your bank can handle a large number of small, fast transactions from credit and cash cards, over a relatively short period of time, around the globe."

"How many transactions, and how long?"

"Perhaps tens of millions of people, or even more, and possibly within only a few days."

He appeared uncomfortable again. "I do not know if we could manage that volume."

"Would your bank split with us the cost of an upgrade in your capacity to handle such an eventuality?"

Klaus thought about my question for a moment. "Again, with the amount of money you hold with us, I am certain we would participate in the cost of an upgrade, although it could be expensive, and I would have to obtain the board's approval. But I think I could do it discreetly."

"Good. It's critical to our plans."

"I'll look into it immediately," he said.

I nodded and continued. "Okay, based on the implementation of such a system, and beyond your commitment to act as our exclusive agent with the bank, will you also act as our representative in negotiating contingency relationships with credit card companies, based on a hypothetical collapse of the United States dollar?"

Klaus's expression became very serious. "That *is* an unusual request." He rubbed his hands together for a moment as he considered the magnitude of my proposal. "I could do that for you."

I leaned forward. "Can your bank engrave, print, and warehouse relatively small certificates of denomination that represent the hard assets we'll store with you? And would your bank continue to print and maintain the distribution of these certificates during the type of crisis we have been discussing?"

He rubbed the side of his face. "I assume you want to take measures to prevent the unauthorized reproduction of these certificates?"

You're beginning to catch on, aren't you, Klaus? "We will, of course, pay a premium to keep the certificates unique and exclusive to our purposes."

"I understand there are some interesting technologies available that we might use to that end."

"Good. Can you also negotiate contingency agreements with two or more overnight carriers to transport large numbers of these certificates anywhere in the world on extremely short notice? We need guaranteed availability and, again, we'll pay a premium."

"We already have similar agreements in place with several carriers." He hesitated, the corner of his mouth turning up in a slight grin. "What is the nature of the corporations we will create, if you don't mind my asking?"

As if you don't already know. I looked at Jack who smiled, and I said, "Klaus, we want to create a private global currency on an unprecedented scale. And I have it on good authority that you are the man to help us."

The grin spread across his face as the implications of my statement hit home; he undoubtedly realized how much his bank stood to profit if my prediction of a financial crisis came to pass. Likewise, if my prediction was wrong, the bank would serve as the warehouse for a vast sum of wealth on which it would still profit handsomely from fees and expenses. It was a no-lose proposition.

He shifted his gaze between Jack and me. "That is very interesting, gentlemen . . . very interesting indeed."

September, Year Thirty

JACK AND I spent the next few months in Switzerland, during which time we formed corporations in two small countries. The first was an island in the middle of the Caribbean Sea; the second was in a small South American nation. Neither country recognized U.S. tax treaties or legal tender laws. Each country also housed branches of Klaus's bank—a convenience imperative to our plans.

Our legal team chartered the corporations to "assist in the management of a large asset group." The lawyers purposely kept the language vague in order to deter potential scrutiny. All accounts were numbered, and a third corporation in Switzerland owned all the shares of the two external companies, creating a deep and confusing trail. The parent Swiss company had only two shareholders—Jack and me—and Swiss law rigidly protected our identities.

The bank handled the creation and storage of all documents, and Klaus served as liaison. We never saw even one of our lawyers or accountants. I was thankful that Klaus took the issue of our anonymity so seriously, but for all our diligence—on every front—there were still forces at work against which none of us could have adequately prepared.

Most mornings, we met Klaus at one of Zürich's many restaurants or cafés for breakfast, going over progress and setbacks, and then instructing him how to proceed. After that, Jack and I would disappear, often taking a routine run around the city. Then we'd usually find some small nondescript place and play chess for hours.

In the late afternoon, we'd generally meet with Klaus at a different place for coffee or dinner—again discussing any issues or setbacks that needed to be addressed. Then Klaus would depart, and Jack and I would embark on our adventures for the evening.

One afternoon Klaus told us about an art gallery near the lake that he thought we would enjoy. After our meeting, Jack and I made our way through the city in search of it, discussing the project as we walked. There had been a sticking point with one of the host countries: its government had recently imposed a limit on the amount of assets that a single corporation could hold. The lawyers thought they could get around the law, but we wanted to know how vulnerable our accounts might be during a financial crisis. If the legal team couldn't confidently rule out a seizure of assets in such circumstances, we would have to form a new corporation in another country.

We turned off a main street into an alley that would lead us almost directly to the gallery, speaking loudly and intently. The issue was important to both of us, and we each had strong opinions about how to handle the situation. I was about to interrupt Jack with some critical thought when my breathing became shallow and my vision blurred for an instant. I stopped talking and slowed my pace, puzzled.

I heard a faint hum, like sweet, sad music. Jack had also slowed his pace, his face somber.

A white van pulled to a stop ahead of us, blocking our exit from the alley. Two men in casual clothes and baseball caps stepped out. One of them opened the sliding door of the van, and they each removed an assault rifle.

Jack's eyes glowed. My heart rate and breathing became slow and easy. Peaceful energy pulsed through me.

Jack stepped in front of me, took my shoulders in his hands, and looked directly into my eyes. In a low voice he said, "There isn't much time. Don't fight it when it comes; it's the only thing that will save you."

I nodded, and he narrowed his eyes, smiling a little. "No matter what you see, you have to understand I'll be fine. If you allow any doubt, it will kill us. Are you scared?"

"No." And I meant it. My fear was nearly imperceptible—a ranting child screaming insults at me from a distance, but having no real effect.

Jack's voice was soothing. "You're ready for this. Don't forget what you've learned."

The men disappeared to either side of the alley's exit, and even though I could no longer see them, I knew there would be no escape through that end.

I heard a noise and turned around. Four more men entered the alley behind us, also carrying automatic rifles. I turned back around.

Jack and I still faced each other in the center of the alley, his back to the van blocking one end of the corridor, mine to the men advancing from the other end. I turned my head again briefly as the four men behind me raised their rifles.

With astounding strength, Jack picked me up like a mannequin and swung me around, placing his body between the gunmen and me. He raised his arms and extended them outward, throwing his head back and closing his eyes.

His body shimmered with the familiar liquid quality, reminding me of a similar scene in the alley in Austin so long ago.

After he set me down, I stood erect and relaxed, allowing the entirety to take control of everything. I closed my eyes and became a calm pool of water, stillness, letting nothing interfere with the serenity of the moment. Shots crackled in the distance, a battlefield somewhere far away . . .

I opened my eyes and everything around me came to a halt.

Jack moved one arm very fast, pointing at the group of gunmen. His movements snapped and stuttered, an awkward, forced dance. His eyes blazed at the four men in front of us, standing motionless, like ancient statues raising their rifles to salute us.

"Without the drug, I can't keep you here," he said. "But I wanted you to see, so you would understand."

"What . . .?" Then I saw them: halfway between the gunmen and Jack several small dots hung in space—the bullets—hovering like black insects. He moved his arm again and I heard a low groan. The bullets moved toward us a little. The groan ceased and the bullets stopped again. "Now you have to go back."

Everything came to life around me and I reeled—dizzy from the sudden resumption of reality, as if I had been thrown suddenly into the fury of a hurricane. I nearly fell, but somehow Jack caught me. Then he was gone.

He moved with the grace of a dancer, so fast it was almost imperceptible, his body shifting back and forth in the alley, effortlessly absorbing the bullets. Each impact made a deep muffled thud.

I remembered his words: *No matter what you see, you have to understand that I'll be fine* . . . Stillness snuffed every spark of emerging fear.

The men with the rifles emptied their clips—perhaps a hundred rounds or more. Then the barrage of gunfire simply stopped, and the echoes of the shots slowly died away. The eerie silence that followed was thick, awkward.

The soldiers lowered their weapons, their expressions frozen in disbelief. We should not have been standing.

Jack stood beside me now, his arms outstretched, his body still rippling liquid. His head hung forward, eyes closed, as though he were nailed to an invisible cross waiting only for death.

"Jack?"

He didn't respond.

"Jack?"

Still nothing.

Then his eyes popped open as if on springs. He raised his head slowly, his expression almost evil, his eyes on fire. He slowly lowered his arms like a bird freshly landed, and his body relaxed. A wicked smile touched his lips.

Then he was gone.

Jack appeared in front of the men, and they jumped back, startled. He swung his arm at the first gunman's throat and the man collapsed, twitching on the asphalt, blood erupting from his jugular.

In the same motion, Jack swung his arm at the next man and the head came off, blood bursting from the neck in a red geyser. I couldn't believe the human vessel might account for the amount of black-red liquid saturating the street.

Despite losing two of their comrades, the remaining men dropped their useless rifles and expertly withdrew knives. Jack severed one soldier's knife-arm with a stroke and, with his other hand, pushed into the man's chest, removing the pulsing heart. The soldier collapsed like a marionette, blood spouting from the hole in his chest.

The last of the four gunman lunged before Jack could turn to face him. The knife plunged deep into Jack's back. I felt strangely calm at the sight—somehow, amid the carnage and sounds of death around me, the stillness maintained supremacy, and I knew everything was fine.

Jack stood motionless.

The gunman removed his blade from Jack's back and the hole where the knife had entered sealed instantly, like thick liquid filling a void. Jack cocked his head and shoved his arm into the gunman's face, his fist exploding out the rear of the head. He retracted the arm and a gaping hole appeared, out of which streamed brains, bone and blood. The body dropped, lifeless.

I moved, but Jack was in front of me—fifty feet in less than a second—his eyes trained on the other end of the alley.

I had forgotten the two remaining gunmen, blocking our escape where the van was parked. I turned.

One of them ran, but the other aimed his rifle at us and emptied the clip, shells spraying from the side of the gun, bouncing on the pavement. Jack absorbed the bullets again, and when the clip was empty he dove at the man, defying gravity across the forty feet between them. His body passed through the man's midsection, cutting him in half between the neck and legs.

Blood exploded, a thousand tiny hoses spewing their contents in every direction. The gunman was still alive, his detached legs flailing on the pavement. He began to scream.

Jack reached into what was left of the man's chest and removed the heart, killing him instantly. Then he stood, leaned back, and inhaled deeply. He brought his head down and fixed his eyes on the alley's opening near the truck.

"*Jack—!*"

He cut me off with a raised hand, never shifting his focus. He stood frozen for what seemed like eternity, fixated on one spot, waiting.

Then I heard it—the one sound in the world I never wanted to hear again: *Click . . . click . . . click . . .*

I took a step back, terrified as the source of that dreaded sound rounded the corner in front of Jack. There was no mistaking Groeden's long, greasy, gray-black hair or his empty, hateful eyes. In his left hand, he carried the same long thin blade he had used to slit Thomas's throat in the vision I had seen so many years before.

He stopped a few feet in front of Jack, and they stared at each other. Jack's shoulders slumped slightly, and he breathed hard, in and out. Sweat dripped from his face, and his eyes were black with exhaustion, anger, and hatred. Yet he still found the strength to allow a smile to spread across his face. "You never can get it right, can you?"

It was Groeden's turn to smile. "Can't I?" He turned his icy stare to me. "Not yet." He pointed the curved blade at me, the steel glinting in the sunlight. "So stupid . . . so vulnerable."

Jack chuckled. "I'm his shadow. You'll never touch him while I breathe."

Groeden's eyes turned back to Jack, calm and steady. "Well, here I am. What are you going to do—violate your precious obligation?"

And suddenly I felt cold. *The obligation. He said that to me, all those years ago . . .*

Groeden laughed with a raspy coughing sound, waving his hand dismissively. "No matter. You and I have business later, don't we?"

Jack stopped smiling and launched himself at Groeden, but the old man vanished.

Jack looked around in frustration. He screamed—a desperate violent noise. He turned to me and the blood froze in my veins. His eyes carried a rage I knew only too well—the same tempest that had driven me to nearly murder Elizabeth, to allow me to think I *might* murder Jefferson.

Jack took a step toward me and I felt a sort of terror I have rarely known in my life: he needed to kill, and I was in his sights.

"Jack? *Please*, Jack!"

He stopped suddenly, back in control—shaken by my reaction. His eyes changed to a mixture of regret and sympathy. Then he was in front of me again. "I'm sorry," he said putting his fingers to my temples.

Jack's hands were clean. Not a drop of blood appeared on him anywhere. He walked to one of the felled gunmen and stood over the body. He looked up at me, his eyes red and swollen with tears. "I hate this." He looked at the body again for a moment.

I heard sirens approaching. Jack turned and began walking rapidly back toward me. "We have to go."

Several policemen moved into the alley, guns drawn and pointed at us. They spoke German in urgent tones.

Jack said, "Do you still feel it?"

I nodded.

"Don't fight it. You have to find the strength."

Time stopped again, everything in the alley freezing like a movie put on hold, and then the scene faded slowly to black. The whole universe merged before my eyes, but the sensation lasted only an instant. "I want to sleep . . ."

"I know," Jack said. "You have to wait."

I felt his presence—the way I had when he held me in his arms as a child—but I could no longer see him.

We were in the hotel room. Only an instant had passed, but here I was on the bed, Jack gently caressing my head.

"Sleep," he said. "You're safe now."

And yet again, into the void.

———◆———

"*JACK!*"

I sat upright.

He stuck his head around the corner. "I'm right here." He walked over and sat on the bed.

"Oh my *God*! What happened yesterday?"

"Yesterday?" He laughed. "That was three days ago!"

"Oh, no—" My eyes darted around the room. "The police!"

"They aren't looking for us."

"But they saw everything!"

"No," he said. "Groeden covered his tracks."

"We have to call Klaus—"

"I've already done it, everything's fine. I took updates from him and told him what to do. I made arrangements for us to handle things from Austin."

"Does he know?"

"Nobody knows."

"But Groeden . . . Those men . . ."

"Those men are gone," he said, looking away.

"Who were they?"

"I don't know. Groeden must have found them."

"But . . ." I looked even more frantically around the room. ". . . if he can find us here—" I leveled my eyes with Jack's. "—how much else does he know?"

"It's complicated," Jack said. "We think he may have some information—just not very much."

"But I thought Groeden's organization hasn't been created yet!"

"We don't think it has been."

"Then who could Groeden contact to organize something like that? How is he doing this?"

"Look, we just don't know very much about what he can do." Jack spoke cautiously. "We think he may have contacted himself."

"But if he changes history—"

"He's unpredictable, Douglas. Sometimes he seems extremely cautious, and other times, he doesn't act like he cares at all. We think conditions are more ideal at some times than others, and that he's willing to take more risks at those junctures. The only thing I can tell you is that he'll do anything to stop us, as long as the risks don't seem too great."

"Why does he want to hurt us? We didn't *do* anything to him! I thought he wanted Jefferson!"

"He knows he can stop Jefferson by killing us. Don't forget the reason we're in Switzerland in the first place: Groeden has somehow orchestrated this global chaos specifically to get a reaction from us."

He paused, clearly choosing his words carefully. "Look, it's going to get a lot worse. He knows you're creating this currency in response to what he's doing, and he knows that this is a huge opportunity for him to find us. He's not going to stop."

The scene in the alley raced through my mind, rewinding, playing again. And suddenly I remembered: "Groeden said something about an obligation."

Jack looked uncomfortable, but he didn't respond.

"He said the same thing to me, years ago, when he got in my head, in Austin."
I hesitated. "Jack, he asked me a question, and I never forgot it. He said, 'Has he
told you who you are?' What does that mean?"

Jack took a slow deep breath, his eyes on fire.

"He said he wanted to tell me."

Jack continued to watch me, his mind churning. "He *can't* tell you. It's the
obligation to history. He'll take risks, but not that one."

"What does it mean? You said something similar once."

He looked down. "Let it go."

"Jack, am I going to do something bad?"

He looked at me again, his face stern. "You have to let it go."

I shook my head slowly, fighting the urge to scream at him. A moment passed
and I said, "What did he mean when he said the two of you have business later?"

Suddenly Jack looked even more troubled. "Look, it's nothing. He failed, and
that's what's important."

"Why won't you just tell me?"

He stood up abruptly. "Let it *go!*"

I stared at him, my face contorted with frustration. I shook my head slowly,
trying to accept what was happening. Finally I whispered, "What happened to
you in that alley?"

His face contorted with sadness, and he walked to the window.

"We don't have to talk—"

"We *need* to talk about it." He let out a long breath. "When I go to that place, I
tap into the energy that drives the entirety. The power is exhilarating, and it takes
every ounce of mental strength to keep it in control." He turned to face me. "I
know you've felt it too."

I nodded slowly, remembering.

"I feel a kind of madness." He lowered his voice. "And I like it."

"I know," I said. "It's hard to stop."

We looked at each other for a long moment.

He walked back over to the bed. "Look, everything's going to be fine. Groeden
and his team know about the currency, but they obviously don't know any of the
important details or we wouldn't be having this conversation."

"So we're going back to Austin?"

"In two days."

"I'll be glad to get home, Jack."

He smiled weakly. "Me too."

WHEN WE RETURNED to Texas a few days later, Jefferson grilled us about the attack, making us go over every detail, looking for anything that might signal aberrations in the flow of history. When he was satisfied there were none, he asked us how things had gone with regard to the currency; he seemed especially curious about Klaus. Finally, in his usual impassive way he simply said, "It looks like everything is going as it should. You both did well."

I stared at him, dumbfounded. "Let me make sure I have this right: Jack killed several men, Groeden showed up and basically threatened my life—*again*—and you say everything is going as it *should*? We did *well*?"

Jack took a deep breath, looked at Jefferson, and left the room. Jefferson stared at me for a few seconds with an impenetrable hardness and merely said, "That's correct." Then he rose and left the room too.

The depth of my frustration was, at that moment, simply incalculable.

We continued shaping our plans through the bank in Zürich, although we ran into some difficulty deciding what to call the currency. Jack, naturally, had an endless supply of ideas. "You know," he said over breakfast one morning, "the Vietnamese call their currency the *dong*. Why couldn't we name it something like that?"

Eventually, when it became apparent Jack was going to be absolutely no help in the matter, I decided to rely exclusively on Klaus's opinion. While it was true we were taking steps to denominate the currency in every precious asset available, we were focusing our efforts on acquiring gold—primarily for its prestigious reputation as a long-term historical store of value. After weeks of consideration, Klaus and I finally agreed on a simple, functional name that would lend an image of faith and stability: we decided to call the currency the Private Gold Unit—which quickly became the PGU, for short.

Jack was, predictably, not pleased.

We didn't advertise the currency's existence; certainly one of our goals was to make money in the long term, but it was by no means the only impetus behind the original idea. No, our primary objective was to stop Groeden at any and all points—to keep him from gaining more power, and to protect the people who would undoubtedly and immeasurably suffer as a result. And so our first priority was secrecy—not only to keep Groeden as far away as possible, but also to prevent trouble with any governments that might feel threatened by the idea of a stable competitor to their own money.

Things progressed relatively smoothly on the bank's end. Credit card companies were hesitant to collaborate at first, but when Klaus and his team showed them how little risk was involved—and how much money they would make if a crisis occurred—they became downright obsequious. Since no money was to change hands before a crisis, the credit card companies had no reason to report our arrangement to any authorities. And so confidentiality prevailed.

Klaus and his team printed and made ready millions of notes. The bank was consistently ahead of schedule on its purchases of gold and other assets, and we responded by issuing healthy bonuses for their diligence, which made them still more efficient. Likewise, once we made our offers to exceed prevailing market prices in the event of a financial crisis, major mining firms and distributors around the world enthusiastically signed contingency agreements promising us a stable flow of hard assets. Klaus even negotiated lower premiums, as he had said he might. Over time, he had proven not only innovative and driven, but also honest—perhaps his best quality, and I grew to depend on him as much as, if not more than, anyone else with whom I did business.

Our plan was sound and our team was strong. Within a year, everything was in place. And so it was only a matter of waiting.

FRUITION

It is not necessary that you leave the house. Remain at your table and listen. Do not even listen, only wait. Do not even wait, be wholly still and alone. The world will present itself to you for its unmasking, it can do no other, in ecstasy it will writhe at your feet.

—Franz Kafka

Happiness is like a butterfly which, when pursued, is always beyond our grasp, but, if you will sit down quietly, may alight upon you.

—Nathaniel Hawthorne

Austin, Texas, and New York, New York
Late Spring, Year Thirty-Two

OVER THE NEXT couple of years, the holding company in which I was the majority shareholder continued to make acquisitions, but I stayed out of the public eye more than ever. The businesses we held weren't flashy or exciting—they simply generated cash, slowly and quietly. We kept the PGU strictly separate from the other businesses; only Jack, Jefferson, Klaus, and I knew the details of the currency's existence.

When I wasn't on the phone with Klaus or traveling, I passed much of my time playing chess and reading, as usual. Playing my cello had become a big part of my life once again, as well.

Groeden made no more appearances and there were no more attacks, but I wondered how long that would last. Jack and Jefferson still wouldn't tell me much, but there was one thing I was certain of: Groeden hadn't given up. The last several years had been a welcome respite, but a sense of imminent danger now kept me and Jack together more than ever. Surprisingly, Jefferson stayed in town most of the time too, so the three of us were frequent companions.

I hesitate to say that I felt any kind of urgency, because nothing ever felt urgent with Jefferson and Jack. Yet something loomed, almost imperceptibly with a little more weight each passing day—growing around us, reminding me that I could never relax. My training helped me maintain a steady calm; I was more alert than ever, always watchful for anything that seemed the slightest bit unusual.

And of course, there were other things consuming me—not least among them the mysterious episode with the little girl. Nothing similar had happened in recent years, but despite Jack's reassurances, I couldn't shake the feeling I was wasting time. Somehow it seemed imperative that I use this gift—or whatever it was—to help people, and yet I had no idea how.

Jack's words tormented me because I knew he was right; if I were going to affect change, it would be in a way that I couldn't yet understand, but my emotions perpetually challenged my patience. Whatever this thing was, it awakened in me an intolerable restlessness. I felt obligated to do something—*anything*.

One afternoon I sat reading in the dining room when I heard a loud thump against the window. My first thought was of caution, and I crossed the room slowly. A sparrow lay on the ground outside, its neck broken.

I stared at the bird's twisted body for a moment. One wing twitched, and I felt a delicate sadness well up inside me. I turned from the window and walked outside. I crouched by the bird's body, staring at it for several moments, puzzled by the melancholy suddenly hanging over me. *It's just a dead bird . . .*

I fought the urge to touch the broken body, but after a moment, I scooped up the bird, closed my eyes, and let go of everything, allowing the familiar warmth to rush through me. I stayed that way for a moment before I opened my eyes again.

I looked at my cupped hands. As if on cue, the sparrow's body moved a little, wriggling, its feathers tickling my palms. I opened my hands, and the bird righted itself, unsteady at first. Then it burst from my hands, a small explosion of wings disappearing into a blue sky.

I wasn't surprised—I had known what would happen the moment I picked up the bird. The sadness had left me as quickly as it had come, but the event still shook me to the core.

I can do it whenever I want to.

I slowly walked to a lawn chair and collapsed, trembling a little, feeling suddenly exhausted. *This is what it feels like to get old,* I thought, wishing that I hadn't tested myself. I could already feel the conflict beginning to roil inside—more ferocious than ever, demanding I find a use for this thing.

During the next week, I tried several times to talk to Jefferson and Jack about it, but they gently dismissed me, assuring me yet again I would understand when it was time. And—yet again—I found myself frustrated nearly to the point of anger.

But there was no point in getting upset. What good would it do? Whatever this thing was, my role would be revealed when it was time.

◆

IN THE LATE summer, after my thirty-second birthday, the United States dollar started to lose value steadily. At first I thought this was the beginning of the imminent collapse I was certain was on its way, so I started doing some research, looking for unusual activity in markets over the past several years.

Sure enough, I found a few destabilizing events I couldn't explain—unusually large short-sales of dollars or U.S. interest rate instruments, in some smaller, more obscure European markets. There was also some erratic behavior by central banks in a few insignificant Asian countries—all precisely timed to maximize negative impact on the U.S. dollar. And this told me the decline in the American currency was calculated, which in turn meant Groeden could very well be behind it. And yet none of the events seemed dramatic enough to justify a total collapse of the currency.

So what was the point? The Fed would make the necessary monetary adjustments, and the economy would be fine. Simply put, none of this was enough to cause the catastrophe I was preparing for.

But something wasn't right. And suddenly it became clear to me that these isolated jabs at the dollar weren't meant to cause crippling damage, but rather to introduce uncertainty and doubt into the economic system over a long period of time—most likely laying the foundation for something else. Groeden had bigger plans.

Of course, I knew Jefferson and Jack would give me no answers—and they didn't—so I had no way of predicting what would bring about the downfall of the greatest currency the world had ever known. All I could do was wait.

Early that fall I was in my room packing for a trip to New York. One of our smaller private holdings was planning an initial public offering, and I had decided to be there, to witness another piece of my dream come to fruition. I had been to New York many times, but never to stand on the floor of the New York Stock Exchange—if only in anonymity—as one of my own holdings graduated to a new level of grandeur.

I heard a knock and turned to see Jack leaning against the threshold, arms folded. "Hey," I said, returning to my task.

"Where are you going?"

"To New York."

"Why?"

"On business. Some of us still work, Jack."

"I love New York."

I stopped packing and looked at him suspiciously. "Why would I care that you love New York?"

He pursed his lips. "I'm just telling you. In fact, I was thinking about getting one of those bumper stickers—"

"What are you getting at?"

He looked defensive. "I'm not *getting* at anything."

"Yes you are."

"No I'm not."

I folded my arms. "Jack."

He inhaled deeply and then released it. "Okay, fine. I'm coming with you."

"Why?"

"Can't I just come with you? Do I always have to have a reason?"

"Why, Jack?"

His face took on a pathetic waif-like expression. "I want to see a Broadway musical. I want to see the MoMA, to go to Times Square. I want to ride in a cab driven by a Pakistani—"

"Jack! Why are you coming to New York with me?"

He leveled his gaze at me and his expression became serious. "Because I have to."

My heart began to race a little; I had long since grown accustomed to the idea that, when Jack came along, it usually wasn't just for fun. But I knew better than to ask more questions, so I nodded in resignation. "You have a ticket? I'm leaving in three hours."

"I'm in the seat right next to yours, you little bastard."

Jack and I had two full days in New York before the public offering of my company, so we made the most of it. For forty-eight hours, he dragged me to every site and event he had mentioned—and then some. I was surprised he knew so much about the city, and I enjoyed myself thoroughly. It was a welcome distraction from the question that hovered at the edge of my mind: why was he here at all?

I managed to quell my curiosity for most of the tour, but the day before the event at the New York Stock Exchange, Jack became unusually somber. Early that afternoon, as we walked through the Museum of Modern Art, I found myself unable to suppress my apprehension any longer.

We stood gazing at a Manet and I turned to him. "Hey."

He gave me a light smile.

"Tell me why you came."

I expected some flippant remark, but he only took a deep breath and continued to smile, not really making eye contact.

"Jack, I—"

He shook his head slowly, putting a finger to his lips. "Tomorrow."

"No, I have to go to—"

He continued to shake his head, still smiling. "Listen to me. Just let it go for today." There was something in his eyes that made bumps rise on my arms. The smile never left his face, but somehow I knew in that moment that he had absolutely no desire to be in this city. And yet, here he was.

I said nothing more. Jack wasn't talking, but I would have my answers soon enough—whether I wanted them or not.

I set my alarm for 5:00 A.M. in order to have plenty of time to get ready and eat breakfast before I had to be at the exchange. When it went off, I opened my eyes and squinted. The room was flooded with light.

I allowed my eyes to adjust, and I saw Jack on his bed hugging his knees, his back to the headboard, his head resting on his forearms. He was fully dressed.

"What's up?" I said.

He lifted his face, pulling his hair out of his eyes. "Good morning," he said in a gravelly tone. He looked exhausted . . . *and sad*, I thought.

"What are you doing up?"

"I couldn't sleep."

"What's going on, Jack?"

He shook his head and smiled, but it wasn't sincere.

"Hey, man, are you okay? I can be a little late this morning, if you want to talk—"

"You're not going to the NYSE today." His voice was emphatic.

This had gone too far. "What are you talking about?" I said exasperated.

He pushed himself off the bed and nodded at the suit I had laid out. "Pack that and the rest of your things. Put on something comfortable. We're leaving in fifteen minutes."

I stared at him for a moment, my mind racing. I looked around the room and noticed his bags were already sitting by the door. I thought about protesting, but instead I got up and began packing.

When I finished, I looked at the clock between the beds. It read 5:13. By now, I was on autopilot, merely following Jack's orders. We flagged a cab outside the hotel, and as we put our bags in the trunk, I vaguely wondered about the bill. Then I thought, *He's taken care of it. This was all planned.*

We got in the taxi and Jack gave the driver instructions, although they didn't mean anything to me. We drove for about twenty minutes. I remember crossing a body of water, but I couldn't have said what it was.

The cab stopped. Jack got out and I followed, mechanically helping him pull our bags from the trunk. He paid the driver, and we walked down the sidewalk for about five minutes, until Jack led us into a restaurant, where we sat at a booth.

The waiter gave us menus, and Jack ordered coffee and breakfast. He looked at me. "Order something. You need to eat."

"I'm not hungry."

He looked at the waiter. "Bring him the same thing."

Jack stared at the table. He seemed older somehow, and I found myself searching for gray hair. *Why would I do that? Jack's not old.*

When our food arrived, he began to eat. I watched him for a moment, but I didn't touch my plate.

"Eat," he said, almost pleadingly. "We're going to be here a while." His eyes seemed hollow, and it occurred to me that he was worried about much more than just my nourishment—Jack needed comfort, and I had none to offer.

If he needs comfort, what am I going to need?

My breathing became shallow, and Jack looked up again. "Listen to me," he said.

I lost focus, and my mind began to drift. *Dad and Thomas . . . Barney . . . Elizabeth . . . why would I think of her now?*

"Hey!" Jack grunted. "We're going to be here for a few hours, and I need you to work with me, okay? Please eat."

He was strong again, at least for the moment. I gazed at him a little while, then picked up my fork, dragging each bite into my mouth, forcing my jaws to grind the substance into something that could be swallowed.

"Thank you," he said.

We finished eating and continued to sit in the booth. The waiter kept refilling our coffees, and the hours seemed to stretch on forever. Jack, for the most part, kept his head hung forward, staring at the table, his brown curls covering his face.

At one point I thought, *This is how a condemned man feels.* Without thinking I blurted, "Are we going to get hurt?"

He looked up, his eyes vacant once more, and he shook his head slowly. "No, you're safe—" He hesitated. "—I've never been here . . . I'm sorry."

"What's going to happen?"

"It'll be over soon." He smiled a little and seemed to regain some control. I had always trusted Jack, and I knew I would have to find faith in him now. There was simply no other choice. And yet, in that moment, I felt as much dread as I had ever felt in my life.

We sat for a while longer, and suddenly Jack pushed himself out of his seat, grabbing his luggage. "Come on."

I rose and grabbed my bags. Jack and I left the restaurant and walked a few blocks to an alley behind a nondescript apartment building. He threw open the top of a dumpster and tossed his luggage in. He turned to me, "Give me your bags."

I looked at him strangely, and he took a step toward me. "Douglas, do what I say."

I extended my arms and Jack took the bags. He put them on the ground and unzipped them, rifling through my things. "Where's your wallet?"

"I have it."

He found some papers in one of my bags and pulled them out, handing them to me. "Put those in your pocket." He looked through the rest of my things, and once satisfied, threw the pile in the dumpster.

"What are you—?"

"It's too difficult to take it with us," he said, walking away from the dumpster.

Jack reached for the handle of a door leading into the building and we entered. He stopped at the elevator and pushed the arrow pointing up. The doors slid open, and we got on.

I stared involuntarily at the numbers as they marked our progress to the very top floor. The doors opened to reveal a sparsely furnished apartment.

"Where are we?" I said.

Jack looked exhausted. "It doesn't matter."

I followed him through the foyer toward a huge expanse of windows overlooking water, in front of a magnificent skyline. Jack looked at his watch, and I glanced at mine. It was 9:35. The opening bell had rung. Our company was now trading publicly, and I had missed it.

Jack placed his back against one of the enormous panes and slid to the floor, lacing his fingers in his hair, clutching his head. "Watch the sky."

I didn't have the energy to argue. I didn't want to be here. I closed my eyes.

"*Watch it!*" he said.

My eyes snapped open and I looked into the sky. Nothing seemed out of the ordinary . . . some clouds . . . a plane floating over the city . . .

Time collapsed, and my senses exploded.

What?

The fatigue evaporated, and suddenly I was ready for anything.

Jack leaned his head back against the glass and looked at me sideways, his eyes roiling with energy. *"Watch it,"* he hissed.

My eyes moved back to the plane. It was a film, a bird gliding in slow motion toward the sea to pluck a fish, falling, falling . . .

I looked at Jack's wide eyes, which had never wavered from mine. Back to the plane, almost to the horizon . . .

A ball of orange and red, bubbling, reaching into to the sky.

"No—" The word choked in my throat. *"No!"*

Jack's eyes still focused on me, filled with anguish. "I'm sorry."

My head snapped around. *"Where is that?"* But I already knew.

"The stock exchange."

"Oh my God . . ." I whispered, putting my hand to my mouth. "Why?" I looked at him, unable to fathom the moment. "Why would you make me watch this?" I could barely form the words.

Jack's eyes were pleading. "So it would be real. So you would know how far he'll go . . ."

I collapsed next to him, desperately struggling against the anger and hatred. I clawed at the window, pressing my cheek against the glass. *"No . . ."* The fireball receded, replaced by a plume of smoke climbing toward the atmosphere.

"I'm sorry," Jack repeated. A tear rolled down his cheek. "I'm *so* sorry."

I don't know how long I sat there before I felt him touch my elbow, gently pulling me. "We have to go, Douglas."

"What have they done?"

"We have to go." His arm snaked around my midsection. I resisted, and then bright lights filled my peripheral vision, like another explosion. *Are they here now? Have they killed us too?*

Time and space evaporated, and I returned to the vapor, floating in nothingness, everything . . . black.

Sound and light.

I inhaled desperately, heaving. I twisted onto my side and my lungs seemed to freeze. The light was too bright. I squeezed my eyes shut.

A hand pressed mine. Jefferson said, "Breathe." Then more slowly, "Breathe."

I heard Jack. "Fuck. *Fuck!*" He sounded like he was crying. "He wasn't ready for that! *I* wasn't fucking ready." He was definitely crying. "Goddamn it. *Goddamn* it!"

I tried to open my eyes, but the light was still too much.

Jefferson said, "Let it go, Jack."

"I—" he sobbed. I heard rapid breathing, then it slowed.

Jefferson's hand squeezed mine again. "Douglas, breathe."

My chest ached, but I felt it loosening. I let go and inhaled again. The relief felt narcotic. I lay still for a moment, then opened my eyes and sat up. I was on the floor of the living room in the house in Austin. Jefferson knelt over me, clutching my hand, supporting me as I looked around the room. *Am I dreaming? How can I be here?*

Jack sat on the sofa, lying weakly against the arm. He was pallid, his breathing labored.

I looked at Jefferson. "How—?"

"You burst," he said. "You're in Austin."

"But—"

"I know what you saw, but you're here now."

"They blew it up."

Jefferson wrapped his arms around me and held me. "Douglas, I'm sorry."

I looked at Jack. He seemed almost incapable of getting enough oxygen. He trembled, and his face seemed to be darkening.

I pointed at him. "Jack—"

Jefferson let me go, but I managed to maintain enough balance to stay upright. He gently touched his forehead to Jack's, placing his hands on Jack's cheeks. Jack's breathing seemed to improve immediately.

I reeled. Then blackness buried me again.

I opened my eyes and tried to sit up. The pain was immense. I slowly pulled myself to my elbows. I was in my room. "*Jefferson!*"

I heard footsteps and he appeared.

"Where's Jack?" I said.

"He's resting. He's fine."

My eyes bounced around the room. "Everyone thinks I was there—"

"I've taken care of it," he said. "They know you're all right."

I looked into his eyes, trying to organize my thoughts. "I have to get to the television. I have to make some calls."

He nodded and helped me out of bed.

"How long?" I asked.

"Two days."

"*Fuck!*"

He helped me to the couch and said, "They didn't open the markets until this morning. Everything is being routed through the NASDAQ."

"And the NYSE?"

"It's totally destroyed."

I caught my breath. Jefferson left the room and returned with a telephone. He handed it to me and I started to dial a number, but then I lowered my hand.

I stared at the television, appalled by what I saw. The images were horrifying. Terrorist had hit market centers across North America, Asia, and Europe. Planes were grounded globally, and every nation on earth had placed security forces on high alert. Commerce and travel had come to a complete standstill.

Global markets were in turmoil—trillions of dollars gone in the blink of an eye. Everything was in chaos. I raised the phone and dialed Klaus.

"Douglas, are you okay?"

"I'm fine, Klaus. Thank you. Tell me where we stand."

"Everything is fine here. As you are undoubtedly aware, gold and other assets are skyrocketing, which means you are making a tremendous amount of money—as you expected."

"Thank you. I have to go."

"I will keep you updated."

And I was already dialing the next number. *All the preparation, the years of anticipation. This is the moment we've been waiting for.*

And yet the victory was Pyrrhic. As we profited, the world economy was collapsing.

The New York Stock Exchange had been obliterated by the attack, along with several city blocks—thousands of lives lost in an instant. The plane had been a military transport, loaded with explosives. Four Caucasian men had appeared in uniform at Andrews Air Force Base in Maryland—all with proper credentials— and had presented orders to fly the plane to Hanscom AFB in Massachusetts. While over New York City, the plane had simply diverted slightly and dived into the NYSE.

An investigation into the identities of the pilots and the ground crew yielded nothing but dead ends. All the attacks around the globe had been orchestrated with similar professionalism, killing hundreds of thousands, and fueling intense speculation about how it could possibly have happened. And yet, despite intense investigation, no one could seem to find any answers. But I knew.

Groeden.

My grief was incomprehensible; so many of my friends and colleagues had been there that day, and I couldn't shake the feelings of guilt and remorse. *I was supposed to be with them . . .*

As usual, Jack and Jefferson gave me nothing, only adding frustration to my already abject sense of loss. "Did Groeden know I was going to be there?" I asked Jefferson a few days later.

"Probably."

"What the fuck do you mean, *probably*? I was supposed to be at the NYSE, and suddenly a plane turns it into a crater? That's awfully convenient, don't you think, Jefferson?"

"It wasn't the only place they attacked."

"So maybe my death would have been icing on the cake?"

His face remained blank. "I realize this is hard for you. We just don't have any idea how much information Groeden has or doesn't have."

My rage grew. "You know what? That's not *fucking* good enough! I lost a *lot* of my friends!"

He bit his lower lip, his eyes remorseful, but he didn't respond.

"*Fuck* this." I pushed myself up from my chair and stormed into my office.

Understandably, stocks continued to melt down as markets around the globe tried to handle the crisis created by the terrorist acts. Over the following weeks, as the full scope of the tragedies bore down on every sector, the U.S. dollar lost an unprecedented amount of value. Government officials did everything they could to stanch the bleeding, but nothing worked.

In the ensuing months, politicians fatuously demanded work programs and increased government spending to stimulate the economy, but their clamoring smacked more of vote-seeking bluster than of substantive solutions to what was quickly escalating into a global economic catastrophe. The dollar had no assets behind it. There was nothing to back the rhetoric; there was no gold—no more "faith and credit." There was only paper.

By the end of the summer, the slide had reached critical momentum, and the dollar lost still more value, at a staggering rate. Foreign governments began to reject its viability. Other currencies fell accordingly, and soon people started looking elsewhere—*anywhere*—for quality.

The Swiss franc—the only governmental currency still backed partially by gold—started a slow rise, which subsequently escalated into a frenzy. It was *almost* the last currency in the world in which people could have faith, but even the franc couldn't support the pressure put on it. Its gold reserves simply weren't high enough.

The U.S. president issued an executive order imposing price controls on basic commodities—milk, bread, and gasoline—to which consumers and business owners reacted unilaterally, ignoring the decree. Black markets developed everywhere until it became obvious the executive order was unenforceable. Prices floated freely and openly again, but the economic fabric continued to fray at its edges.

If the endorsement by Klaus's bank hadn't been enough to give the PGU credibility, indemnification—as well as the demand for regular independent audits—by the world's most trusted insurance and accounting firms removed remaining doubts. Essentially the Private Gold Unit really *was* gold—among other precious assets—only it was much easier to transport and exchange. In recent years, several financial institutions had even taken minor positions in the PGU, and the currency had grown quietly, slowly, and steadily. It now stood ready to provide the world a safe, liquid store of value.

When the dollar's slide began, word quickly spread about a private alternative denomination backed by gold. Institutions were hesitant to take larger positions at first, but as the major world currencies continued to collapse, the PGU began to appeal to an increasing number of banks, and demand rose sharply. We purchased more hard assets and issued the appropriate amount of extra paper, which gave us yet more liquidity and stability.

In order to dispel the notion that we were trying to corner any specific markets, we continued to spread our purchases among a variety of precious assets beyond gold—including silver, diamonds, platinum, and other valuable commodities. They were stored in the vaults of Klaus's bank, as well as other institutions around the globe, diversifying our risk, as well as indemnity.

Jack and I monitored events carefully, working as closely as ever with Klaus. But I was still somewhat numb to the magnitude of what was happening in the world. Maybe, like other people, I couldn't quite believe that *any* economic problem had the potential to escalate into an uncontrollable global epidemic. Reason told me this was going to be bad, but even as I worked to ensure the PGU's solvency, somehow I couldn't get my arms around what was happening. And yet, everything continued to unravel, just as Jack and Jefferson had suggested it would.

Jack recovered quickly from the episode in New York, but neither he, Jefferson, nor I left the house much the following months. I spent days and nights on the phone or in front of my computer, trying to manage not only the situation with the PGU, but also my businesses in the United States, and I found myself so busy that I almost didn't have time to wonder why—or *how*—this had happened.

One day I sat in the living room, on the phone with a gem dealer in Belgium. I ended the call and put the phone down, sighing audibly, sinking deeper into the sofa. Jefferson walked into the room and said, "Tough day?"

"They're all tough days."

"Yeah." He took a seat in the chair next to the window.

I pulled my head forward, not wanting to revisit what was on my mind, and yet also not really understanding how I could suppress it. But it was, I supposed, as good a time as any. "How could Groeden have caused all this?" I said. "Even if he's bursting, he shouldn't be able to put something of this magnitude together. It's too complex."

Jefferson's expression was solemn. He remained silent, letting me draw my own inevitable conclusion. I took in a sharp breath. "Oh my God. The organization has been created."

He nodded. "Sometime in the last couple of years, we think."

"But if he doesn't have the technology, why is he doing all this? How does he know about us?"

Jefferson took a moment, choosing his words carefully. "He's probably in contact with a younger version of himself."

I let my eyes wander around the room, absorbing this disturbing news. I looked at Jefferson again. "They're trying to blame it on *anyone*—the Middle Eastern networks—even the IRA if you can believe that. But really, nobody has a clue. There's no mention of anyone even closely resembling Groeden."

Jefferson raised an eyebrow. "Do you think he would want that sort of publicity? He's not stupid, you know."

"I'm still not sure I understand why."

"Douglas, he wants us."

"But why punish the world just to get us?" I winced, thinking about all of the victims lost in only a fraction of a second—and maybe we were somehow responsible for it.

"Because he realizes we're the only people in the universe who know what he's doing, and he also knows we'll respond, unequivocally, to anything he does. The louder he screams, the louder our reaction. He wants us to make a mistake."

I sighed, disgusted with all of it. "The world is falling apart, and we're making a fortune. How is that supposed to hurt Groeden?"

Jefferson's eyes were bright, almost begging me to understand, and yet I didn't. "You still don't know yourself," he said.

I put my elbows on my knees and rested my forehead on my palms, staring at the floor. "No, I guess I don't." I raised my head and looked at him. "This is so hard."

He nodded slowly. "It's only going to get harder."

"Yeah. You guys keep saying that."

Fall, Year Thirty-Two

FOR A LONG time—stretching back to the years even before the currency—I had continued to work anonymously through the small group of officers who made up the management team of our parent U.S. corporation, which oversaw all the investments I had accumulated. Without this group, I would never have been able to run our companies so secretively for so long, and while I never revealed to them the reasons for my anonymity, it was their cautious discretion—perhaps as much as anything—that prevented Groeden from discovering my identity.

One day late that fall, just as the economic catastrophe seemed to be reaching its climax, I drove downtown to meet with my team. The failing dollar had created tremendous doubt and uncertainty in their minds, and I needed to restore their waning confidence by whatever means necessary.

Near the capitol, demonstrators were gathering—an occurrence that had become much more frequent recently. I parked in a garage a few blocks off Congress Avenue to avoid driving through the crowd, after which I made my way through the developing demonstration.

When I entered the boardroom, every eye turned to me. Lisa Santos, the company's president, and Theresa Stanton, the chief financial officer, sat at a large table in the middle of the room. Gary Foss, the chief operating officer, stood at an enormous window overlooking the city skyline.

The tension was thick; our companies were not immune to the financial calamities developing around the world, and while I wasn't involved with day-to-day operations, I was ultimately responsible for many of the larger decisions. But more than anything, this company was my brainchild, and so my approval was all but a requirement. Lately, however, in the face of this crisis, I had chosen inaction, and no one could understand why. They were starting to become frustrated, if not downright angry.

I got right to the point. "I know you're all concerned about what's happening, and it may seem that I'm refusing to act. But remember, the companies we've placed our capital in—and that we're responsible for—are among the best in the world. With the failure of price controls, our subsidiaries shouldn't have trouble maintaining small profits."

There were some grumbles. "Douglas, forget the speeches," Lisa said. "The dollar's going to hell. We need to talk about survival, not profits." Hers wasn't the only mutinous expression in the room.

I decided to tell the truth. "I've taken steps to protect us."

"What steps?" Lisa asked.

I looked at Theresa. She nodded and leaned forward. "Douglas authorized me to make some transactions that should guarantee our survival." She paused. "No, let me rephrase that. We're not just surviving, we're flourishing."

"What are you talking about?" The question came from Gary Foss.

I answered for Theresa. "Several years ago, I found out about a new vehicle in which we could place our idle assets, and I told Theresa about it. "

Theresa continued, "At first I thought he was joking, but he persuaded me that we should start moving into it. It's called the PGU."

Gary said, "I've heard of it. Everybody's talking about it. Some Swiss bank issues it." He looked at me. "You didn't bother to consult us?" He shifted his eyes to Theresa. "Terry, I don't have to tell you how drastically that breaches the boundary of ethical behavior. I can't really believe you'd just let Douglas talk you into something like this without mentioning it to the rest of us."

Gary looked at me, and I realized I would have to persuade him the same way I had convinced Theresa. "She isn't guilty of anything, Gary. I have a friend who was able to make the transactions for us—someone I trust . . ." I let the last words come out slowly, the way Jack and Jefferson had taught me, and they seemed to hang in the air—the last sweet notes of a long piece of soothing music.

He stared at me for a moment, puzzled. "I don't know why—" He looked down at the table for a moment and then shook his head. "If you trust this friend, then I suppose . . ."

I hoped his acquiescence wouldn't be too obvious. If I handled the situation correctly, they would see the wisdom in my words, but if I allowed any room for doubt, they would never trust me again. Persuasion didn't come as easily to me as it did to Jack and Jefferson.

Lisa looked at me sternly. "I don't know how you managed to hide this, but you had an obligation to include us in your plans." She looked at Gary for a moment, clearly concerned by his capitulation. It somehow seemed unnatural.

It is unnatural, I thought. I had to finish it now or the moment would be lost. I inhaled deeply and let go. "Lisa, the positions have always appeared on the balance sheets as 'extraneous cash and cash equivalents.' They're also in the cash flow statements. You can go back and look—it's all perfectly legal." I hesitated just long enough to let the information settle, and then said, "I had a feeling that the economy might get bad, so I made the decision." I wasn't trying to hide anything from you, it just seemed better to keep things quiet." I held her gaze, desperately hoping this was working. "You understand that . . ."

She looked at me for a moment with the same confused expression that Gary had, and then her face softened. She nodded hesitantly. "Yes."

I let out a breath of deep relief and leaned back in my chair.

On cue, Theresa delivered the brick that would complete the foundation: "Our liquid assets are denominated almost entirely in PGUs, not dollars." She hesitated, looking from face to face. "We aren't the only company doing this. Several Fortune 500 firms have recently revealed similar moves. During tomorrow's conference call, I'm going to announce that we will conduct all future transactions in PGUs to the greatest extent possible. The stock is probably going to go through the roof."

"You're sure we haven't violated any laws?" Lisa asked, the last traces of doubt melting from her eyes.

Theresa smiled. "We are simply holding foreign currency. That isn't a crime."

I looked around the room at my colleagues and I felt dirty. I was disturbed that I had kept this important thing from two of them, and even more disturbed at how easily I had convinced them to support me. It seemed like a strange way to work with trusted friends, even if I wasn't lying to them.

Lisa studied me again for a long moment and then smiled. The relief showed on all their faces.

Finally Gary said, "I don't know how you do some of the things you do, Douglas, but I'm glad we're on the same team."

I walked out of the building, stepping onto Congress Avenue, and into the middle of a throng of demonstrators walking toward the capitol. I felt out of place in my suit, and several protestors glared at me as I worked my way to the garage where I had parked. I was about to turn a corner when a burst of tension hit me. I stopped, familiar waves of serenity now spreading through my body—the stillness that always appeared in the moment before the firestorm.

Something was very wrong.

I twisted my head, my eyes scanning everything. My vision became crystal clear, and even my sense of smell heightened. Time slowed.

Something pulled my gaze to the right. The river of protestors shuffled down the sidewalk, signs slung over their shoulders, faces intent. I watched the crowd for a moment longer, trying to process what I was feeling. Then another onslaught of premonition brutally shoved its way into my thoughts, hitting me with all the intensity of a gale. I scanned the streets, searching for the source.

Without understanding why, I focused on a set of large glass doors at the entrance to a modern three-story edifice. *It's a federal building.* I had no idea where the thought came from, but I knew it with near certainty.

My vision blurred and I shuddered with the energy that rushed through my body. Whatever was about to happen was going to be tremendous.

My vision cleared and my eyes locked on a man walking against the tide of protesters. He was dressed casually in jeans and work boots, striding with his head down, hands tucked in the pockets of his pants. But something about his appearance seemed odd, and as he approached, I realized what it was: the day was abnormally warm for the time of year, and yet he wore long canvas coat.

He reached the building and stopped, looking around nervously. Before I could prepare for it, our eyes locked. My heart started to thunder in my chest, but serenity took over again and the tension melted away.

The man looked exhausted, but his eyes told me two unmistakable things: he was scared, but he was determined.

For a moment, I wondered if this would be another attempt on my life, but then something told me I wasn't the target. *And yet there are no coincidences. I'm supposed to be here.*

The man pulled his eyes away from mine and checked the street around him one more time. Then he walked through the front door of the building.

Why?

A warning screamed in my mind and I spun around, turning my back, falling to the sidewalk.

The explosion shattered rows of windows across the street. A park bench flew over, missing me by a foot, crashing into a storefront to my left.

A few seconds passed, and I rose, calmly watching the scene around me. Bodies lay everywhere. A scorched form stumbled out of the destroyed building and into the street; hair gone, clothing burned away or melted into flesh. It looked like nothing more than a walking piece of charred meat. It took a few more steps, then collapsed.

I heard screaming, shouting. I began to tremble as the first rays of a new thought burned through the mist in my mind. *When people start sacrificing themselves, it's time to pay attention to the message.* Then another thought erupted: *This is what Groeden wants.* If my disdain for him that day in New York hadn't been absolute, it certainly was now.

I shook off the thought. *There's no time.* I scanned the carnage, desperately wanting to help in any way I could. But a bigger force was driving me now, telling me I had to get home. I had to find Jefferson and Jack.

I began walking toward the garage, cutting through a small parking lot. I pulled my phone from my pocket and was about to dial Jack's number when another burst of energy shot through me like a crack of thunder.

Glass exploded. I flinched and dropped the phone, unable to comprehend what was happening.

I turned my head and stared at a figure, perhaps twenty feet away, pointing a pistol at me. Thousands of shards of splintered glass littered the ground at my feet, from the shattered window of a car.

Before I could do anything, the front of the pistol kicked. Then it simply froze. A small burst of flame protruded from the end of the barrel. Time and space ceased; my subconscious had anticipated the event, bringing me here by reflex, and the entirety had responded by pushing back the onslaught of time itself. Even in the face of the attack, I felt a sudden deep appreciation for Jack's training in that instant.

The bullet started moving toward me, slowly at first, and then more quickly. Then it slowed to a stop, three inches from my face.

All the years of preparation came together in one thought: *If you let fear have even a fingerhold, this bullet will find you and spray your brains all over this parking lot.*

I stayed perfectly still for a moment, taking comfort from the serene motionlessness. Then I began to move, slowly, carefully—the way Jack had taught me—stuttering through space and time. I stepped sideways keeping my eyes on the slug suspended in space.

The attacker, a younger man, perhaps in his early thirties, with straight black shoulder-length hair, now stood perfectly still, like a marble statue, holding the pistol in front of him. His expression was an amalgamation of arrogance, anticipation, and fear. Something about him seemed familiar—a disturbing brightness in his dark eyes.

I let go, allowing time and space to resume around me with an explosion of sensory input, like a train passing within inches of my face. I took a deep breath, trying to recover from the effort. The slug had passed my head, shattering another car window several feet away.

"He said it might be like this, you fucking traitor." The man held the pistol steady, still pointing it at me. "I didn't believe him." He seemed excited, almost giddy.

I tried to catch my breath and sputtered, "Who are you?"

"All that matters is I know who *you* are, traitor."

Traitor? My mind spun.

He fired again, and once more time froze. The bullet came toward me slowly, and I simply moved out of its path.

When space and time returned, I heard my phone ringing on the ground where it had landed. I fell against the car beside me, more exhausted than I thought possible, breathing heavily. I could only sustain this for one, maybe two more shots. I made a decision instantly.

I forced time to slow and crawled awkwardly over the car. In the same stuttering motions, I grabbed his arm at the last moment. I had no more energy to suspend space and time. I was back again.

I snapped the man's wrist easily and the pistol fell to the ground. I kicked the side of his knee and heard a crunch as cartilage and bone ripped from their moorings. He screamed and would have collapsed had I not been holding his arm. I towered over him, and when I looked into his eyes, I suddenly knew.

It was Groeden. The eyes were unmistakable.

The revelation took me off guard. I barely caught the glint of a blade before he drove it into my leg.

I screamed and shoved my hand into his left eye. When I pulled my arm back, I felt resistance from the flesh of his cheek. Then it came loose, and I tore half his face from his head.

We both fell to the ground. I grabbed the hilt of the knife protruding from my leg and slowly pulled it out, fighting to stay conscious through the pain and exhaustion. I tossed the blade away, breathing deeply, and again I became aware of my phone ringing—a distant, surreal sound.

I put my hand on my leg and felt warmth pulsing in my fingertips. The act was automatic, just something that had to be done. I leaned my head back, welcoming the energy, and suddenly the wound no longer existed beneath the slit in my pants. The pain vanished, leaving an odd, vacant feeling where the knife had been, as though my leg refused to accept that the damage had been repaired.

I stared at Groeden laying on the asphalt, unconscious, a bleeding mass of flesh hanging from his cheekbone. *I should kill him now.*

But a distant voice, just a whisper, stopped me. *And if you do . . .?*

I dragged myself to my phone. I rested against a car's tire and dialed Jack.

He answered before the first ring ended. "Where are you?"

"I'm downtown."

"Why haven't you picked up your phone?"

The exhaustion was like a fog. "There was a bombing," I said, my speech slurring.

"We know. It's all over the news. *Christ*, we were worried, Douglas!" I could hear the relief in his voice.

"I couldn't answer the phone. Groeden stopped me."

"*Groeden*? What in the fuck are you talking about?"

"He's here. He's younger."

I could hear Jack breathing heavily, thinking. Finally he said, "Is he still there?"

I leaned forward and peered around the car's bumper. "He's—"

Groeden was gone.

I looked around frantically. "I don't—"

Before I could finish the sentence, Jack was there, his back to me, scanning the scene, prepared for anything. I dropped my phone. After a few seconds, he turned and put his hands on my face, scanning my eyes, "Where was he?" His eyes still darted about looking for danger.

"Over there," I raised my arm, trying to fight sleep. "Jack, tell me what the hell is happening."

"I will, goddamn it! Just help me." He rose, again scanning the parking lot. *"Fuck!"* he yelled, hitting the hood of the car. "Are you sure it was him?"

"Yeah, I'm sure. I ripped half his face off, Jack—I took his eye out."

"You did *what?*"

"I got his eye—"

"How bad?"

"Bad," I said. "It's totally gone."

Jack's face became ashen. "You're absolutely positive?"

I nodded, struggling to keep my eyes open. "What is it?"

"We need to talk to Jefferson."

"Jack, what is it?"

He sucked air in between his teeth. "We've all seen him before."

"So?"

"Douglas, Groeden has always had two eyes."

He looked at me for a moment longer, and then he put his arms around me, and I fell into blackness.

I awoke on the sofa in the living room. Jefferson sat across from me, and Jack stood next to him. Jefferson turned to me, his expression troubled. Without preamble he said, "I want you to tell me what you felt after the building blew up."

The suddenness of the question took me off guard, and I gave him a confused look. "What does it have to do—?"

"Tell me."

"I don't know, I felt numb."

"Nothing else?"

Then I remembered. "Yeah . . . there was something else. I saw the guy who did it." I thought about the determination in his eyes. "Did Groeden send him for me?" I considered all the possible connections, and suddenly the implications of the day's events bore down on me with their full weight. "If he did—"

Jefferson and Jack glanced at each other, and Jefferson said, "We don't think Groeden planned these bombings."

I furrowed my brow. "What?"

"Federal buildings were targeted in several cities." he said, staring at me intensely.

"What?" I repeated. "It must be Groeden."

Jefferson shook his head. "If we're right—if his organization is government funded—then he won't attack anything federal."

"You're saying it was just coincidence that I was there?"

Jefferson's face was impassive. "Everything happens for a reason, Douglas. You were supposed to see that today."

I looked vacantly out the window for a moment. "Well, if Groeden wasn't responsible, then who could have coordinated this?"

Jefferson and Jack looked more uncomfortable now. "We think this is the backlash."

I slowly closed my eyes and nodded. "It's starting, then." I took a deep breath and opened my eyes again. "It's more serious than I thought it would be. That guy knew what he was going to do—I saw it in his eyes." I shook my head. "I can't begin to imagine where this is going to end."

Jefferson looked suddenly relieved, as though he had been anticipating the sentence. "You're beginning to understand. Even though Groeden wasn't behind this, he was expecting it. He's depending on this economic collapse to fuel people's fear."

"Like the Nazis . . ." I muttered, staring at the floor. Then I raised my eyes quickly. "Bigger businesses are moving over to the PGU, but we need to make it available to everyone. If we don't, a lot of people are going to die. I'm afraid things are heading toward total anarchy, and we're the only ones who can stop that from happening."

And then my thoughts were abruptly dragged to the next pressing issue: "Groeden wasn't supposed to be in that parking lot today. He changed history."

Jefferson nodded, his face becoming concerned again. "He knew from the book that you would see the bombing. He must have contacted himself. Tell me how it happened."

"Time slowed down, but I didn't mean for it to. It just happened. I ripped his eye out, but it didn't feel like I was doing any of it—it felt like someone else was in control."

I had never seen Jefferson more concerned. "Are you okay?" I said.

"I'm proud of you. I never would have believed you were ready." He sighed heavily. "But this is uncharted territory; it wasn't supposed to happen. Did Groeden see you come out of the building where you had your meeting?"

"I don't know."

"We have to assume he didn't," Jack said, "If he had, he'd know about all of us, and we'd be dead by now."

"You were lucky," Jefferson said, "but we have to be careful now because I'm not sure how much the book is going to help us from here on out." He pushed a smile through his anxiety and glanced at Jack.

"What?" I asked.

Jack laughed. "I'll bet that goddamn snake didn't think he'd have one of his eyeballs torn out."

Jefferson nodded. "This is what happens when we violate our obligation to history. We're fortunate it was him and not us."

"How could he know what I looked like? The younger Groeden had never seen me before."

"I don't think he did know for sure," said Jefferson. "He probably only had a general description from his older self. I think he just got lucky."

"I hope that's true," Jack said nervously. "Because if he knows more, we're in a lot of trouble."

I slept for a short time and then rose, still exhausted. There was something important that needed to be done as soon as possible. I dialed the number and waited.

"Hello?"

"Klaus," I said, "have you heard?"

"Yes," he said in his thick accent. "Jack called me, but we did not get to speak long. Were you hurt? You sound sick."

"I'm fine," I said sluggishly, wanting nothing more than to lose consciousness again. "Klaus, we need to talk about our plans. Things are getting very bad, very fast. Are the suppliers still honoring their agreements with us?"

"Of course. They have given us priority over most other interested buyers. I don't think that will change, because no one else will pay the premiums we are offering." He paused. "Douglas, you should know that they have asked for payment in PGUs. They do not want Swiss francs anymore, and they certainly do not want dollars."

I couldn't help but smile a little through my fatigue. "That's good news. It's just what we need right now."

Now for the hard part . . .

I took a deep breath and held it. I had discussed the next phase of my plan with Jefferson, and he had given his approval, but I was still so uncertain. There was movement in my peripheral vision, and I turned to see Jack standing in the room listening to Klaus on the speaker phone, watching me carefully. He smiled, clearly trying to ease my tension, and yet the weight of my responsibility bore down hard on me. I tensed my jaw, determined not to allow my fear to control me.

After a few seconds, I exhaled and said, "Here's what I want you to do now, Klaus: take our profits from here on and buy precious metals futures contracts. I don't care what exchanges you use, within reason. I also want you to sell puts against as many contracts as possible. Try to get good premiums, because the money you receive will give you more liquidity."

Klaus was quiet for a moment. "Are you sure that is safe? We have never used leverage before. Is this the time?"

His cautionary tone dredged up all the memories from my days as a speculator, and I felt even more uncertain for a second. I pushed the thoughts aside. "You'll have to trust us on this. Those puts will expire worthless and we could use the cash right now. I have a strong feeling that demand for the PGU is about to pick up considerably, and I promise you that any leverage we use will only be short-term. We'll be out before you know it. We're going to need that cash, Klaus; I'm scared that we may have trouble if we don't use everything we have at our disposal."

I hesitated, acutely aware of the power at my fingertips. "Klaus," I said, "If we don't have sufficient assets backing the PGU, our paper is worth no more than any government's—and we all know that story."

"I understand," he said. "I will take care of it immediately." Then he added, "Douglas, some people have been in our bank in the last two weeks—people from your IRS and Treasury Department. They are not being at all inconspicuous. They are demanding to know who you are."

I turned to Jack again. He looked concerned. "How have your people handled the inquiries?" I asked Klaus.

"The way they have been trained to handle them—with silence."

"Perfect. Just keep yourself in the background."

We exchanged goodbyes and disconnected.

"So now what?" Jack said to me.

"Nothing." I rose from my chair and walked toward the door. My feet felt like cement blocks. "Let's let Klaus to do his job. The PGU is about to become available to the public, but until that happens we should sit tight."

He stared at me as I passed him.

I stopped, puzzled. "Why are you looking at me like that?"

He smiled. "I wish you could see yourself right now."

I held up my arms and looked down at my suit. It was filthy, torn in several places, with a bloody, gaping hole where the knife had entered my leg only a short while before. "Yeah, I'm a mess."

He shook his head. "Not that, you little dumbass bastard."

"What?"

He folded his arms. "Well, if you don't see it, I'm not going to tell you." His smile broadened.

I turned around and resumed my trudge toward the bedroom. "Fuck you, Jack. I'm going back to sleep."

Despite the gravity of everything that had happened that day, as I walked away I couldn't help but smile. Jack, in his own goofy way, was trying to tell me he was proud of me.

◆

GLOBAL CURRENCIES WERE now losing value so quickly that vast numbers of people couldn't afford even the most basic necessities. Across the United States, lines formed in front of churches and government assistance centers—none of which could handle the massive onslaught of people in need. And—as it usually does when resources become hopelessly scarce—the violence escalated.

For so long, rioting and house-to-house guerilla warfare had been only distant nightmares—images rolling harmlessly across television screens, viewed by audiences tucked safely in their living rooms. But now, even in neighborhoods that had once been considered middle class, organized factions took up arms and began attacking any symbols of authority daring to remain exposed.

Stories abounded, without precedence, of people being stopped at gunpoint—their cars, belongings, and sometimes even their lives taken. The city where I'd lived nearly half my life had been transformed from an energetic, technology-driven college town to a war zone. And the story was the same, if not worse, all over the world.

While many financial institutions had been taking positions in the PGU for some time, we assumed Klaus would have to approach the largest banks with relief proposals—to convince them of our legitimacy. Instead, we were surprised when two of the biggest money center banks in the world actually came to us with requests for our currency. We naturally offered to provide liquidity, but only under the condition that they allow any clients—from institutions to individuals—to convert to PGUs. The banks agreed and began a campaign to inform the public, placing emphasis on all the steps we had taken to prove the stability, security, and liquidity of the PGU's asset base.

At any other time in history, these bastions of the financial community would have dismissed the PGU as ludicrous. But now, in the absence of any other viable exchange instruments, word spread quickly, and reaction was swift. After the first two banks made their policies known, a surprisingly large number of other money-center institutions around the world followed suit.

The U.S. government, already in a state of havoc, accused domestic banks of violating legal tender laws—until it was pointed out that none of them actually printed the new currency. Lawmakers next tried to argue that the PGU was a violation of rigid U.S. securities laws, but the claims were tenuous at best, and no one seemed particularly eager to seek clarification.

Finally, the U.S. president accused Klaus's bank of undermining the dollar's stability—an indictment ignored by almost everyone, including the Swiss government. The idea was preposterous; while it was true that the nearly interminable sale of dollars to buy PGUs had put an unprecedented amount of pressure on the U.S. currency, the situation was clearly a result of markets at work—not some conspiracy hatched by the Swiss bank.

Without the dollar's integrity, the United States became effete in the world's eyes, and politicians panicked as they felt their power slipping. The U.S. Federal Reserve intervened yet again, but the efforts had little impact on the failing currency's momentum. The PGU helped to allay economic disintegration, but civil unrest continued to gnaw at the threads of the most powerful union in history.

The anonymous attacks against the United States and other countries escalated, accompanied by still more violent protests and demands for action. Domestic and foreign terror groups began to target icons of power—both federal and private—inciting panic as unseen soldiers chipped away at almost every imaginable symbol of stability.

The PGU may have helped balance the vacuum created by the failure of the dollar and other currencies, but turning a world economy around wasn't going to happen overnight. In the face of what was becoming a global depression, the nationalistic furor that had been so prevalent during previous crises took a backseat to survival. The protests that had begun in the early days of the economic downturn had only proliferated, and were now almost invariably turning into violent riots. For the first time since it had all started, I began to hear the words *civil war* being whispered, and the thought left me cold.

The United States Congress held hearings and assigned task forces to discover the identities of the shareholders in the PGU's issuing corporation, but Klaus and his bank were as good as their word. Likewise, the Swiss government stood resolutely by its policy of banking secrecy. What the U.S. didn't know was that the Swiss had used the PGU to help stabilize their own currency in the global crisis. Even under normal circumstances, without solid evidence of criminal activity, the Swiss government would never undermine its own banking privacy laws—along with literally centuries of banking faith. In the current tumultuous economic environment, however, there was no way Swiss authorities would kill the only thing creating any semblance of order. We were the proverbial goose and the Swiss needed our golden eggs as much as anyone else did.

"I can handle angry shareholders and scared board members, but I have no control over what the government does," I said to Jack in the car one afternoon. We had just finished a long phone conversation with Klaus, and our schedule for the rest of the day was uncharacteristically free, so we had decided to head to the Cardinal for a few games—a rare treat anymore.

"It's lost control," I continued. "Do you have any idea how badly they probably want to find us?"

"You worry too much," Jack said, steering us along the route that we had taken so many times from Jefferson's little house to the coffee shop. Only a few years ago, these neighborhoods had been clean, the houses well maintained. Now everything seemed to be falling apart. The scene filled me with melancholy.

Fuel prices had risen astronomically over the past year—yet another vicious component to the cycle of economic turmoil. As currencies became less valuable, oil became more expensive, which in turn only made goods and services yet more expensive. While some people still drove, gasoline had now become a carefully rationed luxury, rather than a staple. With unemployment rising almost uncontrollably, many people literally had nothing to do but mill about, often in throngs, to commiserate about their collective nightmare.

Jack's car was by no means extravagant, but neither was it old or beat up, and as we cruised through these neighborhoods, I noticed people casting glances our way, almost like predators. My thoughts returned to the currency. "What if Groeden did see me come out of that building before the bombing? What if he turns us over—?"

Jack laughed. "Groeden isn't interested in having you detained. He doesn't know your name—it's been hidden from him too well. Look, if he did, you wouldn't be sitting in an interrogation room, you'd be dead."

"If the government finds out—"

"What are they going to do?"

"I know we're not breaking the law, but who knows?" I looked out the window at two men standing on a street corner, watching us. "And even if they don't do anything, our identities would still be compromised. How do you think Groeden would feel about that?"

He scoffed. "Just trust me on this one—" Suddenly his eyes narrowed. "What the *fuck*?" The road in front of us was blocked by debris: tree limbs, garbage cans, bicycle frames.

I felt an electric buzzing in my ears, and I turned to Jack. His eyes were suddenly ablaze.

He feels it too.

Almost in slow motion, a shadow passed in front of us. Something hit the windshield, instantly turning it into a spider web. Jack slammed on the brakes.

Several people appeared in front of us. Then more appeared behind, quickly creating another pile of debris, blocking any exit.

Jack unbuckled his seatbelt. "Get out. Move to the front of the car."

I was so calm I almost felt detached from the scene, as though I were watching it unfold on a large screen. I walked forward, scanning the people in front of us, then quickly turning to count the ones behind. There were seven men and women, total—three in front, and four in back.

Jack and I were now about fifteen feet from the three bandits in front. A haggard-looking man held a pistol, his arm extended toward us. The four behind us moved around to join the ones in front, presumably to get out of the line of fire.

They all look so thin, I thought. *Has it gotten this bad?*

The man with the pistol said, "We're going to take your wallets and your car keys." His eyes were exhausted, almost sad, but his tone was all business. "I'm going to have to ask you not to do anything stupid, because we're very hungry, and this is just something we've got to do."

Jack and I stood there, staring at the group. I looked at the man with the gun. *This violates everything he believes, but he has no choice. None of them has any choice.*

As I watched, a new feeling emerged in me—a level of empathy I had never felt before. These people were scared and defeated. Their world was being ripped apart; the things for which they had worked their entire lives were evaporating before them.

There's a better way. It was as though someone had flooded a dark room with light. Something inside of me changed in that moment, the kindling of a small fire that would lead to an answer to the most important question I had ever asked myself. The picture was starting to come into focus: these people needed more than help—they needed a new way to live.

I had studied philosophy and economics for years, using the tenets to carefully build my own foundation, but as I watched these dejected people, I realized how much I had missed. They weren't merely anonymous numbers in a vast machine—existing merely to be tracked like cattle by an unsympathetic system over which they had no control. *No, these people are human beings, and all they want is to be able to take care of the people they love.*

The man was about to speak again when one of his friends said in a low voice, "Eddie."

He didn't respond.

"*Eddie*," his friend repeated.

Eddie turned his head slightly, his eyes shifting between me and Jack and the man who had spoken. "What is it?" he asked.

The second man pointed at three children standing on the sidewalk, their gaunt expressions a mixture of confusion and fear.

Eddie turned, but I could still see his face—filled with surprise, sadness, and shame. He lowered the pistol out of site of the children. "You all get out of here!" But the children only continued to stare at him. Eddie looked at a woman to his left. "Get them out of here! They don't need to see this!" The woman moved toward the children, and at that moment, I reached up to wipe a bead of sweat from my forehead. The movement was too quick.

Eddie, clearly on edge, quickly raised the pistol, and in that fraction of a second, it went off.

Time and space froze. The bullet headed for Jack's face, but he easily moved out of its path.

The world around us slowly began to increase its momentum, building, finally resuming normal speed. The children and the woman hit the ground, and the group around the car flinched, startled by the shot. Eddie dropped the pistol, horrified by the mistake he had made.

I turned to Jack, and what I saw chilled me. His eyes burned with anger. He snarled viciously, and I knew if I didn't do something in that instant, Eddie, and maybe some of the others were going to lose their lives.

Jack took a deep breath. I could see his muscles tensing, preparing for what was to happen. It was the alley in Switzerland all over again. "*No, Jack!*" I barked.

He turned to me, and the anger drained from him so quickly that it took some effort for me not to repeat the command. His eyes softened in what looked like relief and gratitude. He nodded once, almost imperceptibly, and took a step back.

Something gnawed at me. *Why did he submit so easily?* And then something else trickled in: *Is he being obedient?* The thought was so incongruent I had to force myself not to let it consume me.

I turned to the group, all of whom had clearly seen Jack's eyes and had perceived the danger. Eddie held the pistol again, his arm shaking badly.

My lack of fear was so palpable I almost felt numb. Without even thinking about it, I said, "Eddie, put the gun down."

He stared at me, his eyes wild, his mouth open. "Give me your wallets and then back away."

I looked deeply into his eyes. "Eddie, no."

He gazed back at me for another second, and then fell to his knees, weeping. "What is happening to us?" The pistol dropped to the pavement with a clatter.

I glanced back at Jack, who now leaned against the hood of the car, scanning the scene, his arms crossed.

I walked to Eddie and crouched in front of him. I watched the scared, uncomprehending faces around us. Eddie shuddered and heaved. "I'm sorry," he said.

"Hey," I whispered. "Listen to me."

Eddie stopped crying and lifted his head.

I took him by the elbow and slowly helped him to his feet. I reached into my pocket and extracted my wallet, pulling out a large number of bills. And suddenly Jack was next to me, holding an equally sizeable wad in his hand. We handed the cash to Eddie.

"I can't take—"

"Yes you can," I said.

Eddie looked at the money in his hands, and then at me again. "This is that new money."

I nodded. "Go feed your family, Eddie."

He looked at me again, baffled and shaken.

I smiled and covered his hands with my own. "Things are going to get better. I promise."

It took about ten minutes to clear enough of the debris to get the car out. As we drove away, I said, "What the *fuck* is happening? Why would anyone cause this?"

Jack struggled to see the road through the cracked windshield. "You know why."

"Those are good people. They just can't find enough fucking food to eat. How can anyone blame them?"

Jack didn't say anything.

I sighed. "I had no idea how bad it was. I can *feel* this happening around us. Those people—there was something about their faces, something about their eyes. They're losing everything, and they're *fucking* scared. We're descending into chaos." I coughed weakly and thought for another moment. Then I sat up straight and turned to Jack. "I *fucking* hate him."

Jack stayed quiet for a moment. Finally he said, "Normally I would never want you to feel that way about anyone." He took a breath and pulled the car to the curb. He turned to me, his eyes hot. "He's the one person in the universe I would actually encourage you to hate."

Fall, Year Thirty-Two

ULTIMATELY JACK HAD been right—the authorities had no luck finding us, and meanwhile the dollar held little more integrity than the paper on which it was printed. The United States Treasury was going broke. As the situation continued to deteriorate, Washington, in an act of desperation, threatened Switzerland with economic sanctions, which was anything but rational; the Swiss government was responsible for nothing more than upholding the laws that allowed the PGU to exist.

To further add to the imbroglio, new polls began to suggest the public believed the U.S government only wanted to save the dollar in order to reestablish its previous dominance over global monetary policy, and that it intended to do so by undermining the only currency that still represented value—and hope. To most people, the reality of the situation seemed clear: Washington—and not our currency—had destroyed the dollar through years of poor preparation; the PGU merely stood firm in the aftermath as the only liquid store of value left in the world that offered any real promise for ending the nightmare that now threatened the survival of so many people.

The proposed penalties against Switzerland became less popular with each passing day, but the Swiss didn't seem very concerned in any case, merely ignoring the threats. This only further enraged Washington, and less than a week after the sanctions were proposed, a story broke that the House National Security Committee had briefly discussed limited military action against Switzerland.

The idea was actually nothing more than an abstraction—the product of a purely academic military scenario analysis, never intended to be considered seriously. But the public was outraged at the mere suggestion, and the backlash was so great, the president and ranking members of Congress promptly issued a public apology.

The Swiss, not surprisingly, were not soothed by the fatuous display of regret and summarily placed their own economic sanctions against the United States—a move that turned Washington into a laughingstock around the world. Fresh stories seemed to appear so quickly that I found it almost impossible to get away from the television or my computer, eagerly awaiting every breaking event, snatching sleep when I could.

Jack and Jefferson stayed close, cooking meals, or getting things we needed from the store. They almost seemed to enjoy watching me react to everything happening in the world, and yet there was careful scrutiny in their eyes—more cautious observation than I had ever felt from either of them, as though my decisions now were more critical than all the others before.

Businesses now accepted the PGU almost universally, and soon the global public largely refused to use any form of government-issued currency at all. In a desperate attempt to control the situation, U.S. lawmakers passed legislation forbidding trade in any foreign currency—public or private—but that decree, like all the rest, was ignored. Jefferson, Jack, and I continued to use PGUs everywhere we went with no resistance at all. Nobody wanted dollars anymore.

One day in mid-July, I was sitting in front of the television when a fresh story broke. Earlier that day, an anonymous source in the White House had apparently leaked to the press that the president, in a meeting with key members of Congress, raised the possibility of sending troops into banks to enforce the ban against foreign currencies—a move clearly directed at the PGU.

The backlash was immediate; I watched as report after report returned overwhelming negative reaction to the possible deployment, and it quickly became clear that this was the last indignity many Americans would tolerate. Just that quickly, what had been mere whispers now became angry shouts. For the first time in living memory, impassioned conversations openly revolved around the notion that the United States faced the real possibility of civil war.

A few days after the incident, I sat in front of my computer, working furiously on some projections for Klaus when Jack came into my office.

He looked serious. "Have you heard?"

"Heard what?"

"You'd better come in here."

I followed him into the living room where a "Breaking News" banner flashed at the bottom of the television screen. The anchor related the latest events in a dramatic tone. ". . . the Texas legislature called the emergency session at approximately 9:30 A.M., central time, at which point many businesses and schools across the state closed."

The screen switched to the Texas capitol building. Crowds of people seemed to be gathering. "What you're seeing is a live picture of the capitol in Austin, but other than rumors, we have very little information about the reason behind the closed emergency session. What we *are* hearing from our affiliates in Austin is that people are eagerly anticipating word from lawmakers."

"What's all this about?" I said.

Jack pointed at the screen. "They're debating secession."

I turned to him, "What the fuck are you talking about?"

He gave me a wry smile. "That surprises you?"

I looked at him for a second. "No, I guess it doesn't." I laced my fingers in my hair. "I just didn't think it would happen so quickly."

The Texas legislature had debated separation many times in the decades since the American Civil War, although the topic had never generated anything even approaching serious support. But few people doubted Texas's fortitude and economic strength; as an independent nation, it would rank among the wealthiest on the planet, and public figures in Austin were wasting no time informing the world of that fact.

At first, none of the networks explicitly mentioned what was clearly on everyone's mind. But after a few hours, the veil lifted, and soon everyone was speculating about the implications. For the rest of the day, news agencies scrambled to gather opinion polls, which yielded surprising results: a strong majority of Texans favored independence.

Jack and I remained in front of the television, mostly in silence. I brought my computer into the room and continued my work as analysis poured from the set. At about sunset, I heard the front door open and Jefferson walked in the room.

"I guess you've heard," I said.

He nodded, and we looked at each other for a moment. He seemed to be searching my eyes for something—perhaps my level of conviction or fear. I was about to say something else when I heard, "We have this breaking news out of Washington . . ."

The three of us turned our eyes to the television. The anchor angled his head slightly, his face somber as he listened to the words coming from his earpiece. "We have a confirmed report that . . . the president has put federal troops in Texas on alert." He straightened his posture. "I'm going to repeat that: we are now receiving confirmed reports that the president of the United States *has* placed federal troops in Texas on alert."

Jefferson and Jack turned to me simultaneously, awaiting my reaction. I looked between them, my mouth a little dry. "They're making a mistake," I said.

Jefferson characteristically raised his eyebrows and looked at me over his glasses.

Jack merely turned back to the television.

"I wish you guys would tell me something." I stared at the television screen. "*Anything—*"

But Jefferson and Jack only remained silent.

Within a couple of hours, the Texas legislature put its own state guard units on high alert. Hundreds of Texas soldiers dressed in battle fatigues and carrying automatic weapons surrounded the capitol and erected barricades in a defensive stance. Troops parked tanks and armored vehicles on every side of the building, facing outward, sending a clear message to the world: Texas would decide its own fate by whatever means necessary. In what seemed like the blink of an eye, the conflict had moved beyond mere discussion.

Klaus called us several times in the next few hours, not really to update us, but rather to check in as a show of support. The conversations were short and unemotional, the tension palpable, and I finally just told him to call if anything troubling came across his desk. I assured him I would do the same.

Jefferson, Jack, and I meanwhile stayed planted in front of the TV. A constant, low-level adrenaline flow kept my heart rate moderately higher than normal, my breathing a little more shallow. *It's all happening so fast . . .*

At the capitol, no one seemed to know how to handle the unprecedented situation. City and state police dressed in full riot gear—openly displaying comradeship with the Texas soldiers—patrolled in front of the barricades to control the gathering crowd of civilians. The throng was here to show support for the growing secessionist movement, but their presence created a problem for troops: any violence would certainly bring civilian casualties.

Texas soldiers and police tried to persuade the now enormous crowd to leave the area around the capitol, but the supporters held their ground, undeterred. A token force of federal troops spread out to critical points farther away from the capitol, but they were outnumbered, their morale was waning, and they clearly wished to avoid conflict. Soon rumors began to circulate that some federal troops were deserting U.S. army positions in order to enlist in the state guard, and the news only further soured the U.S. soldiers' moods.

The Texas legislature continued to convene into the night as the world held its breath, and while no more news came from the halls of the capitol building, media crews trained cameras on every square inch of the grounds, conducting interviews with almost anyone who had an opinion, and the crowds only grew. The legislature, however, had locked itself in, refusing to offer any word on the progress of the assembly.

It was well past midnight when I finally decided nothing more was likely to happen before sunrise, so I went into my room and closed my eyes for some much needed rest.

I felt my body being shaken.

I bolted upright. Jack was standing over me. "Get up," he said.

We hustled into the den, where Jefferson watched the television, relaxing in a leather chair in the corner, his legs crossed. I looked at my watch, which read a little past 8:30.

The view on screen was of the capitol grounds, and the voice on the television said, "We are now awaiting word from the Texas capitol, where we understand legislators have reached some sort of decision—possibly on a critical vote taken this morning."

The crowd around the capitol seemed electrified. "Let's go down there," Jack said. "You don't want to miss this."

I looked at Jefferson. He smiled slightly and nodded at us once.

Jack and I had to park more than a mile away, and we walked rapidly in silence toward the capitol. We found a spot on the edge of the crowd where we stopped to watch. Nervous chatter filled the air as everyone waited anxiously for the outcome.

At 10:37 A.M., the governor appeared at the steps of the capitol building in front of a battery of microphones. At first, a pulse of energy ripped through the crowd, but then, just as quickly, a hush fell over the scene. The governor's voice boomed from speakers stacked high on either side of the portico, which now served as a dais.

"Fellow Texans, citizens of the United States, and citizens of the world, I come to you tonight not as the Governor of Texas, but as a messenger sent by the elected representatives of this state.

"As most of you know, the Texas legislature has been hard at work for most of the last two days, carefully deciding our future. I am proud to say that I have been part of that process, and I am addressing you tonight to tell you about a historic decision that has been made here in Austin.

"Earlier this evening our lawmakers agreed that we should do everything in our power to chart the safest and most productive course for the future of every single person in our state, and a few minutes ago I signed an order to that end."

The governor paused for a moment. The hush around the capitol was nearly maddening. Jack grabbed my arm and squeezed as the governor continued. "It is with great pride that I announce the birth of The New Republic of Texas."

The eruption of cheers around the capitol was as sudden and deafening as a thousand cannons firing at once. A chill crawled down my spine. The crowd rocked with waves of ecstatic joy, and when the commotion subsided the governor continued. "I have been appointed interim president of the republic until general elections can be organized, according to the articles set forth in our constitution, and pending its reratification."

Jack looked at me and smiled. "We should go now."

We walked in silence back to the car as I considered the implications of what had just happened. Finally I said, "This a good thing." I felt almost elated, although I wasn't quite sure why yet.

Almost as if he were reading my mind, Jack asked, "Why is this a good thing, Douglas?" He didn't sound like he was disagreeing with me, but rather the tone of his voice seemed to encourage me to form some sort of conviction.

I smiled. "I don't know—it seems like the logical next step. Texas is free to fix its own problems now."

He stopped and turned, looking hard at me. I felt the smile disappear from my face. "It's not over yet," he said.

When we got back to the house, Jefferson looked as though he hadn't moved from his chair. Jack and I sat down in front of the television without a word.

The crowd continued the celebration for about two hours, but the mood suddenly and frighteningly became somber when a battalion of federal troops began surrounding the crowd—and the capitol—marking the beginning of a chilling standoff. The U.S president made a televised request that Texas cease its rebellion, pleading to people's sense of unity and faith, appealing to patriotism and history. But the entreaties rang hollow in the hearts of those faced with starvation and violence.

Texas's acting president responded within an hour with another statement in which he replied unequivocally: the New Republic of Texas would remain independent. A hundred years earlier any U.S. president might have ordered troops to fire, but under current global scrutiny he would never be able to maintain the public support he needed to order such a massacre. In any case, the Texas troops were well armed; a battle would hardly be a quick, easy victory for the United States. Similar circumstances had surrounded the events leading to the Soviet Union's collapse, and the parallel seemed to elude no one. The Texans now hoped for a similar outcome, and so the impasse continued. The number of civilians grew, as did the number of U.S. troops present. Four U.S. tanks drove down Congress Avenue and parked nose to nose in front of several Texas guard tanks, aiming their turrets directly at the front of the legislative building. Throngs of people stood around the federal tanks, screaming insults and throwing garbage. Within an hour, two more U.S. tanks appeared, helping to cover the rear of the building. Rumors began to circulate that many of the people in the crowd were armed, which made the U.S. soldiers even more uneasy. Still no one backed down. I saw movement to my left, and I pulled my eyes away from the television to find Jefferson extending a cup of tea toward me. "Thanks," I said.

He smiled and started to take a seat next to Jack on the sofa, when I felt a bolt of fear run through my body. "Oh, my God—" I put my hand over my mouth, my eyes wide.

Jefferson froze, and I noticed I had Jack's attention too. "What is it?" Jefferson said.

Suddenly an image forced its way into my mind—the man with the shotgun who had tried to kill me and Jack in the restaurant. "Groeden . . . what if he sends somebody out there to set it off?"

Jefferson and Jack looked at each other and smiled, relieved. "You shouldn't worry about that," Jack said.

"Why? He wanted this."

"No," Jefferson said. "He wanted things to get bad. But he definitely doesn't want the federal government to lose control."

I furrowed my brow. "I don't understand."

Jefferson eased himself into his chair. "If violence breaks out, the feds could lose total control, and if that's the source of Groeden's funding, it could all end. He had the ability to cause a lot more damage, a lot sooner, but it was a calculated risk. The book talks explicitly about what you're seeing on television right now. Groeden wanted chaos, but believe me when I tell you that he did *not* want this to happen—he tried very hard to prevent it."

I stared at the floor as the pieces started to come together in my mind. "So the currency—"

Jefferson looked at me expectantly. "It's the glue, Douglas. It's the critical element holding things together enough that people can react rationally—that they can make the right decisions. Unless something unexpected happens—" He glanced at Jack and smiled, and then looked at me again. "I think Groeden is sitting somewhere right now, fuming over the fact that he's in danger of losing most of his support."

"And without that money . . ." I brought my eyes up to meet Jefferson's. "This might be the reason the Bell isn't more advanced."

Jefferson nodded thoughtfully. "It *might* be."

I considered that for a moment. "So there's no chance he's out there—" I glanced at the television screen. "—trying to make it worse."

"It will be bad enough for Groeden if the Union falls apart peacefully, but the last thing he wants is a civil war," Jefferson said. "The implications for his research are devastating." Jefferson chose his next words carefully. "Groeden wants to preserve as much as possible at this point."

"So you don't anticipate this escalating?"

Jefferson and Jack looked at each other again cautiously before Jefferson said, "Anything could happen, Douglas."

"But—"

He smiled. "*But* you should just let things happen the way they're supposed to."

I sighed and shook my head, turning back to the television.

We continued to follow events for the rest of the day as tensions reached critical mass. Violence seemed all but imminent now. The suspense was almost too much to bear, and I finally muted the television and looked at Jefferson. "If this thing does get out of control, Groeden isn't the only one who's going to suffer."

"That's true."

My frustration bordered on anger. "Just fucking tell me how it's going to turn out! I have a lot of decisions to make, and a lot of people to answer to—"

Jefferson nodded at the television screen, and I followed his gaze. A news reporter stood in front of the Texas capitol building and I turned the sound up ". . . these fascinating new developments coming to us in the last few minutes. Apparently a source at the United Nations is quoted as saying that several countries around the globe have simultaneously officially recognized the Republic of Texas's sovereignty." The reporter looked down at a handful of notes clasped in her hand. "From what we know right now, at least some of the countries offering recognition are Russia, The Czech Republic, Mexico, and Cuba." The reporter looked back at the camera. "So the real question many people are asking now is, will this end the standoff?"

"The real question, indeed," I muttered.

Within an hour several hundred more U.S. troops arrived as reinforcement, and a small skirmish finally erupted when some angry Texas civilians threw stones and glass bottles at the arriving soldiers. A rumor flowed through the crowd that U.S. troops had fired, and a great deal of commotion ensued. For a moment full-scale violence seemed unavoidable as many in the mob began screaming for retaliation. But the rumor was quickly dispelled and the crowd relaxed a little. Still, public support for the federals waned faster than ever now. The faces in the demonstration were black with anger, shouting demands that the U.S. troops leave Texas soil.

I sat only a few feet from the television, elbows on knees, literally hanging on the edge of my seat. My stomach seemed to tighten with every passing minute. In the next six hours, the Texas legislature voted to keep its constitution. There were, of course, some obvious minor adjustments, but overall it would be business as usual for the Lone Star Republic, with one notable exception: The new country would adopt as its temporary currency the Private Gold Unit, issued by our corporation, and distributed by Klaus's bank.

It was an incredible show of faith in the PGU and a great victory for everyone—except the United States government. If the world hadn't seen the currency as legitimate before, it would now. Tension, however, still swelled, and violence became more plausible with each passing minute. I paced in front of the television, at times trying to get work done, yet always pulled back to the intensity of the events captivating the world—happening only a few miles from our house. The fact that we were controlling the instrument that had essentially brought about this moment only made me more tense.

The insults emanating from the crowd had turned into furious rhythmic chanting, and both U.S. and Texas troops looked uncertain about what would happen next. Federal troops were becoming increasingly frustrated and impatient with the crowd gathered to harass them. Texas troops, on the other hand, were beginning to resent the U.S. presence on what they now considered sovereign Texas soil. As the standoff continued late into the night, I managed to close my eyes for a few more hours, until I was shaken awake yet again—this time by Jefferson. I sat up on the couch and watched the announcement that Montana's legislature had voted to secede.

Within another hour, news broke that Arizona and Colorado would also depart the Union. For about ten minutes, no one was able to confirm the story was more than another rumor started in the burgeoning crowd. But then a televised announcement from Montana's governor eliminated any speculation, confirming that the three states had indeed voted to depart the Union.

Jefferson and Jack had left the room, so I had no one to talk to, but I knew they would be no help anyway. Once again I sat glued to the television, wanting desperately to do anything—to be anywhere but here. And yet there was no other place in the world I would feel as safe, and so I simply remained in my chair, transfixed.

Nobody around the capitol seemed to know quite what to do. News cameras picked up several shots of U.S. troops looking around in obvious dismay. One network reporter pushed his way through the crowd, shoving a microphone into a confused federal soldier's face. The reporter yelled above the chaotic din, "What will you do if you're ordered to fire?"

The soldier didn't answer immediately, examining the scene like a lost child looking for his parents. Finally he shrugged and said, "I don't know. I guess if they want this place that bad, we ought to just let 'em have it. I don't think I could shoot nobody—some of those guys over there are my friends." He pondered that thought for a moment. "Nah, I don't think I could."

His face broke into a broad smile, telling the whole story—broadcast instantly around the world by the most watched television news network in history. Within minutes, cameras picked up commotion at the capitol's portico. After another moment, Texas's acting president once again stood in front of the battery of microphones. Through the loudspeakers, he entreated U.S. troops to lay down their weapons, guaranteeing their safety.

He ended the short speech with a moving observation: "We're friends—many of us are even related to each other. We speak the same language, read the same books, and listen to the same music. Everyone here wants a peaceful outcome to this historic moment, so let's make this a day of celebration, not a day of mourning."

At first the crowd only hummed with curious anticipation, but within minutes, the first U.S. soldier surrendered his weapon to the Texas Army in front of a battalion of cameras. He saluted smartly, and then shook hands with the officer who accepted his rifle. Both men smiled broadly. Soon all the federal troops began to hand over their arms, and the crowd around the capitol erupted in cheers.

The American Civil War of the 1860s had been geographically feasible. The divisions were clear from the start, and the campaigns had been fought along rigid demarcations. But now states as distant as Oregon and Alaska were proclaiming independence, creating unclear borders. Even if a decision of war had been popular—which it wasn't—fighting it would have been nearly impossible, given the meandering lines being drawn that made the formerly contiguous United States look like a chessboard. And, of course, there was always the question of how the federal government would pay for such a campaign, given the decimation of its currency.

Left with diminishing strategic, political, and economic choices, the U.S. president decided it would be dangerous to go against public opinion. The fact that U.S. troops had given up their arms before the world's eyes didn't lend support to aggression, and within half an hour he met with remaining ranking members of Congress. Without much discussion, they decided states wishing to secede would be allowed to do so. What other choice was there? The vote would be a formality; no one wanted to pursue a violent course.

I watched for another few hours as the crowd around the capitol rocked with celebration, and suddenly I remembered what Jefferson and Jack had said only a short time ago about Groeden—about how badly he needed the Union to survive. And now it seemed as though that possibility was completely dashed.

Just before dawn, the U.S. president placed an informal call to the acting president of the New Republic of Texas, assuring support and requesting an open dialogue to establish strong relations between the two nations. The United States now recognized the new Republic's unconditional sovereignty.

I turned off the television and went to my room, exhausted but also elated. I lay down and stared through the darkness at the ceiling, unable to resist the smile that spread across my lips—or the one thought that overwhelmed all the rest.

Texas was, unequivocally and for the second time in its history, an independent nation.

———————◆———————

IN THE ENSUING months, the United States retained only a fraction of its former self, its new borders mostly confined to northeastern states—with the exception of New Hampshire, which seceded quickly. When the dust settled only sixteen states remained in the Union. Almost all regions of the former United States were now subdivided into new republics. The fledgling countries established treaties and, contrary to fears, nothing really changed.

The U.S. stock markets—including the New York Stock Exchange, which had only recently reorganized in a vague, decentralized version of its older self—had trouble for a short time and then turned around quickly. New exchanges were created in many of the nascent American republics—one of the first and biggest being the Texas Securities Exchange, headquartered in Dallas. Many companies, including our umbrella firm, were listed on exchanges throughout the new nations, and around the world. These trading centers thrived and created stiff competition for the old, established networks in New York, as well as other antiquated financial centers. The new republics' economies bubbled with productivity and growth, setting the stage for global changes yet to come.

I find it miraculous that Jack, Jefferson, and I were able to maintain almost total anonymity through everything. Not long after the collapse, however, a news agency broke a story claiming that the group behind the PGU was a small consortium from Texas. I immediately called Klaus, who already knew of the leak and had begun an investigation. The source, however, was never discovered, and no further details were ever disclosed, so our identities remained unknown.

After Texas adopted the PGU as its currency, many other nations followed suit. Other private issuers surfaced, trying to grab market share, but we had established ourselves universally—entrenched in almost every available economy. We wouldn't be dethroned easily. People used PGUs around the world, and while other private currencies did succeed in limited regional settings, no one could match our recognition and established faith.

Ironically, most people simply ignored the weak legal-tender protection Texas initially granted to the PGU—even if our money did enjoy market supremacy over other currencies. After the closure of its central bank, the Republic of Texas decreed that its citizens could legally transact business with any medium they desired. It was the first time in modern history that a nation had decided not to coin money, and within a decade almost every other country on earth had followed suit.

Politicians and academics spoke with eloquence and passion, but no one listened. The era of centralized authority and planned economies was over; never had a revolution been so thorough, so universal, and yet so nearly bloodless. People were free, and the freedom was real—not merely a slogan tossed casually from the lips of power-hungry politicians.

The avatar of an open society was in full swing, spreading contagiously across the globe, and its roots had sprouted from almost no violence at all.

After things settled down, we began using the profits from the PGU to buy shares in well-managed firms around the world. It was clear that the corporations we had built to manage the PGU would be among the wealthiest on earth in a few years. We authorized a public offering to dilute ownership and sold more than 50 percent of our shares to Klaus's bank, gladly relinquishing majority control.

Klaus asked how we wanted the money split. Jack kept his half intact at the Swiss bank, but I requested something a little different: I asked that Klaus set a large portion of my equity aside.

"How much?" he asked.

I told him the figure and the phone line to Switzerland was silent for a moment before he said, "That is an *enormous* sum of money."

I chuckled. "Believe me when I tell you it's not enough."

"And who will be the beneficiary of this account?"

"Put it in the name of Jefferson Stone."

A few months later, Klaus informed me that Jefferson had failed to return his calls. I told him to keep trying, but he was never able to make contact, so I confronted Jefferson. "Our Swiss friend has been trying to give you some money. I believe I have a debt to settle with you."

"I'll return his call soon. I've been rather busy."

But Jefferson never did call Klaus, and it would be a very long time before I would find out the fate of the money I had set aside to repay his kindness.

October, Year Thirty-Two

THE CARDINAL HAD barely managed to remain open through even the first, milder phases of the economic downturn, and eventually the owners announced they were simply going to close its doors. Then, miraculously, an anonymous benefactor stepped in, offering enough cash to see the shop through the worst of it.

It was, after all, my home.

Jack and I once again spent a great deal of time playing chess at the Cardinal, grateful for the pastime now that things had slowed down a bit. Jefferson even joined us sometimes, and we would often stay for hours, telling stories, laughing, and generally unwinding in the wake of everything we had been through. It was, perhaps, the most peaceful time the three of us ever spent together, and I remember those days with an incalculable fondness.

One day that fall, Jack and I hovered over a board at the shop. "I want to ask you something," I said, moving a rook.

"Yeah?"

I put my hand on my forehead. "Something has been bugging me for a while. I thought we were finished—that I had done everything I was supposed to. But lately I've been getting this feeling. It's hard to explain. I feel . . . incomplete."

He toyed with a bishop nervously.

"Jefferson's supposed to kill him," I said.

Jack quickly lifted his eyes, and just as quickly looked back at the board.

"There's more isn't there?"

He glanced at me again—only for an instant—but in that fraction of a second, I saw a spark of fear in his eyes, and it was enough to turn me cold. "Why did you look at me like that?"

"Like what?" The fear was gone, and he now looked at me as though I were insane. "What the shit are you talking about?"

"What's going on, Jack?"

He took a deep breath and smiled. "Remember who you are and what you've learned. In the end, we all do what we're supposed to do, and that's enough."

"Jack, no—"

He lifted his hand to cut me off. "Please don't push it."

I opened my mouth to protest, but something in his eyes stopped me. This was new territory, and suddenly all the old uneasiness was back, with as much ferocity as ever.

A few days later, I sat in my office going over some company reports. A cool breeze blew through the open window, moving the linen curtains in such a way that the sunlight caught my eyes, pulling my gaze to the gorgeous day outside. I decided that sitting in my office was no way to spend an afternoon like this, so I grabbed a paperback and headed out the door.

I ambled through the neighborhood. The temperature was soothing, and the smell of the changing seasons reminded me that winter was close. A sea of fallen leaves slowly eddied and swirled in the soft breeze, dancing under my feet, and the afternoon sun inspired a lazy feeling that only appears inside me on autumn days like this one.

I made my way to a nearby grocery store where I ate lunch on the patio of the attached café, alternately reading and gazing through the boughs of the magnificent oak trees, watching the clouds float sluggishly through the sky—a herd of giant white bison moving across an infinite blue plain. People laughed and talked easily around me, and I smiled with contentment. Very little could trouble me today.

I finished eating and went into the grocery, strolling slowly down each of the aisles, carefully gathering a few items I needed—along with some I didn't. I was searching for one of the last articles on my list when my vision blurred.

My jaw tightened, and my breathing slowed. I lifted my head, scanning the store, my senses straining for input. I froze, honing in on the source of the turmoil, and my breathing became shallower still.

Elizabeth stood less than twenty feet away from me. She held a jar in her hand, reading the label. She didn't see me.

The familiar pain surfaced, visions of my brutality so many years before. She was as beautiful as ever, perhaps even more so with years of maturity. I gazed at her—mere seconds stretching into what seemed like hours—and I was surprised by an abrupt realization: I had so purposefully set her memory aside for these years that I now found myself wondering about her experiences since our separation. Where had she traveled? What people had she met and shared her life with? Did she live in Austin? Did she have children? She looked content, and I found pleasure in that observation.

She appeared to be alone, but I was careful to stay back, not to call attention to myself—I didn't want to make her uncomfortable. In truth, I wasn't quite sure what to do, so I just waited, watching.

Then all at once my indecision melted. I approached her deliberately and waited silently beside her. For a moment she didn't notice me, but then she became aware of the close presence and turned to see who it was. Her expression changed to shock, her eyes clouding with fear. She opened her mouth to speak, but I raised my hand, stopping her with the gesture. She stepped back, her face cautious, almost angry, and I simply stared as deeply into her eyes as I could, letting her in, letting her see everything.

Something about her shifted and she became confused. She reluctantly allowed me to put my finger to her lips, and the tension instantly melted from her body. I allowed her deeper into my eyes, and she inhaled sharply, her face collapsing into an expression of almost unconditional trust.

She reached up, taking my hand in hers, and I noticed a wedding ring. The sight should have devastated me, and yet my serenity only grew more pronounced, the energy of the whole universe pulsing in my veins as I reached into her eyes. Finally, I released her hand and ran my fingers slowly, gently along her face. She tilted her head to meet my touch and I leaned close, stopping just before my lips met hers. She didn't resist, nor did she seek anything. She merely stood, staring into my eyes, our mouths so close, inhaling and exhaling.

Her breath smelled as sweet as it had the night we met, and my head swam with the memory of that day so long ago. We hovered together in space and time, circling one another before the entirety, saying everything with no words. After a moment, I put my mouth beside her ear and whispered the words I had longed to say for so long. "I'm sorry."

I turned and walked away. I would never see Elizabeth again.

I RETURNED HOME and immediately went for my cello; it was, after all, my first love, and it soothed me now, the notes moving through the air of their own accord, becoming more fluid not at my discretion, but rather when the time was right.

But soon, I was pushing too much, trying too hard to preserve a moment that refused to be preserved, and I became frustrated with the predictable repetitions. I picked up a guitar I had been teaching myself to play and plucked at the strings, hoping it would give me what I was looking for, but it failed to inspire me, and I slumped forward in my chair, the disappointment crushing, the moment slipping away.

I stayed there for a while, defeated, almost unable to move. Finally I pushed myself out of the chair, leaning forward to put the guitar in its stand. Halfway through the motion I stopped. Jefferson stood in the doorway. His face was impassive, but something in his eyes didn't seem right.

"Hey," I said. "I was just about to come find you and—"

"You saw her."

I stared blankly at him for a minute, opening my mouth to speak. Instead, I just nodded. There was no reason to ask how he knew.

We held each other's eyes for a moment, and then he took a few steps toward the cello. He sat in a chair, expertly positioning the instrument between his knees. He ran his hand along the grain and closed his eyes, stroking the strings with the bow. "Play," he said.

"What?"

He lowered his head, and his eyes bored into mine. "Play."

I looked carefully at him for a few more seconds, puzzled, and even a little frightened. Without completely realizing what I was doing, I began to move my fingers over the strings of the guitar.

Several waves of energy hit me. I heard a sound that made me want to laugh and cry at the same time: it was my lovely cello, and for the first time in my life, I heard it played the way it was meant to be played. He pulled the rich notes from the instrument as effortlessly as he might have used his own voice; he *understood* the music, taking it to depths I had never imagined.

I knew any questions would be meaningless, so I closed my eyes and let go, curiosity evaporating from my mind. Nothing mattered now. This was what I had been looking for.

I allowed the music to wash over me in sheets of beautiful sound, and it became like a chess game—a universe of endless probabilities. It was perfect, yet flawed; any path we chose could have gone an infinite number of ways, and still all the paths we did not choose were before us—all possibilities in the entirety. And I *felt* them every bit as much as I heard them.

The complexity of the compositions forced me deeper into the folds of peace. Time stopped, but the music didn't; it was in my soul, no longer linear in space and time, but everywhere at once. The music simply *was*—our beings inextricably bound together in the entirety by the melodies and harmonies flowing between us. Jefferson was the very definition of serenity, and my path was now clear, even if I didn't understand why, or even how.

When it was done, I hung over the guitar, exhausted. I lifted my head, and in the diminishing light of dusk, I could see that Jefferson was no longer in the room. I dragged myself across the floor and collapsed into my bed.

I slept a deep, peaceful slumber. It may have lasted days, but I can't say exactly how much time elapsed. I dreamed of the music, of Jefferson playing my cello, returning me to innocence, restoring the warm security I had never known how much I missed until this moment . . .

The peace dissolved, the way the sun slips behind the horizon, light surrendering to dark. The music faded.

I sat alone on a cold floor, naked. Yellow, smoky light made it impossible to make out my surroundings. The silence was thick in my ears, shattered by a sound that drove waves of panic through me.

Click . . . click . . . click . . .

Each footfall pierced me like a nail, oppressive and maddeningly slow. I struggled to move but something held me fast. Then the sound just stopped.

Groeden stood over me, his long greasy hair twisted and spiked in all directions. His face was sickly pale, but something was different now: where his left eye had been before was now a hollow black socket, the cheek beneath it a mass of scarred tissue where I had ripped his face away in his youth. He stared at me with his remaining black orb, a confident twisted grin full of sharpened, rotting teeth streaking across his reptilian face.

He held his hands behind his back, considering me as he might look at a piece of meat he intended to cook for dinner. "I told you I'd be back." His voice gurgled with hate.

I tried to move again, terror punching at the walls of my veins. I wanted to scream but nothing came. *It's not real . . .*

Groeden laughed softly and tilted his shriveled head. "You're scared. I like that." He continued to stare at me, and I realized that the most frightening thing about this apparition—if it really was an apparition—was the control and calm behind the single remaining glassy black marble that burned into me from the wrinkled, disfigured face.

Groeden slowly brought his arms from behind his back, and dangling from his right hand was the long thin blade he had used to slit Thomas's throat. He held the knife in front of me, turning it slowly, causing light to flicker across my face and in my eyes. I tried to squint against the harsh brightness, to pull my head away, but my muscles refused to respond.

"What is the saying? 'An eye for an eye?'" He chuckled and put the knife against the soft skin just below my left eye, applying pressure. "You think it isn't real, don't you?" He let out a long raspy breath. "Tell me if this doesn't *feel* real."

Groeden put more pressure on the blade. I tried to squeeze my lids shut, but they wouldn't respond, and I watched the smile spread across his face as my left eye popped like a grape exploding underneath a shoe. Warm liquid ran down my cheek as the blade slid into my head, pushing deep into my brain. The pain was immeasurable. I tried again to scream, but still nothing came.

There was something else, now—a familiar presence holding me at the brink of sanity, and I silently begged for it to assume control, to take me away from this. Jefferson's voice broke through: "It isn't real, Douglas. Don't let him win."

My mind was imploding. *Jefferson! Stop him! He's killing me!*

"He's not killing you. He's playing a better game."

And with those words the soothing calmness began to trickle in, because I knew Jefferson was right. I breathed in heavily and pulled my head back. I slowly rose to my feet, my heart rate falling, my breathing returning to normal. I reached up and touched my face, rubbing my left eye. It was undamaged.

Groeden and I stared at each other. I felt no fear at all. "Never again," I said.

"Why did you interfere? Do you *know* what we could do together?"

Suddenly it came to me like a burst of light, so clearly it nearly blinded me. I laughed in spite of myself. "You *need* me. That's why you're here."

He smiled. "You really don't know, do you? He hasn't told you."

"Does it matter?"

"If you had any idea where this started, you wouldn't be so smug. You were with me, once." He glared at me the way a teacher might look at a rebellious student. "We could rule the entirety together. Can you imagine what that would be like?" His only eye brightened and he drew in a breath. "We could be *gods.*" He whispered the words almost sexually.

"It's moot. It defies the obligation."

He let out a frustrated hiss. "Do you know what I'm going to do to you if I succeed?"

"You already have," I said. "But we've succeeded more, and that will never change."

He sneered at me as his image dissolved. "You still have so much to lose."

I bolted upright in my bed, sweat soaked, breathing heavily. The midafternoon sun streamed through the curtains, a cool breeze tickling my face from the open window. I slipped from the bed, and walked into the hallway, and then into the kitchen.

No one was there. "Jefferson?"

I stopped walking. A whisper appeared in my head—nothing more than a soft rustle of leaves in the wind.

What is the significance of you?

I began to walk again, a peaceful energy running through my blood. Visions of my past coursed through my mind, the cars of a speeding train, each catching my focus for an instant, then moving on, giving way to the next fleeting memory.

I saw my childhood and my adolescence. Thomas and Dad were with me, surreal and unmoving. Elizabeth joined them for a second, and then those memories gave way to my destitution and everything that went with it. Within another fraction of space and time, I had relived my recovery, the revelation from Jefferson and Jack . . . *and all the rest . . .*

Everything happens for a reason.

The projection of my life ended as quickly as it had begun, encompassing only a few seconds. I felt as though I were floating, drawn toward something bigger than myself—a balloon being dragged by a child. I went through the kitchen in a trancelike awareness, stopping for a moment to look into the park across the street. It was empty. For an instant, I wondered if I would ever see it again, but then the thought seemed absurd. *Why would something like that come to me now?*

I almost laughed, but the thought reemerged, and I became troubled. I shook my head slowly, confused. Something tugged at me again. I walked toward the living room, and somehow I knew they would be in there together, waiting for me.

I saw Jack first, his expression strangely neutral. Fear crackled in his eyes, and then, just as quickly, it was gone. Jefferson sat impassively on the couch, his face calm. Another person was in the room to my left.

I reacted without thought. Time and space ceased to exist, and I floated in the entirety, a small fish alone in a never-ending sea.

I felt several explosions. The top of my head erupted in pain, and I fell hard to my knees. Stillness pulled itself tightly around me, like a blanket enfolding an infant. Pain receded in the face of the serenity as blood trickled down my face.

I kneeled in awe, staring disbelievingly at the person who had shot me. Now other visions sputtered in and out, interrupting the scene: Jefferson unconscious on the sofa, bleeding. Jack, rushing toward me, shouting. I blinked once, and everything returned to what it had been—Jefferson sitting impassively, smiling. Jack with the same look of serenity, a hint of apprehension in his eyes. *What is this?*

A middle-aged man stood over me, his short gray hair clean, his appearance neat. Only the scars and the patch covering his left eye gave him away. "Did you feel *that*?" Groeden said, a bright smile stretching across his face.

I looked at Jefferson, confused.

As if he had read my mind, Groeden's body began to shift, growing larger and more grotesque. His skin shriveled, shrinking to fit the bones of his face, his hair growing into a tangled mass of snakes and worms, his clean white teeth mutating into sharpened blades. Blackness covered us until we were the only two people in the universe. He stood over me, hundreds of feet tall, snarling, his blade pulled high above his head.

There was a thunderous clap, and then nothing—blackness all around. "This is your time." It was Jefferson's voice. "You must decide who you will be. In a moment, it will all be done."

"I didn't think it would be like this," I said.

"After everything he did to you, and now you discover he is only a man." Jefferson laughed softly. "He never had any real power, Douglas. *You* allowed him do what he did to you. *You* gave him the right to create those visions—you're giving him that right now."

My mind raced, remembering all of it. *How many horrific things have I faced? How much pain have I endured?* "I just thought it would be . . . *harder.*"

"This is the end of the loop. You've destroyed his future."

"*I* destroyed his future?"

"The organization is lost. He has no choice but to confront you here."

"Confront *me*?"

"Oh, Douglas, I'm so sorry it has to be this way. You must do this thing now."

"But I'm not *ready!*"

"Yes, you are."

The air around me began to vibrate, and I felt more explosions. I was back in Jefferson's house on my knees.

I looked up. Jack stood between me and Groeden; he had stopped the rest of the bullets. Again different visions interrupted the scene—vague, apparitions in the background—Jack and Groeden struggling, superimposed over the strange scene of stillness, Jack standing motionless between us, doing nothing. And then I understood.

Jack is just playing his role. Everything else is how it happened the first time . . .

Groeden's remaining eye was solid black, filled with torment and hatred. I could almost taste his anger, and it occurred to me how easily I could have slipped.

How easily I could have become what he is.

He turned to Jack and chuckled. "You don't even bother to struggle anymore."

Jefferson still sat calmly on the couch, his eyes serene. Briefly, I saw a ghostly image of him lying back, a bullet hole through his forehead, his eyes fixed open. Then the image was gone as quickly as it had appeared, and he smiled at me again. It was like some surreal play, and yet this was reality. No escape.

No escape.

"You're the only person here who doesn't know what is about to happen," Groeden said to me. I narrowed my eyes, trying to understand what he meant. "Do you love him?" he said nodding toward Jack.

"Yes," I said without hesitation.

He smiled. "Of course, you do. And that's how you'll pay for what you've done."

I looked into Jack's eyes and suddenly I knew. *Don't do this, man.*

A spectral visage erupted from his body, clutching at Groeden's wrist. And then it disappeared.

"That's right," Groeden said, slowly putting the barrel of the pistol against Jack's head, "Play your precious *fucking* part. It's your *obligation.*" The last word spilled from his mouth like vomit.

Jack gently closed his eyes.

"Fight him, Jack!"

His smile broadened.

I lunged, but it was too late. The gun kicked and made a loud pop. Jack's head snapped sideways, his brains bursting from his temple with the force of the exiting bullet. His eyes opened, staring with a blankness that told me they no longer saw me, his face maintaining its smile. Then his body crumpled, a lifeless sack collapsing under its own weight.

A deep growl formed in my throat, and I grabbed Groeden's arm, slinging him across the room with a force I didn't know I possessed. He hit the wall and fell to the floor, unmoving.

I stood motionless over Jack's twisted form, a pool of blood growing under his head. His body twitched once, and then again. His eyes, staring at nothing, turned to glass.

You were my best friend in the whole world, right, Jack? My best friend? Didn't you take care of me? Always? Jack . . . ?

Jack?

"Jack?"

I fell to my knees and screamed. "Jack, no! Goddamn it, you can't!" I threw myself on his chest, *"Please, Jack! Please!"*

"Douglas . . ."

I pressed myself harder into Jack's body, my grief interminable. I struggled to breathe, but my lungs wouldn't allow it.

"Douglas . . ."

Something pushed its way through, soothing . . .

"Douglas."

I raised my head and pulled in a breath. I turned and looked at Jefferson, sitting on the couch. The serenity in his face further quelled my anguish. "There's something you have to do," he said.

The forms around me moved slowly now, phantasms swirling in every direction. Jefferson crawling toward Groeden, blood saturating his shirt. Groeden pulling himself up, leveling the pistol at Jefferson.

I shook my head hard, and everything reverted: Jefferson on the sofa, still smiling. Groeden crumpled on the floor, slowly regaining his bearings. Then more images, different outcomes converging in a hazy dream, spinning shadows. The fleeting snatches reminded me of my addictions—how very clouded my perception had been. I covered my mouth and stifled a scream. I looked out the window, and then back at Jack's body.

The intimate voice of the entirety broke through, a clear thought piercing the static, pulling me out of the nightmare with the strength of its sweet presence.

What is the significance of you?

I am . . .

Space and time evaporated.

I stood before my own image, each of us staring at the other. Blood soaked my hair and ran down my face. The image opened its mouth and spoke, but the words came from all directions. The voice wasn't mine—it was the entirety. "What is the significance of you?" The sound was so close, devoid of any echo, startling in its immediacy.

I stared at myself for a moment, unable to react.

It repeated the question: "What is the significance of you?"

I don't . . . I am . . .

"Don't you know?"

I looked closer at the person in front of me. *You aren't me . . .*

It smiled. "Are you so sure?"

I was confused. *You want me to see something?*

It nodded slowly. "What is the significance of you?"

I snapped back into reality, still kneeling over Jack's lifeless body. Tears ran down my cheeks, mixing with blood, running into the corners of my mouth.

Groeden pushed himself to his feet, pointed the pistol at me, and pulled the trigger. It only clicked. He ejected the clip, reeled, and reached into one of his pockets, his movements slow and exaggerated. He removed a fresh clip and clumsily tried to push it into the gun.

I began to grow angry. *He killed Jack . . .* The thoughts came as overlapping whispers in my head, the anger now bordering on fury.

My hands flew up, almost of their own accord, and began grabbing bloody clumps of my hair, pulling. I squinted, my body tensing from the stress. I fought back the tears of rage, looking at Jefferson for support, pleading with my eyes.

He only smiled and shook his head.

It all seemed like an evil hallucination, and yet something in my mind—some presence—insisted on keeping me acutely aware that this was reality, its authority unassailable and absolute. The anger bubbled in the back of my throat, offering its final thrust, and my body tensed again as I prepared for the madness that would surely overtake me. But at the peak, a deluge of serenity spilled over me, washing everything else away.

I looked at Groeden, and a new realization broke through: *He wants me to feel this rage. No—he* needs *me to feel it. It's his only hope.*

My vision blurred, spinning me. I closed my eyes, and for a split second I could see myself again. The image of my own bloody face broke into a slow peaceful smile. Then, as quickly as it had appeared, it vanished.

But the voice remained.

What is the significance of you?

I shook my head, clearing my thoughts. Groeden's clip found its mark. He pulled the barrel back, chambering a round. He lifted his arm. Time froze.

What is the significance of you?

I am . . .

The last vestiges of doubt dissolved—the thickest morning fog giving way to a rising afternoon sun.

I am everything . . .

Yes . . .

And I am . . . nothing . . .

I opened my eyes and they stung with the intensity of my purpose. Time resumed around me with a violent hiss. The realization had taken only an instant, but it was all I needed. I exhaled sharply and stared at Groeden, my faculties now decidedly intact.

I stood erect and allowed energy to invade my body with a fierceness I had never known. I leaned my head back and sucked air into my lungs, smiling at the miserable man in front of me.

I whispered, "I am everything, and I am nothing at all."

Groeden reacted as if the statement were poison, cringing at the words that pounded him with all the savagery of a lead pipe. He had spent most of his life dreading this one sentence with the very fiber of his being, but I had released each syllable, and now they hung in the air like smoke, ensuring his fate, driving him further into the grip of insanity.

"You fuck!" In an act of final desperation, he pulled the trigger.

I fused with the entirety. The bullets thudded into my body, becoming part of my soul, melting and reforming. Then light and sound thundered around me as space and time resumed their flow.

I was still on my knees, my knuckles supporting my upper body. A second passed. Then another. One more. I drew a breath.

My head snapped up, and my eyes fixed on Groeden the way a starving leopard might look at a wounded gazelle. We stared at each other for an incalculable amount of time, his single eye wide with panic as my obligation became clearer to both of us with each passing instant.

I leapt at him, surprised by my agility and control. I grabbed his throat and lifted him off the ground, pulling his face into mine, and for an instant I wondered if I wouldn't tear out his jugular with my teeth. I uttered a low short snarl, yet my emotions obeyed every command.

Groeden resisted, struggling, trying to break my grip, but the steadiness with which I held him before me—nearly a foot off the ground—had nothing to do with physical strength. His resistance was useless.

I meticulously spoke the last words he would hear in this world. "I will *never* let you have more."

Groeden's face became swollen and dark. He began to flail more violently, his remaining eye darting about in its socket, pleading silently for mercy. In response, I pulled his face closer to mine, dumping my soul into his. And I delighted in knowing what he saw as the last spark of his life faded into oblivion.

His body collapsed in an emotionless thud to the floor, and I wondered for a moment if I might kick it. Instead, I gave up control, allowing the energy to seep out of me. I bowed my head, humbling myself to the balance restored.

Groeden was no longer my responsibility.

The entirety would know better than I what to do with such a creature.

———◆———

JEFFERSON DIDN'T MOVE. He held his hands over his stomach, covered in blood. He slumped, his head falling sideways on his shoulder.

I ran to him. "It's over—"

He grabbed my wrist. "It's not over, it's only started. I have to go now. You've learned everything I can teach you. You're strong enough."

I put my hand around his. "We'll talk about it later, okay?" Panic returned, full force. "I'm *not* going to lose you both! Jefferson, *no!*"

His body took on the familiar shimmer, and he began to wheeze. Yet he managed a smile. "You haven't lost us, Douglas. You have to . . . allow it . . . accept it as your fate." He coughed, blood spilling from his mouth onto his chin, small spots splashing onto his crisp, white shirt. "Do you trust me?"

I fought back the panic. "Of course. Yes."

"I'll be here . . . *always.*"

I nodded, and suddenly the panic was gone again. Jefferson's smile broadened as he recognized the transition on my face.

I said, "We'll see each other—"

He raised his hand, cutting off my words. His body melted, fading into the entirety. "Goodbye, Douglas."

I squeezed his hand. "Goodbye, Jefferson."

And then he was gone.

I walked across the room to Jack. His head lay in a pool of coagulating blood, his eyes hanging open, grotesque in their inertness. The lids drooped over the glassy spheres that had for so long made me laugh with only a glance. The peaceful smile remained frozen on his face.

A tear formed, overflowing the rim of my eye, and rolled down my cheek. I sat beside his body and put his head in my lap, caressing his hair, his skin growing colder under my touch, his muscles stiff and lifeless. I tried to make the energy form in my hands, but nothing happened.

Please . . . please come . . . Let me bring him back.

Still nothing.

Blood covered my hands and clothes as I rocked back and forth weeping softly. "It wasn't time for you to go . . ."

I looked down at his face, blank and unmoving. A tear hit his cheek, making a line in the drying blood as gravity pulled it downward.

I inhaled deeply and shuddered. "*Why?*" I stroked his hair, holding my breath. Then I leaned close to his ear and whispered, "Please don't go, Jack."

Through the haze of my despair, a vague notion tapped at my mind. I was only dimly aware of its presence, an insect buzzing around my head. I tried to focus, but sadness drowned everything.

I looked at Jack again, and my throat felt like it would swell shut from the pain. *There's something else . . . right in front of me . . .*

Then it came, and any reservations I ever had simply evaporated. Relief passed over me, replacing the immeasurable weight of grief.

What is the significance of you?

Warm contentment seeped through me, spreading slowly. I leaned my head back and inhaled as warmth permeated my limbs. A smile came to my lips, and in my mind I felt the words that defined my place in the entirety, from a source so ancient it defied time: *I am everything and I am nothing at all.*

RESOLUTION

Let us forget the lapse of time; let us forget the conflict of opinions.
Let us make our appeal to the infinite, and take up our positions there.

—*CHUANG TZU*

October, Year Thirty-Two

MY BODY HAD endured so much in so little time that I was hardly surprised when I slept again for days. This time, though, the sleep was fitful and confusing; I wasn't sure where reality began and ended. I awoke often, but I don't know how many times, or for how long each time. I felt alone and vulnerable, unprepared for the future. Even in my sleep I sought answers, but nothing helped me find what I was looking for.

I heard the music, distant and beautiful, but I was no longer in control of its course. Jefferson was playing.

I saw Groeden laughing, rage filling his face.

I opened my eyes. I was alone in the darkness, and for a moment, terror seized me as I tried to regain my bearings—to understand where I was, the state of my universe. My mind reset but I remained disoriented and confused, sitting up slowly, my body aching. I rubbed my hand over my head and felt the scar.

Has it healed?

I allowed the serenity in, taking several deep breaths. I slipped from my bed and went into my office, moving to my computer. It seemed to demand my attention, and I stared at it for a moment, wondering why it was suddenly so important. I looked to the left of the screen, and I saw it: an envelope with my name on it.

The memories flooded in: *The notebook, the letter in the hospital room. Even after he's gone, he finds me . . .*

It was the final component—the last piece of the puzzle that would complete the picture. I finally understood how Jefferson had so easily anticipated every detail of my life, how he had been so confidently prepared for every possible outcome. But more than anything, I finally understood that Jefferson Stone—as he had promised—would never leave me. The connection between us—the probabilities—blurred any lines of distinction in space and time.

Douglas,

I remember how quickly the questions formed in my mind the first time I read the letter you're holding, but you mustn't panic. Everything will be fine. I'm proof of that.

The book is your roadmap, so read it carefully. It is the guide that will keep you from corrupting the future. As I have said many times, small details will change as you move through your life, and you must accept that as part of the loop.

I'm sorry I had to mislead you about so many of the particulars of our lives, but had you ever suspected the truth, it would have destroyed everything. Going forward, you will find a number of inconsistencies with the explanations I have given you. Rest assured, they were by design. Don't try to find out more than you are ready for.

I hope you won't underestimate Groeden's importance. Never forget that he always exists—even if only in his younger form. He won't be able to find you all the time, but you should still be constantly prepared for surprises. One thing is certain: you will see him again, and I encourage you to prepare for that. I also want you to understand that there are things about him you don't yet understand. He is stronger than you believe.

I know there is one question burning in your mind, but I won't be able to answer it to your satisfaction. I don't know whether I lived after I was shot. I hoped to return to my universe—to finally break out of the loop for better or for worse. Unfortunately, I can't tell you anything beyond that, which is certainly for the best. But I think we both feel strongly about my future, and I'll leave it at that.

If there's anything I want you to have, it is the knowledge that I was never scared, and you won't be either. If I live, I will live, and if I die, I will return to the place from which I came.

Until I see you again,

Jefferson

I finished the letter, folded my arms on the desk, lowered my head, and wept.

After a time, I became calm and allowed the truth a tentative hold, thinking about the ways this knowledge would change my path forever. I took deep breaths and reread the letter, beginning the enormous task of understanding who and what I am.

Something made me look up. There it was, on the far corner of the desk. Non-descript. Ordinary.

Did I see it before?

It was a book. Nothing more.

I reached out and touched the cover, just once, pulling my hand away. And in that motion I found the energy to put the confusion and despair aside. I knew I had to rise to the obligation, to move forward and start my life anew. There was so much work to do.

Every single word will define your path.

Even these . . .

So now I will ask the question I began with. If you caught a glimpse of your own death, would the knowledge change the way you live the rest of your life?

TRANSITION

MANY EVENTS IN my life have been sudden and painful, and without a doubt their impact was lasting. But the transitions that have had the most profound effects are the ones that came slowly and subtly, without my even understanding the shift was taking place.

One spring afternoon, I was running in downtown Austin, when suddenly I just stopped, although I couldn't have said why. There was a sea of movement around me, and I made a circle where I stood, breathing deeply, watching the currents of people and automobiles flooding the streets and sidewalks. It seemed the city was never more alive.

I leaned back and looked up at a skyscraper, marveling at the feat of human accomplishment it represented, running my eyes slowly down its glass side to a small grocery occupying part of the building's first floor. Colorful blooms burst from boxes below the store's enormous plate glass windows, and people sat on iron chairs on the sidewalk under striped awnings, eating lunch.

An old man in an apron stood outside the small store, hanging signs that announced the day's specials. He finished with one of the signs and slowly turned around. Our eyes met, and we stared at each other for a few seconds, the throng of people around us almost coming to a standstill. He smiled at me, as if we shared some deep secret.

I turned my eyes away and the epiphany finally drenched me, drowning me in its lucidity. I had always had all the pieces, but now I finally understood completely. *The money was never the only goal.*

I looked blankly at the sidewalk and basked in the warmth of the thought. We had done everything we could, not because we wanted to win, but because we knew we were *capable* of winning—because we had the power to mitigate the pain before it ever really started. We never sought an ounce of fame, and while we unapologetically made a great deal of money, the wealth was never the true objective. No, from the beginning it had been about human action and progress, preserving the creativity, prosperity, and happiness that would keep the fabric of humanity from disintegrating. We did it all for the growth of knowledge, and that was what *really* destroyed Groeden.

I looked back at the grocer and his smile widened.

This thing we created isn't merely currency, it is an entity that flows through humanity, and we made it because we were supposed to.

I turned my head slowly and took in everything around me, watching the masses of humanity flowing through the streets, like an army of busy insects, building, innovating . . . *living.*

The currency saved all of this . . . I let the thought linger for a moment.

The grocer's eyes narrowed, but the smile didn't leave his face. He turned back around and resumed his work, and I watched him for another moment before continuing my run. Energy vibrated through every cell in my body.

Now I was near the intersection where the car had taken the little girl's life. *Did I mean to come here?* I looked around the area, inundated by the images of her death—and of her revival.

My eyes stopped on a bench ten feet away. A sparrow perched there unmoving. I watched it for a moment, and then leaned back and looked at the sky, closing my eyes.

Jack had been right about everything; it was so much bigger than I ever could have imagined. What I possessed, everything I *was*, all my abilities, my insights, they were incidental—mere indications of something far more significant. The sun was warm against my eyelids, peace rippling through me like a breeze dancing across water. I had never felt more alive.

I brought my head down again and opened my eyes, but the bird was gone. I smiled, nodding slowly. Then I turned and headed for home.

———◆———

FOR DECADES I could have driven myself insane pondering Jefferson's fate. I might assume he didn't make it back to his universe, because I haven't heard from him since the letter. On the other hand, I might assume he did make it back and simply has no reason to contact me. And then it is equally possible that any answer to the mystery would simply disrupt the obligation. So I have had to—and will continue to—draw my own conclusions about everything beyond the book. It is clearer to me.

Experience is everything.

I now approach the future just like everyone else—because no one will hand the answers to me. And that may be the best explanation for why Jefferson hasn't contacted me. There are an infinite number of probabilistic outcomes, all of which have occurred somewhere, at some time, in the entirety. Jefferson left me precious few clues about how to navigate the next several decades of my life, and I have always been grateful for that.

My life as I know it is built on the strangest of paradoxes: I have become nearly omniscient and ubiquitous—if I chose to, I could see everything. And yet I choose to see very little—and I manipulate even less—because to do so would disrupt the very set of conditions that have made me what I am. And besides, to know *all* the answers would defy the joy of the experience. So I merely drift, taking what I am given, and nothing more.

The entirety doesn't live; it doesn't make decisions; it simply *is*. The entirety is balance—all things having their counterparts in space and time, settling into equilibrium. It is the way. It was here before time began, and it will be when time no longer matters. I finally understand that I have no mission, no imperative. I simply exist, and I am not alone.

But if there is an explanation for my presence—a reason for my existence—it is this: I am here in anonymity, and I have offered humanity a set of alternatives—choices that didn't exist before. Maybe history will ignore what we've done; perhaps most people will merely continue to cling to irrational fears. But there will be others, and if we've come too soon, we will simply lay the foundation and then return to where we began—to the entirety. The future will know what to do with our work.

I cannot begin to fathom what comes next. The little girl, the dog in the river—those things were but a spark. And while I know that we were the only ones who could do what had to be done, I also know that there is so much more.

I possess something I still don't fully understand, and yet I know I have no choice but to use it. Groeden is gone in this universe, but he haunts me in the endless void that makes up the entirety, and although I don't know exactly how things will unfold, I am sure of one thing: the rest of the answers will come, as they always do.

But they won't come now.

Not yet.

———◆———

I SAT IN my office, holding the book in my hands. I had been there for hours, studying every sentence, every detail, driving myself to exhaustion. My eyes stung. I needed a break.

I heard something and turned my head. I looked at my watch and raised my eyebrows in surprise. I rose from my desk and walked into the living room.

He was there, in front of the chessboard, just like almost every other night. And as always, the probabilities unfolded in the entirety, dancing in front of me, begging me to play. His pawn stood alone in the center, demanding my response, so I sat down, pushing my own queen's pawn. The two pieces met in the middle of the board, and I watched them, waiting for the next move.

I smiled as the familiar peace rippled through my body—contentment, and maybe even a little bit of security in the knowledge that everything happened exactly the way it was supposed to. Then something distracted me—glimmering in the afternoon light, pulling my eyes to the edge of the board, gently reminding me. There, shining in the autumn sun, rested a solitary quarter.

And never, I think, have I understood my life more clearly than in that moment.

QED, Austin, Texas

It is so good to be back, to be home again.

I have seen so much since the last time I was here, yet it is the same in all the most important ways. It makes me feel like a child again; I remember the haughtiness, how oblivious he was to the mistakes he would make. And I relish the memories, desperately aware of how critical they are to what I have become. I am at peace as I face this task.

There is Barney sitting alone, chatting idly to no one. I wonder if he's talking to himself, or if they are with him now. Thick snowflakes fall outside and Saul wipes a glass behind the counter. My eyes move from table to table, finally stopping on the one with the chessboard and the paperback. I walk to it and sit down, flipping through the pages of the book.

Someone is staring at me and I lift my head. He approaches, confused, a question looming in his mind. And so I speak the first words. "Is this your chessboard?" A chill spills down my back, spreading into my limbs.

He nods. "Yes."

"I thought you might be up for a game." I rub the scar on my head almost without realizing it. "I hope you don't mind that I was looking at your book."

"Yeah, I'd love a game," he says.

Something compels me to look at Saul, still wiping a glass behind the counter. He raises his head slowly and our eyes meet. His mouth turns up in a slight smile, and he nods once. Then he simply looks back down at the glass in his hand.

I extend my hand to the boy across the table. "I'm Jefferson."

"It's nice to meet you," he says, shaking my hand. "I'm Douglas Cole."

Suggested Reading

Boaz, David. *Libertarianism: A Primer*. New York: The Free Press, 1997.

Bohm, David. *Wholeness and the Implicate Order*. New York: Routledge, 1980.

Buffett, Mary, and David Clark. *Buffettology*. New York: Rawson, 1997.

Capra, Fritjof. *The Tao of Physics*. New York: Bantam, 1975.

Cleary, Thomas. *The Taoist Classics*: Vol. 1–2. Boston: Shambala, 1990.

Csikszentmihalyi, Mihaly. *Flow: The Psychology of Optimal Experience*. New York: Harper Perennial, 1990.

Dali Lama and Howard C. Cutler, M.D. *The Art of Happiness*. New York: Riverhead, 1998.

Dawkins, Richard. *The Selfish Gene*. Oxford: Oxford University Press, 1976.

Deutsch, David. *The Fabric of Reality: The Science of Parallel Universes and Its Implications*. New York: Penguin, 1997.

Ebeling, Richard M. *The Austrian Theory of the Trade Cycle and Other Essays*. Auburn, AL: The Ludwig von Mises Institute, 1996.

Fine, Reuben. *Chess the Easy Way*. New York: David McKay Company, 1942.

Fisher, Philip A. *Common Stocks and Uncommon Profits*. New York: Wiley, 1996.

Friedman, David. *Law's Order*. Princeton: Princeton University Press, 2000.

———. *The Machinery of Freedom: Guide to a Radical Capitalism*. La Salle, IL: Open Court, 1973.

Gordon, David. *The Philosophical Origins of Austrian Economics*. Auburn, AL: The Ludwig von Mises Institute, 1996.

Graham, Benjamin. *The Intelligent Investor*. New York: Harper Collins, 1973.

Graham, Benjamin, and David Dodd. *Security Analysis*. New York: The McGraw-Hill Companies, 1934.

———. *The Warren Buffett Portfolio*. New York: Wiley, 1999.

Hagstrom, Robert G. *The Warren Buffett Way*. New York: Wiley, 1995.

Hanh, Thich Nhat. *Peace Is Every Step*. New York: Bantam, 1991.

Hawking, Stephen W. *A Brief History of Time: From the Big Bang to Black Holes*. New York: Bantam, 1988.

Hayek, F. A. *The Road to Serfdom*. Chicago: The University of Chicago Press, 1944.

Hofstadter, Douglas R. *Gödel, Escher, Bach: An Eternal Golden Braid*. New York: Vintage, 1979.

Jung, C. G. *The Basic Writing of C.G. Jung*. Edited by Violet Staub de Laszlo. New York: Random House, 1959.

Jung, C. G. *Synchronicity: An Acausal Connecting Principle*. Translation by R.F.C Hull. Princeton: Princeton University Press, 1960.

Kilpatrick, Andrew. *Of Permanent Value: The Story of Warren Buffett*. Birmingham, AL: AKPE, 1994.

Laotse. *The Wisdom of Laotse*. Translated and edited by Lin Yutang. New York: Random House, 1948.

Lowenstein, Roger. *Buffett: The Making of an American Capitalist*. New York: Doubleday, 1995.

Mansfield, Victor. *Synchronicity, Science, and Soul-Making*. Chicago: Open Court, 1995.

Mason, James. *The Art of Chess*. New York: Dover, 1947.

Mises, Ludwig von. *Economic Calculation in the Socialist Commonwealth*. Auburn, AL: The Ludwig von Mises Institute, 1990.

———. *The Historical Setting of the Austrian School of Economics*. Auburn, AL: The Ludwig von Mises Institute, 1969.

———. *Socialism*. Indianapolis, IN: Liberty Classics, 1981.

Murphy, John J. *Technical Analysis of the Futures Markets: A Comprehensive Guide to Trading Methods and Applications*. New York: New York Institute of Finance, 1986.

Popper, Karl R. *Objective Knowledge: An Evolutionary Approach*. New York: Oxford University Press, 1972.

Popper, Karl R. *The Open Society and Its Enemies*: Vol. 1–2. Princeton: Princeton University Press, 1962.

Popper, Karl R. *Realism and the Aim of Science*. New York: Routledge, 1956.

Popper, Karl R. *Selections*. Edited by David Miller. New Jersey: Princeton University Press, 1985.

Popper, Karl R. *Unended Quest*. La Salle, IL: Open Court, 1974.

Pratt, Shannon P. *Cost of Capital: Estimations and Applications*. New York: Wiley, 1998.

Rand, Ayn. *The Ayn Rand Lexicon*. Edited by Harry Binswanger. New York: Meridian, 1986.

Rand, Ayn. *The Fountainhead*. New York: Signet, 1943.

Reinfeld, Fred. *The Complete Chess Course*. Garden City, NY: Doubleday, 1953.

Rothbard, Murray N. *The Case Against the Fed*. Auburn, AL: The Ludwig von Mises Institute, 1994.

———. *The Case for a 100 Percent Gold Dollar*. Auburn, AL: The Ludwig von Mises Institute, 1991.

———. *What Has Government Done to Our Money?* Auburn, AL: The Ludwig von Mises Institute, 1963.

Simon, Julian L. *The State of Humanity*. Cambridge, MA: Blackwell, 1995.

———. *The Ultimate Resource*, Volume Two. Princeton, NJ: Princeton University Press, 1996.

Stanley, Thomas J., Ph.D. and William D. Danko, Ph.D. *The Millionaire Next Door: The Surprising Secrets of America's Wealthy*. New York: Pocket Books, 1996.

Steele, David Ramsay. *From Marx to Mises: Post-Capitalist Society and the Challenge of Economic Calculation*. La Salle, IL: Open Court, 1992.

Taylor, Thomas C. *An Introduction to Austrian Economics*. Auburn, AL: The Ludwig von Mises Institute, 1980.

Teweles, Richard J., and Frank J. Jones. *The Futures Game: Who Wins, Who Loses, and Why*. New York: McGraw-Hill, 1987.

Watts, Alan W. *The Book: On the Taboo Against Knowing Who You Are*. New York: Vintage, 1966.

———. *The Tao of Philosophy*. North Clarendon, VT: Tuttle, 1995.

———. *Taoism: Way Beyond Seeking*. North Clarendon, VT: Tuttle, 1997.

———. *The Wisdom of Insecurity: A Message for an Age of Anxiety*. New York: Vintage, 1951.

Zukav, Gary. *The Dancing Wu Li Masters: An Overview of the New Physics*. New York: William Morrow, 1979.

For more information about Paco Ahlgren and *Discipline*—
including the *Discipline* web log, more suggested reading, news,
events, and future publications—please visit www.pacoahlgren.com.

MALM TIUM TIUM